TANGLEWIRE

TANGLEWIRE

a women's prison novel

by Patricia Coyne

BEACON
publishing + design

TANGLEWIRE: a women's prison novel
a Beacon Publishing & Design Book / October 2017

Published by Beacon Publishing & Design, LLC
3201 C Street, Suite 302, Anchorage, Alaska 99503
www.beaconmn.com

ISBN: 978-0-9831644-5-6

Printed in the United State of America

www.patriciacoyne.com

INTRODUCTION

JANUARY 1997

Pay me eighteen cent an hour
Gonna work me like a He-brew slave.
Tak-en sick the doc he grin, he diagnosing me my ear-ly grave.

It's the annual talent show at the Danbury Federal Correctional Institution for Women, and the auditorium overflows with gray commissary sweat suits. All the folding chairs are claimed, the bleachers are filled, and inmates lean against the walls.

Mother loving tangle wi-re
He twisting lazy in the sun.
He got them thousand razors calling,
Ya'll come…and take that ru-un…hon.

The singer is white and not a typical high-security prisoner. In another life she composed folk songs and performed at organic cafes. Now she, composes blues and performs in the penitentiary recreation building.

She's here because few years ago, when the feds raided her house, they found a hydroponic grow in her basement along with a Browning 12 gauge pump action in the stairwell. The weapon upped her time and security level so now she serves out her eleven years behind the razor wire.

She's quite a sight. She's gone butch here at Danbury, but for tonight's performance her girlie friends have femmed her out.. They've dusted her freckles with talcum powder dyed with instant coffee-crystal, lipsticked her cheeks and craft-glittered her eyelids. To finish her off, they spiked her hair with microwaved, tickle-me-pink Crayola.

She's dressed in the standard Danbury performance outfit—kitchen-worker whites—but she's very tall, and this year she couldn't find her size. She's made do with pant legs tucked into lace-up work boots and a shirt that swings loose over a cutoff thermal.

Transplant the singer seventy miles north to the late-nineties streets of New York City and she'd be taken for a crazy person. But in a penitentiary where street norms have faded, where points are given for resourcefulness, and where the inmate eye is starved for color and variety, she's fantabulous. She's the bomb. She's all that and a bag-a chips.

The singer attracts an avid group of fans—and not just simply because she identifies as a penitentiary guy. She's a guy with a guitar—albeit a guitar that she checks out from recreation on Tuesday, Thursday, and Saturday between six and seven thirty.

She composed "Tanglewire Blues" here in the gymnasium, impressing and enamoring the groupies gathered around her, and she has performed it for the last three talent shows. Time served here confers status, so the veterans in the audience are profiling their familiarity with the lyrics by joining in. Newer inmates try to mouth a few lines.

But not everyone in the audience is a fan. It's a white thing, and white inmates are in the minority. The Spanish, mostly Colombian, are not particularly carried away; still they are respectful. Their culture has been properly represented tonight, most recently by a salsa dance number. They sway and clap politely.

The black women, however, are not impressed. The song's phony ghetto-speak annoys them, the tune is Dallas, not Delta and that yodel, coming out her mouth on the chorus is straight-up cracker. This is no kind of blues blues. This is just another off-brand whitey, trying to dry-hump the blues.

They yawn and study the ceiling. They pick lint off their sleeves. They turn to berate a chair-kicker.

Yet although the performance does not please everyone, no one would think of leaving. They're all eagerly anticipating the closing act.

The recreation department has gone against policy and allowed in some gangsta rap—a recording of Notorious B.I.G. The Fatback Sisters have been working on their lip-sync.

It's going to be awesome.

TANGLEWIRE

a women's prison novel

Outside the penitentiary's recreation building, it's a wintry night but there are no dark corners on the compound. It's kept ablaze with twenty-four-hour floodlights. But even though it's brightly lit, the place is somber. And now, with the inmate population out of sight, it looks like a declining World War II military base. Except there's a dark watchtower and double-rowed tangles of razor wire.

The five-acre center of the facility is laid out in a strict rectangle—half a football field framed by low-slung, white stucco. The track, a misshapen oval and out-of-bounds after dark, lies off behind the recreation building, The central square under the floodlights is crisscrossed and outlined with sidewalk, now black against white. Last night it snowed again. This morning in the early dark, a crew of yard workers had been on the shovel, lining the walks with banks of snow.

On a normal Friday night, even in the depth of winter, the grounds are alive with inmates in brown prison-issue jackets exchanging inmate banter, calling to each other, and pacing the square to the beat of their commissary headsets. But it's talent-show night. The grounds are deserted.

On the far side of the compound, a door opens and two uniformed officers emerge. The younger is white and has recently transitioned from the army, bringing his GS-5 rating to the Bureau of Prisons. He has yet to lose his upright, arm-swinging drill and his military buzz cut. He has just graduated from orientation, and the lectures have quickened his get-tough resolve.

The other officer is older and taller, an African American. He's has been a correctional officer for over a decade and bears hardly a trace of his former military stride or military physique. He moves with an easy slouch and he's put on extra pounds. Both officers have their walkie-talkies and handcuffs clipped to one side of their belts. On their other side is a retractable reel of keys so that—although their walks are different—they sound the same. They move with a distinctive correctional-officer jingle.

From across the compound wafts a note and a twang, and the big man nods toward the recreation building. "You ain't going to find much up in these units tonight. You just need to document that you accomplished your walk-around."

"I hear you. I'll take Unit Ten on over to Two."

"Roger. Be back at you."

The older officer moves away a few steps, then stops and turns around. "You probably need to be aware that on these activity nights, you might could happen on a couple of them up in here getting busy—you know?"

The younger man's ears turn red.

The older officer expands. "You be here awhile, you bound to come up on all that. Some of these ladies? The way they carry on up in here is shameless."

"I'm ready for them." The young man pats his belt possessively. "I got the cuffs right here."

The older officer pauses thoughtfully for a moment. "Look, word to the wise. You just starting out." He shifts his weight to the side and holds up an instructing finger. "You got to be tough, but you also got to show some flex. Be my advice, you going to walk into your buildings a little bit heavy. Let your keys loose so they be aware you coming up on them, know what I mean? Provide them a little time to get themselves correct. You do that way, you save yourself a whole stinking pile of drama."

"I hear you."

"And a stinking pile of paperwork."

"I hear you."

The rookie turns marches off.

He reaches the door of Unit Ten, stops, and turns back. The veteran officer has disappeared. He opens the Unit Ten door—but gently. He covers his keys with a quieting hand, slips inside, and eases the door closed.

Back in the auditorium, the performer is winding it up and her fans in the audience clap and sing along with the chorus.

> *The feet don't never touch the free world while the*
> *Body's doing Fed-er-al time.*
> *Yo' feet ain't never feel no freedom 'fore you*
> *Finish up your Fed-eral time.*

She bows to receive the cheers and whistles, swings her guitar aside, and shrugs the strap up over her pink spikes. The clapping continues as she turns to rest her guitar against the sound system. She walks offstage.

Outside, up the square and past the rec building, the two duty officers are still at their rounds. The older one opens the door to Unit Four and—keys jangling, humming a tune—strides through. He lets the door slam.

On the other side of the compound, the younger officer, hand muffling his keys, is easing the door closed behind himself into Unit One. There've been no busy inmates yet, but it's too soon to relax. Unit Two's coming up, large and unruly. It's the unit where they place the incoming inmates and the troublemakers. Everyone calls it the projects.

Back on the recreation stage a pair of African Americans, the Fatback Sisters, have warmed up the audience through an interlude of sound-system dysfunction. They are positioning themselves for the evening's final act.

They are magnificent. Especially from behind.

No one knows if their AKA—the Fatback Sisters—came with them from the streets or was penitentiary born, but by now even the staff uses it. And although the two are inseparable and nearly interchangeable, it's unclear whether they are actual sisters. They share a last name—Washington—but they claim not to be related. It's a claim, however, that is inevitably compromised by mysterious, conspiratorial looks and giggles.

The two are compound mascots. In an institution full of separated mothers, they are especially appreciated for their childlike spirit and energy. They have been allowed to bunk together, are never apart, and can be seen of an evening holding hands and skipping the compound square, counterintuitively light of foot. They sing, correcting each other's rap lyrics, and acting out playground chants.

But tonight on stage they've turned into grown-ups. Male grown-ups. Menacing male grown-ups, only slightly diminished by their accessorized kitchen whites. One sister has a handkerchief laid kitty-corner on top of her cornrows. The other holds a construction-paper cigar stuffed with painted-yellow toilet paper. Both wear paper chains encrusted with gold glitter. So the menace does not radiate from their costume but rather from their posture and their attitude. They've turned bad.

They wait glowering downstage beside the loudspeakers while their backups, four lanky African Americans, gym shorts drooping, circle upstage in random, loping prowls. As the synthesized beat opens they stop, tug up their shorts and, finding imagery mics, they lean into them and call out in unison.

"It's Biggie!"

The audience cheers and, in a rhythm that breathes street, the Fatback Sisters stalk center stage. They tilt their heads, raise their chins, and look out through drooping lids. They are no longer giggly girls but world-weary gangsters, ready to tell it straight.

The audience cheers again.

"Yo aah," the sisters lip sync into their mics.

One raises her hand and does a four-finger sign; the other, elbow up, uses her cigar as a microphone.

"Mother[bleep]er's better kno-ow... huh, huh." (The transgressive word has been censored by the staff, but the Sisters and backups all lean forward and overtly mouth it.)

The audience whoops.

I'm-a bad bad.

Lock your windows, lock your doors.
Biggie Smalls,
Huh... yeah.

Although they enjoy it, the action confuses the majority of the rap illiterate audience. The Fatbacks seem to be syncing to a single voice but with a double identity. The enlightened, however, understand that that they are being presented with alternate stages in the life of Biggie Smalls—young Biggie, stage right, mature Biggie, left.

Recreation Specialist, Mr. Castagnola, polices the room's double-door entrance. He feels obliged to project boredom—posture careless, arms folded, chin superciliously raised. But as he watches the act, his eyes start to dance and his lip twitches.

A one-to-three, he be home the end of '93.
I'm ready to get this paper, G, you with me?

Out in the compound, the younger night officer enters his final building.

Unit Two is cavernous with it's three tiers of cells rising to the right, a twenty-four feet wall of cinder block to the left, and a group of aging institutional table-chair sets in the common area between. It's emptied out now, but still it echoes with faint clanks and groans.

Its look is hardcore prison—concrete and bars and tiers—and until recently it was the protective-custody wing of the hole. But a couple of years back, when Danbury turned female, fewer isolation units were needed and the wing was turned over to general population.

To accommodate women, the cells were refurbished. The iron-slat bars looking out on the passageways were hung with multiple yards of white-vinyl shower curtain and the steel toilet/sink unit at the rear of each cell was privatized with curtains on U-shaped runners. A set of bunks replaced the narrow segregation cots and a pair of lockers was squeezed into the remaining four feet of floor space.

Tonight the common area between the cell tiers and the concrete wall is deserted, and the rookie is used to seeing it that way. He has officiated at count, and at count the inmates are in their rooms. But also at count the curtains are open. Now they're closed. The officer approaches lightly and whisks the first one aside.

Empty.

The next.

Empty.

As he approaches the third curtain, he hears a creaky-voiced cry. "Get your policing self up on over here, Mister Officer. Evil be on the loose!"

The guard stays his hand. There a question whether he should rightfully respond.

"Mister Officer! Where you *at*?"

Just as he reaches again to slide the curtain open, it opens on its own. He spooks and jumps back.

A heavy black inmate face, eyes large with emotion, peers out at him. Her body is hidden behind the curtain she secures under her chin. Her face glistens with baby oil and is garnished with a twist of white tissue paper packed into a nostril.

The officer recognizes trouble and tries to move on past.

"Officer! Officer!"

He turns and rolls his eyes.

"Officer, you best be quick getting yourself on up there. Evil on the loose!"

Ms. Caruthers drops the curtain and steps out into the walkway. She's wrapped in a white-sheet toga; she clutches it to her breast and points with the other arm down the common area to the iron stairway.

"*What?*"

"Something evil transpiring. Up in that room."

The fleshy upper section of Ms. Caruthers arm quivers.

"What room? *Where?*" protests the officer.

"Up there," insists the woman, impatient. *Fool just standing there.* "Up to the third tier. Up in there next-side the TV room."

The officer hesitates uncertainly, and she stamps a rubber flip-flop. "You best don't be shifting on your feet, fidgeting. Get yourself on up. Look-see *to* it like you supposed to do. That's your *job*."

She looks off into the distance as though to confirm vibrations and nods her head in dark affirmation.

"Hurry-up. Get up there. Evil doings."

The officer's recent orientation classes failed to offer skills in correcting African American grandmothers with premonitions.

"What? Evil *what?*" he asks and his voice slides up an octave.

"Well now, Mister Officer, how'm I supposed to know? I ain't up in there, and I ain't about to mount up them stairs. That's your business."

The officer snorts and turns and strides swiftly toward the stair case.

On his way up, he slows near the second tier. He almost ignores Ms. Caruthers. He almost makes his normal exit at the second tier landing. Instead he rolls his eyes again, sighs, and continues up to the third.

"Crazy old bitch," he mutters, then corrects himself. His orientation has emphasized that female inmates are always referred to as ladies—not women, not girls—certainly not bitches.

"Crazy old lady."

Down on the first floor Ms. Caruthers stands in her doorway, head tilted out, waiting . . . waiting.

"What the fuck!" comes the booming bellow.

Ms. Caruthers nods in satisfaction

"Jesus Chr-rist!"

Ms. Caruthers pulls in her head and pulls her shower curtain closed.

INMATE DOWN! INMATE DOWN! INMATE DOWN!

The loudspeaker echoes across the deserted compound.

ALL OFFICERS. UNIT TWO. PROCEED. IMMEDIATELY.

The penitentiary staff—caught nodding through an easy, activity-night shift—is electrified, and the compound comes alive. Doors fling open and a dozen silhouettes, male and female, emerge. They proceed at double time as the INMATE-DOWN order demands, around the square and across the sidewalk's X.

A few of the guards are trim; most are not. A very large, round man tips forward, arms pumping, posture impersonating a gallop. His actual pace is barely a trot. A heavyset middle-aged female tries to run, but she's slowed by the unforgiving polyester of her uniform. A more athletic guard attempts an off-sidewalk short cut, but he flounders in a snowbank and turns back.

The older of the original pair of duty officers is first to arrive at the door. He throws himself through it.

On stage in the auditorium, the Fatback Sisters are lost in the two ages of Biggie. The Sister wearing the hankie-rag—the young Biggie—struts and puffs her chest.

Huh, word to mother, I'm dangerous—

Crazier than a bag of [bleep]ing Angel Dust.

When I bust my gat, mother take dirt naps.

I'm all that and a dime sack. Where the paper at?

Old Biggie with the cigar steps forward.

Big up, big up, it's a stick up, stick up

and I'm shooting niggas quick if you hic-cup

INMATE DOWN! ALL OFFICERS REPORT

IMMEDIATELY TO UNIT TWO. INMATE DOWN!

The loudspeaker comes in under Biggie's rap. The sixties-era sound system crackles with static but Mr. Castagnola, the recreation specialist, heeds and exits at a run.

The performers, deep into the act, ignore it. The four backups carry on ambling around the stage, weaving their way in and out of the two Biggies, tugging up their shorts and halting now and again as the mood takes them to fling up their arms in a cross between a free throw and a cheer lead.

Older Biggie claims center stage. He syncs into his mic-cigar.

One in the chamber, 32 in the clip.

Mother[bleep]es better strip, yeah nigga peel before you find out how blue steel feel.

The show goes on, but the announcement has caused a certain amount of restiveness in the audience. For one thing, even under the static and crackle, they can tell that the message's voice lacks its usual air of ironic boredom. And for another, all but the very newly arrived know that if an inmate is DOWN, it does not mean that she is resting. It means she is hurt.

Eyes widen and inmates begin to exchange glances. They stretch back and forward on their seats, peering around one other.

Who's missing?

On stage, the Biggies remain oblivious.

Ooh Biggie, let me jack her, I kick her in the back,
Hit her with the gat,

Old Biggie answers.

Yo chill, Shorty, let me do that . . .
Just get the [bleep]ing car keys and cruise up the block
The bitch act shocked, getting shot on the spot
(Oh shit! The cops!) Be cool, fool.

A murmur moves through the audience.

"Ottilla and Dessie? Big O and Dessie?"

"Shh!"

"Who?"

"Cassidy and Johansson."

"Who?"

"Shh!"

"Ottilla Cassidy and Desiree Johansson!"

"Hey, girl, how Dessie gonna split? I was just now seeing her up *in* here."

Outside, at the door to Unit Two, the veteran duty officer guards the entry, blocking those who would enter. On the sidewalk in front, the rest of the officers don't know what to do but they know that they should do something. They shift back and forth.

And now trotting down past recreation from the medical building and bearing an empty gurney come the institution's two medics. They are short, dark-skinned, pudgy, and set apart from the staff by white health-service jackets. And now, by the fact that they are the only staffers with a goal. They move with determination and their eyes are filled with urgency.

But as they approach, their jog is impeded in front of Unit Two by the hovering crowd of tense and agitated personnel. The medics, India nationals on work visas, are underdogs in the institutional hierarchy and normally they would defer, but tonight, mission trumps rank. They hunch and crouch to enact an their apology but they push forward with determination.

"Hip-hip!" they call in continental singsong. "Coming through, sirs! Out of the way, sirs."

Their passage forces guards off the sidewalk and into the snow banks.

The medics ignore the curses.

Before they can reach the steps leading up to Unit Two, however, the door opens. The guarding veteran officer recoils and steps away as a tall inmate, clad in a beige, polyester prison-issue uniform stands in the entrance.

She's a light-skinned African American, tall, slim but wide-shouldered, with close-cropped hair. Her arms are in submission behind her back, but her head is up. Her face is utterly blank, as though unaware of the wounds on her face and neck—deep scratches with rivulets of blood down her throat and into her collar. She is empty of expression.

Almost hidden behind her is the short, rookie officer. He's holding fast to the chain of his prisoner's cuffs, and he tries to push her forward. She resists, stays immobile. The congestion of personnel below her on the sidewalk crowds her path and offers no passage. It only glares up at her in hostility.

Another shove. "Get the fuck going. Move!"

She sways forward, but stays rooted. The staff radiates fumes of adrenalized hostility and refuses to make way. A bare flicker of emotion disturbs the inmates blood-streaked face.

"I said move it!"

She steps forward but only to brace herself. She keeps her ground.

For an instant the scene under the arc lights is frozen into stark tableau. The only movements are billows of icy breath wafting into the night air.

But now the scene is broken by the medics. Heedless of the tension, still in obsequious crouches, still issuing a duet of Bengali apologies, they drive through the cluster. The only concession they make is in the position of their stretcher. They have shifted it to ride vertically.

The officers swear at them but grudgingly step aside, and the medics persevere. They start up the concrete steps where, at the top, poses the bleeding, handcuffed inmate. The medics ignore her and push past.

And with that the spell is broken. The officers and staff step off the sidewalk into the banks of snow to allow the wounded captive passage. But to demonstrate their hostility, they make a show of stiffening their bodies away from the contamination of her.

Yet from the prisoner's expression, she might be walking a country lane. Her attention is focused over their heads, out into the night. She seems oblivious to the hostility, unaware even of the guard at her rear who is harrying her and harassing her forward. She ignores the crowd, casually moving through it.

Back inside rec, the two lip-syncing Biggies and the loping backups are still at it. Old Biggie commands center stage.

And if he start to scream 'Bam! Bam!' Have a nice dream.

Hold up, he got a [bleep]ing bitch in the car.

Fur coats and diamonds, she thinks she a superstar.

Young Biggie steps forward.

Ooh Biggie, let me jack her, I kick her in the back

Hit her with the gat...

Suddenly the music grinds down in midbeat and halts.

Mr. Castagnola, back in the rec building, is squatting over the sound system. He rises and shoves past the Biggies to center stage. His face is taut. An eye twitches.

"Settle down, ladies," he bellows, his voice cracking, "Remain calm. Settle down."

The admonition, called out to an only mildly restive room, causes waves of panicky alarm. The inmates begin to rise and scatter and call out to one another. From the Spanish section comes a scream in contralto, another in soprano.

But on stage the performers go cool. The lopers assume elaborate attitudes of unconcern. They relax into casual, pelvis-to-the-side slouches. The side-glances they exchange are utterly neutral. Young Biggie rights a slipping do-rag, but very languidly. Old Biggie is so relaxed his cigar slips from his fingers.

LOCK DOWN. ALL INMATES RETURN TO YOUR UNITS.

Behind the fuzz of the aging sound system, the announcement radiates angry accusation. The inmates pick up its tone and begin to elbow and push toward the door. Their voices—Spanish and black and English—are shrill with alarm.

LOCK DOWN, LOCK DOWN, LOCK DOWN.

The distressed inmates take note of the loudspeaker's wrath. They don't know what they have done; they only know that one of them has done something. Something very bad.

Outside the recreation hall, the compound had been regaining order, but now the double doors of the rec swing open, and the swarm of exiting inmates creates chaos again. The inmate line divides into a fork—some few headed toward the north-side units, the majority southbound toward Unit Two.

The officer parade policing the handcuffed hostage has been moving north to the captain's office, but it halts in the face of the advancing swarm. It swears, and the officers in the lead close in around the captive. A female guard steps out in front of the prisoner and spreads her arms, although it is unclear whether she is protecting the captive from the swarm or the swarm from the captive.

"Get back, get back," yells another officer. He motions with one hand and reaches for his walkie-talkie.

The front flank of inmates falters.

ALL INMATES, REPORT TO YOUR UNITS IMMEDIATELY!

LOCKDOWN, LOCKDOWN, LOCKDOWN!

It's mass confusion now. A minority of inmates are headed away from the action's center, but the majority live in units located beyond the uniforms. It would be theoretically possible for them to achieve their home buildings by turning away from the spectacle and taking the long way around the compound. But they very much do not want to do that. They see the bloodied, handcuffed inmate, and if they can get closer while at the same time, not disobeying a direct order....

So instead of turning away and retreating, the southbound line stops and steps off the sidewalk and up onto the snowbank. Some, in overcompensation, skid down the back side. They are on edge and excited, but they all know their best chance of being allowed witness to drama is to project indifference to it. They hush and become incurious. They wipe expressions and cast eyes downward.

In the meantime, the last of the inmates emptying the recreation hall still pours out into the night, loud and eager. But immediately they catch the mood. Even the new ones know enough to move off the sidewalk, remain silent, and lower their eyes.

So finally, the scene regains order. The cuffed and bloody captive, with staff front and rear, swings at a deliberate pace between the rows of inmate and on down the sidewalk. The inmates bow heads as though in prayer.

Then suddenly the mood changes. The team of medics emerges from the door of Unit Two. They struggle with a gurney now draped in army blankets. The canvas sags. It bears weight.

"Emergency! We are on our way, sirs," they sing out. "Move off the path immediately, sirs! Hip-hip, please. Passing through."

To get to the medical building they must trot their burden beyond the guards and up through the lines of inmates. Undeterred, they lower their heads and jog forward.

With the trotting medics now at their heels, the officers marching the tall African American past the rec to the captain's office have two options: they can up their gait to a matching trot, or they can move to the side and surrender the sidewalk. They choose surrender, but with face-saving curses.

The line of inmates, on the other hand, is quiet and sedate. Like falling dominoes, they have cleared the sidewalk all the way to the rec entrance. As the stretcher moves past they keep their heads down.

But not all the way down, for from the gurney a bare female arm flops loose and falls. The arm is white under the flood lights, but the index finger skimming the sidewalk is dark with blood. The inmates can't help but raise their eyes. Some even raise their heads, only to be nudged back down by peers. An untoward movement and the medics will be ordered to retreat and they will be banished.

The wiser choice for the medics now would be to keep moving, let the arm drag. But the rear medic—the one with a view of the arm—cannot allow it.

"Halt! Halt," he cries in a yelp tinged with panic.

The lead stops and looks around. He makes lowering motions with his chin and the two, bearing the weight of the stretcher, drop into a squat. The rear medic tilts the stretcher down to rest its handles on the sidewalk.

The staff swears again, and the inmates become very alert.

The rear medic stretches out and repositions the arm under the army blanket, but as he rises again with his burden, he fails to note that a corner of the blanket trails on the sidewalk. The two resume their trot. Almost immediately the blanket whips off and is yanked to the ground.

A few of the officers yell. Gasps escape from the inmates. Several of them erupt into sobs. One Spanish girl issues an involuntary wail, and a companion reaches for her, pulls her in close, and rocks her.

The buzz-cut Rookie officer standing in front, his back to the action, jerks around now at the disturbance. He is the one to have discovered the contents of the gurney, and he is trying not to think about it.

Here it is again.

He forces his focus away. It lands on the embracing inmates.

"Inappropriate contact," he barks.

The young inmate jumps away; the older raises her chin and glares at him.

Otherwise, all attention is on the body. The medics have decided not to pause and cover it again—just to hurry it home.

Until recently the thing on the gurney, flopping to its jouncing ride, was a well-shaped and sensuous young female. Now it is only vile. The face of the body has teeth bared, tongue protruded. The whites of the eyes are blossoming red and the bruises around the neck are already deeply purple. Wisps of blond curls once decorated the body's face; now they only highlight the horror.

A cropped, torn tee shirt fails to cover a breast and a bare midriff. Both lie white and exposed under the arc lights. The waistband of the thermal long johns has slipped down, and reveals hand-stitched, prison-issue panties refashioned into a thong. The toenails are painted contraband pink.

Someone in Unit Two has illegal nail polish; she is selling pedicures. Ordinarily this would be worthy information but now no one bothers to take note. All focus is on the body.

It's obscene, but not sexually obscene, for there is no humanity in it. Its obscenity resides in the sprawl of the posture—the utter absence of the human impulse to present itself. It once would have cared deeply—now not at all—that its features are twisted and contorted, that its breast is exposed, that its torso is awkwardly laid out, that its limbs fall into ungainly positions.

"Hip-hip. Out of the way."

The rough trot jiggles and bounces the body in a repulsive parody of restlessness.

The inmates know that staring in fascination as they are doing is an infraction that lies beyond the penitentiary rules—is an ultimate off-limits, an absolute out-of-bounds. They are ashamed that they stare, and yet they stare.

The body, repellent in its fitful repose, bounces and flops past. It disappears through the entrance to the medical building.

LOCK DOWN, LOCK DOWN, LOCK DOWN!

The harshly lit compound is quiet now. The hushed and shaken inmates move, heads down, toward their units.

Finally, all is still.

PART 1: CHAPTER 1

1996
SIX MONTHS EARLIER

"What in the world is the matter with these girls?"

The question comes from a bench on the grounds of the Danbury Federal Correctional Institution. The bench sits outside of Unit Twelve and overlooks the compound. The question is directed at a Unit Twelve resident, Iris Engels, an inmate in her late forties.

"They're not girls," Iris says tightly, avoiding eye contact. "They're ladies."

"Then why don't they act like it?"

Iris doesn't respond.

She is, by prison standards, neat and well put together. She's tall and slim. Her brown hair, streaks of gray around her face, is cropped close at the nape. She has prominent cheekbones and a small, delicate nose—a high school graduation gift that she regrets. Her eyes are a light brown—almost khaki. In this late-morning light they match her uniform.

Lunch hour is winding up, and the penitentiary compound is congested with inmates. Very few look anything like Hollywood's rendition of babes-in-bondage. In the first place, very few of them are babes. The average inmate is in her midthirties. Many are middle-aged, and there are even a few elders.

And the compound doesn't sound like a Hollywood prison either. It lacks a hush of muted sorrow, the *Nobody Knows the Trouble I've Seen* soundtrack. Indeed, it is raucous. It rings with good cheer, and half of the good cheer is in Spanish. There are also small and less-clamorous groups of Vietnamese and Chinese, and over a third of the compound is descended from Africa—African Americans largely, but a portion of the blacks speak Spanish or speak with Nigerian and Jamaican lilts. English is a minority language, and among the English speakers the women conversing in standard—as opposed to urban or island or African vernacular—are a minority within the minority.

"Where are all these Spanish coming from?"

"Colombia."

"Why are they all here? What are they doing?"

"Their time."

The answer hangs in the air.

The questioner is a few years younger than Iris but now she looks older. Her face is bare of cosmetics and shows strain. She's dressed in gray scrubs, meaning that she came in this morning and has yet to be dressed out. The shimmer and shape of her hair means that she's a white-collar self-commit. She arrived of her own volition, not in travel shackles. By extension it means that she avoided doing her presentencing time in a county jail or at a Metropolitan Correctional Center. She had money and the judge granted her bail.

An incoming inmate's hair tells a lot about her, and the general rule is that the better the hair, the more difficult the adjustment. The rule applies now; this one is going to be a pain.

It is obvious, as she looks over the compound with a condescending air, that she is clinging to her pre-prison social position. She is assuming that she can bring her education and her occupational stature in with her.

She is wrong.

Also, at this moment, she is offending prison etiquette by claiming, uninvited, a space on Iris's bench. She is assuming that they are peers—that the two of them will naturally sit together and patronize the population.

She is wrong.

"Why are all these women acting like they're at some kiddy party or something?"

Iris sighs and responds unwillingly. "Because maybe they're carefree? Safe?"

"Safe in a *prison*?" exclaims new commit.

"Absolutely," says Iris, defensive and responding in spite of herself. "A lot of these ladies are violence-free for the first time in their lives."

"That doesn't sound right to me. I did my research. Prisons are dangerous places. For every hundred inmates, there's over—"

"Men's prisons," interrupts Iris, still not making eye contact. "No one's going to hurt these women. Their guards aren't allowed to; their men aren't allowed in."

"Yes but... aren't they always beating up on *each other*?"

"Oh, there'll be a girl fight every couple of weeks. Mostly hair pulling and scratching. Hardly ever serious."

The new commit is confused by the whole scene. These women have committed criminal acts, (obviously of a baser nature than her own) but they look like regular women. And they aren't acting the way they should. It's their attitude. They're too boisterous. They move too loosely. Some are almost romping. They look as if they fail to grasp that they are being punished. The penitentiary doesn't seem to be having a penitential effect. Indeed, it seems to be having a carefree, just-a-kid-again effect. The inmates shout to one another. They break into involuntary half-skips. They playfully push and aim slaps and dart away. They laugh loudly and tease. The younger ones—and even many of the middle-aged—move with a loose stride, unburdened by the obligation to present themselves as graceful or sensual.

"Aren't they even a little bit unhappy about being locked up?"

"They'll all certainly tell you that they are," says Iris noncommittally.

The new woman waits for Iris to expand. When Iris doesn't, she adds lamely, "Well, they don't act like it."

They sit in silence.

Then, when Iris begins to talk, it's almost to herself. "A lot of them—the Spanish and the Asians, some of the white women too—are out from under their families and their husbands for the first time in their lives. They'll admit, if you can get them to talk about it, that they actually have more freedom now than they did before. Free of domination; free of responsibility. And they are absolutely not going to get *pregnant* again."

Over beside the rec building a group of middle-aged Colombians are at play, laughing and pushing one another. A trio of white women need one another's support in the fall-out from a joke. Up the sidewalk a pair of huge young black women hold hands and skip past. The newcomer watches the pair with condescending amusement and tries to catch Iris's eye.

She can't.

"Well," she finally observes, "they must be unhappy by the way the guards treat them. I personally have never experienced that kind of rudeness."

"Maybe--do you think it's because you came in treating them like underlings? Like they're part of the wait staff?"

The new inmate frowns and ignores the suggestion. "I just don't see how anyone can stand being talked to that way."

"The guards are rarely abusive."

"It depends on how you define abusive. Perhaps your standards are . . ." She trails off.

Iris refuses the bait. "It's like the military. None of us particularly likes it when we're ordered around or yelled at, but the people doing it aren't supposed to love us. It makes a difference."

Outside of Unit Six a trio of young African Americans are now competing in a happy little race.

NO RUNNING ON THE COMPOUND, LADIES.
NO RUNNING ON THE COMPOUND.

They falter and continue, but at a speed-walk.

"I should think they'd want to pull themselves together and grow up. Maybe they wouldn't get yelled at if they didn't act like a bunch of kids on a playground."

Iris ignores the speculation and looks over her shoulder at the door of Unit Twelve. A young inmate with long dark hair carrying a canvas bag is just coming out.

"And here she is now. Emilia, this is . . . I didn't get your name?"

"Rebecca Kaplan."

Emilia Rivera smiles sweetly at her. "You are welcome to Danbury," she says in Spanish accent.

"I was just explaining that she was taking your place."

"Is okay," says Emilia, flipping aside a curtain of hair, "It is plenty of space."

She perches on Iris's side of the bench and shuffles her hips to make room for herself.

Iris throws her a look.

Emilia smiles back. Her eyes dance.

The population that Iris Engels and Rebecca Kaplan have been discussing could, in tableau, pass for an ordinary American street-side group of women.

Maybe a little more ethnically diverse? Less than a quarter are white.

A little less polished? The commissary has yet to complete its change-over for the new female population. It offers only a few basic cosmetic and hair-care products.

A little less trim? It lists a generous half-page of junk food.

But probably what most firmly situates the population in a penitentiary is its day-dress. Everyone is in the same beige, polyester pull-up pants and button-down shirts—some long sleeved, some short—over thermal underwear. Everyone has on heavy, black prison-issue boots or oxfords. A few of the inmates have thrown brown zip-up jackets over their shoulders or hung them, sleeves tied at the waist, but most are in shirtsleeves on this warm New England day in early fall.

Just emerging from the dining room is a second newcomer. This one, unlike the self-commit on the bench, has already been processed but her uniform is still stiff with factory sizing. Her hair has been crudely chopped off—blond for only a jagged inch at the ears and neck. The rest is brown, detention-center root. Three days ago and fresh off the airlift it had the same roots but was long and blond down her back. It needed its ends trimmed, but it was still long and blond.

The hair salon over beside the laundry room is (unofficially) segregated, and the pair of African American inmate beauticians keep it that way. A new white girl comes in with long untrimmed hair and before she can protest—

Yesterday this one had sat in shock, her blond strands on the floor, while the beauticians—exchanging mischievous twinkles—had cooed and fluffed at the hack job and told her how cute it was.

Now, as she leaves the dining room, her hairdo is not contributing to her adjustment issues. She's still dazed by the overcrowding and the chaos and, paradoxically, by the isolation. The veteran inmates act as if she doesn't exist, and her roommate doesn't speak English. As she emerges into the sunlight she sees two uniformed officers lining up inmates, doing pat-downs. She has no idea why.

In front of the line, a sheepish Spanish lady—forestalling the officer—removes a small plastic bag of salad-bar vegetables from under her shirt.

"Don't be pulling this shit again, Sanchez," the male guard growls, and he drops the bag onto the pile at his feet. "Next time I write you up. Now outta-here,"

The second pat-down guard is female—a fierce African American nearly six feet tall. Her hair is a high wedge-cut; her eyes are set wide apart. That, together with the length of her legs starting high on her torso, gives her the look of a space invader.

"You! Get your ass over here." She snaps her fingers and points at the ground.

The new inmate looks left and right with panic behind her eyes. She points at herself—me?

"Yes, you. Do you see anyone else?"

She does. The penitentiary, built to hold a population of six hundred, now houses over twelve. They're everywhere. Indeed, at this moment a someone-else is tripping over the heel of her shoe.

The alien's lunatic question coupled with the entire madhouse atmosphere causes the new inmate to fear that she's been assigned to do her time on another planet.

Back on Iris's bench there are still three, but the composition has changed. On one side is still Emilia Rivera, the light-skinned Colombian with long, blue-black hair. In the middle is still Iris Engels, the thin and middle-aged inmate with a graying crop. But Desiree Johansson has replaced the paper-crime self-commit.

Desiree, like the newbie over at the pat-down line, has blond hair but hers is natural. She has curls down her shoulders and a clear Nordic complexion. It has been suggested that she is the best-looking girl on the compound.

Well, okay. The best-looking *white* girl.

Desiree moves in a different circle from Iris's, but she had been encouraged to approach her: "You really need to talk to her about your case. Just go up—introduce yourself."

"She looks scary. She'll probably try to blow me off."

"No, really, she's not like that."

Desiree Johansson had broached Iris tentatively, but to her surprise, she was welcomed. Iris made room for her on the bench, telling the new self-commit that they had personal business and shuttling her away.

"Oh-oh, watch," Iris comments now, leaning toward Desiree, "Uranus is going after fresh meat."

Back at the dining hall exit, at the front of the pat-down line the inmate with the new prison cut is visibly shaken.

"Hurry it up. Get your ass over," in a voice that rises above the hubbub. "Spread your arms. Spread your legs." The bark carries over to the Unit Twelve bench.

"Now just watch the way Uranus pats her down," says Iris.

Desiree shakes a curl out of her eyes. "Da-y-mn. I'm just glad she's got somebody else to go after."

"Yeah, I noticed back when how she used to mess with you. So, she isn't still on your case?"

"Actually, not so much anymore." Desiree pauses and ventures a little sass. "But she's still hating on me ba-aad. Because I'm so beautiful and she can't have me."

Iris and Emilia laugh.

"But now she's working her way past it," suggests Iris.

"She's trying," agrees Desiree, happily.

The three women on Iris's bench watch in detached sympathy as the new inmate faces Uranus and spreads her arms and legs.

The officer impatiently twirls a finger. The inmate looks confused.

"I said turn the f—turn around!"

The pat-down drama continues, but the view is blocked now as two African American inmates approach Iris's bench. The elder of the two addresses Iris with an attitude of respect.

"Ms. Iris? Er, Ms. Iris? Uh, can I...?"

"Sure, Asia, no problem, but just a sec."

The petitioner is middle-aged, of matronly build with a stiff do of black hair. The one she is leading is a young, slim tomboy with close-cropped head. In spite of the older one tugging her along by a shirt tail, she walks with a springy step, her shoulders back, her chin up.

Iris leans around the pair and holds up a finger. "We're watching some B.O.P. action here."

"What's Be-Oh-Pee?" asks the young inmate.

"Shh," says the older.

"Girl, you *are* new," exclaims Desiree.

"I keep hearing Be-Oh-Pee, Be-Oh-Pee, Be-Oh-Pee," complains the tomboy.

"Shh," admonishes the matron. "That's how we call the Bureau of Prisons up in here. Now you pay attention. That uniform up over there? You want to stay back from that one. That's Williamson, working her bad-ass pat-down."

"What's her problem?"

"Just bad-ass attitude. Right this minute she's wanting to scare herself some of that new-cracker white-trash," The older woman catches herself and flicks an apprehensive glance at the white ladies, but they are laughing and taking no offense. Their attention is focused on the exit.

The officer looms over her prey. The new one hastily turns her back and re-spreads her arms and legs.

"Watch how Uranus does her now," says Iris.

"Who Uranus?" asks the youngster.

"Shh," hisses the older.

"Shee-it, why you shushing? I just ask—"

"Stop popping your lips." The older one throws a half-hearted mother-swat. "You ain't need to ask nothing."

The young inmate raises her fists and dances nimbly.

"Hey, Big Momma, you try-a shush me? You know who you addressing? You addressing Number One."

"I'll number-one your ass," threatens the Big Momma.

Desiree intervenes. "Uranus is just the nickname we all give to that lady officer over there."

"Why?"

"Because she looks like she comes from Uranus."

"Your anus?" The youngster asks in genuine bewilderment.

"No, fool, *U-ranus*," corrects the older.

Pause.

"What's *U-ranus?*"

"SHHH!"

Over in front of the dining room exit, Uranus is being thorough to a fault. She handles her way down her victim's shoulders, then with a trained side-of-hand, she firmly demarcates the breasts—between and underneath.

"Uranus knows the inmate's clean," explains Iris. "She's just tormenting her—getting herself off on a little newbie intimidation."

Uranus is on one knee now, lingering around the inmate's upper thighs.

"Go, Uranus," Desiree mock-shouts.

"She couldn't get away with all that if she were a man," observes Iris.

"Just got to lo-oove those officer dikes," agrees Desiree with a touch of TV valley-girl. "They are so totally thee worst."

Uranus moves to the second leg, but this time she starts higher. The new inmate jumps at the crotch bump, and her three-women audience on the bench can almost hear a small, involuntary squeak.

"It's happy days for Uranus if she can get her fish to cry," says Iris. "But oh dear, no. No tears for Uranus."

"Po-or Uranus," chimes in Emilia.

Desiree frames her mouth with her hands, "Maybe next time, Uranus!"

Uranus rises and fixes her attention over the shoulder of the newbie, demonstrating the extent that she is not worth looking at. She curls her lip, twitches her nose, and sniffs. She dismisses the inmate with a withering wave.

Now that the drama is over, Iris turns to the newcomers. "What's going on, Asia B? You ladies know Asia—Asia Applebee?"

Asia B, the matronly African American, pushes the youngster forward. "This here is Rogo—Rochelle Gooden. She come in couple weeks ago."

"You are welcome to Danbury." Emilia smiles, giving a little dip with her head.

"Ms. Iris, Rogo here is needing some legal work done if you got the time. The Feds went and enhanced her up an extra sixty months for an illegal silencer. Except what I hear is, it ain't illegal to *own* a silencer."

"Depends on the state. Where's she out of?"

"Virginia. That's where she caught her case is Virginia."

"Wasn't even my weapon!" says Rogo with indignation. "My cousin, he come up, drop it off at my crib, He be going to his auntie's funeral."

"Okay, now wait a minute, back up," says Iris. "What I'm hearing is that the Feds came and they searched your place and found a weapon? With a suppresser. And this took place in Virginia?"

"Roanoke. But it was not my weapon."

"And I'm assuming they found drugs? How much?"

"Not no big stash or nothing. They got a few little grams of powder, ain't got rocked up yet."

"Lucky," says Iris.

"Yeah, I know, huh? And just a little couple ounces of weed which they *saying*, weigh out at ten, which I just purchased, so I *know* is coming right in at eight, know what I mean? I ain't pinch it yet."

New inmates can overflow with the details of their crime story, and it can be wearying. Rogo notices the distancing expressions but misreads them.

"Don't get me wrong, I ain't come up here in the penitentiary bitching on my drug weight. That was my shit, and I'll take my time for my shit. But that was *not* my weapon and that weapon got me *fucked up*. I kept telling the po-lice—I'm saying, 'Just check it out for prints. I ain't never even *touched* that gun,' but they acting like I just moving my lips, know what I mean?" Rogo makes a talky-talk gesture. "They say unless I'm ready to testify on Mojo—"

"Okay, stop. Who's Mojo?"

"That'd be my cousin, Modell—Modell Johnson. My lawyer, she's telling me how I got to roll over on someone or she can't do nothing for me. Except me, I'm thinking it's more like she and that prosecutor had a little something going on, you know?"

Iris protests. "No, Rogo, you actually want your attorney to have a good relationship with the prosecution...."

"Not with that piece of shit. He trying to do me, like, for eighteen years! And all the time those two be like—whispering, laughing—shit like that. Be planning out their shit together, trying to fuck me over."

Iris sighs and Asia B interjects. "Rogo, Ms. Iris don't need to be listening to none of your theories. Just talk about your specifics."

"Okay, okay, so anyway, like I say, the time they giving me on the dope? That's cool—that's all good. I accept my thirty-six months, know what I mean? But they going wild on my ass, sticking me on those hundred twenty. They saying, like, sixty for the Glock-9, then they go and enhancing me up another sixty behind the suppressor and none of that wasn't even *mine*. I never, ever in my life even kept no weapon."

Rogo is no longer hip-hopping. She's stiff with the injustice.

"Who was the gun registered to?" asks Iris.

"Some dude doing his time up at Jessup. Never heard of the dude."

"But it was in with your belongings."

"That's on account of Mojo. He didn't want to be carrying up into the church where his auntie is having her funeral, know what I mean? It was a respect thing. The auntie wasn't my people—she from the other side of the family-- so he knew I be staying at home—up in my crib watching the game and he riding on past, so he just run upstairs, boop-boop, stash it up in my closet. Then after the burial he had to go sit with Grandma Johnson—she's grieving and shit—so he never come back over to my place that day. So then the next morning, four a.m.—*BAM-BAM-BAM.*"

Rogo, animated with narration, is hip-hopping again, acting out the BAMS. "BAM-BAM-BAM! I'm like, 'What the hell?'"

Iris sighs. Desiree's eyes are starting to wander off onto the compound. Emilia reaches for her bag.

Asia interrupts. "Tell Ms. Iris about your security designation."

Rogo halts the SWAT-team dance.

"Oh yeah, see, behind those weapon enhancements? They got my security upped so I ain't never going to be camp eligible. Otherwise, I get down my time below ten years, I'm transfer over to Alderson. That's just up the road from where my mom's at. She be able to come up there weekends, but she can't be expecting to drive all this way up over here. She get lost on those big super highways, the DeVille ain't even *trying* to make it, know what I mean? Be busting up along the highway, she be standing there—car's tearing past"—Rogo swings her head—"*Zoom, zoom.* If they make me do all my time up in here, Moms—she getting on in her years. She might be never see me again."

Iris responds with genuine sympathy.

"I'll try to see what I can do. But I have to warn you, it doesn't really matter who owned the gun. They found it with drugs, period. So we wouldn't get anywhere trying to fight the weapon charge. You didn't try to brandish, did you?"

"Brandish, hell, no. They busting in, I ain't even know it's up *in* there."

"Good. I'll have to see if your lawyer objected; if not we might be able to claim ineffective and then ask for relief over the enhancement. I think," says Iris focusing into the distance, "that Asia's right—silencers are legal in Virginia. I'll have to check. If they are, that'll give us something to work with because the Feds are supposed to comply with state law." Iris waves her hand. "So, if we're right, eventually the court may be persuaded to take off the suppressor enhancement. Do you have priors?"

"Just some juvie shit."

"Good."

LUNCH BREAK IS OVER.

ALL INMATES, REPORT TO YOUR WORK STATIONS.

REPEAT: LUNCH. OVER. INMATES: BACK TO WORK.

They all rise. Desiree dusts off the seat of her pants, and Emilia zips the canvas bag. Rogo cocks her head. "Why that loudspeaker up in there always be trying to be talking like it's on M*A*S*H* or something?"

"Because the officer behind it *watched* M.A.S.H.," says Iris ruefully. "Too *much* M*A*S*H."

Rogo is intrigued. "That loudspeaker's an officer?"

"Hush! What you think?" Asia B gives Rogo a shove.

"No, actually," teases Desiree, "it's a recording. No, I know! It's the Wizard of Oz."

"No shit. Wizard of Oz doing time here at Danbury." Rogo looks pleased with the attention.

Iris turns to Emilia. "Hey, we've got to go. Johansson gave you her paperwork, right?"

"Yeah, I did," says Desiree. "She put it in her bag."

Iris turns back to Rogo. "Now, your paperwork—your PSI. Has it come in yet?"

"Nah, I just got up in here. My attorney, she saying I can only bring in my Bible with me."

"Well, I can't do anything without your PSI. So your task, should you choose to accept, is to write to your lawyer."

"She hates my ass. I be sitting all those months up Roanoke County? Mojo, he stop upping the money flow, she stop accepting my calls, know what I mean? She ain't about to send me no—"

"No, she'll send it. She has to. That's part of her job. But you've got to put in the request. Write to her. You've got her address? Get it from your folks."

Iris, Emilia, and Desiree start to walk away.

Iris stops and turns back to Asia B. "Remind her. We've got a year to file, but we want to get on it."

"I'll be at her," promises Asia B.

ALL INMATES, REPORT TO YOUR WORK STATIONS. NOW!

Asia tugs at Rogo's sleeve. As they start across the compound together, Asia B begins: "See I told you Ms. Iris going to help... hey, don't you be looking at that white lady."

Rogo looks innocently left and right and points at herself. "Me? What white lady?"

"You know."

"You referring about that *lawyer* white lady?"

"*Shh!*" Asia swings a pelvis bump. "No, I'm not talking about no lawyer white lady."

"You talking about that Spanish lady?"

Asia swats. "I'm talking about that yellow-hair."

"Yellow hair?" Rogo dances away. "Oh-hh, *that* yellow hair...."

CHAPTER 2

Desiree, blinking from the sunlight, enters the laundry. The front room is a combination office and reception area. Under its flickering, buzzing banks of fluorescents it has aged gracelessly. The Sheetrock walls are blotched with patching plaster; they crack and buckle under layers of yellowing paint. The floor, '50s gray asphalt tile, holds a faint buff in the middle but is edged with grime-embedded wax. The room is crowded with a pair of oversized metal desks and a bank of files. The only natural light, now that Desiree has closed the door behind herself, creeps in through its mesh-covered pane.

To the left is a large darkened area—the cage—sectioned off with a wall of woven steel links. The front wall features a window looking out onto the grounds which slides open to. distribute sheets and uniforms and underwear issues to lines of inmates. It's shuttered now.

"Johansson, you're late again."

Desiree extends her commissary wristwatch out to Mr. O'Donnell, head of laundry. "Not by the time *I* got."

O'Donnell is standing, leaning on one of the desks, his arms crossed. He wears operations-staff gray, which differentiates him from the blue-uniformed correctional officers and the caseworkers in street clothes. He is thirty-something, tall, on the heavy side with blue Irish eyes.

He ignores the watch. "Yeah, yeah, be on time. Work on it. I need you in the back this afternoon. Ramirez has a medical and Gomez... I don't know where the hell Gomez is."

"Is called out on a writ, boss," chimes up an inmate leaning languidly on Desiree's desk. She is light-skinned with darkly mascaraed eyes, brows a thin-penciled arch, Wet 'n Wild lips, and high, colored-in Colombian cheekbones. Her shoulder-length blond hair, dark at the side part, is crisp and turning orange at the ends. She is shapely and her pants are hand-altered—pegged, with pockets stitched closed to conform to her pelvis. Her crossed legs are extended as she faces the room, propped against the desk, arms stiff and palms down in a pose that emphasizes her breasts.

She addresses O'Donnell in proprietary reproach mixed with little girl. "I am telling you this morning, Mister Boss. Gomez is packing out last night."

"Yeah, yeah, whatever," waves O'Donnell in dismissal. "Just get back in there, Johansson, and help fold."

The coworker uncrosses her legs and rises in victory. Now she can claim Desiree's desk.

"Apaza," O'Donnell interrupts before she can sit, "there isn't anything going on out here."

"I needing to reconcile files," protests Apaza.

"No, Johansson finished this morning. I want you over in the cage."

Apaza puts on a sulky face. O'Donnell ignores it.   "The floors in there need mopped," he tells her. He reaches to his belt, pulls a key from the retractable reel, and unlocks the cage's oversized mesh door.

"Perez is having the mop bucket," Apaza protests in little-girl pout.

"Well then, wait till she gets done *having*. Get in and straighten out the shelves."

In laundry-department hierarchy, the reception desk is pinnacle, the cage is a few steps down, and the back room where Desiree has been sent is the pits. It's a cavernous windowless room, redolent with hot-fabric and detergent. Its floors are an uneven concrete with cracks and paint dribbles and oil stains. On the right is an aging line of hulking, wheezing, vibrating machines; on the left is a pair of long folding tables.

As Desiree enters, a middle-aged Spanish woman is mopping the floor of her passage.

"Wet! Wet floor!" the woman shrieks at Desiree at a flames-in-the-dryer pitch.

Desiree stops and, heaving a sigh, leans against the doorframe. She paradiddles her fingers and rolls her eyes up in a silent plea for patience.

Perez, the middle-aged mopper, is concentrating on an area needing special attention that borders Desiree's work boot. Desiree shifts out of the way.

In the back room a cart piled with freshly dried sheeting has been wheeled to a folding table and a team of four Colombians, all matronly and—to the North American eye—looking very much alike, are doing the sheet-folding salsa. A couple of them swing out stretches of fabric, flick it to snap, then, with flair, swing back together, aligning the hem and selvage edges.

Desiree is finally allowed in, and a white girl beckons her to the second folding table. She's in her late twenties, busty, a little on the heavy side, medium-ash Clairol hair with a roll of bangs. She's holding the hem of a sheet.

As they begin to fold they discover on moving apart that the sheet is twisted. They both adjust and spread for a second try—twisted again—and again for a third. They fall into giggles.

One of the Spanish matrons, stern, clucking in disapproval, comes over. She firmly removes the sheet, gathers up the rest, and walks the pile over to the adult table.

The two make naughty-child faces at her back.

Perez wheels over a cart of beige uniforms, and Desiree picks out a shirt in a mock show of apprehension. "If we don't get this one right she's going to come over and rap our knuckles."

"She's bringing the switch."

The two, giggling together, start on the pile of shirts.

"I'm Dessie. You're Lydia, right? Aren't you in the drug program?"

"Not anymore," says Lydia. "I'm back over in Unit Two. They flunked me out."

"Oh, that's right, I heard another one of you programmers bit the dust. That was you, huh? So what bad-bad thing did *you* do?"

"Relationship, they *said*. Except we never did really *do* anything."

"So how'd they prove relationship?"

"They didn't, actually. I got caught out-of-bounds over at her unit. We weren't actually—you know. We were just barely even fooling around. I snuck in because she was getting transferred up to camp the next morning and we were just wanting a little minute—you know. Whatever. Except then someone went and snitched us out to the guard."

"So you didn't actually get cuffed up or anything."

"No, just a write-up for off-limits."

"But, oops, curtains for the drug program, huh?"

"Yeah, they were trying to boot me anyway, because I had already gotten snitched over the relationship. So now that was all the proof that they needed."

"I heard how you ladies were dropping like flies over there," says Desiree, starting to fold. "You were like number three in your cohort, right?"

"Yeah, but I don't care," says Lydia. She notices that Desiree is struggling with a shirt and reaches across to fasten the buttons for her. She slides it back. "I probably wasn't going to get my year off anyway. My son—he's with his dad in Sacramento. He just got diagnosed with non-Hodgkin's lymphoma."

"Oh, I'm so sorry,"

"Yeah, I'm putting in for a family medical transfer, trying to get out to California."

"FCI Dublin?"

"Right."

A washer, with a screeching of gears, moves into a violent spin cycle.

"He had this swelling in his groin area," Lydia continues, yelling over the machine, "and I guess he was kind of embarrassed to tell Sandra—that's Spider's girlfriend."

"Spider is..."

"My ex, Conner's father. And Spider, he was in training up in Portland. But then he finally got back home, and they got Conner in and they caught it in time."

"So how old is he?" yells Desiree. The whole room is vibrating.

"Conner? He just turned nine in September."

Desiree is having trouble folding and talking at the same time. Lydia reaches across the table for her pants. "He's got a good prognosis. They're putting him in the low-risk category."

"So, you're trying to get out there?"

The spin cycle is slowing, but Lydia still has to raise her voice. "Yeah, except it's this big fucked-up, fuck-up because now Snodgrass—that's my case manager—she says she can't put in any transfer for me or anything until I've gotten all my documentation together. And so I'm saying, 'exactly what documentation?' and she's totally, like, *useless*. At first she goes on about how I needed a signed letter from the doctor. So I relayed that information back to Spider, so then now she's saying, 'never mind the letter; I need the medical *transcripts*.' Except now Sandra isn't accepting my calls anymore because the last bill came out to whatever."

The washer is cycling up again.

"So, I wrote explaining about the transcripts," Lydia yells, "but Spider has never, ever, wrote a letter in his life, and so now I can't even find out anything unless Spider picks up, and he won't when Sandra's there, and she works nights which on our time zone is after count. Plus I'm almost out of my phone minutes anyway."

"Girl, you need some help."

"You can say that again."

"Girl, you need some help. Girl, you need some help. Girl—"

"Shut up!" Lydia mock threatens with pair of pants and Desiree feigns a duck.

"No, really. Do you know Iris Engels?"

"She's that lawyer lady over in twelve, right?"

"Yeah, out on the streets she used to be this, like, big deal New York criminal-defense attorney, so she really knows her stuff. Before I had actually met her, she kind of, like, intimidated me. Like I was thinking she'd act all, 'Who are you?' or whatever? But I finally just went up and asked and, you know, she was actually nice. You probably should talk to her."

"I can't really afford—I had to quit UNICORE to be in the drug program." Lydia looks down at the table. "Mom is sending me in a few bucks every now and again but..."

"No, really," says Desiree, reaching across to pat her hand. "If you tell her you don't get any money in, she's totally pro bono. I told her I've got a little bit, but she told me, don't worry yet, after she's looked over my paperwork and finds out whether she can do anything for me, Emilia will just give me a list—that's her roomie. She works over at the law library too."

"Engels is working for you?"

"She hasn't actually started. She's in the middle of something else, and I only just got her my paperwork."

"So what's she doing? Your 2255?"

"No, I'm way too late for that by now. Plus, right after I got here, Mom sent my case up to some university--to these guys that do post-conviction whatevers? They said forget it; not going to fly."

Desiree reaches for a pair of pants and continues. "See, my problem is, they stuck me with a violence, so even though I'm qualified for the drug program, the B.O.P. says I'm not eligible for my year off. So Iris says she can't promise anything, but my violence was a B.O.P. designation—it wasn't the judge or anything—so she'll see if there's any way to get them to lift it."

"So you have your usage documented and all?"

"Yeah, I got a drunk driving in '89."

"Lucky you! It took me forever to get qualified. I'm in here for credit-card conspiracy except I didn't want to tell my presentencing lady about how I had any drug-usage issues or anything. I was thinking it would make me look bad."

Lydia separates the shirts from the pile and moves the pants over to Desiree's side. "So then all's I had was—I had done this little treatment gig back in '91. And mom finally got them to document, but it was like pulling teeth because I didn't graduate—I took off out of there early—and they kept thinking mom was trying to get them to say I'd *completed*. It took forever to finally get it into their heads that she just wanted them to write and say I'd *been*. So now, of course, she is totally pissed over how I flunked out."

"Bummer."

The washer has settled down and shuddered into silence. Perez opens it and starts pulling wet clothes into the laundry cart. Down at the far end of the folding table, the Spanish ladies have finished their pile of sheets. One of them has picked up a Spanish newspaper and is reading aloud from its horoscope section. The prognostications are inspiring gales of merriment.

"And that's really too bad about your kid." Desiree says sincerely. "You really need to talk to Iris."

"I don't know. I don't want to just walk up out of the blue. Can I get you to introduce?"

"Absolutely. Catch me tonight at chow hall. She's almost always out front of twelve. I'll walk you over."

"So what's up with her and that sexy little Spanish?"

"Emilia's like, her secretary or whatever. Iris writes it all up and Emilia does up the typing. So they're like, partners. Plus, you know they're roommates."

"Yeah, actually I was roommates with her sister for a little minute last year. Claudia? She seemed nice, but I didn't know her very well. I moved in right before she got deported."

"When was that?"

"Last January, I think. Yeah, January. I couldn't figure what her issue was, but that lady was not happy to be getting out of jail."

"Probably wanted to stay and finish up her time with sister."

"Yeah, probably." Lydia is working her pile of uniforms. "About the sister and Iris? I was hearing a couple of the black ladies in my unit, they were saying how both of those two got under ten years but they still got placed in preferred housing. They were wondering where they were getting the juice from."

"Huh! I just assumed they were long term. Maybe their Team is rewarding them for services they perform or something?"

"That doesn't sound like them."

"Whatever."

"Whatever," agrees Lydia. They fold.

"What's with the two of them—Iris and Emilia? Are they like, *together*-together?" Lydia asks.

Desiree shrugs and puts her palms up. "Who the hell knows? They're tight, except whether they're actually in an actual relationship...?"

A pause. The two inmates work on the last of the uniforms.

Lydia, folding: "Probably are."

Pause.

Desiree, folding: "Probably are."

CHAPTER 3

It's liver on the menu tonight, and the dining hall is only half full. Most of the inmates there have changed into sweat suits and tennis shoes. One is marked as new by her daytime beige.

"Mom said she sent in my money, like, two weeks ago. But it still hasn't shown up on my books, so how long's it usually supposed to take, anyway?"

"With the B.O.P.? Who knows? Could be months."

Beyond the salad bar is the serving window, and behind that a pair of inmates in kitchen whites—hair pressed under woven-white nylon nets—load plates with off-color liver slabs and scoops of processed mashed potatoes.

A designated pair of street-clothed staffers stands mainline. They're to be available for inmate requests (hopefully short; hopefully minor) and they're just leaving. At the far side of the room, a single officer remains on duty.

Iris and Emilia, dusting cupcake crumbs from their fingers, are seated at one of the long rows of bench-and-table sets. The room is well heated, but Iris wears her winter coat. She glances casually at the officer. He's looking at his watch and edging toward the door. She reaches into her coat pocket and surreptitiously pulls out a small plastic trash liner. Palming it and reaching under the table, she hands it off to Emilia.

Emilia shakes out the bag under the table and works at finding its open end. All the while she looks nonchalantly around the room.

Iris hails a passing inmate exiting with a tray.

"Hey, Rodríguez, I want to ask you something. You're still orderly over at administration, right? So, what's the scoop on Coleman? What's she like?"

"She seem, uh, very, very nice. I am very, very happy, now she is the warden they are, er, finding for us."

"Yeah, I hear she seems okay. They say she's even volunteering on the piano at Protestant services."

"Uh, is…?" Rodrigues is not comprehending.

All the while, Emilia pretending a polite interest, is filling the bag under the table with carrot strips and broccoli from her plate.

"You know, the piano? At Protestant?" Iris mimes piano playing and elbows her own plate over to Emilia.

"I am, er, no... I go to Catholic."

"I hear she really gets rolling on those spirituals."

Rodriguez bobs her head uncertainly. "Is very, very nice," she agrees.

Emilia, with quick and delicate fingers, has gathered up a last clump of chopped green onions and drops it into the bag. She passes it under the table to Iris. Iris flicks her eyes over to the officer again. His mind is elsewhere.

Iris knows that she and Emilia probably don't need this level of subterfuge, but there are contrabanding protocols to respect. She swings around and, disentangling herself from the bench, she stretches, and satisfies an underarm itch. The vegetables find a resting place behind her coat lining, settling against the bottom hem.

Carrying their trays with slabs of liver and mashed potato intact, the two make their way to the tray disposal window and the exit.

Outside only a single female guard is on pat-down duty. Emilia walks up, stretches out her arms and turns. The officer pats her in a dilatory fashion and nods her away.

Iris steps up. They lock eyes and the officer responds with a flick of recognition. Iris turns and spreads her arms. The officer's hand pauses at the vegetable bag, then continues, sweeping on down over Iris's sweatpants.

"Okay, Engels, out of here," and she waves a dismissal.

Iris and Emilia swing on over to Unit Twelve.

CHAPTER 4

Unit Twelve's upstairs art room is crammed with rows of tall metal lockers, labeled and padlocked. Its table-chair sets have been pushed aside, and the floor space is filled with a row of a half dozen women practicing facial exercises.

Emilia stands in front, facing them.

"Okay ladies, we are finish up tonight with the forehead." She raises her arms, elbows extended and thumbs at her brows.

The women in the room do likewise.

"Okay, frown—release. Frown—release. Okay ladies, finger resistance is facial weight. So we are pulling down with the fingers—move the forehead muscle up. Okay, eyebrow up? Okay, one-two-three-four-five and *release*. Again. One-two-three-four-five and *release*."

Emilia lowers her arms and claps her hands. "That's it! You ladies are very, very beautiful! You will be Miss America."

The class laughs and chatters as it gathers up plastic cooking bowls, cans of mackerel, and packages of ramen noodles. They all exit the art room, move past the silent TV room packed with inmates in headsets immersed in *Touched by an Angel*, and make their way down the hall to the microwave area.

The microwave space is crowded. Women mill around, waiting their turn, holding bags of popcorn kernels and squares of ramen. The second of the two microwaves is given over to an African American production line.

At the far end of the work table the first inmate pours nacho chips into a plastic wastebasket liner. She presses out the air, ties off the bag, places it on the ground, and grinds it underfoot.

Next, a lady tips a foil of ramen flavoring into a plastic water bottle, adds oil, and—thumb over the top—shakes. She pours it into a bowl of steaming water. The oil-water mixture goes into another white plastic bag lumpy with corn chip. It is kneaded into dough.

Next in line, a woman flattens ping-pong-ball sized circles of nacho dough between layers of saran wrap. She peels back the top and sends the flattened patty down the line for a spooning of commissary salsa and a squeeze of jalapeno cheese.

At the end of the line, a woman doles out a sprinkle of diced, cooked chicken. She rolls up the dough in saran and positions the rolls on a tray fashioned from a cardboard box.

Emilia stands at a table away from the production line, massaging her sealed bags of ramen into crumbles. She opens them, shakes the pieces into a bowl of water, and adds her salad-bar vegetables.

The microwave buzzes. The large, motherly African American overseeing the operation removes a finished tray and a half-dozen inmates, bowls in hand, line up.

Off to the side, a lady with a legal pad is keeping book.

Emilia approaches the head cook and, with a playful tap to the shoulder and a deferential expression, indicates the oven.

The woman sighs but reluctantly gives way. "You be cooking for Ms. Iris, right? You just doing that one bowl, I let you cut if you hurry it up. I got to get finished up in here. See all these hungry ladies?"

"Just four minutes, Ms. Jefferson." Emilia puts her bowl in the oven and turns the timer.

"Do you know," ask Ms. Jefferson, in an offhand tone, "if Miss Iris be hearing word on my 2255?" Her attention is fixed on the tray of rolls making small adjustments to their placement.

"No, Ms. Jefferson, is too early. So far is nothing."

Ms. Jefferson, without affect is ready to load the tray as microwave beeps.

On the way out of the room, Emilia selects four of Jefferson's plastic-wrapped rolls. She rests them on the lid of the ramen bowl.

"Oh right on! Chilaquitas," exclaims Iris.

Emilia, her hands full, has rolled through the door of the ten-by-ten room on the first floor of their building. It has its own toilet/sink unit, two metal footlockers, and standard bunk beds framed in iron pipe. The two thin mattresses are spread with bright, multi-colored crocheted coverlets. A plastic rosary hangs from a top bunk post.

Iris, propped up in her bottom bunk, takes off her reading glasses.

"Those are Jefferson's, right? How are we standing with her?"

"After these ones, she still owing to us six more."

"Oh, good. That lady knows how to cook." Iris dog-ears her *New Yorker* and places it under her bed. "And to think," she continues lightly, "only eighteen months ago she was in her kitchen, putting the same love and commitment into cooking batches of crack."

Emilia is standing at her locker, "Aye, yi! Caliente," as she gingerly unwraps the still steaming chilaquitas. "She asking about her case."

"Any day now, sorry to say." Iris sighs ruefully. "They're just going to dismiss. The ineffective was pretty weak. I'll be shocked if they even ask for a response." Iris massages her scalp in frustration. "First offense nonviolent, she takes a plea and she still gets two hundred and twenty-seven months! It's insanity! This country is going out of its mind!"

Emilia dishes out half of the ramen. She places two of the chilaquitas into the bowl, pops open a warm can of Pepsi, and, after she hands the meal to Iris, goes into mock attention. "Is a drug war going on," she recites, saluting.

"Is a drug war going on," agrees Iris.

"What-cha gonna do?" asks Emilia, palms up helplessly.

"What-cha gonna do?" Iris agrees.

The overhead lights in the rooms of Unit Twelve have been turned off at the main switch and the banks of fluorescent lights in the hallway of have been dimmed. The commissary clock on Iris's locker reads 11:54.

Emilia is under her blankets on the top bunk. She is curled into a tight ball, her rosary twisted around her fingers. Iris on the bottom bunk, pajamaed in thermals, glasses on, is reading a paperback Zuckerman novel under the dim beam of a battery-operated book light. She rubs her eyes now and looks at the clock. She nods to herself as she hears the shriek of metal and the outer door opening and slamming shut. Down the hall comes the clump-clump of heavy boots, and the loud guffaw of male laughter, followed by a female snicker.

Iris marks the Roth with a strip of artlessly decorated cardstock, puts it on the floor under her bed, turns off her book light, covers herself, and waits.

The door to her room is thrown open, the beam of a flashlight hovers over the top bunk and then moves down.

"Thirteen, fourteen," mutters a male to himself. He slams out.

Almost immediately it reopens.

"Thirteen, fourteen," murmurs the female.

Iris and Emilia lie quiet. They hear guards finishing the first floor and mounting the stairs. Their footsteps are overhead now, pausing, moving on, pausing, moving on. Finally they tromp down the back stairs.

The voice of the female guard ringing out as though to the unit in general, "Pe-ew. Stinks in here. Smells like a used tampon."

A bark of male laughter, the door slams shut, then quiet.

Iris turns to the wall and settles down to sleep, but her eyes snap open. There's a barely detectable shaking of the bunk and a barely detectable stifled sob.

"Emmy," whispers Iris loudly.

The sobs continue.

"Emmy, come down here." Then sternly, "Come. Right now."

Emilia climbs down the bunk.

"I so sorry I waken you up," sobs Emilia.

"You didn't, darlin'."

"Me, I just so scared!"

"I know, babe, I know. I'm trying to fix it. We've still got six months. *Over* six months. I'm working it."

Iris lifts the covers to welcome her. Emilia crawls in.

CHAPTER 5

It's after dinner and the dozens of Unit Twelve inmates are gathered in the front common area for mail call. The officer pulls a pre-opened manila envelope from the bottom of the mail crate.

"Gomez. Maria Gomez."

"Is out on a writ," calls an inmate.

The officer tosses the letter back into the basket.

"Uh, Gra –Gra— jewski," he calls. "Dorothea Grajewski."

Dorothea retrieves, then, back in her group, rips through the mailroom's perfunctory retaping job and pulls out an ill-folded clump of childish flower drawings.

"Oo-oh, cu-uute," says the inmate next to her, admiring the lopsided row of daiseys.

"Al—men—derez," falters the officer. "Tamera Almen—derez."

Tamera's friends crowd around as she opens the floral card.

A sister is a special treasure sent from God.

I am just so in awe of you and so proud to

call you my sister.

They all sigh and glow.

The officer tosses the few unclaimed pieces back into his mail crate, slings the crate under his arm, and moves to the door.

Iris and Emilia, standing at the rear of the common area, look at each other in disappointment and shrug.

"Maybe we hear it tomorrow?" asks Emilia.

"Maybe we hear it tomorrow," agrees Iris.

ATTENTION ON THE COMPOUND: ALL INMATES RESIDING IN UNITS THIRTEEN, TWELVE, AND ONE, REPORT TO UNIT ELEVEN. REPEAT: THIRTEEN, TWELVE, AND ONE. REPORT TO THE DRUG BUILDING.

The inmates look questioningly at one another. The Drug Unit is off-limits to the general population. Most have never seen the inside. The few who accidentally stumble in are immediately accosted by a programmer, eager to practice her assertiveness-training skills. "Uh, this is the *Drug* Building? This is your out-of-bounds."

"Yeah," another will chime in, "you get caught up in here, they be *writing* your ass up."

The guard with the mail crate calls over his shoulder. "You heard it. Better hop to it, ladies. Drug building."

The Danbury Drug Building's central hall is a large open space with high ceilings. Up on either side are second-level balconies. Doors line both levels.

As the strangers from the surrounding units enter, they eye the space with wonder. Their own cramped, cacophonous living quarters were conceived for half their number of beds. This, in comparison, seems expansive and gracious and serene.

The drug programmers, haughty with program exclusivity, are already gathered and are not happy to be invaded.

"What's going on?" the outsiders ask.

The residents don't hear the question--s ploy intended to signal the inconsequential standing of the intruders. And to disguise that they don't know either. Everyone mills.

Before long the outer door opens and an, African American woman, forty-something, with a confident air, enters and steps up to a waiting podium.

She wears a full-figured pink flowered dress under a purple suit jacket. The jacket is enhanced with a large rhinestone broach. The frames of her upswept glasses are embedded to match. Her hair extends past her shoulders in multiple shiny, synthetic braids. Her expression is full of good humor and good will.

The inmates have yet to be formally introduced, but everyone recognizes the new warden. She accesses the compound through the back off-limits entrance beside the parking lot, but she has been observed on her way to the chapel-- a spot of brilliance on the beige-dull compound. No one has seen her up close.

"Good evening, ladies, I'd like to introduce myself. I am Camellia Coleman. I am your new warden, and we are all going to get along just fi-iine."

The inmates exchange glances of cautious optimism. Their previous warden, Charles Taterchuk, had been a pale, elderly ghost of a functionary whose only discernable personality trait was a disinclination to come into contact with an inmate. The inmates referred to him as Chucky—sometimes Chuckles. They would do impersonations of him, shuddering in horror and shrinking away from each another.

Taterchuk retired in early summer, and Danbury has been warden-less for months. The population has felt no particular lack—indeed, they have been quite happy without—but word is that Coleman is going to be okay. Even nice. She is nothing like Chuckles.

"I'm sure we'll be getting to know each very well." The warden laughs. "Perhaps in the case of some of you, very well indeed."

She pauses to let her words settle.

A few of the white women, most especially the paranoid-by-nature biker chicks, widen eyes at one another. Is this supposed to be a threat?

The Spanish women—with a more developed acquiescence to power—nod approvingly.

The black women take the statement as a promise. Under this new regime they've been anticipating a more favorable distribution of privilege.

"I'll be standing mainline all next week," the warden continues, "and if any of you have questions or concerns, I hope you will feel free to come up and introduce yourselves and express yourselves. And also, starting this next work-week, my office hours will be extended for one-on-ones: every Tuesday and Wednesday afternoon from two to three-thirty. Repeat:" She leans forward, "Tuesdays and Wednesdays between two and three-thirty," She raises a purple-fingered nail and adds in punctuation, "Twenty-four seven."

Iris, standing in the back of the crowd next to Emilia, puts on a whimsical expression. She mouths, "Tuesday and Wednesday, *twenty-four seven?*"

Emilia looks uncomprehending..

"Forget it, Babe."

The warden's voice rises now, braking into cadence.

"It is my personal mission [*pause*] on this compound [pause] to build a generous measure of confidence and trust [*pause*] extending down to each and every one of you [*pause*] here in this room today and extending up into the very highest office of this facility."

"And a—*men*," breathes Iris, but then she looks over at Emilia whose eyes are warm.

The warden steps away from the podium and stretches her arms out toward the audience, beckoning them in with long, purple-nailed fingers. The preacher intonations switch to down-home. "Now, come here. I want you ladies to hear a li'l story."

She folds an arm over her chest, using it at prop for the other. A finger is pointing upward.

"Now, when I was Assistant Warden over at Bryan? On my previous work appointment? One of the Bryan ladies came to see me because she had herself li'l problem. She was a little bit afraid to talk to me about it; she didn't *want* to talk to me about it. But my office had worked on building trust in and amongst the population. And so this lady was going to try-yy to trust me just a te-eeny-tiny, li'l bit." The warden squeezes a thumb and finger together to demonstrate trust size. She holds it for a moment.

"The inmate—this lady—no," Warden Coleman admonishes playfully, shaking a finger at them, "I'm not going to tell you her name."

The audience, unaware that it had wanted to know, is still intrigued.

"Anyway, she was scared, but she was starting to trust and she was starting to verify."

The warden continues, conversationally. "Now her li'l issue was—and it wasn't a little issue—it was a *big* issue." She pauses and looks around. She drops into a whisper, albeit a loud, carrying one. "Her issue was, there was an officer [*pause*] assigned there at Bryant [*pause*] and he was harassing her. He was *sexually* harassing her. And so she was afraid. She was afraid and she just didn't know where to turn."

Warden Coleman has their attention.

"But you see, she was scared because she also had another issue. And that other issue was that she had family in the area. And that family came for a visitation with her every other Sunday. Every other Sunday of the *month*. So she was cementing her bonds. She was cementing her bonds with her husband and her children, every other weekend. And you-all ladies know—I don't have to tell you—you know how important *that* is. Don't you?"

Pause. The audience, still back with the harassment, fails to respond.

"Don't you, ladies?"

She wrings few nods.

"So naturally, she wants to trust me to protect her from the harassment, but she's thinking that if she tells me, we're going to follow our standard procedure; we're going to transfer her to another institution. At another institution so far away that she couldn't enjoy any of her visitation rights and privileges."

Warden Coleman pauses. She had been leaning forward in intimacy. Now she straightens and pulls herself upright. Holding the silence and turning, she stalks a few paces left, then turns right and stalks. She stops and faces the audience. Her voice, when she finally speaks, is official.

"When an officer [*pause*] has contact that is sexual in nature [*pause*] with an inmate…"

Long pause.

"Ladies."

Long pause.

"That. Is. RAPE!"

The loud pitch of the word echoes through the room and, causes the audience to startle.

"When an officer or any other prison official [*pause*], engages in sexual activity [pause] with an inmate [*pause*], he or she is committing an act of *rape*. Upon the *person* of that inmate. So, ladies. If you *ever* find yourself in a situation of intimate sexual contact with an officer [*pause*] or with a staffer [*pause*] here at this institution [*pause*] or at any *other* institution [*pause*], you are a victim. You are a victim of a *rape*."

There is general stirring now, along with a whispering that comes from one side of the room. Warden Coleman looks over in annoyance, but her face clears. A Spanish woman is translating for the others. She nods in approval.

"You are a victim, and therefore *you* will not be held responsible," she continues. "You are not in a *position* to be responsible. You are an inmate and therefore, in the eyes of the law, that law says that you are being victimized by a predatory officer. He is breaking his trust with you. His mandate is to keep you *safe*, but he is not *fulfilling* that mandate. He is not *keeping* you safe; He is perpetuating a *harm*. He is premeditating an act of *rape* against you. You are his victim, and I'm here today to give you the courage to realize and acknowledge that you don't have to be that victim."

Warden Coleman leans toward the audience again, and lowers her voice.

"Just because you are an inmate, that doesn't mean you got to be a victim, does it?

No response.

"Now, does it?"

A few hesitant headshakes.

"That's right, it doesn't. I want you to come to me, and I want you to talk to me. And any of you, here in this room? If you come to me to report an act of sexual aggression against you, and *if* you can help me gather up the sufficient proof for a conviction—you understand that the system cannot act on your say-so alone—but if you can help me get sufficient evidence. . . ."

The warden pauses.

"I see you're a little confused. Well, here. Let me give you an example."

She looks around the room. "It's just us ladies here tonight, and that's a good thing because I'm going to have to get just a li-t—tle bit explicit. Just a little bit. I hope none of you ladies mind."

No one minded.

"There was an inmate at Lexington, she was in segregation—I believe she failed a urine test or some-such. That's not the issue. What *is* the issue is that the officer who was supposed to be protecting her in segregation, he started *harassing* her in segregation. He wanted her to engage in an—" she makes air quotes—"oral act of sex. Now, I'm sure all you ladies know what that means."

They know.

"And this lady, she understood she was being victimized and so she waited until he was gone and she just—she *spit*. Into her li'l dixie cup. Then when she reported, she had that li'l cup for her backup. Now that's the kind of proof I'm talking to you about. So if any of you ladies—now, I'm not implying," the Warden looks around mischievously. "I'm not saying that any of you ladies have anything to spit."

There is relaxation and general laughter. Even Iris laughs.

"But that was just one example of retaining proof. And as I'm saying, if there are issues—any issues at all? You come right to me and we can, and we *will* work it out together. Because if you do come, and if you help us to catch a predator, then I personally am going to be in a position to help *you*."

She scans the room, holding their attention.

"I can petition right up there to Washington, DC, and then I can petition to your judge and I can say to your judge, 'Here is a lady that stepped up and cooperated with us. Here is a lady that assisted us in the conviction of a criminal act.' And I can say, 'Here is a lady that is deserving of a little assistance from us. In the person of maybe [*pause*] a little reduction?'"

The warden holds up her finger and thumb again.

"'Just a li-iittle bit of a time-reduction off of her sentence?' Now I can't say how *much* of a reduction. That depends on the situation. But I will tell you that the average in cases such as this can extend up to [*pause*] twenty-five percent. You do the math."

They did.

"So now you think about that, ladies," the warden continues. "But before I ask for any questions, I've got a little supposition that you might be saying to yourselves, 'But Warden Coleman,' you're saying to yourself. 'Whatever happened to that lady in Bryant? What was *her* outcome?'"

The warden smiles at the upturned faces. "Well, in the particular case that I was referring to, there was no prosecutable action because that lady had come to me— you're going to be relieved to hear — before a *tragedy* could occur."

There is no relief visible.

"And because," chants the warden, holding up a finger, "she was willing to trust, she avoided, praise the Lord, being the victim of a crime."

If there is disappointment visible, the warden doesn't notice.

"And I'm happy to report," she continues, her face radiant, "that through my interventions—and I had to work a li'l bit, pull a few li'l strings—but through my intervention, that officer who committed that harassment was transferred to another institution and that lady got to finish up her time at Bryan. She finished her time—" the warden consults her wristwatch and holds up a finger—"as of now [pause] she is back home with her husband and her children."

The evening compound vibrates with humor.

"So keep your cup on your person at all times."

"Just remember: don't swallow."

"I won't swallow if you don't swallow."

"Yep, direct order: Don't swallow.

"Don't swallow! Spit!"

Warden Coleman has finished her second talk in Unit Nine, and the inmates are out comparing notes.

"Hey," says an inmate from Unit Eight, "she never did get around to telling the end of that Bryant story."

"Yeah, whatever happened to the Bryan chick?"

"She told us in the Drug Building. She said that she prevented the nasty and the chick got to stay."

"Whew!"

"So . . . no dick for the chick?"

"She must have swallowed."

"No way. No swallowing! She didn't even get a chance to *spit*."

Desiree has approached Iris and Emilia's bench, and Iris has invited her to sit. Desiree isn't joining in the humor. The warden's talk has turned her serious.

"So what do you think, Iris?" she asks, a slight strain in the casual question. "Is she going to be catching any predators?"

"Maybe. Sounds like she's going to try. This is signaling to me that there's some kind of shift inside the halls of the BOP. Something's changing. Staff and inmates have been cohabing forever and administration pretty much overlooked. Now from the way she's talking, someone up above…hmmm."

"Do you know about anything like that happening here?" asks Desiree idly.

"There's always talk. Emmy says there's rumors about the captain. I know back when I was at Lex, it was going on all over the place. Even the warden had a girl-friend. Which turned that lady totally insufferable, I might add. She would have gotten snitched out but who you going to snitch to?"

"But the Bryan guard was *harassing*," protests Emilia.

"I don't believe it," says Iris. "I can't imagine a situation where a guard is messing around with an inmate who is trying to get away. Enough so that she has to go to the *warden*? I mean, come *on.* To save her virtue?"

"Maybe is truth."

"No! How's a guard going to harass? Where's he even going to find a *place* to harass? It's just as crowded there. No private rooms. Everyone's always *around*. Where's he going to corner her?"

Iris asks it of first Emilia, then Desiree. Emilia shrugs, Desiree keeps a blank face.

"So, like," Iris continues in a sarcastic tone, "she's sees him coming and she's scared and she's trying to get away from him, so she leaves her friends and she runs and runs--into a broom closet?"

Emily laughs.

Desiree looks thoughtful.

"Plus he's a man. Inmates there are just like here. He could be a hunchback, you know? They'd be after him just like in here." Iris twirls a finger to encompass the compound. "All the players in here are trying to bend a guard. Bryan's not going to be any different. He could have had his pick of dozens—hundreds. All he has to do is just--She beckons with a finger.

"Not all inmates." Desiree seems upset and Iris looks at her thoughtfully.

"Okay, you're right. Fifty *percent* of the inmates. There's always a couple of nuns. There's the butches. There's the grannies. There's *me*. I'm not counting me."

Iris gives Desiree a sidelong glance and continues. "All I'm saying is, guards don't have to harass. They just have to figure out how to find a place to go."

Desiree is without expression again.

"Except now we got a new warden pushing the issue. Hmm," Iris speculates to herself, "I can't imagine she's going solo on this. If she were riding her own hobby-horse, she probably wouldn't have gotten bumped up to warden. So I'm thinking maybe the BOP up-top? Someone up there has decided that the big push isn't going to be drug prevention any more; it's going to be rape prevention. Hmm."

Emilia looks at Iris with a question. "Is it really rape happening, even when the lady is saying is okay?"

"If she's an okay *inmate*, yeah. Statutory. That's been on the books for forever. We're all underage in here. We're children who need to be protected from ourselves. But"—Iris is talking to herself again—"I'm just remembering. I think last year there was a prison case that changed the legal definition of 'administration's deliberate indifference to a substantial risk of serious harm.' Hmm. I'll have to look that up."

The sky is darkening, and the floodlights have come on. The off-limits areas are in shadow, but the main square is bathed in bright light. Inmates are gathered in gossiping circles. They have a lot to talk over.

Iris continues. "If there's any part of that Bryant story that's true—if she's not making the whole thing up—then I'm thinking the inmate and the guard might have been having a thing going on. Then the inmate starts getting too demanding and the guard tries to drop her. So she goes to the warden."

Thoughtful pause.

Emilia speaks up. "So the lover guard, he is, er, kick'n her to the curve?"

"It's a curb." Iris continues, deadpanning. "This is a serious story, babe. We've got to get our terminology right. So here's how it happened. I'll bet. The inmate started insisting that he had to bring her in some pot. Or maybe some tar? He decides it was getting too risky and he calls it off. So she goes to the warden and puts on her scared-little-inmate face and does a revenge snitch on him."

Still no response from Desiree.

"So happy ending: the inmate trusted the warden, and with the warden's help she retained her virtue and got rid of the predator and—Dessie, *what in the hell is bugging you?*"

Desiree pulls herself together. "Nothing. I'm just not feeling it tonight."

"You feel some kinda way?" twinkles Emilia.

Iris, still deadpan: "That would be Ebonics for on the rag."

Desiree forces a laugh. "Yeah."

Iris's attention is caught to her left. She leans forward and looks over past Desiree, down to the benches of the next unit over. "Hey, I thought Ferguson was pulling graveyard this quarter."

Desiree jumps, starts to look over, then focuses down at her shoes.

A slim officer—African American, midthirties, evenly featured with large tortoise-shell glasses, and carrying a pair of textbooks—is standing in front of the next unit, talking gravely to the inmates.

He leaves them with a serious nod. "Good luck with that, Ms. Wilson. Keep trying. You're councilor is going to listen, but you got to keep on pestering. It'll work out as long as you be keeping the faith."

He moves on down to where the three are sitting. "Ladies, Ms. Engels and Ms, uh, Rivera? It's Rivera, right?" he greets them. "How are you two ladies on this fine evening?"

He finally includes Desiree with a perfunctory nod.

Desiree's head is still down. She's having trouble with a cuticle.

"Miss Rivera, you must be almost due to be getting back home now, right? To Bogotá? How's that pretty little sister of yours doing? I bet you're missing her. What do you hear from her? Ah, what was her name?" He snaps his fingers, in search.

"Claudia," says Emilia in a small voice that Iris overrides.

"Ferguson, what are you doing here at this hour? We're not supposed to see you until eleven."

"I'm subbing for Jameson, pulling a double. So I'll be right here tonight at my regular time, counting all you fine ladies in your beds."

He flashes a quick glance in Desiree's direction and shifts his books. "Miss Engels, you still keeping it real over at the law library?"

"Oh yeah, totally real. So what you studying there, Ferguson? Aren't you about ready to graduate?"

He sighs. "Just a couple semesters. It's been a real hard slog, but I'm seeing the light at the end of the tunnel." He shifts *Methods of Social Research* so that the title faces outward. "Now you have a fine evening, ladies." He nods to Iris and Emilia and in the vague direction of Desiree. He moves on to another group of inmates.

"So anyway," Iris continues, her eye on Desiree. "Back to the warden. I'm guessing this is coming down from Washington and sexual harassment is their next new thing."

Her eye stays on Desiree who is gazing expressionless off onto the compound.

"And if the warden is telling *us* how criminal it is for staff to fool around with *us*, can you imagine what she's saying to staff?"

Desiree snaps her attention to Iris. Her eyes widen.

"Yeah, huh," she agrees.

CHAPTER 6

The walls of the law library are lined with volumes—*The Federal Sentencing Guidelines*, *Shephard's Federal Citations*, bound editions of the *Criminal Law Reporter*, fat copies of Ballantine's and Blacks law dictionaries.

At the far end, Emilia is at work at a large IBM Selectric. Iris is at her desk consulting with a middle-aged, dark-skinned inmate, identified as African by a set of symmetrical scars at her cheekbones.

"I'm sorry, but you're not a citizen so there isn't really anything—" Iris shuffles through the paperwork on her desk, "Ms., uh, Akosua—"

"*Philomena,*" corrects the lady. "In English it is Philomena will be my name."

"Your paperwork says Akosua. Okay, so, Philomena—uh, first can I ask you how you got the name Philomena?"

Philomena laughs deeply. "My grandmother, uh--when my grandmother will be a small child? That missionary lady from England—is English—she take a travel to Ghana to teaching my mother in her village. She will be having this name, Philomena. This thing is not, uh, English name?"

"Well, it's a little out-of date."

"That will be the bad thing? Out-of-date?"

"No, it's a beautiful name, Philomena. It's a fine name."

Over at the typewriter, Emilia issues a Spanish curse and removes a ribbon cartridge from her typewriter.

"Uh, excuse me, Philomena. Emilia, don't throw that cartridge out. There's supposed to be a lady over in four who knows how to rewind the ribbons."

"Bueno, se." Emilia tucks the spent ribbon into her canvas bag and takes out a new one.

"Okay, sorry, Philomena, but I'm a little curious. How in the world did you manage to hide three ounces of heroin in your *hair*?"

She looks at Philomena's close crop.

Philomena's voice fills with woe. "My husband, he is marry a new wife, this one very evil. So the whoonga man is coming to our village. He discovering who that lady will be transport to JFK? That evil one, she is saying, 'Akosua, is that one for transport.' My husband is saying, 'Yes, is correct. Akosua will be transport to JFK.'"

Beyond Philomena's back, over at the small window of the front door, appears a big, male African American face, peering in. "Captain Carter, Head of Security" reads his name tag. He lifts a finger and twirls Iris a wrap-it-up.

"I am weep very much," continues Philomena. "I am weeping, 'No, no, Akosua will not be that lady.' But that evil one, she whisper my husband, 'Akosua will be that lady in our village for transport.' My husband, he listen to that evil one and then he say to the whoonga man, 'Akosua, my number one wife, she transport for JFK.'"

The captain in the window wraps it up again.

"The whoonga man, he have the heroin for my hiding inside in —" Philomena makes a wig shape with her hands and acts out putting it on her head. "Lady hair? And the whoonga man, he saying to my husband, 'See, this thing is very good thing. She is wearing, she will not apprehend.' So my husband say to me, 'Akosua, you will be the one for transport to JFK.' Then he taking me to Accra for application passport."

"Uh, just a sec." Iris looks at her watch. "Emilia, what time is my medical?"

Emilia turns around with a question on her face. Iris slides her eyes over to the door.

"Is now," says Emilia.

"Philomena, I'm sorry." She points at her watch and rises. "I've got a medical appointment. Besides there isn't really anything I can do for you."

Philomena rises. "Miss Iris, I am requesting that I be permission to remaining in Dublin F.C.I. That is the thing I ask you for help."

Iris shakes her head but Philomena overrides. "I am living in Danbury penitentiary, so F.B.I. are saying, 'Philomena, she will being okay to remain in our country, because she, uh, she—*agree*—she will remaining at Danbury FCI.'"

"I don't think so, Philomena. I don't think it works that way. When it's time to go, you've got to go."

"I am apprehend in JFK, my husband not receiving money from whoonga man.

If I returning to my village, my husband is angry to me."

Iris puts her head in her hands and messages her temples. She slides a glance at the door. Captain Carter gestures another impatient wrap-it-up.

"Philomena, come back tomorrow and we can talk it over."

The African woman gathers her things. "He angry, he go get his stick, he beating me. That is, uh—that is very hurting me."

Iris sighs and rises. "I'm sorry."

Philomena is gone and Captain Carter fills the doorframe. He leans back, throws a conspiratorial left/right scan onto the compound and steps into the room. "All right, Engels, let's go."

His eyes flick over to Emilia, who has her head down, totally engrossed in her typing.

Captain Carter strides purposely across the law library, and Iris rises and follows. There is a door at the end of an alcove between the library shelves. He selects a key from his pulley-chain, unlocks the door, and—looking over Iris's head—he holds the door open for her. The captain takes the lead again, and the two wind their way through a storage room stacked high with cartons of shrink-wrapped toilet paper, sanitary pads, and jugs of liquid hand soap.

The captain yanks at his key collection once more and opens a back door leading out past an out-of-bounds sign to grassy area. To the left, just inside the razor wire, is the staff parking lot and Iris, almost jogging to keep up, has time to snatch a quick survey.

Where are all these SUVs coming from?

Is everybody driving an SUV out there?

. . . huh, black-green—new color—ni-iice!

. . . Uh, Kia? What in the hell is a Kia?

The captain unlocks a back door, makes a stay-there gesture and, half entering, peers in left and right again. He waves Iris in. They climb two flights of stairs, the captain ascertains another clear coast, and finally waves Iris through a door. It leads into a waiting room and beyond, the open door of the warden's office.

From her desk the warden offers a big smile, rises, and beckons Iris in. "Thank you, Captain Carter," she waves a dismissal. "But you may want to stay on standby. Ms. Engels will need you again after we've finished our little talk here."

The captain issues a disgruntled noise and leaves.

"I'm so glad we can meet, Ms. Engels." The warden walks around her desk with an out stretched hand, but then retracting it just before contact. "I've been reading what Evelyn, uh, Assistant Warden Powell, has to say about the contribution you've been making here at Danbury, and I must say, I have been impressed. Come right in here and sit down."

"Why thank you, Warden Coleman."

Close up, the warden's affect startles. Iris's eye is used to unadorned inmate in monochrome. Here are glossy synthetic braids interwoven with bright beads, purple-dangle earrings, sparkle-frame glasses.

"You know that it's inmates such as yourself," the warden is continuing, "who volunteer to step forward and assume a leadership role. You're the ones who turn these facilities into *feasible* facilities."

Warden Coleman bestows a smile that reminds Iris of a kindergarten teacher.

"The staff can't be everywhere at once," the warden continues. We rely on some of our more mature and responsible inmates—such as yourself—to help us keep these institutions viable."

The warden sits behind her desk. "Please take a seat, Ms. Engels." She fingers some paperwork on the desk in front of her. Her nails are deep-red acrylic. Her rings flash. "I see here that due to your assistance and the information you provided in the aftermath of that unfortunate, uh, incident last year, administration was able to discover exactly how that paraphernalia was getting in."

"I couldn't track down the heroin, but…,"

"You did fine work, Miss Engels. When we have one of our case managers—a case *manager*, mind you—on the loose, distributing hypodermic needles!"

Iris accepts the thanks with a modest nod. "You understand he thought he was doing his bit to fight AIDS. . . ."

". . . It threatens the very foundations of what we are trying to accomplish." Warden Coleman ignores the interjection and leans forward. "If it had resulted in an actual *fatality*, I'm not sure, but with that kind of an incident on Taterchuk's record. . . I'm not sure he would have been eased out qui-iite so smoothly. I gather that the fact that he 'uncovered' the source . . ."

The warden taps the file with a long nail. "Reading between the lines here, I can't see where you had any actual face-to-face with him, did you, Miss Engels?"

"No, Warden Coleman. I never even met the man. He was more of a big-picture kind of guy."

Warden Coleman chuckles.

"Well, you will find that my management style is very different from that. Ve-eery different. I'm hands on. I'm up close and personal." Warden Coleman, elbows on her desk, clasps her hands tight to illustrate. "I like to establish actual *relationships* with my ladies."

Iris nods.

"Now I know that you and A.W. Powell established a relationship of mutual trust. You know, of course, she's on leave, but you may not be aware that she's awaiting her transfer. She's moving up to regional. So from here on out, it is my intention that the two of us will establish a similar kind of report."

"You mean *rapport*." Iris leans back in her chair and crosses her arms. "I don't know, Warden Coleman, if that is going to actually be able to happen. I can't guarantee that I'll always be in a position. I suppose I can try to keep my ear to the ground, but it kind of depends."

The warden's smile had frozen with the correction. Now she stiffens.

Uh-oh!

Playing hard to get had worked with Powell, the aged-out flower child with a romantic weakness for Iris and her avant-garde background. The smarter Iris hyped herself, the better Powell liked it. And a display of reluctance was Iris being real.

Not this one. This one is displeased. Warden Coleman's lips are set, her are eyes hard as she inspects Iris closely. There is a very long pause.

Shit!

Iris wishes she could start again. She sits up straight, rests her hands in her lap and studies her fingernails.

Here it comes.

"Ms. Engels," says the warden finally, "tell me about your work."

"You mean," says Iris cautiously, embedding as much meekness as she can muster, "in the law library? Rivera and I have just started a project, going through and weeding out all the duplicate reference material. You know, they send the new casework in paperback and then they duplicate in hardcover, so we're trying to weed out the duplication to clear up space…."

"No, Ms. Engels," interrupts the warden, "that is not what I am referencing. I am referencing the legal work you do for other inmates. Here on the compound."

The warden has managed to turn her purple lips sinister. Along with her eye shadow. Her braids—instead of their aren't-we-having-fun jiggle—vibrate with menace.

"Very occasionally, Ms. Coleman" Iris keeps her head down. "I will work with the general population in an advisory capacity but—"

"As I'm sure you are aware," interrupts the warden again, "the BOP has assumed a more skeptical attitude over that sort of practice. We no longer encourage—in fact we are attempting to *discourage*—inmates filing legal paperwork for other inmates."

The warden pauses to let the statement rest for a moment. She leans across her desk, her extensions a-quiver.

"Now, as I suppose you are aware, Ms. Engels," she says, allowing her voice to fill with weary scorn, "the courts insist that administration may not impede the ability of inmates to perform their own legal work [*pause*] but it is currently BOP policy to depreciate any inmate-on-inmate legal assistance activity. To all extent possible."

The act of reiterating policy has taken the edge off of Warden Coleman's hostility and Iris is relieved to note it.

"Again, I'm sure you're aware of the new policy that now considers it to be contraband? A second inmate's paperwork located within the instigating inmate's property?"

The warden's voice becomes lavishly benevolent. "Now, I'm sure you wouldn't have anything like that in your property, would you, Ms. Engels? Or in Miss Rivera's property? Because," her voice goes back to stern, "if there is even a suspicion that an inmate is in possession of contraband such as the variety that I mention, we can… and we do implement a regime of room inspections. On a regular basis."

Iris keeps her head down.

Okay, how do I turn this thing around?

"And furthermore, Ms. Engels, the BOP mandates—and this is written policy—that if an inmate who works in the law library and is, at the same time, known to be acting as legal council…' The warden's leans forward, and her sternness dissolves into sympathy. "Why, in that case the BOP strongly urges that that inmate, or inmates, be relieved of the position and assigned to other duties. The kitchen always has openings, Ms. Engels. And winter will be here. The yard is going to need bodies for its snow-removal crew."

Iris remembers the first time she saw Emmy, flat on her back on the sidewalk tangled in her shovel. She never had learned how to walk on ice.

"Furthermore, Ms. Engels, I'm not altogether sure that you and Ms. Rivera actually meet the qualifications for our preferred housing. That might be something we need to look into. We might find that we've got ladies on the waiting list who actually *do* qualify. We may need to transfer you over to the projects." Her voice fills with mirth. "I believe that's what you ladies call Unit Two?"

Emmy had been in two when they met. She was a top bunk, and it was the habit of the gang-girl on the bottom to practiced leg-ups against the underside of Emmy's mattress.

"Now, as far as the problem with your legal work, I do not know what kind of understanding you had with Assistant Warden Powell. I'm sure it was highly irregular."

"Ms. Powell was aware that I helped the inmates. She moved me into the law library when the position opened up. She also saw to it that Rivera was assigned to help me."

Warden Coleman nods sagely. "And into preferred housing. Yes."

"But I do want to emphasize," Iris continues, posture upright and eyes respectfully down, "that I follow policy. I do not accept payment for my work. Everything I do, I do pro bono. You can check. The only money on my books is from my sister."

Iris looks up and allows their eyes to meet, but for only a sincere second. She lowers them again.

Ms. Coleman nods, takes off her cat's-eye glasses, and twirls them.

"Perhaps . . . perhaps there is some accommodations we can work out? But you know how it happens in here, Ms. Engels: you help us, we'll help you." She leans back and chuckles again. "You seem like an intelligent individual. We don't have to play games with each other, now do we?"

Iris raises her head and locks eyes. "No. No games."

The warden sits back. She lays her glasses on her desk. "Ms. Engels, my aim—and I'm hopeful that you can help me accomplish this—my aim is to stop any and all illegal sexual contact as it occurs. [*pause*] On the compound. [*pause*] Here at Danbury. Now I understand that up to now, everyone has had pretty much free rein in here. I understand that Warden Taterchuk did not undertake this sort of misconduct as his priority."

Iris takes a chance. She keeps her head down and speaks formally. "Uh, Warden Coleman? He may not have known what it was. It's doubtful that Tatterchuk had ever actually *had* sexual contact."

There is a pause.

Damn, damn, damn. Keep your mouth—

Coleman breaks into a peal of laughter.

Whew!

"I didn't say that." The warden's voice rings out joyously. "*You* said that!"

Iris has affirmed once again that she can rarely go wrong, disparaging one staff member to another.

The warden nestles happily back down into her chair. She turns serious again.

"I'll tell you this in confidence, Ms. Engels. Now, you didn't hear this from me, but I am not in an altogether trusting relationship with our Captain Carter here. I've sent out notification that on certain disciplinary matters, I intend to bypass his office altogether. I wouldn't be surprised if he isn't himself involved in impropietous activity."

"I think your instincts might be right."

The warden leans forward avidly. "What do you hear?"

"Nothing specific. Just snatches of rumors out of the Spanish community. I'll keep my ears open."

"Do. Be sure to. And I'll go further, Ms. Engels. I'm saying now—and you can quote me—that some of these inmate-on-inmate relationships, these unnatural relationships? They have got to stop. And they *will* stop."

She takes on the black-preacher rhythms. "Any sexual contact—that means any and *all* sexual contact [*pause*] on my compound [*pause*] will no longer be tolerated. And I have instructed my staff to see that it is no *longer* tolerated. It is against BOP rules and regulations and under my watch and on my compound, those rules and regulations are to be—and they *will* be—enforced."

Good luck, lady.

"I know on some institutions these things are overlooked. I'm thinking specifically of a female institution near San Francisco whose name I will not mention."

You don't have to. There's only one.

"Out there they're allowing the inmates to have it any which way. I've walked that facility and I can testify that it is *Out. Of. Control.* The inmates walk around handholding—kissing? Whatnot? I hear they even perform their little play-wedding ceremonies."

"That's California for you."

Maybe I should transfer.

"Yes, that's California, but that is not Danbury. That is not Danbury under *my* watch. That kind of nonsense isn't occurring on my compound because I intend to enforce *all* the rules. I don't pick and choose the rules. I don't say, 'Now, some of these rules, they're just little, itty bitty rules.' I *respect* the rules. And I demand that same respect out of my staff and my inmates."

The warden looks at the clock. "But the first thing on my plate—the first objective of my tenure here at Danbury—is to stop officers from preying on inmates." She leans forward. "Uh, Ms. Engel, are you aware of any of that kind of activity going on?"

"Well, not directly, Warden Coleman, but I've kind of been observing. I've been watching a guard, an Officer Ferguson?"

"Ah, yes," says the warden enthusiastically, "LeBron Ferguson."

"The scholar. The one taking the college classes."

"Ms. Engels," and Warden Coleman's voice fills again with mirth, "that man is no kind of scholar. He got a GED back in '84, period. That is the extent to his education. Those books he's toting around? They are sheer exhibitionism. I expect he's picking those books up at a yard sale."

Iris and the warden's eyes meet for a brief moment, enjoying the vagaries of human nature.

"Now what you hear that boy's up to?"

"Well, just rumors. Him and one of the inmates."

"Which one?" pounces the warden.

"The name is Desiree Johansson."

The Warden picks up a ballpoint and jots. "Johansson?"

"Yeah. Desiree. She's over in Unit Five."

"And you suspect that she and Ferguson got a little-sup'in going on?"

"Maybe. Just little hints so far."

"How well are you and—is it Johansson? How well are you two acquainted?"

Iris studies her lap. "Some, actually. Right now I'm putting in a petition for her to get the BOP to redesignate her. You know, Warden Coleman, working with inmates on a legal basis—within the lawyer-client relationship? It's a good way to establish trust. It gives me a platform from which to become aware of certain situations." Iris pauses and chances a glance. The warden seems receptive.

"I can sometimes gather," Iris continues, "information that I would not ordinarily have access to. Now, in the case of Johansson I've only just started to open lines of communication. The relationship is not, at this moment, on a confidential level."

"Can you change that?"

"Maybe. I'm not sure."

The warden frowns.

Iris looks her in the eye. "I can certainly try."

CHAPTER 7

"Hey Des, do you have a minute? I'd like to get some information on your case. Want to go over and do the track?"

It's the next day, Saturday lunch, and Iris and Emilia—on their way to the tray disposal window—have paused. Desiree is sitting with a group of women.

"Are those new?" asks Iris as she exits with Desiree. "I haven't seen them before."

"They're campers," explains Desiree. "They just got transferred down here for the drug program. They're all, 'Oh, God, behind the wire! Big, bad penitentiary.'"

Iris gives Emilia an eye signal. Emilia nods and turns and heads back to her unit.

"Scared of us, huh?"

"Yeah, they're thinking that now they're up here with us real criminals. I had to explain how no one is going to shank them or rape them with a broom stick or anything."

"I'll bet they were happy that you even talked to them."

"Yeah, they were getting the silent treatment over in the Drug Building."

"Good for you. I used to try to help out the newcomers but it's just too exhausting anymore—all that new-inmate hysteria. I'm glad you're taking over."

Desiree colors lightly. "They were totally freaking out behind all the foreign languages. They say everyone down at camp speaks English."

"You know why that is, don't you?"

"They passed some new law or something?"

"Yeah, a while back they passed the mandatory deportation thing for noncitizens, and the Colombian camper guys started walking away so they pulled all of the deportables out of the camps. Transferred them behind the wire."

"I kind of heard, but it was all happening when I was first down and at the time, everything seemed like just a big old crazy mess anyway."

"Yeah, as of '94 I think it was? Everyone who's going to get deported is a security risk and has to do his or her time behind the wire."

"Did any of the women escape?"

"No, probably didn't even occur to them. Spanish women aren't—let's just say they aren't particularly of a defiant nature."

"You mean they're suck-ups?" ventures Desiree.

Iris laughs and Desiree looks pleased with herself.

"Anyway," says Iris, "it caused the mass redesignation."

Iris and Desiree are past the rec building and approaching the track. It's a beautiful New England fall day. The trees have turned, and most of the leaves have fallen but the grass is still green. The sun is warm but mixed with a cool fall breeze.

"So that's probably why we're so crowded over here, huh," says Desiree, brushing at a curl.

"One of the reasons. That plus mandatory minimums. They've upped everyone's sentence so we're all doing so much time that there aren't many camp eligibles in the first place. That's why Unit Two and the all cubicles are double-bunkedup that way."

"Yeah, just try getting a shower in Unit Five."

The two are out on the track, walking the half-mile circle. It's the only place on the crowded compound where inmates can hold private conversations. There are scores out exercising, but the majority of these are closed off inside their headsets. Plus, track etiquette dictates a generous space between each inmate.

"It's beautiful out here," says Iris, looking out at stretches of green no-man's land separating the track from the razor wire, "but God, I miss the city."

"You're New York, right? I've never been there. Everyone in Iowa was always saying how it's so dangerous and everything."

"Used to be. It's not so bad any more. From what I hear these days it's been pretty well cleaned up. Things were actually starting to turn around before I got indicted."

"So you don't get mugged just walking down the street any more?"

"I guess not. Our own dear Nazi is taking credit, of course, but crime was dropping under Dinkins." Iris breaks off. "You probably aren't that interested in New York politics."

"I know nothing about any politics," admits Desiree, "but I've been thinking that its time for me to become more aware."

"Well, don't mind me, I was just talking local mayor stuff. I can get really irate whenever I think about Giuliani—Mayor Giuliani. He was head prosecutor during my investigation. If it weren't for him, I wouldn't even be in here."

"What did they get you for?"

"Defending the wrong people, basically."

"That was your crime? That's what they charged you with?"

"I don't usually like to talk about it ."

"Oh, I'm sorry. You totally don't need to."

"No, actually, it feels good to talk to somebody. You don't really want most of these women in here to know too much about you. I mean, I've got Emmy—I'm close to her—but she's from another culture. I guess we all need someone to unload on every now and then."

Desiree colors again and glances over at the khaki-colored eyes, the classy cheekbones, the pertly carved nose.

"Besides," Iris continues, "I usually spend my time focused on other people's cases. It's really rare that I get a chance to talk about my own."

"I'm really interested," says Desiree eagerly. "Tell me about it."

"If you really want to know."

"I really do."

"Okay, so, you know how the Feds are, Dessie. If they decide to go after you, they'll always find something. Giuliani, our dear mayor—he was trying to convict a quote-unquote drug lord under some very shaky evidence. The gentleman in question was African American, so Giuliani calculated that he'd naturally avoid facing a jury that was not necessarily of his peers."

"That was almost like how it happened to me," interjects Desiree. "Well, a little bit like it. I'm sorry. So go on, then what happened?"

"They offered my defendant seventy-two months to plead out. I convinced him to take it to trial. If we'd lost, he's have probably gotten twenty to thirty years, so he had to trust me. But I knew they didn't have—long story short, we won. I got him off. So then they came after me."

"So what did they ever find to charge *you* with?"

"Basically, money laundering. They claimed that the fees I accepted were dirty. Defense lawyers usually are protected that way—kind of—but Congress passed an exception for drug money. Which wasn't passed until '89, which was after the majority of the incidents in question, but Giuliani decided he was Giuliani and he could get away with applying retroactively. Which was in itself totally illegal."

"Now wait, I don't get it. You got paid to defend this guy and then they said he was paying you in drug money? Then you got him off, and then they put *you* in jail?"

"Well, not quite. They couldn't do anything about the money I got from *him* because the jury came back innocent. That turned it into clean money. But they did a grudge investigation and established what they called a pattern of what they called 'racketeering.' Like I say, the Feds can always find something."

"So you took it to trial."

"No. I couldn't take the risk. They were taking down a local Crip chapter, and they found what they called "ties," and they were threatening to include me in the RICO? Corrupt Organizations? I bargained them down to nine years and I pled."

"So if you lost at trial, how much time were you looking at?"

"They were threatening thirty-eight. Don't ask me how they came up with that exact figure. Probably they researched and found out it was the number that sounded the most ominous. It worked. I pled."

The two of them are rounding the loop past the outdoor weight area. No one is lifting, but a couple of inmates are on the bench discussing it.

"Besides," Iris says lightly, "unwritten rule: you never act as your own attorney, and I figured I was the only lawyer in town who was good enough to get me off."

Desiree laughs.

They hear a pair of joggers coming up from behind them and they step out of the way.

Desiree asks, "So if you got them down to nine, why didn't they put you at camp? I thought ten years and under."

"The prosecution told my PSI investigator that they considered me a flight risk. I never turned in my passport. I said I lost it, so maybe they thought I actually was a flight risk—who knows? When I got here and had my first Team, they told me to keep it clean and in a couple of years they'd redesignate. But now I don't even want to *go* to camp. The law library's better down here. Up there at camp it's all dorms. Here I have a room with an actual door on it."

"Yeah," says Desiree, "this girl I was talking to over at the laundry—she was wondering how you and Emilia managed to get into preferred housing."

Iris laughs easily. "Actually it was Powell—remember the Assistant Warden who just left? She hated the sentences everyone was getting, she supported the legal work Emmy and I were doing, and she got us moved over into a place where we could do it more effectively."

"Yeah, that's what I said."

"Hey, Dessie, enough about me. I've gotten you out here to talk about you."

"But you told me back *when* that you didn't want to hear."

"I didn't want to hear about it *yet*. At first I try to focus on just what's laid out in the paperwork. But they'll be responding soon, and it's very possible that the BOP will challenge and I'm going to have to answer. So I need to hear your whole story."

"Okay," says Desiree hesitantly.

"If you'd prefer not to talk about it. . ."

"No, it's not that, it's just that if I tell you, it's going to make me look like this big, fat dork. You're going to think I'm a total idiot."

"Oh, *please*, Dessie, we're women! We've all been total idiots at one time or another. I've certainly been. I'm assuming you're referring to, what was his name? Mr. Dixon?"

"Danté Dixon."

"From your paperwork I got that you admitted to organizing a bank robbery, planning, issuing instructions."

"Ha!"

"Yeah, it didn't read right."

Desiree snorted. "I didn't even know it was going to *happen*. I was asleep in the back seat of the *car*. I didn't even know he was even going to *do* it. I woke up and . . ."

"Okay, stop. Let's go way back. Tell me about him. How did you two meet?"

"He was from Chicago—he grew up in the projects. And the Hawkeyes gave him this football scholarship."

"Hawkeyes? What's—"

"Oh that's the University team. Iowa City. That was the city just down the road beside Cedar Rapids, where I grew up."

"Okay, so, Danté's a football player and—"

"No, actually all that was before I met him. He was defensive line and he was like this big star on television and everything. Except he had gotten this neck injury. His top two vertebrae in his neck were damaged or whatever, and so he wasn't able to go professional. He was forced to retire from the game."

Desiree has slowed her pace to talk and a jogger is approaching from the rear.

"*Beep, beep!*" the jogger projects loudly over her ear-phones, and the two move hastily to the edge of the path.

"I remember back when I was young and my father and my uncle— they would be talking sports and they would be saying his name because he was like this rising star."

"How old were you?"

"Like, junior high? And I remember thinking that that was, like, *thee* world's most romantic name—*Danté Dixon.*"

Desiree's voice drips with sarcasm. "I used say to myself, I used to go 'Danté-and-Dessie. Danté-and-Dessie-Dixon.' Boy, talk about your lamebrain."

"When did you two finally meet?"

"I had just graduated."

"High school?"

"Yeah, high school. I was, like, prom queen which was so totally no big deal except then the TV got ahold of it and it was all like, *Prom Queen Turns Bank Robber. Metro High Prom Queen arrested* for Bank Robbery. And somehow they got their hands on a picture of me in my prom dress. My parents were pissed. God, they were—my mom totally wanted to die. Dad had less than a year for his thirty at Quaker . . ."

"Quaker?"

"Quaker Oats—the plant—but since mom couldn't face the neighbors, they had to put the house up. They moved out to Arizona."

"Okay, back up. Let's start again. You graduated from high school and . . ."

"And there was this kind of a nerd that I used to know, and he would make up these fake IDs? He had this equipment in his basement or whatever. He usually charged, like, fifty bucks a pop, but he did mine for free—I guess he kind of liked me or something. So I had this ID where I could get into all the clubs. So me and these other girls that I used to hang with, we used to hang down at The Tycoon. It was like this 'dangerous' C.R. dance club. And one time this one girl I knew came up and she was like, 'Someone wants to meet you.' And I was like, 'Who?' And she was like, 'Danté,' and I was like, 'Who?' because the music was loud and everything, and she goes—she yells it out, '*Danté Dixon,*' and I'm like, 'No way!'"

Desiree, wrapped in her narrative, has slowed. She doesn't notice that there's a jogger coming up again behind. Iris tugs her sleeve to move her off the path.

"So anyway, one thing led to another. He was like, you know—holding the bag, and I'm like, I'd done lines before but I'd never smoked. And before you know—well, Dottie, she was getting nervous about the whole scene, so she moved out and Danté had been mostly hanging there before but then he moved all his stuff in."

"So obviously you had your own place by then."

"Yeah, my mom, when I first started going out, she was all, 'You're living under my roof, you're following my rules.' So my dad, he had already gotten me on at Quaker so me and Dottie, we had found this apartment in Czech Town."

"And Dixon started dealing out of your place," states Iris as a fact.

"Yeah . . . well, yeah. Danté said it was because so I didn't have to go to work every morning, and at first I didn't quite realize what was going on because probably during that period I was getting high quite a bit? It was kind of like—all of a sudden my apartment was where it was all happening. Like big time. And I was Danté's *wo-man*, you know? And we had the traffic—all these people in and out."

"What was he dealing? Crack?"

"Yeah, he was getting his powder in from this cousin in Omaha—like, ounces at a time, and he got this one friend of his—Rochelle? She taught me how to rock it up so he was moving rock, but then every so often we would have to do these runs up to Chicago for Danté's downtown."

"Downtown?"

"Yeah, heroin. *Uptown's* cocaine. You know, it's like so—when"—Desiree holds up an air phone—"they're listening in? 'Are you going to go *downtown* tonight?' So that's what they just called it. But the product he was getting in Chicago—it wasn't that shiny white-powder stuff like they have in the movies. It was black tar. It was like, base. Up from Mexico. I tried smoking it once. Ha! I was like, barfing into the toilet bowl all night. Never again. But Danté was really in need because of how he had gotten tackled wrong and gotten his neck all messed up. So he was experiencing constant pain. He needed it just to survive."

"How long did this go on?"

"It was over a year, probably. I wasn't paying a lot of attention to the time in those days, but yeah, when I went back over the whole thing with Calvin—"

"Calvin?"

He was my lawyer, Cal. He had used to hang in the clubs before me and Danté hooked up. He would be like, at closing time he would always be asking me over to his place for lines. I was kind of dumb back in those days. I hadn't actually been with anybody—just fooled around, you know?"

"Yeah, I know."

"Now I'm realizing that he was thinking all along that I was going to be with him or whatever. But he was kind of, you know, not that good looking? And I never would make out, except there was this one night. It was like, right before I hooked up with Danté. Cal got all weird on me and so I finally had to sneak out when he was in the bathroom. So anyway, I already knew him and so naturally when the shit came down he was my choice of lawyer to call."

"Naturally? He might not have been the wisest choice," says Iris wryly.

"I know but I was kind of like, ashamed. I didn't want to tell some strange person how I was in all this shit and everything, and I didn't really know anyone else."

"Beep, beep!"

"Want to sit down for a minute?" asks Iris, tugging Desiree toward the bench beside the weight area. The talkers have moved; there's a pair of lifters on the weights, but they're out of earshot.

"Okay, so you're living with Danté now and he's dealing dope. So how do we get from there to robbing a bank?"

"It was on the way home after a Chicago run that had went bad. See, I always used to stay in the car when Danté went upstairs to this place to cop. He said the people didn't trust a white girl up in their business, so I always waited in the El Dorado and he was usually just like, in-and-out—bang. But this time he comes back *cussing*. He's all 'Motherfucking niggas, motherfucking niggas.' And he has his Glock under the seat and he's reaching down there and he's acting like he wants to go back in or whatever and I'm like, 'Can't you just go to another spot?' and he's like, 'Motherfuckers come up on my bank,' and then he's like, 'What you got in your purse?' and I'm like, 'You're the one keeps the money,' and he's like, 'Dig around the bottom.' And then he's like, driving around looking at the gas gauge, and he tries this one place and no one's home, and he's slamming on the steering wheel, 'Shit, shit.'"

They're both sitting now. Iris is quiet, letting the story flow.

"Then finally he's like, 'Here, babe, you don't need to be going through this shit.' He's like, 'Here, eat this, baby,' 'cause he always keeps a couple of zees—"

"Zees?"

"A couple of Xanax in his wallet just in case, so I'm like—by then the sun's already been up and I'm zonking, so I'm climbing into the back seat and the next thing I know, this big old cop is right in my face—this far—and he's shaking me, 'Wake up, wake up.'"

"According to your paperwork the bank was on the west side of Davenport."

"I have no knowledge. I was like, *out*."

"But you pled guilty."

"Yeah, well Cal, he explained to me that it was going to be my word against Danté's. He said if it hadn't been the Feds and it had been the state of Iowa that was handling it, they wouldn't have been able to charge me because the teller was saying that Danté was alone and no one saw me driving away or anything. But it had went federal, and the Feds have this conspiracy law so they could get both of us. And at first I'm like, 'I didn't do anything. I'm not pleading guilty. I'm taking it to trial.' And Cal's like, 'Miss Johansson'—now he's calling me Miss Johansson! Ha! He's like, 'Miss Johansson, you do that, they're going to put you away for twenty-five years.'"

"Shh," cautions Iris, indicating the weight pile with her eyes.

The two lifters have moved into earshot and are suspiciously silent. Desiree has been projecting, lost in her tale, but now she lowers her voice.

"Then he was telling me how they'd gotten Danté for this *other* robbery in Newton—they had traced the prints or whatever. And Cal said that Danté was trying to testify how I had planned out that one too. Plus they had found this one other dealer who had sold to an agent and he was sitting there in jail, and he was ready to testify that he had heard me *doing* the planning. And Cal was like, 'I know you didn't plan anything, Ms. Johansson, but the jury—they might not actually believe any of it—but this is Iowa. They're going to want to convict you, just because you're a hometown prom queen cohabitating with a black man.'"

"He might have been right."

"I'm like, going—I'm like, 'So I'm supposed to stand up in court and tell the judge a bare-faced lie that I planned a bank robbery?' And he was like, 'Yep, that's the way the system works.' And I'm like, 'So why would that not make me be committing perjury?'"

"What did he say?"

"He just *laughed.*"

"I'll bet he did." Iris gazes out past the razor wire. "I am not particularly impressed with the deal he worked out—first offense, ninety-three months? He did get them to drop the gun charge, but still."

"So if they dropped the gun charge, why is the BOP trying to say I had a gun and got me designated violent?"

"Because there's language in your presentencing report that suggests you in the role of organizer with a weapon involved. They didn't give you any kingpin points—well," Iris talks to herself, "actually they couldn't because they didn't have a third conspirator, and so it couldn't be an enterprise. And the courts didn't give you a weapon enhancement."

They are back walking the track again. The sun is getting low, glittering off the tiny blades in the tangled scrolls of wire.

"I'm not pretending," interrupts Desiree, "that I understand about any of the legal or anything, but I have still never gotten why I'm violent."

"Your problem is that your PSR language indicates that you are the organizer, which they say *implies* a weapon. They didn't say why it *implies*. It's pretty shaky. I think we have a good chance."

"Could Cal have made it so they wouldn't have put that in there in the first place?"

"No, but he could certainly have gotten a protest on record. I would have. The way he let it stand, he left an opening for the Bureau of Prisons to classify you violent. Which they were happy to do. If he had filed a competent protest, it's doubtful that you'd even be behind the wire right now. You'd be up in camp. Oops, erase that. By now you'd be back down here for the drug program. And you'd be out—let's see, you've done fifty-six? If they let you right into the program, you'd be out just over a year from now. That's if you graduated."

"Oh, I'd graduate. I'm keeping my nose clean from here on out."

COUNT. COUNT TIME.
ALL INMATES RETURN TO YOUR UNITS FOR COUNT.

The loudspeaker is sovereign, and the joggers and walkers stop in their tracks and reverse course. Iris and Desiree on the near side of the field quicken their pace toward the entrance.

"You do understand why Danté lied about you, don't you?"

"Actually me and Danté got to talk for a little minute while we were getting transported in the van to the airlift. He said it was because I was so fine, and while he was away all the brothers would be after me, and he loved me so much he couldn't stand to do his time thinking like that. So this way I'd be safe and waiting for him."

Iris snorts. "What a dream boy! Actually, Dessie, he lied about you because they told him—how much time did he get?"

"One hundred twenty-three months. They ran the Newton thing consecutive, but they upped him on weapons."

"Yeah well," said Iris, "it would be my guess they told him that he was looking at twice that amount—maybe even thirty years—unless he gave them somebody else. And he had a problem because they didn't have him for any of his drug activity, so if he gave up any of his drug people that would mean exposing himself. So you were the only name he had to give."

"Yeah, I don't know. Cal pretty much told me that, except all that time in county, I had thought I was going crazy. I was sitting there—Danté was my first real boyfriend, and I was sitting in jail wondering how he was going to do that to me. Then finally when we got in the van and he told me, you know—that other stuff? I probably at the time wanted to believe. It made me feel better."

COUNT TIME, LADIES. RETURN TO YOUR UNITS.

Iris and Desiree are off the track and about to separate. The compound square is alive with inmates heading for their rooms, casting long shadows in the afternoon sun.

"We've got to get together again," says Iris. "I'm going to need to flesh things out a little more."

"Okay, cool. Meet you at chow?"

"I'll wait for you. And Dessie, before I go I want to say that I like how you don't try to present yourself as anyone other than who you are. I respect that."

"Yeah, thanks, but it's probably because I don't *know* any better. I'm just an Iowa girl." Desiree curls her fingers into a little wave and turns toward Unit Five. She walks away smiling.

CHAPTER 8

"This cornbread is scary."

Desiree and Iris are together in the dining hall.

Iris nods. "Don't breathe in or you'll get crumbs in your lungs."

The dining room is sparsely populated. It's Saturday evening, New England baked beans, and the majority of the inmates are in their units cooking for themselves. The few who are there take note: Iris and Desiree are eating alone together? So, where's Emilia?

Iris leans over. "I'm glad you told me your story. It makes it easier for me if the BOP comes back with an objection."

"I'm still embarrassed about how it makes me look so totally *stupid*," says Desiree.

"Babe, we're in here, so we've all been stupid at some point in our lives. Someday I'll tell you about some of the stupid things that I've done."

"Ha! I can't imagine you ever getting suckered the way I did."

"You'd be surprised." Iris takes a bite of coleslaw. "I'll tell you someday when I'm in my more confessional mood. Right now I'm focused on how sorry I am about the way Danté screwed you over. You shouldn't have had to go through that. I'm hoping it hasn't made you bitter. I'm talking about African American men in general."

Desiree looks down at her plate.

"All of them aren't creeps like that, you know. Most of the African American men I've met have been very sincere people. And well, you know about how they're virile and passionate."

Desiree's cornbread lies in crumbles on her plate. She's moving the slaw around with her fork.

"So I'd hate to think," Iris goes on, "that just because of the one bad experience . . . With your looks and your personality, you could attract the best, and being with a black lover can be a wonderful experience. It would be too bad if you rejected it out of hand."

Desiree keeps her eyes on her food.

"Of course, I'm saying all this on the assumption that Danté is the only black lover you've had."

Desiree pokes her Jell-O to make it quiver.

"Sorry, Dessie. You don't know me that well, and this is absolutely none of my business. You have no particular reason to trust—"

"No, really, Iris, it's not that. Really. I totally trust you." Desiree looks around the dining hall. "I just feel funny talking about shit like that in here."

"Oh, I understand, Desiree. But if you ever feel the need to unload, I'm always here."

"Okay."

"Sometimes you just need to get stuff off your chest."

"Yeah, huh."

"We can talk more out on the compound."

"Does she really think she's going to catch anyone stuffing their pants full of baked beans?" asks Desiree.

Iris and Desiree that evening watch the dining room exit from the bench. The tall black guard they call Uranus is alone tonight, patting down inmates.

"Good one, Dessie," Iris laughs. "Actually I'll take male guards over females any day. They've got more compassion."

"I know, huh. Why do all the dike officers have to act like such bitches?"

"Trying to prove they're tough. They're all ex-military, which attracts the lesbians. In the army it was don't-ask-don't-tell, so they were all scared of getting accused. They had to demonstrate how tough they could be on one another. And now in here, where it's us helpless little inmates, they really have to be tough on us."

"Does the BOP do don't-ask-don't-tell?"

"No, you can be gay in the BOP; you just can't be nice."

Uranus is picking and choosing her prey. She beckons to a suspect who, the jig being up, sheepishly reaches to her waist and pulls out a garbage bag of salad greens. She smiles ingratiatingly. Uranus, stony faced, tosses the bag to the ground, curls her lip, and spins her finger, ordering a turn-around.

"See, now she's doing a punishment pat-down. A male guard would have said okay and waved her past."

"Yeah," says Desiree impulsively, " you know, I actually like some of the male guards."

Iris's face stays casually blank. She waits. Then, when Desiree doesn't expand, she says, "Some of the men take a real personal interest in us. I heard one of them say—I think it might have been, who? Officer Ferguson? Anyway, someone like him said that half of us don't belong here in the penitentiary in the first place."

Pause.

"Actually, I think that *was* Ferguson."

No response. The Fatback Sisters, holding hands and singing, skip past. Iris tries to share a smile, but Desiree's mind is elsewhere.

The usual pairs and trios of inmates tonight are walking the inner compound circle in casual conversation. Most of it is in consonant-rolling streams of Spanish, but every now and then there's snatches of English. Iris and Desiree sit in silence, catching wafts of conversation.

"Bitch trying to be the step-momma, but she best don't be thinking she going to keep my babies. Time I get up on out of—"

"—Works over commissary? She was saying that Hanson just reupped and forgot to order the white-girl foundation and the polyfill *again*. I guess the men didn't need it, so we don't either."

"She sure remembered to order tampons."

"They don't want us bleeding all over the government property."

And, dancing to the beat:

...*running for your jewels.*

Lil' Cesar, go ask you homie how I'll leave you

Iris breaks the silence. "I heard Ferguson's put in for a transfer. Have you heard anything about that?"

"No!" exclaims Desiree. She grabs a hold of Iris's arm. "Who told you? Did *he* tell you that?"

"No, I don't *think*. I don't remember."

"Really. Who told you?"

"I can't remember. They might not have even been talking about Ferguson."

Desiree is still clutching Iris's arm. Iris untangles it and puts it around Desiree's shoulder.

"Hey Dessie, something's going on, huh."

"I haven't ever mentioned a word to anyone. Is he really leaving?"

"You know, come to think, Dessie, it might have been Laughton they were talking about. Actually, I think it was Laughton."

Desiree's body slumps in relief.

"But what's with you and Ferguson?" asks Iris in gentle concern. "Is it something you need to talk about?"

"No," says Desiree.

They sit in silence.

"If I tell," says Desiree, "you've got to promise you won't tell anyone. You can't ever, *ever.*"

"Dessie, I keep client confidentiality. That's what lawyers do." She looks around. "Come on. The track will still be open for a while. We probably shouldn't be talking here."

CHAPTER 9

It's just after 3:00 a.m., and the inmates are asleep.

Unit Five is sectioned into a series of cubicles. The walls are six-feet high and inside each cubicle are two bunk-bed sets and four gray metal lockers with dangling padlocks. The majority of the beds are covered in multicolored, crocheted coverlets. The coverlets lie over khaki-colored army blankets, and these over the humps of sleeping inmates.

It's time for count. There's the sound of the front door unlocking, and two officers with flashlights enter the unit. They move through the ground floor, passing the flashlight beam over each hump. The count is very nearly ceremonial. No one tries to escape; there is rarely even an out-of-place inmate and never at 3:00 a.m. Still the officers murmur the numbers to themselves as they sweep down the aisle that divides the cubicles.

They finish the first floor, make a note, and climb the stairs. As they move down the second floor, breathing numbers, one of the officers falls behind. He pauses at a set of bunks near the middle. He rests his hand on the ankle of a top-bunk sleeper and gently squeezes.

With a start, Desiree props herself and blinks into the flashlight. Officer Ferguson trains it back so that she can see his face.

"Shh," he cautions and Desiree nods in response.

He moves along, catching up with the other officer. At the far end of the second floor is the television room.

"Let me check up in here." Ferguson unlocks the door. He flashes his light around the room, then slams the door closed and pantomimes relocking it. The pantomime is gratitious. His partner is already on his way down the back stairs.

The TV room is only barely lit with low-watt bulbs fixed under the sprinkler system running along the upper edge of three of the walls. Desiree makes a lonely figure in her long underwear, huddling on a metal folding chair. She looks down at herself and eases up her thermal top to adjust to the curve of a breast. She checks her breath with her palm and slushes saliva around her gums. She finger combs her hair.

Footsteps.

By the time the door opens she has positioned her body into a gentle S shape, one long leg extended, toe pointed. She holds the pose for a beat and then rises. Ferguson moves forward to embrace her, then looks furtively over his shoulder at the camera mounted over the door.

"It's dead, LeBron," whispers Desiree is a tone of fond exasperation. "It isn't working. You know that."

The cameras were installed in the penitentiary's public areas almost a year ago, but funds for the film have never been allocated. It's a joke among the staff and therefore common inmate knowledge.

"I can't be easy with that cold glass eye staring on me."

He leads her to a door behind the TV set, unlocks it, lets Desiree in and follows. The closet is a large walk-in with brooms and mops and a pair of toilet plungers. On the deep side-shelves rests a tangled stack of venetian blinds, an old television set, and couple of dead microwaves.

Now Ferguson, after moving a mop bucket with his foot, leans Desiree against the back wall.

"Oh, baby, baby, baby," he whispers into her hair.

"They're saying you put in for a transfer, LeBron. Are you doing that?"

He pulls away from her. "Now, that's a damn lie. I ain't about . . ." He freezes. "You been talking to anyone?"

"No, Bronie. No! I haven't said—I would never, ever . . ."

"You sure now? My name fly around up in the warden's ear? My ass is going to get transferred."

"No, I never said anything. I just overheard some of them talking."

"They're talking about somebody else, baby. I'm not transferring anywhere. How could I transfer out of here? You're my life, baby. I can't live my life without my baby."

He nuzzles her neck and moves his hands up and down her back under the thermal. "You the reason why I take my first breath in the morning."

"It was probably just a rumor, but it scared me, Bronie. I've been just sick."

"Oh, my poor baby, listening to a cold-hearted lie. We going to be together, baby. You get on up out of here and we are going to find us a nice, pretty little place. Be surprising if I can even find the strength to get off to work in the mornings. Leave you there in bed? We going to be together every minute we got for ourselves."

"Have you told her yet, Bronie?"

"I'm working on it, baby, I'm trying to find the right . . ."

"You always say that."

"Hey, pretty woman," and he holds her away and looks deeply into her eyes. "You know how essential it is that I am needing to be a daddy for my boys. When the time getting closer . . . Right now, you just worry about getting your pretty little ass up over into that drug program—get your time over with."

He gathers her close again and moves his hands around to her breasts. "We ain't got time for conversation, baby. I got to get back to the station; ol' Wilkins be thinking something happening. Here you go, baby, you just la-ay yourself right on down here . . ."

CHAPTER 10

"Are you certain?" asks Warden Coleman.

Iris is amazed at the warden's collection of glasses. The one's she's wearing now are cherry-colored cat's-eyes with an exaggerated upsweep. Her hair beads are lime, but the cherry reemerges in her lips and her nails. And under the lime green suit in the pattern of her blouse.

Is this what they're all wearing out there now?

Back when Iris was on the streets, everyone had dressed in black. She tries to picture herself in a Juicy-Fruit wardrobe.

She can't.

"Perhaps this individual—uh, Johansson—is expressing some psychological fixation. You're sure it's really going on?"

"Oh, I'm sure it's going on. She's upset with him because he's promising to leave his wife and he hasn't. If it were all a fantasy, that wouldn't be part of it."

The Warden tap-taps her desk with a pencil.

"And this *predatory* sexual activity, which I think we can safely characterize as rape—this rape is taking place in Ms. Johansson's unit after the 3:00 a.m. count?"

"He leaves the TV room unlocked. She waits for him in there."

"We can prevent the activity, but I want to get this verified on paper. I want him to be an example. I want everyone to be assured that any officer who abuses an inmate on my watch—I will see that officer prosecuted to the fullest extent of the law. Now, Ms. Engels, how are we going to accomplish that?"

"It will be a challenge. The way the situation is right now, she'll never say a word.

And even if she did, it would just be an *inmate's* word. She can't produce sperm. He uses a rubber."

"How does he dispose?"

"Flushes on the way out."

"My, my. You did get that child to talking."

"Once she started, I couldn't turn her off."

The warden chuckles, and her hair extensions quiver. She taps her pencil again and looks off into the distance.

"Those cameras are set up in there. I could buy me some film."

"The two of them go somewhere else. Off into some closet, I think she said, where the cameras can't track. He's paranoid."

"We could get maintenance to set a camera up in the closet."

"Without the whole unit knowing?"

They look at each other.

"If I bring her in," says the warden, "talk woman-to-woman, help her to understand about how she's the victim of a predatory abuser? Offer her a little bit of incentive, maybe?"

Iris experiences a jangle of horror. "That might not work out so well, actually."

"And may I ask . . . ?"

"If you were to call her in," interrupts Iris, trying to keep the panic out of her voice, "and tell her that you're aware of the situation? She'd be sure to know you got it from me. I'm the only one she's talked to."

Powell, the assistant warden under Taterchuk had assured Iris—then *reassured* her—that a penitentiary administrator's primary obligation is to hide the identity of an informant. Not this new one.

"But if that's the only means," objects the warden, "by which we can prevent an ongoing rape situation, our hand might be forced."

Stupid bitch!

"There's that, but on the other hand she'd be pretty apt to let the population be aware that we're in collaboration. In which case I'd be unable to assist you any more. I would lose my effectiveness."

"The warden drums blood-red fingernails. "We wouldn't want you to lose your effectiveness. But still, my first priority is the safety of the ladies under my protection."

She wants the credit. Stupid bitch.

"I'm afraid, Warden Coleman, that you'd be putting out all that effort, trying to talk to her, and it wouldn't work anyway. I know how persuasive you can be, but can you be certain you'd convince her? He's the love of her life, remember? They're going to get married, remember?"

"Hmm."

"With all due respect, Warden Coleman, and I'm not trying to suggest that I know how to do your job, but you may have to settle for simply transferring Ferguson."

"That would not be my preference, Ms. Engels. We need to make an example."

How are you going to get yourself out of this one, Iris? Think, Iris!

"Hmm," says the warden, still drumming. "Maybe if we could get her placed in segregation?"

"Why?"

"Scare her? Leave her in there awhile to go over her options? In which case we may not have to compromise you. We could simply give her a chance to understand that if she's has information for us, we'll be able to let her out without a write-up? Or loss of good time."

"You know, that might be a great idea, but the problem is, she's not involved in anything."

"Not involved!" the warden exclaims.

"I mean," Iris adds hastily, "besides Ferguson. So you may have a problem convincing her that she's actually in any kind of trouble—I mean other than her relationship, and of course you wouldn't be able to use that."

Come on, Iris, work this.

"So you may have to focus," Iris continues, "more on a transfer type of solution."

"She needs to be in some kind of violation," the warden muses, taking off her glasses and swinging her chair around to look out her window. "Could we maybe," she asks herself, "put a little something in her property?"

No! Stupid bitch!

"You know, um, begging pardon, Warden Coleman, but I'm pretty sure that she would suspect a plant."

"Now, how's she going to have that kind of suspicion, Ms. Engels?"

"Okay, here's the problem, and I'm afraid we have to get into the weeds of inmate politics here."

The warden snorts.

"Johansson knows," explains Iris, "that obviously someone put them in her property and she doesn't have the kind of enemy who would waste their drugs on her to get her into that kind of trouble. You'll find this distasteful, Warden Coleman, but drugs down among the population are pretty valuable."

The warden snorts again.

"Inmates aren't going to squander without a high level of motivation. No one's motivated and Johansson and she knows it. On top of that, inmates are always repeating stories about staff planting drugs on them. I know, I know! They're paranoid! But the thing is, she'll automatically go there."

This piece of insight is not pleasing to the warden. She puts her glasses back on and narrows her eyes. "If I hear you correctly, you're suggesting that I am unaware of what's going on in my compound?"

Exactly!

"Not at all. In fact, Warden Coleman, the population has been impressed with your understanding and your level of concern. Now, your predecessor? I don't want to disrespect him but his style was more one of …disengagement? I actually think some of the inmates felt that when all was said and done, he just really didn't care. But since you've come, I sense more of a feeling of security."

"Yes, I've always been responsive to the needs of my ladies. Now that's not to say I won't be firm. My administrative priorities are fairness and firmness."

Here it comes:

"My leadership style is to be fair but at the same time to be firm."

The virtue chant.

" I've never felt those two priorities should cancel each other out. I've never been convinced that they need to cancel each other out. I am convinced that they can coexist, and under my watch I intend to see that they do coexist."

Yeah, yeah, yeah.

"Warden Coleman, I agree. I absolutely agree. And there's no way you should be expected to submerge yourself in some of these more neurotic mind-sets."

The warden is not quite mollified, but Iris plows forward. She moves closer and puts her elbows on her desk and locks eyes.

I've got to get this through her thick skull.

"So as all this relates to Johansson, if you place her in seg under the conditions you suggest? She's not involved in drugs; she'll know someone set her up. And then you start grilling her? Even if you don't directly mention Ferguson, she'll know why. Because what other reason would you have to be planting drugs on her? She'll clam up. And again, she'll suspect it's coming from me."

"I can see you think you've thought this all the way through, Ms. Engels." The warden pushes her chair back and away. There's a chill in her voice. The cat's-eyes take on a menace.

Rats! She's thinking I'm calling her stupid.

Iris quickly moves her elbows off the desk and sits back and hunches her shoulders.

"Well, you know us inmates. We have a lot of time. We can sit around and work this stuff out." She studies her tennis shoes. "Plus, our minds go in devious ways. That's why we're in here."

Warden Coleman relaxes and allows herself a small chuckle.

"You may have a point. You do have the time, yes you do. So how we going to go about getting that child into segregation? Getting her to cooperate? Has that great mind of yours come up with any devious ideas?"

"Well, actually, an idea is coming to me. I think I may be able to get her into seg without her knowing that it's you wanting her in there. But you'll have to give me a week or two."

The warden looks interested.

"But the way I'd go about it," warns Iris, "wouldn't be terribly ethical, and—pardon me if I'm being presumptuous—but, you don't seem like the kind of person who would actually want to know that sort of thing."

The warden leans over her desk and folds her hands. Her glasses are friendly again. "You probably right about that, Ms. Engels. I believe I'll be leaving all that devious inmate behavior up to you."

CHAPTER 11

"Hey Ms. Iris," says Rogo, "you looking fine. Got your boyfriend coming up in here to visit?"

Rogo and Asia B, the African American mother/child couple, have stopped by Iris's bench to chat. The question is almost drowned out by the loudspeaker:

MARIA TRUJILLO, SHANNA WILLIAMS, AND MARIA CASTRO

REPORT TO THE VISITING ROOM.

REPEAT, TRUJILLO, WILLIAMS, CASTRO. VISITATION.

It's Sunday. Emilia and Desiree are sitting on either side of Iris on the bench. They're in sweat suits while Iris wears a crisply ironed uniform.

"Now Rogo, don't be bothering the lady," chides Asia B.

The weather has turned, and there is a sprinkle of snow in the shadows of the lawns. Asia B shivers. She wears her prison-issue jacket over her suit, her collar over her ears, and her chin tucked inside the zipper.

"I ain't messing with her," Rogo protests, jigging from side to side. Rogo's wearing her coat as a partial sleeping bag, her left arm tucked inside. "I just seeing the lady looking all fine that way, expecting her boyfriend for visitation."

PATRICIA BUDDAMER AND TATIANNA HERNANDEZ, REPORT TO

THE VISITING ROOM. BUDDAMER, HERNANDEZ, VISITATION.

Sunday is prime visiting day, and the compound is scattered with day uniforms among the sweat suits. The inmates in uniform are further singled out by elaborate makeup and hair. The Spanish and Caucasians prefer highly constructed updos with stiff, elaborately entwined curls. The African Americans, other than the dread and the corn rowed ones, lean toward standaway straightened caps. Even Iris's simple cut has an extra poof in the back. She has on lipstick and shadow heightening her khaki-colored eyes.

"Nope, no boyfriend, Rogo. My sister's coming."

"From New York?" asks Desiree.

"Outside of Philadelphia."

"Tell her I said hi," says Rogo and dodges Asia B's lazy slap.

"Ms. Iris sister," scolds Asia B, "ain't want to hearing no hi's out of *your* mouth." Rogo dances out of reach. "Now, Ms. Asia B? You miscalculating. That sister be loving her some Rogo," she slides a glance at Desiree, "cause Rogo's got the pimp juice."

Emilia titters and Desiree allows herself a smile.

"Rogo! Don't you be talking that way in front of these nice ladies."

"Rogo, have you heard back from your lawyer yet?" interrupts Iris.

Rogo pulls herself up to attention. "No ma'am."

"How long has it been now?"

"Been going on two weeks. Haven't heard word-one. I told you she don't like me."

"She might have misplaced the letter. Write to her again. She has to send it. It's required. Asia, see that she gets another letter out."

PAMELA PETERSON, IRIS ENGELS, TWANIA GAINS, REPORT TO THE VISITING ROOM. PETERSON, ENGELS, GAINS . . .

Iris rises. "Whew, finally." She starts to leave.

"Your watch!" cries Emilia.

Iris, making a face, turns and tugs at the Velcro band and hands it to Emilia.

"Tell your sister," says Rogo, flicking another quick glance at Desiree, "that her loving Rogo be remembering after her."

"*Get* your sorry self . . ."

"I'll tell her, Rogo."

The visiting room is crowded. The small table-and-chair sets overflow with women, children, and here and there a man. It also clatters with conversation. Voices are raised in excitement. Children wander away only to be corrected by the caretaker and the inmate mother each trying to over ride the other. There is a small gathering in front of the snack machines and the photo area. A female guard sits at a desk at the front of the room.

"McCarthy, don't touch the machine," she calls out. "Get back." McCarthy hastily steps away and, from a distance, points her visitor to the box of Gummi Bears.

At the far end, back in the corner, Iris sits with her sister: a smaller, softer, more domestic-looking version of herself with society-lady blond hair tucked behind her ears. The sister is in an animated monologue.

"He's feeling better, but Goldstein says there may be some blockage developing now, if you can believe, in the *right* ventricle. They want to schedule him in for a follow-up, but Josh told them, 'Wait until after the holidays.' They're short-staffed at the office. So anyway, what with all that on his plate, he's being a little bit of a grump these days."

Iris, elbow on the table, hand cradling her chin, listens attentively. "And the kids?" she asks.

"Noah's been invited into the honor society—I told you that, didn't I? Chelsea's just got her braces. Remember last year how she said if we had the dentist put them in, she was going to yank them out? So now she won't admit but she *loves* them. All her friends have them. They all get to complain together."

The sister leans nearer and pretends to whisper. "She's starting to develop. I got her a training bra, but we don't talk about that, okay? Josh refuses to discuss." She sits back again. "And poor Dillon—his arthritis is getting so bad sometimes he can't even stand up by himself. We have to haul him up by his rear rump. He's half-blind—keeps bumping into the patio door. We have to remember to keep the curtain shut."

"Huh, Irene . . ."

"We're going to have to put him down, but say it in front of Chelsea? She goes into hysterics."

Iris takes a breath, "Irene, did Weldon's office ever get back to you?"

"Yes, I forgot; I should have mentioned. They say no. They lack any kind of congressional mandate. All those decisions are made over at Immigration. They say, nothing they can do."

"I was hoping that since Josh had volunteered to bundle all that money . . ."

"Weldon made a personal call and he was really nice and apologetic and everything, but he said that immigration policy is out of congressional hands. So how about Schumer? Has his office gotten back?"

"No," says Iris, "and it's been almost two months. I guess I'm going to go ahead and hire an immigration lawyer. How are my funds doing?"

"Iris, I told you before that Josh really doesn't recommend that. He's concerned about you having enough to get yourself reestablished."

"This is more important, Irene. It's my money."

"You could write and ask him, Iris, but he says that with the way he has it set up you'd be a fool to try to withdraw early. Honestly? I'm pretty sure he wouldn't go for it. He says a decent lawyer is going to want five thousand up front and it would amount to throwing the money away."

"It's my money."

"I know, but he called this old college roommate in the Department of Justice who knows immigration policy. I think Josh said his name was Spike—probably a nickname, but anyway—Spike told him forget it. He said she'd have a chance for a hearing if we were talking paper crime—Europe or China. But Colombia narcotics? No way."

"So he's not going to take the money out for a lawyer, even if I insist?"

"I don't think so, Iris. He's protective of you."

Iris puts her head in her hands and massages her temples.

"I'm sorry, but you know Josh when it comes to taking care of his family. Do you want a Dr. Pepper? Let me get you a Dr. Pepper. SunChips? You want Sun-Chips, right?"

While Irene is gone, Iris rubs her face, sighs, and pulls herself together. She looks around the room. At the next table is a family with young children.

Iris is back with the snacks.

"Thanks, Irene." She nods toward a child. "It's so strange to come into the visiting room and see these undersized heads. You don't realize until after you've been seeing adults for month after month how miniature children are."

"Oh Iris," says Irene, stricken, "I know I should get down here to visit more often, but with the kids and the shop and Josh being sick . . ."

"Irene! I didn't it mean that way."

"I'm always thinking I don't get over here enough."

"I'm lucky you can even come at all—ever. So what time is the plane taking off tomorrow?"

"Not until noon. It'll be getting into Miami at three. I called, and Cabot House says it can extend visiting hours because I'm out of state."

"At $4800 a month, they better extend."

"Well, the place is clean. Some of those places when we were looking around? You wouldn't believe."

"And mom's happy there."

"As far as I can tell. I just hope she recognizes me this time. I told you about last time how she was having a bad day? She kept saying, 'Now, do I know you? Tell me again, am I supposed to know who you are?' A whole trip, and she didn't even know it was me. I suppose we should have moved her up closer to us but she was already acclimated, and getting her on the plane in a wheel chair . . ." Irene sighs. "At least she isn't asking where Dad is any more."

"Or me."

"Or you."

"My name does not cross her lips."

"No, and actually it's a little hard to tell if it's because she's still rejecting you or because she can't remember you existed in the first place."

"Well, either way I'm sure that's no great loss for her. I never was exactly her golden girl."

"Iris, you can't blame her. You were terrible to her. You kept calling her stupid—"

"I was sixteen!"

"No, I'm talking about later when you came home from college. You sneered at everything she ever stood for."

"I got into Colombia Law, didn't I? She's a Jewish mother. She stood for that, didn't she?"

"Yes, and she was really proud until they found out who you were advising. You were always going on and on about your artsy friends, and then we come to find out all that time you were just a sleazy—"

"What do you mean, sleazy. How can you . . ."

"Because we found out about your 'clients'!"

"Everyone deserves representation."

"Drug-gang members? They deserve . . ."

"That was never proven. I got the guy off, remember? He came back innocent."

"Not innocent enough, apparently." Irene spreads out her hands and turns her head left and right to encompass the visiting room. "Here you are!"

Iris bows her head.

Pause.

"I've done it again. I'm sorry, Iris."

Pause. Iris sniffs.

"Iris, really, I'm really sorry. Iris?"

Iris looks up. "No, that's okay, I was the one who started it. Do you have a tissue?"

"Where's my purse?"

Off to one side, an inmate with her camera is collecting chits and taking photographs. Next up is a Spanish inmate with a pair of visiting sisters. Friends? The inmate's prison pants are crisp and formfitting, her side pockets sewn closed. The two visitors are in black stretch pants and platform heels. Giggling, the three line up facing the wall. They prop their hands against it, extend back a pointed toe and turn their heads in exaggerated provocation.

"Do you think we should get a picture?" asks Irene in an upbeat voice.

Iris shakes her head and laughs. "Get a cheese cake of the two of us? Now that would be a sight." She does a final sniff, wipes her nose, and stuffs her tissue into her breast pocket.

"Hey Iris," Irene says brightly, putting her purse back under her chair. "What's with all those"—she flutters her hands—"all these shirt-decoration, creasy-things going on in here?"

Irene nods to a table to their right, where a pretty African American inmate has ironed an intricate pattern of chevrons onto the back of her shirt. She indicates with her eyes to the left. The shirt there is a checkerboard. "What is it? Some kind of jailhouse fashion trend or something?"

"Actually, kind of. On the streets, gang members used to have different identity creases. They'd have their girlfriends take lessons on how to iron them, so then in here the girls kept it up."

"It doesn't look easy."

No, it isn't. I couldn't do it. It actually turned into a controversy last year because all of a sudden the BOP identified it as gang related. I don't think by that time it even was any more. But they got all panicked and thought it needed to be stamped out."

Irene is interested.

"But then," Iris explains, "there was another competing theory from the councilors about how pride in appearance is an intrinsic part of the rehabilitation process. Which is total nonsense. I never saw anyone take more pride in appearance than an un-rehabilitated gang member."

"You should know."

Iris stops and looks at her.

"Oh, Iris, don't take that wrong! I was just . . ."

"No, that's okay," says Iris, smiling. "Anyway, the upshot was, inmates got to keep the creases and the BOP settled for just continuing to not let us have sweat suits in gang colors. Which is pretty much all the colors sweat suits even come in. For a while they were letting us have olive green. Then they heard how green was a color out in Milwaukee or someplace, so everyone had to send the olive green home. Apparently there aren't any gray gangbangers, so that's us."

"So is there very much gang activity in here?" Irene scans the room, trying to do it casually.

"No, not for women. The rule is, 'We're cool with each other in here. When we get out, we can go back to banging each other.'"

"So everyone gets along."

"No, I mean obviously the girls have problems, but it doesn't have anything to do with their street affiliations."

Irene is scanning the room. "Who in the world? Who is that crew?"

Irene indicates a group of women in the far corner. A half-dozen visitors wear long, flowered pioneer dresses with bonnets over wraparound braids.

Iris laughs. "Those are the Branch Davidians down from Canada. They're visiting Ruth—see? That inmate they're talking to? That's Ruth Rydal. She was one of the Waco crew that jumped out the window. She says they just ignored that her skirt was on fire until after they got her cuffed. She has scars up and down her legs."

"Nutcase, huh?"

"No! Sane! A really stable person. You'd be very happy if your kid got her for a teacher. She's still believes in the leader—what's-his-name. Koresh? Probably after all she invested, she's got to. I don't really know her that well, but I do know she's calm and rational about everything. I've talked it over with her a little bit, and I can feel she's carrying trauma—I mean, who wouldn't? But she isn't resentful or sorry for herself. I like her."

"Are you doing legal for her?"

"No, and she's got grounds. There was blatant prosecutorial misconduct at that trial, and that's just what I gleaned from the papers. But in here, for the ones who took it to trial, even if you can afford to pay for the transcripts, it's really hard to store them. There's so much of it; they take up boxes, and you've got to get special permission to keep them under your bed. When she first got here, I offered to hook her up with the pro bonos at Yale Law School. She said no. She's getting out next year, anyway. They'll be sending her back to Canada."

"Wow. You certainly are rubbing up against an interesting cast of char—uh, Iris," she whispers, "is that normal? For an inmate and another woman to kiss that way?"

A young black inmate and her guest are just breaking away from a clinch. Iris leans over to her sister and speaks quietly. "You just witnessed a drug pass."

Irene gasps and, elbow on the table, puts her bent-bsack hand over her mouth. She follows the pair with her eyes.

"You probably didn't notice, but when that gal—I forget her name. I think she's actually in the drug program. Anyway, when she first got here—to the visiting room? She didn't come right in; she stood there at the entrance. Then her inmate friend—no, another one over there. That one. She came up to the guard and asked for a deck of cards. And so at that point the inmate swoops in when the guard's vision is blocked, and her visitor kisses her in a drug balloon. Now watch. Watch inmate one with the balloon in her mouth."

Irene, shifts in her chair and attends from the corner of her eye. "A balloon?"

"Yeah, balloon. It's stupid, actually, to kiss a woman like that when they could have just passed it by hand. See there? The inmate is trying to swallow. Oops, can't . . . Whew! She got it down."

"Uh, can I ask how she going to get it out?"

"You don't want to know. If she lives in Unit Eleven like I think, she has a toilet in her room. She'll probably wait until her roommate isn't there and stick her finger down her throat. If that doesn't work, she'll have to wait for it at the other end."

"You mean—eww."

"It's courtesy for a roommate to step out when you have to take a—when you have to defecate. But you don't want her to catch you fishing around in the toilet bowl, so sometimes you have to go down to the shower with a garbage bag. And you never know for sure when it's going the balloon's going appear. It's not easy being a penitentiary druggie. She's in the drug program too, so if they catch her, she going to lose her year."

"Her year?"

"Yeah, you get a year off your sentence if you complete the drug program."

"So how would they catch her?"

"Urine test. You get called over and they watch while you pee—uh, while you produce."

"Well, I'm certainly going to have some interesting stories to tell at Woman's League," Irene says archly.

"Won't you, though."

"Now Iris, who's that one—no, more to my left. She looks so normal. Like someone at Shabbat dinner or something."

Irene indicates the new white-collar inmate with the good haircut—a haircut which by now has lost its luster and needs a trim.

"Aha, you're talking about Kaplan. Rebecca. Hmm, that must be her husband. She's Savings and Loan. According to her—she *says*—the guys above set policy and they were all doing it—cash-for-trash, flip-loans. She was just taking orders. She says. Then when it collapsed the guys got off by cooperating with the investigation and saying it was all on her: she was on her own; they knew nothing."

"You mean the men just *blamed* her? How could they get away with it?"

"In some of these thrift cases, the prosecution team looks into it and it's like the end of a daisy chain. Could go up—who knows how far. So when they get handed a scalp, they stop there. I don't know if that's true in her case, but I'm assuming.

But I'm also assuming that she's more culpable than the way she's remembering it now."

"Is she asking you for legal help?"

"No, she's got a high powered post-conviction team out of New York. I know them—they're big bucks."

"She certainly doesn't look like prison material."

"She doesn't think she does either. She walked in here with an attitude, and they're giving her a hard time for it. Especially the African Americans."

"How do you mean? Are they hurting her?"

"Oh no, just tormenting."

"Like what?"

"Like, crowding in front of her in line. Stepping on her toe as they walk by. Elbowing her. Spilling Pepsi on her bag in the laundry line."

"Poor thing. Can't she complain to the authorities? "

"She's tried that. They just ignore her and she makes it worse."

"Isn't there anything you can . . ."

"Not until she learns to ignore it. As long as she keeps screeching, and stomping off to the unit manager's office, she'll just make it worse. I tell her to not react. Sail above. They'll lose interest. But she can't. All she's doing is turning herself into their toy. They poke, she squeaks."

"That poor lady. It's the kind of persecution—my heart just goes out."

Iris shakes her head. "No, you're thinking it's a Jewish issue. It just isn't. I'd be surprised if they even know she is. All they know is that she's white and she's middle class and she needs to know her place. Which is probably up the hill to camp, but she's not going to be camp eligible for a while. She doesn't have a clue how do time behind the wire."

"It's that different from camp?"

"More attitude here, less middle class. Probably she came in scared, so in compensation she strode in trying to look like she was in charge. Worked fine in the boardroom; in here it's a signal she needs to be knocked down to size."

"Why do they care so much?"

"Because in their eyes, she's the stand-in for all their past humiliations. She's the teacher who flunked them and the social worker who reported them and the clerk who followed them around Woolworths. So now it's payback time. She's on *their* territory now. Now *they're* in charge."

"Is it just the black ones who are like that?"

"No, some of the white girls try, they just don't do it as well. And it's not even all of the blacks. The Islanders and the Africans—they're polite—well, they're polite to whites. Not to the other blacks necessarily, but that's another story. And then there's the Colombians, who have different issues entirely. They have their own tribal arrogance thing going. But it's more apt to bump up against blacks. Let me put it this way: it's complicated."

"Did they ever try to give you a bad time like that?"

"No, I got a pass," says Iris wryly. "My crime story preceded me. Plus, I was the only lawyer in here, and lawyers are gold. I hit the ground helping to write up their BP-9s."

"BP-9's?" Irene looks at her watch and unhooks her coat from the back of the chair.

"Inter-penitentiary grievances forms," explains Iris, rising. "Then I started 2255s—filing appeals. So no, I did fine."

The last few visitors are filing out of the visiting room, waving and blowing kisses. Two officers stalk past them to begin their contraband search, upending tables-chair sets and sifting through the trash. A pair of inmate orderlies hovers at the edge, waiting for the officers to finish.

Irene has left and Iris stands in line near the visiting room exit, waiting to be cleared. To her right is a separate room for inmates singled out for a strip search. The rest, after the usual pat-down, are only required to finger-comb their hair, open their mouths, and take off their shoes.

Iris turns to the inmate next to her—a forty-something African American.

"And how was your visit, Ms. Rice?"

"Why, it was just wonderful, Ms. Iris. And how was yours? That was your sister? My son and his wife and my little grandbabies drove up over from Baltimore. Going to try to make it back tonight."

"That's a long drive with kids."

"They're good babies. Uh, say, Ms. Iris, you hearing yet on my camp eligibility?"

"I won't. You're case manager with notify, but I think it'll go through. You came in with just a failure-to-appear, right? You've got a couple of years clean. You'll be okay."

"I hope I get it. Like I told you, I got a cousin over there in the camp. I'm hoping to do my time with her."

"Uh, Alicia, you're still living in Unit Five, aren't you?"

"Yes, ma'am."

"I need to talk something over in private with you. Do you think that during the day when the law library isn't crowded that you would have time to stop in? I've got a little problem. I need some advice."

Alicia visibly swells. "I can surely try, Ms. Iris. I'm over CMS under Woodrow. He ain't about to let his people walk away any-old time, but I know someone, work over in medical. She can get me on the call-out."

"That'd be great, Alicia. By the way, that girl over there?" Iris indicates the corn-rowed kisser who is now being beckoned into the strip-search room. "I never can remember that girl's name."

"Oh, that's Tamika Henderson. She just got accepted into the drug program."

"Oh, that's right, Tamika Henderson."

"They almost wasn't going to let her, but she saying how she run some game on them."

"Okay, Engels," calls the officer.

Iris steps up to her and shakes her hair. The officer, without requesting that she either open her mouth or to take off her shoes, simply twirls her finger. Iris turns and spreads her arms for a very perfunctory pat down.

COUNT TIME, LADIES. COUNT TIME.

RETURN TO YOUR UNITS FOR STAND-UP COUNT.

Iris throws an a-okay gesture to Alicia Rice and hurries to her unit.

CHAPTER 12

In the law library Emilia is at the typewriter and Iris, at her desk, listens in as two older African Americans exchange compound news.

"Angela, she got snitched to the chaplain. He say the choir be expecting to set an example on the compound, so they can't be having no choir director be involved in no relationships. But now I hear where Ms. Angela, she be behaving herself. She broke it off with Cynthia, she getting her life all clean and proper, asking the chaplain to let her back into her position."

"How long those two be broke up now?"

"Hasn't been a month but the chaplain, he considering the request. He tempted because the new warden, she be complaining on the choir be dragging, ladies ain't showing up, be a little bit raggedy. Angela, she got that leadership talent."

"So when she going to hear for . . ."

The door opens and there's a breeze. Alicia Rice, the lady Iris consulted last weekend after her visit, room, blows in with a scatter of yellow leaves.

"Hey, Alicia! Ain't you in the electrical shop? How you be walking up in here like a free person?"

"Got my name on the call-out for medical but Ms. Iris, she asking me to stop by. Hope they ain't whistle-blow my ass."

"Don't worry, Alicia," says Iris from her desk. "If they blow the whistle I'll tell them I called you in. It'll be on me."

"Yeah, you be relaxing, Ms. Alicia. Ms. Iris, she got the juice."

"Okay, ladies, sorry, but Ms. Rice and I have some business we need to talk over."

The two rise from their table and make their way out of the door.

Emilia leaves her typing to find the broom and dustpan.

Iris moves out from behind her desk and pulls up a chair at the long oaken table. "Ms. Alicia, I'm glad you could get away. I need to talk to you."

"Behind my camp designation? It still ain't gone through."

"Any day now, Alicia, but no, it's something else. You're in Unit Five with Dessie Johansson, right?"

"Yeah, she be on my floor. Across the aisle and down a ways."

"Listen," Iris pauses and sighs. "What I'm going to talk to you about—it's highly irregular, but I couldn't think of anyone else to go to. I need someone I can trust." Iris lowers her voice almost to a whisper, and Alicia bends in eagerly. "Have you heard anything about Desiree in connection with the shower?"

"The shower?"

Iris sighs again. "Someone told me—I can't mention names—it was just before her release. She wouldn't have said anything except she was on her way out the door."

Alicia nods.

"Anyway, she felt that she needed to let me know that Dessie has a habit of urinating in the shower. She could smell it whenever Dessie got out."

"Oh! Nasty!"

"Yeah, I know, Alicia. It's not a pleasant thing to have to live with."

"Come to think, Ms. Iris, I thought I detecting some kind of odorish thing going on in there."

"You do know, I'm sure, how it can get to be a habit and after people develop it, it really takes over and they have a terrible time breaking themselves."

Alicia nods hesitantly, then with assurance. "I believe I have heard."

"Now Alicia, Dessie's my friend. The only reason I'm here even mentioning it . . ." Iris lowers her voice. Alicia bends in further. "I did some work for her, and I saw her paperwork from County Correctional. Now, please don't tell anyone I told you this, but she tested as a possible for AIDS."

Alicia gasps.

"Not positive. *Possible.* They reran the tests, but she got transferred before the results came back."

"Oh, my sweet lord! You mean that nasty, yellow-hair bitch—"

"No really, Ms. Alicia. Dessie's a good person. I can't hear you talking that way. She can't help if she has the habit, and her health may be just fine. Probably it is just fine."

"You say she be pissing her AIDS up into my *shower?*"

"I would never break client confidentiality like this but after Ms.—after the other inmate—told me about how Dessie has that shower issue . . . It's been just eating away at my conscience. If any of you ladies over there have a cut on your foot or an ingrown nail or—"

"Oh my, yes. Oh my. You did right coming to me, Ms. Iris."

"Please, Alicia, let everyone know so they can watch out for themselves. But *please* warn everyone not to let themselves get too upset. They must *not* lay a *hand.* It's too dangerous. If she ends up biting or scratching . . ." Iris pauses. She looks off into the distance and does a little shudder.

Alicia is mesmerized. She nods her head slowly.

"When they catch her at it, tell them no confrontations. Tell them to turn right around and go straight to the officer station and report. Immediately."

Alicia, eyes wide, keeps nodding.

"Alicia, I thank you for coming over. I needed someone who could warn the other ladies. I know you, and I know you won't tell anyone, ever, where this is coming from. If people in here find out that I'm breaking confidentiality and repeating their information . . ." Iris puts her head in her hands and messages her temple.

Alicia nods and tentatively reaches out for Iris's hand.

Iris grasps it. "I came to you because you're the one lady in Unit Five who knows how to keep things to herself."

"You can trust me. I'll take care of it for you, Ms. Iris."

"Remember, nothing physical. Tell them to just go over and report."

CHAPTER 13

In Unit Five's shower room a small group of African American inmates are gathered in front of one of shower stalls. A terrycloth towel and robe hangs on a peg alongside of it.

The sound of water stops.

The group watches as a pale arm reaches out around the white plastic curtain. They exchange glances and wait. The shower curtain opens and Desiree—turbaned, robed, and flushed—steps out.

She's greeted by hostile faces.

"*What?*"

Two of the inmates, one on each side, push around her and lean into her vacated shower.

Desiree has to bend herself left and right to avoid them.

"*What?*"

The two pull their heads back out of the shower, turn to their companions, and nod.

"Smelt it."

"Yep, sure did."

"Smelt it."

The group turns and as one, gallops out of the bathroom.

Desiree stands, one hand clenching her robe, the other at her loosening towel-turban, staring after them.

"What?"

CHAPTER 14

Outside of Unit Five's shower room it's a mid-November early evening, and the compound square is bright under the floodlights. It's getting late, but the square is still alive with brown-jacketed inmates brightened by colored, handcrafted scarves and hats. It snowed a few days ago, but today there was an early winter thaw and while the lawns are still blanketed white, the sidewalks are dark. Here and there a large patch of melt gleams under the floodlights.

Iris and Emilia are on their bench, both wearing matching crocheted scarf and hat sets with teal, yellow, and purple stripes. The colors shouldn't work together but they do.

"Is late. Me, I am freezer," says Emilia, shivering inside her jacket.

"Freezing, Babe, you are *freezing*."

"Is colder. I am *freezer*," insists Emilia.

Iris shrugs. "If you want to be a kitchen appliance, go for it." She reaches over and tucks in a lock of blue/black hair into Emilia's hat. "They'll be along any minute now, and then we'll get you in so you can go be an oven." She lays a motherly finger on Emilia's chin, then leans past her, and peers across the compound. On the far side, to the left, is the door marked *Receiving & Discharge*.

"I don't know what the holdup is. Probably because they've got so many of them coming in."

Down the compound square Asia B and Rogo, brown-coated and wrapped in matching red-and-yellow scarves, emerge from rec and head toward the bench.

"Incomings be through yet?" asks Asia.

Iris scoots over and nods an invitation to sit. "No, still processing. Dessie said laundry sent over eleven bedrolls, so there's going to be a pack of them."

"Rogo's bottom bunkie packed out last week," says Asia settling in. "The child, most likely getting her replacement tonight. We trying to look over the merchandise."

Rogo, off to the side with her headset, is moving to its beat, a combination of hip-hop and boxing-ring footwork.

"Any minute now," replies Iris, but her attention is caught by a movement in front of Unit Five. A group of inmates is emerging at a run. They remember not to and slow themselves into an arm-pumping power walk. They are heading toward the captain's office.

Asia also has been down long enough to recognize potential drama. "Those women's got a little something on they minds."

"What can you see, Ms. Asia B?" sings Rogo improvising to a song from her headset."

"Rochelle Gooden, I see you acting like a crunked-up fool."

"You is cold, Ms. Asia. You is a cold, cold woman," Rogo sings.

"I show you cold. You going to be cold."

Rogo jabbing and boxer-pivoting: "This here Danbury what's cold. You gots to get your child in outta the weather, Ms. Asia B."

"You just hush you mouth. Your new bunkie coming through, you need to get yourself a first-hand."

Iris's attention is elsewhere.

"Oh rats! It's Uranus."

A tall black officer is silhouetted in the open door of the captain's office. Her warrior body fills the space for a moment, then she turns left and follows the group back toward Unit Five. She moves casually, with a lazy gait. Even from across the yard it radiates menace.

"What's going on over there?" asks Asia.

"I'm not sure, Asia. Looks like trouble in Unit Five."

"Here they come. Here come the fish!" sings out Rogo.

The door to *Receiving & Discharge* swings open, and a group of new inmates emerge. They were off-loaded from a van and entered the compound through the back entrance. This is their first real view of their new home and they pause to peer around, hesitant and insecure.

"That's them," says Asia.

They have been issued temporary coats—ragged cast-offs—until laundry can dress them out. Under the coats they wear gray travel scrubs and rubber flip-flops.

All of them clutch army-blanket bedrolls.

A female officer, short and stocky, steps out in front of the group and beckons them with a theatrical follow-me-into-battle. Their destination is Unit Two—the projects—the three-storied, tiered unit that shares an entrance with segregation. It's actually only a few buildings down from R & D, but the officer in charge, in the spirit of tour guide, leads the group the long way around the compound square.

"Uh oh. Now there's a big boy."

One of the newbies, a light-skinned African American, rises a good five inches above the rest. She has the build of a man—long limbs, wide shoulders, and a deep, flat chest. But her face is smooth. It's soft. Like an adolescent boy and not adult man. But does not she move with the rugged, stiff-joints of a woman trending male. She walks with the ease and the looseness of a young man. On the streets she would surely pass for one.

Iris's attention has been centered to the left of the parade, on Unit Five into which Uranus has disappeared. But now, along with the others, she is arrested by the tall new inmate. She especially notes the self-possession.

After an arduous Con Air journey, hand and foot shackles connected by a chain, and multiple times strip-searched, an incoming inmate's confidence is at its lowest ebb. Now, for her first appearance, she wants to appear cool and unfazed. She almost never succeeds.

But this one, taking her first steps out onto a federal penitentiary, seems at home. Even in her ill-fitting travel scrubs, her toe peeking through a hole in the white athletic sock and curled against the cold, one side of her jacket zipper hanging loose, she is serene. The ten others clutch their bedrolls protectively; this one finger-hooks the twine and swings it at her side. The others cast apprehensive, fearful glances at the watchtower and the razor wire; this one's eyes are on the horizon. She might be on a nature walk.

"Now that, there? That is one manly lady," comments Asia B.

"Whoo-ee!" agrees Rogo. "All them hos up in here? They to be loving some of *that* one. They grabbing it up like government cheese."

"Is very, very handsome," comments Emilia.

"There might be something wrong with her," speculates Iris. "There's something eerie going on. She may just be a little bit crazy."

They watch the group of incomings led by the jaunty female guard as it turns the corner, passes the dining hall, and heads their way.

Asia chuckles. "See a sight like that, bring out the girl in me."

"They placing her up in here at Danbury," comments Rogo in a low voice as the parade passes, "gots to be a coochie up in there somewhere."

The comment is loud enough for the lead officer to hear. Her lips twitch.

Iris and Asia smile but Emilia isn't in on the joke. "Rogo!" she exclaims, "That is maybe will your new bunkie!"

"Be okay by me. Long as she ain't got no dick on her."

The procession passes. Iris, Asia B, and Emilia sit in contemplative silence. Rogo, standing beside them, is engrossed. But the silence is broken by a sudden, wild commotion.

"Oh, rats!"

Everyone's attention snaps to the entrance of Unit Five. A loudly protesting Desiree is being pushed out of the door. Her hair is wet, she's dressed in thermal long johns, her hands are behind her back, and she is being prodded forward by an angry Uranus. Both voices—the inmate's and the officer's—are raised, but only the pitch carries.

"Now, that is a cuff-and-stuff right there," informs Rogo. Unnecessarily.

"Don't try to fight!" Iris calls out.

The four of them watch, electrified. The busy compound halts and becomes still. A cuff-and-stuff on her seg walk always draws compound attention, and this one promises to be a doozie. Usually a handcuffed inmate on her seg walk tries for a breezy attitude. She swings her shoulders and strolls down the sidewalk because let them. She really doesn't really care *what* they do to her. Whatever.

But not Desiree Johansson. First she fights; then she refuses to move.

"No! I'm not going! I didn't do anything!" comes wafting across the hushed compound.

"Move it!" Uranus gives her a violent shove.

Desiree almost looses her footing, but her fall is averted by an angry, socket-straining yank.

Desiree wrestles and twists around to protest. Uranus yells back and, to the horror and fascination of the compound, Desiree attempts to land on Uranus's shin a backward, flip-flopped kick.

"Don't! Don't!" shouts Iris.

Danbury's occasional girl-fight is humdrum compared to an inmate fighting staff. This is the highest drama a female penitentiary can offer, and it's the first time any of the inmates here have seen such a thing. They know they are privileged.

But not the parade of the incomings. They are horrified. This is the final leg of a fraught trip. Con Air in the wrist-to-ankle shackles, the patronizingly humorous attitude of their guards, the leering jeers and cat calls of male convicts. The flight hops from landing to landing, and at each hop the circle of armed marshals pointing high-power rifles. Up at them!

Now finally, this is their introduction to the penitentiary but, since their destination shares an entrance with the segregation unit, they happen to be at ringside. They have no notion whatsoever of normal life here, and their horror is sweetened by the impression that what they are seeing is commonplace. It could happen to any of them at any moment and for any reason. They shrink into a protective huddle.

All but the tall one. She is still apart from the rest but her faraway look is gone. She is focused now on Desiree, and she is riveted.

Desiree struggles and tries to back kick Uranus once more.

"Don't! Don't!" screams Iris again, but too late. Desiree lands a kick, and although it is a weak one—more of a parody of a kick than an actual kick—it's enough to enrage Uranus. She swings Desiree by the cuff chain, skimming her feet across the sidewalk and flinging her into a pile of slushy mud.

Emilia buries her face in her hands and Iris, in a rare public gesture, puts her arms around and draws her in. Emilia, from Iris's chest, turns her head for a glimpse and immediately turns back. She buries her face.

INMATE DOWN.

INMATE DOWN ON THE COMPOUND.

Desiree is in the fetal position in the mud and Uranus towers over her, swinging a steel-toed boot. She lands a body kick.

The female officer who has been leading the incomings runs into the fray, but she's at a disadvantage. She's short and pudgy; the attacker is a splendidly fit six feet tall. Uranus brushes her aside with a back-arm. The intervening officer back peddles and almost falls.

Desiree is curled in the slush with her arm protecting her head. Uranus swings back for another kick. Desiree jerks away at the last moment, and the kick grazes the top of her skull. But the recoil unbalances the attacker. Uranus slips in the snow and barely manages to keep upright. Which further enrages her. She swings to kick again.

The staff has poured outdoors at a run. Uranus is in mid-kick, and the first to arrive is a pair of male officers.

"Williamson! Stop! Cut the fuck—"

"Jesus Christ! Williamson, what in the fuck you trying to—"

The first grabs her waist; the second tries for an arm.

"Motherfuckers. Get your fucking hands off," Uranus snarls and struggles, utterly determined to land a head kick.

The compound is electrified watching the officers wrestle.

Finally and with great reluctance, Uranus yields and aborts. She straightens, throws off the restraining hands, shakes herself, tosses her head, turns her back on them all, and stalks away.

LOCKDOWN, LOCKDOWN, LOCKDOWN.

ALL INMATES RETURN TO YOUR UNITS.

The incomings are still huddled to the side, as far from the action as they can get. Desiree is left lying in the snow, but the tall new inmate moves and stands over her.

Their lead officer, her face deeply red but her demeanor professional, begins to herd her group through the doorway and into their new home. They're happy to be herded.

All but the tall one who stays beside Desiree as though standing watch. Desiree is very still, curled into the mud.

"Back! Back! Get the fuck away!" yells an approaching officer. The new inmate doesn't move. "Get the fuck away!" He shoves her. "What the fuck you—get the fuck into your unit!" He shoulders past the tall inmate, bends, and lifts Desiree roughly to her feet.

Desiree almost crumbles. He catches and sets her back upright. The tall new inmate has backed *away,* but only a few steps.

"Get! Get into your unit!" the guard roars.

Desiree is standing on her own now, tottering. Her thermals are mud-coated, and her head is bleeding and her face is smeared with mud and blood. A clump of muddy curls dangles in her eyes but, as her wrists are bound behind her back, she is unable to remove it.

LOCKDOWN.

RETURN TO YOUR UNIT IMMEDIATELY.

LOCKDOWN. CLEAR THE YARD.

The guard shakes Desiree's chain roughly and angrily pushes her into the unit's entrance—the one through which the incomings have disappeared. The vestibule behind the entrance reveals a pair of options. To the left, propping open the door with her body, stands a woman in street clothes and a clipboard, documenting the incomings. She studiously ignores the officer prodding his bloody, dirty captive toward the right—toward the locked door.

Desiree is hobbling and bent over, which only serves to increase her guard's anger. He shoves her roughly through the door he has unlocked into the segregation unit. When she stumbles, he tightens her chain to hold her up. He's furious at her. She has tempted—coerced—a fellow officer into an act of flagrant unprofessionalism: an assault on a female inmate. He holds the inmate entirely responsible.

Desiree, no fight left, moves through the open door. She is focused, eyes a bit crossed, on her muddy clump of hair. She tries to shake it away, to blow it away. She cannot. The shaking and blowing simply causes it to shed mud into her lashes.

As she is prodded down the segregation unit's walkway, her eyes are finally flushed clean by her tears.

CHAPTER 15

The common area of the general population side of the projects--of Unit Two-- is a cavernous, twelve-foot-wide passageway. The three stories of traditional prison tiers on the left are shrouded in white plastic shower curtain. To the right a concrete block wall rises some thirty feet. A large window is set up high in it. The window, grilled in iron, consists of a dozen small, paint-encrusted panes of glass with embedded wire mesh. Well below the window bank, clusters of inmates congregate among the table-chair sets, all excited, raising their voices, comparing notes. The acoustics are terrible; the accents and languages echo and blur together, but they are all on the same subject-- the fight.

A third of the way down the passageway and across from the common area in a six-by-eight room, Rogo crawls into the bottom bunk, making—as a welcoming ritual—the tall newcomer's bed for her.

"Don't know her last name," she responds. "They just calling her Dessie. Why you asking?"

"Dessie?" the newcomer exclaims, and her face lights with wonder. She closes her eyes for a moment and moves her lips. Her face is bathed in awe.

Rogo is kneeling on the bed, tying the end corners of the sheet into a knot. "Why? You *knowing* her?"

The newcomer gives an involuntary shiver, "I do, I think. From way back. You don't happen to know where she's from, do you?"

Rogo, holding the knot under her chin, bows the corner of the thin mattress to accept it.

"No idea, but I do know the bitch gots to be fucking crazy, fucking with the guard that way. That was some traumatic shit right there. Welcome to the penitentiary."

Rogo turns to pull up a white thermal blanket.

The newcomer stands in the narrow space between the bunks and the footlockers. "Do you see that sort of shit—excuse me, that sort of *thing*, happening here on a regular basis?"

Rogo crawls to the foot of the bed, then realizing that she needs to get around her new roommate, moves back to the head. The newcomer sidesteps as Rogo crawls off.

"I only been down a couple months, know what I mean? But Ms. Asia B, she been down over ninety, she saying she ain't never seen that kind of drama in all her time."

"Who's Asia B?"

"That's my prison momma up in here. A while back, this one messy bitch over in six? She talking smack, try to spread it how we in a relationship. Asia B, she hear how the bitch talking dirt, she come right up at her, tell her if she don't put away that nasty mouth, she going to mass destruct it for her."

Rogo chuckles at the memory.

The tall inmate has no way to process this glimpse into penitentiary politics. She frowns in slight perplexity.

Rogo, in stocking feet, springs lightly up onto the toilet seat, then the sink, and hops over onto her top bunk.

"But where were they taking her?" asks the newcomer after a pause.

"Taking who? Ms. Asia B?"

"No, Dessie."

"Oh, her. They take her to the hole. That's segregation, right across the hall over there. I don't know why they arresting her in the first place, but I expecting she be up in there awhile, mixing it up with a guard that way."

"She didn't do anything to that guard. I was there."

"She did enough. Ms. Asia B saying how Uranus looked like she caused some visible hurt, so they going to have to document Dessie with a violation."

"Like how long, you say?"

"How long what? Oh, I don't know. Depends on what is the severity of the original infraction, which I don't know what it is. I never hear anyone up in here doing hole-time more than a couple months. Know what I mean? It's mostly like a couple weeks. But then I never hear no one trying to mix it up with a guard."

The newcomer sits on her bunk, bows her head, and closes her eyes. Then she lies down.

Rogo lying down as well but on her stomach, hangs her head over the side of the bunk. "See how I left the top sheet folded up down there? We most all just leave our beds made up and sleep top of the blanket. Then get up in the mornings, fold the sheet up—bang—ready-made for inspection."

"They inspect the cells—"

"*Rooms.* That's just the men up in cells. We ladies up in here? We living in *rooms.*"

"Okay, rooms. They inspect every day?"

"No, they come round usually about once a week. But they ain't about to announce theirselves. Could be happening any moment, know what I mean?"

"What if you don't pass?"

"Nothing." There's a pause. "You leaving the place all nasty, they going to give you a shot."

"An injection?"

"No! A shot is like when they write you up and your consequences are going to be like, they remove your commissary privileges or your phone privileges or like that."

"Forever?"

"No, not forever. For as long as they decide. Maybe a month or something? Of course, if you really doing stupid they put you in the hole."

"Like stupid, how?"

"I don't know—piss coming back dirty? Making hooch? Fighting? Know what I mean? You in a fight, ain't matter who threw the first, both your asses going to get stuffed."

"Unless one of you is a guard."

Rogo snorts. "Right."

They are silent for a moment.

"So anyway, long story short," says Rogo, resuming her role of initiation coach, "you see the street cloths walking up in here holding their clip boards, you know it's room inspection. Cup on the locker? *Check.* Book on the bed? Check. The unit coming out with the smallest number of checks gets let first out for dinner.

"Is that good?"

"Very good."

"Why? Do they run out of food?"

"No. I don't know. Just everybody wants to be first, know what I mean? They say Unit Two—"

"Unit Two?"

"That's us. They say we never been first. Bitches up in here still nasty. They ain't learn how to do their time."

The new inmate, exhausted, is stretched out on her bottom bunk over a white thermal blanket. Her army blanket and sheet are folded at the foot. She's dressed in her travel scrubs and an expanse of café o-latte flesh shows above the ankles. Her toe through her sock nudges the iron bed frame.

Rogo's head hangs over the edge of her bunk. She is still eager for conversation. "So where you say you're from?"

"I come up in Cedar Rapids, Iowa. Caught my case out of Chicago." The new inmate's eyes are starting to close.

Rogo watches her for a moment. Then: "You change up your mind, want to live up-top here, just let me know. Uh, you Cassidy? What you say your other name?

"Ottilla."

"I ain't never heard that one before."

"That's a name back from my mother's people. My great-great-grandma—her name was Tilla—she was off-the-boat Irish, so in school the kids called her O'tilla. So I guess instead of being ashamed or whatever, she claimed it. Added another 't' somewhere and it hopped down to my grandma, on then over on to me."

"So you come up white?"

"Yeah."

"I can tell how you talk." When Ottilla doesn't respond, Rogo says, "Anyway, it's a nice name—Ottilla and all."

"Actually, I was about to go down to the courthouse and change it to Omar. I'm glad I never did get around. It would have been a total hassle for the courts. The Lord intervened."

"Intervened? How you mean, 'intervened'?"

I was in the process of transitioning when I caught my case.

"Trans-what? What's 'transitioning'?"

"Sex change. I was transitioning to male. I'd been on the testosterone over a year—almost a year and a half."

"Testa-what?"

"Testosterone. It's this male hormone medicine they give you for your transition."

"Oh. Okay."

"I had already had my top done, I was scheduled for my bottom, but then the feds came."

"Oh, yeah?" says Rogo trying to sound casual.

Ottilla sits up. There's a Bible resting on the top shelf of her locker along with her laundry-issue soap and shampoo and toothpaste. She picks it up now and lies back down. "So my lawyer, he said forget the transition. He said he wasn't going to be able to get me bail, so even if I went to trial and he got me off, I was looking at a lot of pretrial time, and they weren't going to let me keep me up on my hormones in jail." Ottilla rests the Bible open on her chest. "So while I was still on the streets, waiting for them to arraign me—during that period is when I weaned myself off."

Rogo's upside-down face is turning red, but she remains there, silent, adrift in this new wealth of information.

Finally she latches on to a neutral observation. "Now all that right there? You staying a woman? That's a good thing. Them men prisons, they ain't no joke."

"That's what my lawyer said. But in the end, it was the Lord who stepped in. After the indictment when I was first locked up in MCC Chicago? That's when Jesus came to me in my cell. He poured his understanding onto me, showing me how it doesn't matter—male, female? He thinks I'm perfect just like how I am."

Rogo is silent. Her eyes move from side to side, absorbing the data.

"It was the best thing that ever happened to me in my life," continues Ottilla. "It was . . . wonderful." Her voice trails off.

"Getting thrown into jail?" asks Rogo tentatively.

"The whole thing."

Rogo, with no idea how to respond, finally brightens. "You going to be doing some easy time up in here, anyway. The bitches be after you. I ain't nearly that hunky, they still be coming-up all over me."

"Oh yeah?" says Ottilla with polite interest.

"Yeah, but me," says Rogo sitting up now and dangling her legs off the side of the bunk, "I'm biding me my time. I didn't come up into prison to play games with no bitches. Got me my Ms. Asia B—she a friend of my momma-cousin—so she be waiting for me inside the gates. Know what I mean?"

Rogo sits swinging her feet off the top bunk.

"She having everything I need for myself. She got me my Pepsi six-pack and my hygienes and she borrow me my Walkman until my money coming in. She even found me some kicks—ain't in bad condition—those ones down there. Got me my new ones on order. Commissary be giving you the Reeboks; ain't be selling no Nikes but that's fine, that's all good."

Ottilla has unfolded the khaki army blanket and pulled it up, her Bible on her chest. Her eyes drift closed.

The lights click out in all the rooms down the tiers, leaving Rogo and Ottilla's room in shadow. Florescence seeps in from the common area.

"Do you mind me asking," says Rogo, still sitting, "how much time they give you?"

"Forty-one," says Ottilla neutrally, her eyes closed.

"Forty-one? Now that ain't bad. The judge, he giving me one-forty-eight. That's fourteen years, but I'm trying to get five of them lifted off of me—take me down to nine. So you got forty-one? That's good."

"No, I . . ."

"Yeah, it's good for up in *here*. Know what I mean? I'm surprised you even here behind the wire. You be up on out of here in no time."

"No. I got forty-one years."

"Forty-one years!"

There's a pause.

"She-*eeit*, man! Forty-one *years*? Fuck, dawg, what you do? Homiciding a dude? You . . ." Rogo's voice trails off. "Beg pardon, but you ain't look like you fit that particular M.O. is all." She lies back down.

"I used to."

"That's heavy. What's that in month time," wonders Rogo to herself. "Forty-one *years*," she marvels.

"Easy time," says Ottilla. "The Lord promised he'll be right in here, doing it with me."

Up the end of the hall, at the entrance to Unit Two, the doors clang open and a pair of guards, keys a-jingling, begin their clomp down the hall.

"Now that's a good thing." Rogo punches her pillow and fluffs it.

"Yeah, I'm blessed."

"Forty-one years," Rogo whispers to herself in wonder.

By the time the flashlights have beamed in—by the time the officers have breathed the numbers, and exited the building, the two inmates curled under their army blankets are still.

CHAPTER 16

The evening after Desiree's drama, toward the end of the compound's evening mealtime, Iris and Emilia—finished eating—are on the bench watching the pat-downs. There's a female officer on duty tonight, working alongside a short, buzz-cut rookie.

"El Cachifo," comments Emilia to herself.

"Yeah, he's a raw one. I hear he's still pretraining. He's waiting to get sent down to Tallahassee for orientation classes."

The rookie's body language radiates discomfort; still, he tries to project that it's nothing unusual—this business of running his hands down the bodies of various-ly-shaped women. The female officer with him sends glances his way.

"Poor baby," murmurs Emilia.

"Oh, he'll toughen. Wait 'til he gets out of training. He'll be back with a whole new attitude. He'll be impossible. The more insecure they are when come in, the tougher they've got to be. You watch."

"Not watching for me. I am probably not being in here by that time."

"No, training's only a couple of months. You'll still be here." Iris pats her leg.

They sit in silence.

Asia B and Rogo emerge from the dining room with Ottilla. Asia, at the top of the rookie's line, spreads her arms, and the rookie's face reddens as he moves his hands down her generous outline. He has less trouble with Rogo. His companion officer dismisses Ottilla with a wave.

"Hey, the big boy's bonding already," observes Iris.

The three approach Iris and Emilia's bench.

"This here is Ottilla," says Asia B. "She just moved in. She's Rogo's new bunkie."

Emilia tips her face up to Ottilla coyly and looks up through her eyelashes. "You are very welcome to Danbury FCI," she says in a lilting voice.

Iris stiffens, and Emilia flops over onto her shoulder in laughter. Iris grins sheepishly at the top of Emilia's head. The scene lasts for only a moment. Iris pushes Emilia upright and Ottilla steps forward.

"Ms. Iris? Ms. Applebee here says that you know the girl that got attacked by the guard. Can I ask what her name is?"

"That would be Desiree Johansson."

Ottilla's face radiates delight. "She's from Cedar Rapids, right?"

"Yes." And then, in wonder, "You know her?" Ottilla's face is shining. She looks off between the buildings, over past the razor wire. "Yes ma'am. I grew up just down the street." She looks back to Iris. "Dessie was my babysitter back in the day. She was really good to me. She was my favorite person."

Iris is still surprised. "You grew up next to Dessie Johansson? Really? How strange." She looks away. "I thought we were supposed to have six degrees. What's this—*one* degree? No, it must be zero."

"Zero what?" asks Rogo.

"You hush," says Asia B.

Ottilla ignores the interchange. "What did she ever do to get in here?"

"I'll let her tell you about her crime."

Ottilla nods and, looking off again, says in wonder, "When I was coming in and saw her down on the concrete getting beat up, I almost—I couldn't even believe it was her. I thought I was losing it—like, having visions or something."

"Really wacked her out," agrees Rogo.

"How long is she going to have to stay in the hole?" asks Ottilla.

Everybody shrugs.

"We're not sure," says Iris. "It's too early to know. So, did you catch your case in Iowa then?"

"No. I've been in Chicago since I was eighteen. Got popped out of there."

"Oops, wait!" Iris, leaning to one side, is craning to look around past Ottilla. "Could you move over just a second? We're going to want to watch this one."

Ottilla hastily steps out of the way. "What's going on?"

"That's our Yani—Yanina the Cabaret Queen. I think she's getting ready to do her number on the rookie."

Over at the dining hall exit, a fortyish, lushly figured Spanish woman walking with a hip-swaying, provocative showiness, presents herself to the rookie. She moves in close and the rookie involuntarily steps back half a pace.   T h e female officer flicks an assessing glance over and elects to ignore the situation.

Yanina turns her back to the officer, spreads her arms and legs and shakes her shoulders as though loosening up for a tango. A gathering of her friends—a half-dozen Spanish women—have come out of the dining hall and are in line behind her.

She throws them a wicked grin and shimmies again. "Apresurarse. No puedo esperar!" she calls. Then she looks over her shoulder at the rookie and says with half-closed eyes and a deep and throaty voice, "Hurry. I am waiting for you!"

The rookie, intuiting that he might be in over his head, tries to proceed casually. He begins at her shoulders.

Yanina throws back her head and shakes hair down her back.

The rookie runs his hands down Yanina's arms. She starts to breath heavily. She issues a suppressed moan and, at the sound, the rookie jerks his hands away as though electrified. He flicks a glance over to his fellow officer. She is studiously involved in her own pat-down. He returns to the job, mustering a businesslike manner.

Yanina moans again.

He frowns intently as he moves his hands under her arms and down her rib cage.

She starts to pant.

The rookie is a deep red now, but he is determined to retain his professional manner. Still he avoids the area under Yanina's breasts.

"No!" Yanina calls over her shoulder. "You must not forget my bosoms!"

He ignores her. He drops to one knee and proceeds to outline the hip.

Yanina quivers.

The rookie moves down to a thigh, inside and out, while Yanina struggles to control herself. She can't. There escapes a small sob of ecstasy.

The rookie, still kneeling throws a desperate look to the female officer.

She is carefully unaware.

He goes grimly back to work, and with the second leg he brings Yanina to a full-throated, body-shaking climax.

He rises, red down into the neck of his uniform. Yanina slumps and bows her head and whimpers, then hugely sighs.

The female officer over to the left, waves an inmate past. Her expression has remained noncommittal, but now she turns away to hide a twitching lip.

The rookie's brow is furrowed, and there is a gleam of desperation in his eyes but he assumes an at-ease military posture. He's intent upon demonstrating that he's impervious to spent and trembling Spanish women. He raises his chin and looks off to the horizon.

Yanina recovers with remarkable ease. She saunters away. Her friends have casually, one at a time, drifted out of the pat-down line and are gathered over beside the dumpsters.

"Muchas gracias, Senór Officer," she calls over her shoulder. "Is good for you? Is very, very good for me."

The rookie's color had been receding but, although he doesn't hear her, he starts to redden again.

He choses to wave the next inmate past.

Back on the park bench, everyone has considered it a fine show.

Everyone but Ottilla, who shakes her head in wonder. "What was *that* all about?"

"Yani is messing up a new officer," says Emilia.

"I'll say."

"That wasn't all just play," says Iris. "You also have to understand, those other Spanish women behind her—did you see them slip out of line? I'm guessing they were body-packing. It's chicken-thigh Thursday. That's when Yani performs."

"She does this every *Thursday*?"

"No, just when she can get the right searching guard. Tonight was perfect."

But Ottilla still finds explanation wanting. "*Chicken* thighs?"

"Don't try to comprehend none of this," advises Rogo. "Just chill, know what I mean? This place, you coming up onto it, it makes no sense."

"That group she was with?" Iris explains. "Those aren't connected Colombians. They're—I think they're Guatemalan. Honduran? Anyway, they work in UNI-CORE and send their money home to their kids. They support themselves in here by making chilaquitas and selling them."

"Oka-ay. But . . ."

"Yani—she used to be a nightclub singer—she's kind of taken them under her wing. Which is good of her since they're all mestizo and she's light skinned. That's a big deal there. Anyway, I'm pretty sure she was helping them get chicken out for the chilaquitas. They can charge more for the ones with chicken."

"All that fuss for a couple pieces of chicken?" exclaims Ottilla in wonder.

Iris laughs. "It's all relative. A couple pieces of chicken in here equals—out on the streets maybe? An ounce of weed?"

"Yeah, and a bag of bud in here," chimes in Rogo, "be like winning a lottery ticket. Other shit's easier getting in. The smoke's bulky. Harder to body-pack."

"When you first come in," says Iris, "you look at the commissary list, and it doesn't look very exciting: Pantene shampoo, a pint of ice cream. But after a few months, stuff like that turns premium. A headset or a Casio watch? That's like designer jeans."

"Yeah," agrees Asia. "And some of the kinds of contraband they mule up into here? Like maybe some cheap little Kmart earring? It's going to value up like Tiffany. You get your hands on a beat-up little raggedy-ass Penny's bra? You got yourself a Versace."

"Inmates put in the same amount of game as they used to on the streets," says Iris. "If they don't have any support coming in and they don't have their GEDs, just getting someone to buy a bar of Dove is a hustle."

"What's GEDs got to do?"

"If you can't document a high school diploma, you've got to take GED classes. They put a limit on your salary until you graduate. I think it's seven cents an hour."

"So the GED ladies, they got to get their hustle on," puts in Asia B.

"So, what do you mean, 'hustle'? How do you do you that?"

"Offer services. Clean rooms. Iron," says Iris. "Sometimes they will try to intimidate a new inmate. Or pity her into buying for them. It doesn't work for long. The new ones smarten up."

"Anyone tries to jack you up, talk to me first," says Rogo.

Iris laughs and goes on, "A couple of times I've seen little street hookers? They'll come in trying to proposition older white ladies like they used to do men on the streets? Boy, does that not work. The indignation! It's funny to watch."

"Whew," says Ottilla, looking up past the roof of Unit Twelve to the darkening sky, "Thank God I'm out of the game. I'm a child of Christ."

There's an awkward silence. No one knows how to respond.

"All that struggle to get *stuff?*" she goes on, "That's all in my past. That's not where my heart is—" Ottilla looks down at the row of faces, and her voice becomes tentative. "—any more," she finishes.

The faces stay blank.

"But that's not me making any *judgments* or anything," Ottilla adds quickly. "It just applies to me, personally."

The silence is getting uncomfortable. Emilia stirs as though to respond, but Iris elbows her.

"Because now I've got Jesus in my heart."

Silence.

"Hey, sorry if maybe I'm getting too . . . I'm not trying to preach . . ." Ottilla, arms stiff, hands in her pockets, moves a brown leaf off the sidewalk with her black oxford. She looks up and looks at the faces. "I guess I'll be getting on over to the room." She turns. "I'm glad to meet you, Ms. Iris. Is it Emily? Emilia. Glad to meet you."

"Welcome to Danbury FCI," calls Emilia to her back.

"I'll be right along," calls Rogo.

They watch her walk away. No one says anything for a moment.

"Is nice?" Emilia finally offers.

"No, is *not* nice," snaps Iris. Then, "Sorry. I have trouble with Jesus freaks. They give me the creeps." She shudders.

"Hey, Tillie's okay," protests Rogo.

"I know, I know," admits Iris, her eyes away, studying the compound. "It's probably just my own issue. My heritage? It's—it's not the kind of thing that has always worked out well for us. It can make us Jews nervous."

She rises, dusting off the seat of her pants, and Emilia rises with her. Asia B tugs on Rogo's sleeve but Rogo, genuinely curious, resists.

"What's Jews got to do with it?"

Iris turns as though to explain. She takes a breath, then helplessly expels it and turns away again.

"You hush," says Asia B.

CHAPTER 17

"But before we begin our planning session," says Warden Coleman, "I want to thank you for alerting us as to how we have that little issue of narcotics coming in through the visiting room."

Today her suit is baby pink. Her glasses are cat's-eye again, but this time a neon baby blue. They match her eye shadow but not the red and purple beads, interspersed up and down her braids.

"Has she copped to it yet?" asks Iris.

"Unfortunately," evades the Warden, "we can't prove how she got the drugs in, so we can't suspend her visiting privileges. But we'll be vigilant now that we're alerted. I intend to turn this environment into a one hundred percent drug-*free* environment. Under my watch this is going to be a zero-tolerance institution. The ladies of Danbury are going to learn that there's a new fox guarding the henhouse."

A what guarding the what?

Iris, face carefully blank, is enjoying the mangled metaphor.

"You certainly seem," says the warden," to have your ear to the ground in some of these regards."

"Some," Iris agrees. "The women do come to me when they see things that bother them. When their environment is being destabilized it gives them a sense of discomfort. They need to unload and of course I'm there for them."

The warden nods sagely.

"Actually, Warden Coleman, since you've taken over, I sense that they're starting to feel a little bit more secure."

"Now, that's good to hear," carols the warden. She sits back with a smile. "It has been my observation that inmates are like ch . . . are like members of a family in that they need to thrive in a stable situation."

"I agree. But I hear that you didn't find any actual product in Henderson's property."

"We found burned residue on the back of her mirror. We've sent it out for testing. Actually," says Warden Coleman, chuckling, "the lady outsmarted herself. She ripped a seam on her mattress and hid the mirror way up inside. If she hadn't done that, that mirror might have been overlooked. Of course we would have had her as soon as her UA came back, but this way we were able to isolate her immediately."

"I don't suppose she told you how she got it in."

"No, of course not. She is trying to implicate the source as being a recent release. But she knows she'll be coming back positive, so she's given us a few names to test and soon as we get those results, there will be a few more heads biting the dust."

"People in the program?"

"Now, Ms. Engels, I'm not at liberty . . ."

"No, of course not."

"But I *can* say this. I can say that my-my—wouldn't it be interesting to find actual *drugs* circulating around and among that fabulous new recovery treatment of theirs? My-my."

The warden chuckles to herself and then becomes serious. She leans forward, folds her hands in front of her, and takes a breath. "We here in the administration want to thank you for stepping up the plate. You're keeping your ears open and your eyes open, and we commend that."

Uh-oh, she's working herself into a chant.

"We appreciate that you're assisting us in turning this compound into a restorative environment for the population. Even if the quote/unquote *drug program* isn't quite living up to its mission."

Iris's attention is caught by the warden's fingernails making air quotes. *Blue nails?*

"But that would be neither here nor there."

Are they painting fingernails blue out there?

Iris is bright-eyed and attentive.

"What is important is the general environment of security, not just for yourself alone but for your fellow inmates as well."

They must be. Or else, how would she getting the polish?

"You're down there with the inmates and we staff--we're up here in our offices. We can't do it all alone. We need the participation of a few of the more mature inmates such as yourself."

Iris looks at her lap.

"Now then, about Johansson."

Iris looks up eagerly.

"I admit," the warden continues, "that you certainly did assist us in getting your little inmate friend into segregation, but we've come up against a stone wall. I've been questioning her one-on-one, face-to-face."

"And?"

The warden sighs. "Up until this point in time she has not been what I would call 'responsive.' So we're wondering, do you have input on getting her to be more cooperative?"

"I'm not surprised she isn't in the mood. Can you blame her? Your guard didn't exactly sweet talk her," Iris allows criticism to creep into her voice. "That was some pretty rough foreplay. What's she saying? 'Not tonight? I've got a headache?'"

The Warden stiffens and frowns. "I'm not sure that being facetious is particularly helpful at this point in time, Ms. Engels. It was an unfortunate occurrence. Williamson stepped over the line. I'll be the first to admit it. But—and this isn't general knowledge yet—*but*, for your information, Williamson has been placed on administrative leave. She has entered a drug treatment program—"

"She was *high*?"

"Officer Williamson has entered a drug treatment program," overrides the warden. "We will be accepting her transfer to another institution. In actual point of fact, Ms. Engels, we are all disappointed in Williamson, but remember, she acted in response to inmate aggression. My information is that Johansson started kicking—"

"Yeah, in her flip-flops. She was pretty dangerous."

"And," overrides the Warden again," it has opened doors. Had Johansson not chosen to respond with aggression in response to a direct order, she would have been out of seg as of last Friday. We could not have held her beyond the requisite investigatory period. So all your ground work would have been for naught."

Iris can't help but feel defensive.

You wanted her in seg; I got her into seg.

The Warden continues in a faux-humorous chiding tone. "Apparently I need to remind you, Ms. Engels, to consult your handbook. Look at the section covering inmate infractions. Do you see any mention of the employment of a shower as a toilet? Is that in your list of sanctionable offences? Because it certainly is not in mine."

"Maybe. But maybe she'd be talking to you if Williamson hadn't . . . ."

"So now," overrides the warden again, "we can charge her with assaulting an officer."

Okay, no more pushback, Iris. Cool it.

"Aha, very smart. That didn't occur to me. But even at that, you say she isn't cooperating?"

"Not so far. The young lady—let's just say, she is being obstinate. She assaulted an officer, and we're warning her about the consequences if we choose to charge her—up to a year in segregation, loss of good time, etcetera. But alongside that, we've given her to understand that if she can provide assistance of value . . . ."

"Not working?"

"So far she is refusing to move past her perceived set of injuries," admits the warden.

"She did get pretty banged up."

"Johansson claims to have suffered some kind of a minor rib problem," overrides the warden again, "which medical has not confirmed. She is still attempting to use that plus a few minor marks on her person as the focus of our conversations."

That's Dessie.

"We're giving her a couple of weeks to think it over."

"I'm not sure you're going to persuade her, Warden Coleman. She might have been more receptive if Williamson hadn't stomped her. You didn't see it. She was down in the mud. Williamson was kicking her in the head."

The warden rears back defensively.

"Even though," Iris continues hastily, "Williamson obviously didn't do any real harm. But you know inmates. They can get very aggrieved over that sort of thing."

The warden decides to relent. "Yes, I do, but there was no real damage whatsoever. Medical is in total confirmation."

"But even if she gets over her perceived injuries, she is still going to be convinced that Ferguson is going to leave his wife for her. She's thinking the two of them are going to walk off into the sunset. You're threatening her with a year in seg, so now she's probably thinking that Ferguson will get himself transferred to segregation—"

"That's not going to happen."

"But she doesn't know that. She may be thinking they'd have even more time together. I suspect she's going to keep hanging tight."

"Yes," says the warden, tap-tapping a pencil. "So how do we break the impasse? Do you have any more of your brilliant suggestions?"

"Actually, I've come up with a plan B."

"Aha! And just what would that new plan B, ah, be?"

"Again, Warden Coleman, I'm not sure you want to know the details, but I've been working with another other inmate. She's put in for a family/medical transfer to California. Her case manager isn't giving it much hope—warning her it's probably not going to get approved. I don't know how much influence you have," says Iris, flicking the warden a glance, "but if you have any sort of connections . . ."

The warden smiles. "You give me the information, and I'll make the calls. I'm in position to make those things happen."

"Okay, good. But first I need to know something: Do they double them up in seg?"

"Pardon?"

"In segregation. Are the rooms singles? Or are they doubled up the way they are in Unit Two?"

"Aha. I might be seeing . . . I believe all the rooms in our special housing unit contain bunk beds."

"Okay, good. I'll get you the inmate's paperwork, but I'll need a week or so to get her prepped."

The warden nods. "Drop me a cop-out when the lady's ready."

CHAPTER 18

"Dang, girl," Lydia exclaims, "Is this cookie sheet going to be popping all night long?"

Lydia, Desiree's old folding partner from laundry who is wearing an orange jumpsuit, crawls around making up the top bunk. Her mattress rests on a thin sheet of steel, and now as she shifts position again it emits another ping.

"Hey, it's a groovier sound than the lady down the hall singing *hymns* all night long. '*Ne-eear-er my God to thee*,'" Desiree quavers in falsetto.

Desiree's segregation cell is identical to the rooms in Unit Two, but with orange curtaining and with the iron-slatted door rolled shut. The meager floor space is strewn with a pair of dirty dish trays. Under the bed a splayed paperback with a picture of a woman in a hooded cape fleeing a castle rests among the shower shoes and boots. The steel sink over the toilet bowl is cluttered with cheap, Special Housing Unit, off-label soap and toothpaste. The toothpaste is labeled *Lucky Morning Fresh*.

Desiree, in matching orange, is standing at the rear of Lydia's mattress tucking knots of sheet corners around the thin, plastic encased mattress pad. Her forehead is bruised, and a scabbed-over cut shows under her hair.

"So I'm not going to lose my laundry job?" she asks. "You're saying O'Donnell isn't going to replace me?"

Lydia, on the top bunk, maneuvers to smooth the blanket. "Last I heard, no. Castro was trying to get one of her friends in, but I heard him telling her that he was holding the job for you."

"He's a doll." Desiree tucks in the other corner. "I suppose he's probably letting

Apaza park her ass at my desk?"

"No, actually Apaza's not even in laundry anymore. She put in for over at administration. She's the captain's new orderly."

"Ha! She couldn't get anywhere with O'Donnell; now she's going to shake her ass for the captain."

"Oo-oh yeah, that's our Apaza. But you know, this time it might work. They say that Carter goes after them right before immigration comes."

"Huh. No blowback, huh."

"Yeah, I heard he was messing around with this other Spanish inmate who just got deported. So I bet that's how Apaza's thinking she can get in there."

"Is she short?" asks Desiree with a pillow's edge under her chin. She's easing it into the pillowcase.

"Pretty short, yeah. Someone told me her date's coming up right after Christmas."

"Well, that might work out for her except good luck trying to do Carter with the new warden sniffing around. Maybe they'll let her watch."

Lydia snickers. "Probably not. The way I hear it, the warden and the captain are super hating on each other. They're, like, these bosom enemies or whatever. The captain is even bad-mouthing her in front of the inmates. And then someone heard the two of them last week up in her office, and they were totally screaming at each other."

"Like over what?"

"Like over whether she was going around his authority or whatever." Lydia takes the pillow and fluffs it at the head of her bed. "Inmate coming down!" She scoots off the top bunk, reaching around with her bare foot to find the sink edge. On her way down she slips on the rim of the toilet bowl and almost plunges in.

"Shit! That's all I need. Fall into the frigging toilet bowl!" She tries to recover with a ta-tum pose, and in doing so she steps on a tray and scatters the breakfast dishes. Within the dearth of amusing segregation incident, the misstep passes for a carnival.

The two recover, and as the Lydia restacks the dishes, Desiree arranges herself into a yoga pose on her bottom bunk. Her head almost touches the overhead steel sheet. She spreads a face towel across her lap and, gesturing with a pair of toenail clippers, she snip-snips a beckon at Lydia.

"You asked."

Lydia starts to sit with her but remembers her prison etiquette.

"Can I?"

"Of course." Desiree shifts herself back to demonstrate hospitality, but in doing so, distresses her ribs. She winces and holds them.

"You okay?"

"I'll live. I'm better now, but I can tell that the bitch broke at least one of them. This other long time ago when I was skating? I fell and broke my ribs, and this is the exactly same feeling."

Lydia crawls onto Desiree's bunk and tries to match her yoga pose, but she's bigger and not as limber. She finally props her shoulders against the bed's iron-pipe frame and extends a bare foot.

"Oh my God, Lydia, you're right," says Desiree examining the foot on her lap. "You are growing horns. You nailed it. Ha, ha. Get it? Nailed?"

"Dessie's got jokes!" crows Lydia and the two settle into intimacy. Desiree begins with a little toe.

"God, I can't believe," says Lydia, looking around, "that you've been sitting here in this creep-hole for two whole weeks."

"Fifteen days. I'm scratching Xs on the wall."

"And they're not even telling you how *long* or anything?"

"They say the incident is still under investigation. I keep asking for a BP-9 so I can write a protest. They keep saying, 'Yeah, yeah,' and then they never give me one."

"Out on the compound we all thought they maybe might have shipped you out. Or maybe you had *died*."

"I felt like I was going to. I'm okay now, but that first few days I couldn't hardly move."

"You met with your case manager yet?"

"No, I haven't actually. I don't know what's the right protocol or anything, but it's weird because just the warden keeps coming over. I really must rate."

"She's probably on her friends-with-the-sorry-inmate mission."

"Whatever!" Desiree stops in mid-clip to explain. "They keep marching me up the hall into this little room past the officer station and then I sit and wait and then she comes in. After that first time she told the guards not to cuff me up anymore. It's been like four times now."

"Wow. You do rate."

"Yeah, she keeps asking me how I am and I'm like, 'When am I getting out of here?' and she's like—she's all trying to give me this shit on how she's trying to help me because they're trying to do an investigation over me assaulting an officer. I'm like, 'The officer assaulted *me*!' she's like, 'Officer Williamson is claiming she was responding to a perceived threat,' I'm like, 'Bull shit!'"

"You can document. You got, like, three-hundred witness."

"Yeah, *inmates*. You know how us inmates lie."

"You got any medical documentation?"

"Ha! The bobble-heads are like, (bad imitation of a sing-song) 'we do not require an X-ray; your rib-bones are not fractured. You suffer from only minor contusions and mild skin discoloration.'" She caps it off with a head wag.

"You should still sue. You got a case. You do know Williamson got sacked, don't you?"

Desiree sits up straight, scraping the top of her head. "No!" She winces and tenderly touches the cut on her scalp. "She *did*? How do you know?"

"It's all over the compound. Even the officers are saying it. She's gone."

"Thank you, Lord. I would die if I ever had to face that mutant whack-job again. She scares the shit out of me."

Desiree, about to work on another toe, stops. "Like she came marching into the unit, you know like how she does? And she just comes stomping over to my cubical, and she's like"—Desiree twirls the clippers—"'Turn around, Johansson.' No explanation. Nothing. I kept going, '*What? What?* and the bitch wouldn't even tell me what I was even supposed to have even *done*." Then she starts trying to shove me out the door, and I about lose it."

She bends her head over Lydia's big toe.

From down the hall comes the rattle of the dish cart.

"We're supposed to put our trays out through the slot," says Desiree, making motions to remove the foot so she can get up.

"Stay. I got it." Lydia hops up, steps into her flip-flops, organizes the trays, and passes them through.

The cart moves on.

"What I'm trying to figure out is why they stuck you in here with me," says Desiree as Lydia and her toenails settle back.

Desiree is still on the original foot.

"I mean," she adds hastily, "believe me, I'm really happy to have the company and all, but I go down to shower and I see, like, seven empty rooms down there."

"There have been lawsuits about keeping prisoners in isolation for extended periods of times, and the BOP's instigating a new double-up policy in the hole," Lydia recites.

Desiree looks at her curiously.

"That's just what someone told me," Lydia hastens to add.

"Sounds like you been talking to Iris."

"*No!* I mean, yeah, actually, about my transfer. She was the one that got it through for me."

"See, I told you she could. Except I'm still not understanding why they wouldn't let you wait out on the compound."

"Paperwork issue. Whatever."

"Usually it's the other way around. They put you in here when you first *arrive* because your paperwork hasn't caught up or whatever."

"Yeah, some mix-up. Maybe they sent it on ahead by mistake? I have no understanding, but I'm fine with it as long as I can get out there where I can have my visitation with Conner."

"So he's okay? Here, give me the other foot."

"Stabilized condition for now," says Lydia struggling and finally getting her other foot onto Desiree's lap. Desiree starts on the little toenail.

"Changing the subject, " Lydia says, "but did you ever find out why Williamson came for you?"

"I keep asking. The warden just keeps acting like my lips are moving in silence."

"Out on the compound everyone's saying—now, don't trip. I know this isn't true so don't freak out, but everyone out there is saying you got snitched out because you got AIDS and you'd been pissing in the showers."

"Wha-aa?"

"Now, don't freak!"

Desiree does.

"WHAT?" she screams.

"Shh, they'll come running down."

Desiree throws Lydia's foot off her lap, tries to rise, bumps her head again, and clutches her ribs.

"What?" she repeats in an only marginally muted scream. *"Oh. My. God!"*

She takes the information in again and slumps back on the bunk in horror. *"Who's* saying. Who's *saying* that?"

"All those black ladies over out of Unit Five. But Ms. Iris, she told me personally that she'd seen your paperwork and you don't have any AIDS. Not Hep C—nothing. She…"

"Oh. My. God!" cries Desiree in despair. *"Oh my God! So everyone's saying that I'm supposed to be pissing in the showers? With AIDS! Where in the . . . How in the . . . How did that—Oh. My. God. I am going to die!"*

Desiree slouches over and wraps her arms over her head. She begins to rock rhythmically.

"Don't worry," says Lydia, tentatively touching her shoulder. "Iris got your back out there. She's telling everyone how you're clean and it's all a scurrilous lie from Alicia Rice."

"Alicia Rice? Alicia!" Desiree jerks up. "I thought Alicia was my *friend*. We were always borrowing each other's shit. Why? Why did she go and make up a total lie. Out of the pure thin *air*?"

"Iris is saying how Rice knew she was packing out for camp, so she got all her people hysterical before she left, just to stir up the drama. She says it's probably just a blonde-hating, black thing. Words to that effect."

"Yeah, but Alicia and I were . . . Now everyone's thinking . . . Oh, God. I. Want. To. *Die*!"

"Everyone's going to forget about it. Just yesterday in chow hall, I heard Iris reminding all the ladies that you'd been down long enough for everyone to know how that is not your M.O.—pissing in the shower."

Desiree remains inconsolable. She's slumped over onto her lap and rocking again.

"It's okay," comforts Lydia.

"No it is *not*!"

"Everyone's going to forget."

Desiree, her face in her knees, grabs her pillow and wraps it around the back of her head.

"I just want to die," she repeats—a muffled moan.

CHAPTER 18

It's the next afternoon in segregation. The lunch trays have been pushed into the cells, emptied, and then fed back through the slots. A recovered Desiree, with Lydia, is cross-legged; they are facing each other on the bottom bunk. Desiree lays down a card.

"Eight and I call, umm, hearts."

"Oh, you bitch!"

Lydia crosses both fingers and murmurs a prayer to the overhead sheet metal. She picks a card from the stack in the center.

"Shit!"

"Lo-*ser*," taunts Desiree as she slaps down her last card. "What you got? A seven and a three. That's ten." She starts to scratch the number on the back of a copy of the inmate handbook. "I'm up by eighty-nine. You are so gone."

"I'm through," agrees Lydia, throwing her cards down.

"Sucks to be you."

They sort the deck, then straighten the kinks in their limbs and lean backward. They face each other in a companionable tangle of legs.

"Day two. Wow, seems like a life already."

"No shit. Try day sixteen."

"Yeah, but you get perks. You get to be best friends with the warden."

"Yeah, best friends. Thrills!" says Desiree in disgust. "She wants me to, 'partner with her in providing a safe and secure environment.'"

"Okay, best partner."

"Best partner, Right! Ha! How bout best snitch?"

"So just snitch her some shit if it will make her let you out. Jump on it, girl."

"I don't have any shit to *snitch*."

"Okay," says Lydia, still lying back, her head down at the end next to the toilet bowl, "I've been thinking about this, and I've got some dirt you can pass on to her. I'm so out of here, I really don't care."

"Cool! Tell! Lay it on me, girl!"

Lydia takes a breath and lets it out. She starts and stops again.

"Well?"

"I haven't been giving up the whole story of why I was requesting a transfer."

"Something besides your kid?"

"Yeah, well, Conner was my actual reason, but there was this other '*thang*.'" She pauses and studies the cookie sheet over her head.

"Yes?" says Desiree. "And?"

Lydia reaches up and scratches at a drip of paint on the iron bed frame. "Only reason I can even say anything now is because I'm so out of here."

Desiree paradiddles her thigh. "Yes . . ."

"Okay." Lydia takes a deep breath. "I've been having this thing with this one guard."

"No-o," exclaims Desiree in delight. She untangles her legs, sits up, crosses them, and leans in. "Tell!" She claps her hands in a parody of childish delight.

"Well, truth-to-tell is I was starting to feel like I needed to get away, you know?"

"No."

"He was like, perving out on me or whatever. It was almost like he was stalking me, you know?"

"Like *how*?"

Lydia pauses. She turns aside to focus on the stainless steel of the sink. Finally she turns back and sits up and rests her chin on her knees.

"See, back when it all started out, it was like—fun and games. Or at least on my part. But then, like, he starts to get really serious, you know?"

"Was this while you were still in the drug program?"

"Uh, yeah, well, then and after."

"But I thought you were telling me over in laundry how you had something going on with that other *inmate*. That one who went up to camp?"

"Yeah," answers Lydia quickly. "But he never knew about her."

"Girl, you get around."

"Not really. Well, kind of. Yeah, I guess."

"So, anyway, perving like what? What was he doing?"

"Like following me into rec—this was when he was on evening shift. He was like always standing there watching me work out on the bicycles, then getting all jealous whenever I even said one little word to Castagnola—like, *really* coming *down* on me."

"You poor you. I hate when they get like that. So then what?"

Lydia is looking down, playing with her big toe under a stocking. "Then he, like, turns into this total asshole. He starts, like, whenever I'd go over there to work out, he's all, like, 'How you trying to come on to that honky faggot?' Then, when if it's not even Castagnola's shift, he's like," [sneering] "'Too bad your boo ain't coming in today.' Like that."

Desiree becomes alert.

"So he's black?"

"Oh, yeah, he's black. I was with a couple of the brothers out on the streets, and like they're say, 'Once you go black, you never go back.'" Lydia peeks up through her eyelashes.

"So," Desiree says, studying the footlocker, "what was his na—no," she corrects herself. "When—I mean, was all this shit still going on when they popped you in here?"

"Oh yeah. Let's put it this way: I'm actually happy to be in here right now where he can't get at me. Fer—" Desiree jerks, but Lydia doesn't notice. "This *officer*, he was getting way too serious, know what I mean? Going on about us being together after I get out? I'm like, 'Look, this is fun and games,'"

Lydia isn't looking at Desiree. She's still playing with her toe, talking to it. "I'm like, 'I've got family out there.' He's like, 'That don't mean nothing when two people are in love. I've got family too. If I'm willing to leave my wife and my sons, you got to be willing to do that for me.' So I'm thinking—I'm like, whoa there, big fella. This is getting out of hand."

Desiree's face is frozen. She says through tight lips, "Maybe I'm out of line? To be asking his name."

"Oh, I don't mind telling you who he is. Then you can give up his name to the warden. Be my guest. I'm so out of here, I don't need to keep it secret one way or the other."

It's later that evening in segregation. The dinner trays have arrived and have been pushed back through their slots. Lydia on the top bunk rests a paperback on her chest and looks at the ceiling. It rises ten feet above her, woven with a network of piping—some for water, some enclosing wires, half of it now derelict. A fat pipe with painted-over insulation runs down the wall behind the toilet bowl.

Desiree, on her back on the bottom bunk, stares up at the steel mattress platform.

From down the passageway comes a voice singing an off-key hymn.

When the ro-o-ol is called up yo-oonder,

When the ro-o-ol is called up yo-onn-der,

When the roll is called up yonder I'll be there.

"Shut up, Jacobson," came a voice from up the passageway.

"Hey, Santana, why don't you shut up?"

"Settle down, ladies," warns an officer, paroling past.

What a friend we have in Jee-su-us

All our sins and griefs to bear

A tear is forming in the corner of Desiree's eye. It follows a glistening, demarcated path down the side of her head.

What a privilege to ca-rr—yyy

Eve--rything to God in prayer.

The tear trickles into Desiree's ear. She grimaces and rubs at it furiously.

PART 2: CHAPTER 1

Christmas is a few weeks away, but the women are getting ready. Unit Two, the projects, is alive with busy women in sweat suits and thermals, excited and totally committed to Christmas.

Virtually all of them are Spanish.

When Danbury turned female, the arts and crafts section of the recreation department turned Spanish. Acting on the demonstrable truth that theirs was the more creative and aesthetic-minded culture, the Spanish inmates took control. They have retained it, and thus the annual Christmas decorating project is Spanish. No one else would think of encroaching.

Some of the women are cutting out tree and stocking silhouettes; others are contributing to the heap of red and green construction-paper chains. All three tiers are getting the treatment. On the bottom level an excited trio, laughing and calling out to one another in Spanish, are looping the chains from cell to cell. They work with a mixture of momentousness and merriment.

Ottilla stands in the doorway of her room watching down the row as the three women deck the hall. The leader on a step stool, holding a section of the chain in place, snaps her fingers.

"*Inmediatamente! Cinta adhesiva!*" she calls out imperiously.

A second team member, wielding a roll of cellophane tape, cuts a strip and affixes it to her nose. She stiffens herself into an exaggerated toy soldier and extends her face upward to the leader. The third member, tasked with the mission of steering inmates around the step stool, poses, hand extended. The step stool lady plucks the strip off of her partner's nose, and all three fall into near-crippling gales of Spanish joy.

Ottilla shakes her head. "Man, I been picturing prison in my mind for a while now. I never, ever pictured this."

Rogo is lying up on her top bunk.

"Oo-ooh yeah, the bitches be into their thang," she agrees. "They deep in the comp-a-tition, know what I mean?"

"No. Competition for what?"

"Week of Christmas, staff is going to be coming round judging. Best decoration-unit going to be first out for Christmas chow. Them Spanish bitches, they be into it. They be taking *off.* They be *flying.*"

Ottilla shakes her head again in awe.

"This isn't like any penitentiary I've ever heard about. Everyone's supposed to be all sitting around sad, regretting their sorry, wasted lives. This place is a crazy house."

"You right on that one."

The common area is abuzz with Spanish conversation and inmates with scissors and construction paper and bottles of white glue. A few with headsets are singing along to Spanish carols. One, her headset volume rendering her the more oblivious, power sings of a *silencioso* and a *sagrado noche.*

Off to Ottilla's left, beside the back stairs, a group of crafters is crawling on the floor putting the finishing touches to a life-sized snowman. One of them has happened on a stray square of construction paper. She rolls it into a tube and, nudging the others, tries to balance it upright on the prone snowman's crotch. The gesture inspires an overflow of helpless mirth.

COUNT TIME, LADIES, COUNT TIME.

ALL INMATES RETURN TO YOUR AREAS FOR STAND-UP COUNT.

REPEAT: LADIES. AREAS. COUNT.

The Christmas workers scatter in frenetic haste. They call out to one another Spanish reminders and warnings as they gather their scissors and glue. Some are halted midscurry, assigned to rush back and retrieve. Still they leave behind a mess. It's the kind of mess, which, in any other season, would call down condemnation and mass retribution. Christmas gives special dispensation.

Still, Christmas or no, they are all vitally aware that if they are not in their rooms and in standing position when the uniforms come through, there will rain down a storm of consequence. Standup count is inviolable.

Ottilla moves back into the room, and Rogo slides nimbly from the top bunk to the floor.

The whole unit stands at silent attention. The pair of officers pass through pointing and muttering numbers, then move up the stairs.

There comes a small voice. "*Qué menú de centa?*"

The query brings a storm of inmate reprimand. It rings with righteousness, being as it is, within earshot of the guards."

"*Silencio*! Shh, Shh."

"Shut up, *estúpido*!"

"Quiet, ladies!" Booms down a guard from over the second-tier railing. "Quiet down there! No talking." He pauses. "Quiet," he repeats into the silence.

Rogo, in her first floor room, leans toward Ottilla to whisper. "See that roll of scotch tape over there on the floor? No, way over in that corner under the table. Guards out the door, I'm snatching that puppy. You shoot jiggers."

"Hey, wait a minute," whispers Ottilla urgently. "What do you want it for?"

"Ms. Asia B ask me to keep a lookout."

"What's she going to do with it?"

Rogo looks thoughtful and shrugs. "Tape something up?"

"But what if they come inspect before you get it to her, and they shake down our room?"

"They ain't trip over that kind of shit."

"Yeah, but I don't want us to be breaking prison rules. I'm trying to be straight."

"Shit girl, you gots to loosen up, know what I'm saying? You can't live up in here without you break a rule or two. Think back yesterday morning: You borrow that white girl some of your coffee? Now that there—*bang*—you just broke a rule. Handbook say you can't be giving or selling property to no inmate."

Ottilla slumps and sighs.

"You trying to be a rule-freak up in here," Rogo continues, "you be turning yourself into some kind of hard-hearted individual."

Ottilla shakes her head to defuddle her mind.

The officers are clomping down the stairs and the inmates are starting to stir.

"Quiet down, ladies."

"Now don't get me wrong," assures Rogo, in a whisper. "That's a good thing, you trying to rehabilitate yourself and all. Ain't nobody up in here be on your case for self-improvement. Unless you trying to turn yourself into a snitch or something. But you got to keep it cool and pick your issues."

Rogo indicates with her chin. "That tape over in there?" She lowers her voice even more. "The officers, they ain't *care*. They shake you down, they going to confiscate but they ain't going to give you no write-ups or nothing. Only kind of shit get your ass written up is shit come in off the streets. Or from the tool room. They gots their major issues with their tools."

"Okay," sighs Ottilla. "What is it you want me to do?

"Just do a little diversionary."

"How? Like shout *fire* or something?"

"No, you just stand there in the doorway looking studly. The Spanish bitches be checking you out, they ain't noticing me."

"So what are they going to do if they see you taking it?"

"Ba-aad shit come down on my head. Be worse than me putting my feet on their wet floor, know what I mean? They be all"—she squawks some Spanish-sounding syllables—"up in my face."

The outer doors close and relock. As the unit starts to come alive, Rogo is out like a flash. She scampers and scoops the tape, and in a single motion tucks it under her sweatshirt. With the inmates swirling around, Rogo, headed back to the room, turns the act of wandering back through them into a performance. Fingers snapping, she whistles and jive-saunters to the room.

Ottilla has to laugh.

The evening's crush of impatient inmates, gathering around the unit's door waiting for it to be unlocked for dinner, has started. Ottilla watches bemused as more and more of the unit's hundred-odd women crowd in front of the door, pushing and maneuvering to get closer to the front.

"Maybe I'll understand after I've been down awhile," she says to Rogo, "but I sure don't get it now. I don't see why they all got to be up there on top of each other every night. You say food never runs out. Nobody goes hungry."

There's a lack of floor space in their room, and Rogo has climbed back up to her bunk.

"Not that I've ever heard," she agrees, swinging her legs off the side. "Spanish ladies going hungry? Now that there? That would result in a riot. Spanish ladies be screaming their heads off, stomping, breaking shit. Know what I mean?"

"It's not just the Spanish," points out Ottilla. Look at them all jam-packing themselves: Spanish, African, white."

"They all be getting the Spanish competition up in their blood," says Rogo sagely. "They catch it like the Spanish flu."

Suddenly there's the sound of Unit Two's entrance being unlocked. The crowd pushes excitedly.

"Out of the way, ladies," shouts a guard as the door swings open. "Clear a path. Out of the way!"

"Something's coming down," says Rogo, crawling to the end of her bed and pushing aside the top drape of shower curtain. "He ain't be releasing for no chow."

"Clear it, ladies. Clear it. Let the inmate through."

"Holy shit! That's Dessie. They busting her out of the hole!"

The crowd goes silent and parts and allows the officer to lead Desiree through the common area. A path has cleared down the center and Desiree, with a duffel bag over her shoulder and a sleeping roll under her arm, marches behind. Her head is up and her posture is proud. She carries herself with attitude.

In the center she stops. Inmates are pressed on either side. Others hang over the tiers. All are quiet.

Desiree takes deep a breath. "Hey ladies," she calls out boldly, ringing her voice through the unit, "I'm here to piss in all your showers."

The crowd stirs uncomfortably. There is a single uneasy bark of laugher, then a hush. A group of out-of-the-loop Spanish women are hugely puzzled. The other inmates cast looks around, searching among themselves for signs of how they should be reacting.

As the officer starts up the stairs, Desiree turns back from the foot of the staircase to face the silent cavern. She looks up and calls out to the top tier.

"Hey, Unit Two! I'm here to piss all my HIV germs into your shower!"

The silence is deadly. Then from up front, there comes a clap.

Instinctively Rogo pulls at her roommate's elbow to quiet her; then, thinking better, she puts her fingers to her lips and blows out a piercing whistle.

The crowd relaxes. A flood of relief flows through and a gush of laughter. A few other women start to clap, then more. The room erupts into applause.

"You go, Johansson."

"You *tell* it, Ms. Dessie."

"You the bomb!"

The guard leading Desiree remains utterly noncommittal. He ignores the cheering inmates and mounts the stair landing and turns. Desiree, following, tries to be indifferent but her face is flushed with triumph.

By the time they've climbed to the third tier, the crowd has stopped applauding and is merely in happy conversation.

Desiree and the officer two pass the TV area and stop outside a darkened room. The officer pushes the shower curtain aside to reveal two naked bunks.

"Woo-wee! Lucky me!" Desiree swings down her duffel bag and flings her sleeping roll through the door.

The officer turns to go.

"Thank you, sir!" She calls to his back. "Swe-eet!" she crows to the empty bunks. "I've got me my own private room!"

"Most definitely?" Rogo asks.

"Most definitely," replies Ottilla. "You think there's going to be two Dessie Johanssons from Cedar Rapids, *Iowa*?"

Rogo and Ottilla are back in their rooms, standing beside their bunks.

"So when you going to approach the lady?" asks Rogo.

"I don't know. She probably might not even remember me. I was just a little kid."

"Don't mean you can't be reminding her."

"I'm going to wait."

"She probably be real happy."

"I'm going to wait."

"What? Scared?"

Desiree is back downstairs and gathering a crowd in the common area.

"Dessie, you bad girl, you. Welcome to the outs!"

"Dessie, you did you little stretch up in there."

"Hey, bad girl, I hear you kick Williamson's ass."

"Yeah, right!" Desiree snorts, in jubilant sarcasm. "I got her good. She's not going to mess with *me* anymore."

The women laugh in unreserved approval.

As the two roommates leave the room, Ottilla confesses quietly, "Yeah, I am. I am scared."

They move to the back of the crowded common area. The group has made space for Desiree up front beside the door.

"Step your sorry self up *to* her," urges Rogo. "Introduce your sorry self, know what I mean? What she going to do? Spit on you?"

"Maybe."

"She ain't going to spit!"

"Yeah, I know, but be a total downer if she just stares and goes, '*Ay-nd*?'"

The door is unlocked, and the crowd, with Desiree at its embracing center, swarms out onto the late-afternoon compound. It fast-walks, double and triple file down the sidewalk, around and across the compound, and over to the line extending out from the dining hall door.

"No offense," says Rogo, "but that there? That is some weak-ass thinking."

"Now ain't *that* the truth," says Ottilla.

CHAPTER 2

After the meal that evening, a wan half-moon hovers behind the floodlights, and an evening star just barely pricks its way through. The compound is more crowded than usual. The sidewalks are full of brown-jackets: not in the usual stroll but walking at a pace.

No pat-down guards. Desiree, surrounded by admirers, exits the dining hall.

She sees Iris and Emilia on their bench and swings over. She turns to her group. "Hey, guys, I've got to talk about my case to Iris."

Iris welcomes her. "Hey, you. You survived!" She shifts sideways to make room. "Good to be out of jail?"

"Whew!" agrees Desiree, sitting. "Hope that's the last time I ever see *that* place. I was going nuts in there."

"What in the hell happened? I heard some insane story about you urinating in a phone booth or something?"

"No, not the phone booth. The *show-er*," corrects Desiree in school-teacherese.

"Oh-hh. You pissed in the *shower*! That explains it!"

The two sit in silence for a moment contemplating the perversities of penitentiary living.

"Bunch of black bitches," Desiree says, "hating me for my good hair."

"Shave your head, solve all your problems," agrees Iris. "Don't even have to do it yourself. Go over to the hair salon. They'll shave it for you."

"Speaking of which"—Desiree runs her fingers through her hair—"Emilia, do you know anyone in Unit Two who can check out the scissors? Now I'm out of

Unit Five, I've got to find me a new lady to trim my hair."

"In Unit Two? I will be asking."

"Beep!" A pair of power walkers bounce past; their arms pump and their po-nytails swing. They're moving at just under the compound speed limit. They beep again at a group of chattering Asians, who scramble off the sidewalk. Then, as the Asians recover, a second pair powers down on them.

"Why are all the track bunnies out *here*?" Desiree asks.

"Track is close," says Emilia.

"Yeah," says Iris, "you didn't hear. You were on your va-cay. They dug up a big garbage bag full of hooch out of the horseshoe pit."

"No shit! How'd they find it?"

"Oh, somebody snitched. You know how it is."

"Ha! Tell me about it. Place is pack-full of snitch'n bitches. God, I can't stand this place! I've got to get *out* of here. Speaking of which, have you heard anything about my redesignation?"

"Not yet, but I'm pretty sure it will be coming through. I'm expecting it any day."

"I hope."

The Fatback Sisters, skipping along the sidewalk in front of the rec, now halt as one in midskip, responding to an inaudible signal. They face each other and raise their hands.

Miss Mary Mack, Mack, Mack

All dressed in black, black, black

[Slap-crossover-slap]

With silver buttons, buttons, buttons

All down her back, back, back.

The stream of walkers powers down and steps off the path to pump around them. The sidewalk, by some unwritten rule, belongs to The Fatbacks.

One of the sisters, putting her everything into a slap, misses and stumbles into the other. It is cause of much happiness. When the two recover, they join hands and resume their skip.

"Okay, guys," says Desiree. "I probably should go unpack my shit. They're put-ting me in Unit Two, but they're telling me how it's supposed to be just temporary."

"Who's saying that?" asks Iris casually.

"Oh," Desiree looks around and slightly lowers her voice. "Just, you know, the warden? She came over, like, this one time. Just while I was getting out."

Iris nods. "I hear she has a heart for her seg ladies."

"Yeah, huh. Anyway," Desiree continues casually, her eye following the Fatback sisters skipping past, "she was saying how the investigation cleared me up so I'll only have to be in the projects until another bed opens. She says I can have input on where I want to move to, but I'm thinking I'm going to be happy where I am. They put me way up out of the mix on third, and, guess what, girls?" Desiree turns to both and raises both index fingers. "I'm in there alone. No roommate."

"Congratulations!"

"Good on you, sister!"

"I guess that would be my compensation for them letting their insane guard stomp me."

"Yeah, they probably do want to keep you happy just now. They don't need you sending any grievances up to regional. Enjoy while it lasts. I'm expecting before long you'll be moving over into the Drug Building, anyway. Getting yourself all recovered from your addiction."

"God, I hope." Desiree rises. "Hey, ladies, got to go. I'm traveling a little bit heavy." She indicates with her chin under her jacket. "Got to unload before another one of their guards goes crazy on me."

"What are you packing in there? A semiautomatic?"

"Ha! Just a bag of mozzarella. Valencia on kitchen duty asked if I would carry out. She'll be getting off any minute, looking for me. Got to get on over."

"Is free chilaquita tonight?" asks Emilia.

"Yeah, a couple of them," says Desiree, patting her waistband under her jacket.

"Mozzarella in chilaquitas? Does that even work?" asks Iris.

"Yeah, pretty good, actually. Sure as hell beats that crap that the kitchen's trying to pretend is lasagna."

"Enjoy!" Then Iris calls her back. "Hey Dessie, for the next laundry detail, try to talk O'Donnell into sending you out so you can drop into the law library. You've got to fill me in on all the unit-two scuttlebutt."

"You got it. If I catch any of them of doing each other, you'll be the first to hear."

"I better be! That's your job."

"All righty then" Desiree strolls away, attracting a group of fans. Iris and Emilia watch them gather around her.

"See," says Iris, "I told you she'd be okay. It's a lot better for her this way. Ferguson was going to get tired and ditch her anyway."

Emilia doesn't look convinced.

"Or else they were going to get caught. With the new warden crying rape, that stuff isn't going to be under the radar any more. Someone was going to snitch them out sooner or later."

Emilia is looking away.

Iris nudges her. "Come on, Babe, lighten up. I know you've been upset but trust me: Dessie was going to get caught. They were going to dump her in the hole anyway. Then they were going to ship her out. Down to Tallahassee, probably. Lose her drug program; lose her year."

Iris reaches over, puts a finger under Emilia's chin, and turns her face. "And we wouldn't be able to help any more. We'd be shoveling snow. We'd be over in the *projects* shoveling snow."

Emilia, whose eyes have stayed rolled away, finally locks gaze with Iris.

"Dessie's going to be just fine," Iris says emphatically.

"She be just fine," Emilia agrees.

CHAPTER 3

It's dark in Unit Two, and the pair of guards with flashlights enter through the rear door to count.

The concrete-block walls of the common area are covered in Christmas. A giant snowman reigns, his eyes and shirt buttons crumpled-up balls of carbon paper, his nose an askew cone of orange. Over the plastic-curtain doors the steel slats are outlined with glitter-sprinkled red and green chains. On the cinderblock separation between each room rest Santas and trees and stars.

"Looks like a god-damned kindergarten in here." The unmuffled comment echoes through the common area. Ferguson behind, grunts in agreement. The lead officer shines his light on the dark heads of Ottilla and Rogo sleeping in their first-floor bunks. He moves down the line of rooms, counting under his breath.

Ferguson scans from bunk to bunk. He pauses at the heads of khaki-blanketed humps, lingering occasionally. He moves on.

By the time they have attained the back stairs for the second-level count, Ferguson has fallen behind. On the second tier a spun-blond kitchen hairnet on a sleeping head catches his light for a moment, but he passes to the next room. Finally he mounts the rear stairs to the third floor. His partner is halfway down the tier. Ferguson's flashlight finds a bare mattress on a top bunk. Below is a tousle of blond curls.

Ferguson glances quickly out onto the passageway. He steps into the room, bends down, and squeezes Desiree's shoulder. She jerks awake and rears up, disoriented. Ferguson whispers and focuses the light back up onto his face.

"I didn't think I was going to *find* my baby-girl." He reaches over to finger a curl, then fondle a cheek. Desiree squints in the light, her eyes fixed past his shoulder. Then her lips form a smile.

She bends her head into the snuggling hand.

CHAPTER 4

It's just after the noon meal, and Danbury is filled with daytime-beige inmates milling around the compound, exchanging news and banter, and waiting for the call to return to afternoon work detail. Iris and Emilia, both carrying canvas zip-up satchels full of paperwork, have stepped out of their unit.

Iris turns to Emilia. "Do you have Jefferson's PSI?"

"No. Me, I am not see it."

"Oh rats, I might have left it in the law library. I hope it isn't sitting out. We better go back to the unit and check."

As they turn, Iris notices unusual staff activity. "Uh, oh. Something's happening," she warns.

A large group—a combination of uniformed officers and street-dressed councilors—are moving with determination past the administration building and across the compound. They spin off in pairs toward the individual units to station themselves at the entrances.

CLEAR THE UNITS. CLEAR THE COMPOUND.

ALL INMATES, REPORT TO THE RECREATION BUILDING.

REPEAT: ALL INMATES CLEAR THE COMPOUND.

REPORT TO RECREATION.

All around the compound, inmates stop in their tracks. They are accustomed to their days marching forward in predictable rhythms. A disruption in the routine means nothing good. They question one another in alarm.

"*What?*"

"*Recreation* building?"

New inmates turn to long-timers for guidance. Long-timers shake bewildered heads.

The recreation building?

Inside the living quarters, the a.m. kitchen and yard workers—just off duty—had settled themselves down in their bunks, tucked their hands under their cheeks, closed their eyes, when:

CLEAR THE UNITS. CLEAR THE COMPOUND.

Then, to add to their indignation and resentment, at the unit door they are halted by a pair of staffers, lining them up and patting them down.

"Over to rec. Over to recreation, ladies. Move it."

Iris and Emilia turn back to Unit Twelve. By now there's a case manager and an officer stationed at the front door.

"Can we put these back in the room?" Iris asks indicating their canvas. "We've got legal paperwork here."

The officer looks to the case manager, who nods and waves the pair back into the unit.

Just as Iris and Emilia, empty handed, step back out onto the compound they hear it. Barking dogs!

The compound is electrified. It's a sound that many of them have not heard in years. Then, just as exotic, come the whistles.

"They're bringing in the dogs!"

"Oh my God, shakedown!"

"*Big*-time shakedown!"

At the far corner of the compound the inmates see three German shepherds out in front, straining at the leash, while behind them swarms a team of men clothed in camouflage.

"CERT team," identifies a long-timer.

"CERT? What's CERT?"

"Correctional . . . something, something."

"Correctional Emergence . . ."

Everyone is stirred by the exotic sounds of barking and whistles and the calling out of training orders.

"Those are dope dogs!"

"Dope dogs? What are they looking for?"

"*Duh.*"

"*Duh.*"

There is also, among the CERT team, a man in ordinary maintenance coveralls carrying a folding ladder and a toolbox. He's hardly noticed. Everyone's attention is fixed on the novelty—strange uniforms, strange animals.

ALL INMATES CLEAR THE UNITS AND THE COMPOUND.

REPORT TO THE RECREATION BUILDING.

ALL INMATES, HOP TO IT. NOW!

Finally all the inmates, thoroughly patted and searched, are herded into the rec building. They mill and speak in a higher-than-normal register. For a CERT-team-level shakedown, as opposed to the more laid-back officer shakedown, almost everyone has vulnerable property.

"I left my wedding ring on my locker."

"They're going to snatch it, trust and believe."

"Do the paperwork; you'll get it back."

"Eventually."

"Yeah, eventually."

"My Christmas money come in, bought me an extra Marlboro carton. They're not going to confiscate, are they?"

"Who knows? The handbook calls for one carton at a time."

"I've got an onion stashed up in my boot."

"Dog's going to sniff that bitch right out of there."

"What you think? They ain't teaching no dogs how to sniff no *onions!*"

The rec's auditorium is congested. The upstairs craft area and first-floor weight rooms have been cordoned off with yellow ribbon. Some of the inmates have found bleacher space; others are sitting against the wall.

Ottilla stands at the entrance beside a row of craft lockers. Rogo swings away to join Asia B. She weaves her way through the inmates to a group of middle-aged black women exchanging shake-down lore.

"Pay heed," advises a long-timer, "you trying to hide some of that good shit, here's how you going to go about: Number one, you stuff that shit way down deep inside your laundry bag. Number two, you get out your issue razor—you give your finger a little nip? You drip it all over the crotch of one of your panties, spread it up over top your laundry. That be keeping your shit reeal safe."

"Good idea!"

They exchange high fives.

"Good idea!"

"Except ain't going to work; they bringing in the dope-dogs."

"No, Mr. Sniffy Dog, he going to hit right on your shit."

Rogo joins the conversation.

"Hey, ladies, I got me a roll of tape up in my locker. Is these uniforms going to freak out?"

"You new, so you ain't be having the experience," says one of the women. "These kind of uniforms coming up in here today? They take it but ain't got time to be tripping out on no office supplies. Dogs ain't be hitting on no scotch tape. Over Carswell when I was there? This one lady, she was making up hooch in her thermos. Dogs, they move right on past, ain't even let out a yip."

"Yeah, CERT team—they be searching for your drugs and your weapons. It's your regulation-old female *duty* officer—that one be the one you look out for. Officer Monroe? Now that one, she be the searching witch."

"Amen. She be the searching witch, all right."

"She be up in there tearing your sheets off-a your bed. She be yanking up your mattress. I seen her this one time, she shaking Unit Two? She standing up on the top bunk fumbling and poking the ceiling pipes."

"That woman *crazy!*"

"Yeah, the men on their search duty? You just need to put out a little something. Little penny up off the sidewalk? Little crust of bread? Then they stop looking and throw it in the bag, and document their search; they go on to the next locker. That ain't work on Monroe. That woman going *through* your shit!"

"I heard where she confiscate Ms. Lawson's photo album right after she transferred up into here cause they be selling a different color over at Lexington. She got all of her grandbabies inside there. That evil bitch, Monroe? Snatch it right up."

"Lawson ever get it back?"

"After about . . . months. She didn't have no receipt—how she trying to keep her commissary paperwork, she pack out of Lexington? They denied behind the 9, so she had to submit her 10 all the way up to regional."

"They hating on giving us back our shit. Once they get their hands, they be hanging on like a motha—oh, oh, Rogo, just look at your new bunkie over there. They be flies on shit all over her."

Across the room at the lockers, Ottilla is surrounded by a group of animated younger inmates.

"She ain't going mixing it up behind no coochie," predicts Rogo. "She give her life over to the Lord. She be up in her Bible. She just be doing her time praying, going to chapel."

"That's good."

"That's real good. Can't be having too much Jesus up in this place."

"Hope she know how to keep up her faith. They be swarming—all those bitches with their hot little asses."

"What's her name, did you say?

"Ottilla Cassidy. She say on the streets they calling her O or Omar, but she ain't wanting to have no street-affinity no more. She just answer to Ottilla. "

"Ottilla? She don't look like no Ottilla."

"She a big boy. Looking more like A-ttila. Attila the Hun."

"Yeah. That be about right. She be Attila the Hon-ey, for all-a them flies buzzing up-round."

They watch the honey-buzzers with disapproving glares.

Asia B speaks up. "Rogo here, she say on the street how that one be changing herself over into being a man. She was having some kind of hospital process done on herself."

"She don't go into no detail," says Rogo. "Just say she got her top done. I left it there. I ain't about to ask. Do any of you all know anything about sex-change transitioning or whatever?"

A couple of the older women look wise and nod, but no one ventures an explanation. "Oh-oh, look, she breaking free from the coochie. Looks like she going on a mission."

Ottilla is heading across the room, weaving in and out, moving toward the back bleachers. Desiree sits on the ground-level row with a group of younger inmates. They see that Ottilla is heading toward them, and they nudge one another.

Ottilla comes to a stop in front of Desiree.

"Pardon me. Could I ask you a question?" Ottilla's voice is formal and she holds herself stiffly.

Desiree's companions lean forward on the bleachers, but Desiree pulls back and looks wary. Ottilla makes a small move to turn, then catches her breath and thinks better.

She addresses Desiree again. "Did you used to live Cedar Rapids, Iowa, by any chance?"

Desiree nods cautiously.

"You lived on Fifteenth, just off Mount Vernon Road, right?"

Desiree nods again slowly.

"I don't know if you remember me, but you used to babysit for me. I was just up the street."

"*Tillie!*" Desiree screams, leaping to her feet.

146 | PATRICIA COYNE

The surrounding inmates go silent. The silence radiates out to cover the room.

"*Tillie!*" screams Desiree again.

She gives Ottilla a big hug, then pulls back and scans her face. "Oh. My. God! I can't believe. Tillie Cassidy! Oh. My. God." Desiree's face is radiant. "Of course I remember you." She gives Ottilla a full hug now. Ottilla stands stiff but very happy. She pats her carefully on the shoulder.

"You used to be my favorite little kid!" enthuses Desiree. "Let me think—you weren't in the Brickstones. No, that's right, you were up in that little yellow house on Seventh."

Much of the rec room has focused attention. It watches Desiree embrace Ottilla; it watches Ottilla hold herself awkwardly, smiling and coloring. It understands that it is witnessing a street-recognition scene. It's a scene certain to warm the inmate heart.

Desiree holds Ottilla away to study her again. Her face is still alight. "You were my little buddy."

"Yes, ma'am, that would be me," agrees Ottilla, a-blush with pleasure.

"Tillie Cassidy," Desiree repeats in wonder. "You were my favorite kid. You were absolutely adorable."

"Then I grew up."

They both laugh.

"I was always trying to act adorable around you," Ottilla admits, "so then you'd take me to the pool again."

Desiree laughs with joy. She takes Ottilla's arm, and the two begin to weave their way across the crowded rec floor. They're lost in each other and they don't notice that they are the center of attention. They don't notice that a pathway is cleared for them.

"Remember Darryl? Darryl Compton?" asks Desiree. "The big kid that lived over in the Brickstones?"

"Yeah, he was always after you."

"I couldn't even stand him." Desiree does a little-girl finger gag.

They laugh.

"Remember," says Desiree, "how whenever he was coming around I always used to tell you, 'stay right here?' I was always using you for my protection."

"Yeah," says Ottilla with a glowing smile. "I was happy to be of service. Remember Linda Lawton? How she would go into those fits?"

"She must have been an epileptic or whatever."

"Yeah, Dessie, I remember how you were the only one who would stay with her and help her. Everyone else was always freaking out and screaming away."

"You didn't. You were always the one I would send to run over and get her mom."

"I was just wanting to get out of there."

They laugh.

"Remember Shannon Watkinson?" asks Desiree. "How she and Bumpy Neilson used to sneak off behind the Watkinson toolshed and Shannon would take off her underpants and then all us kids used to crawls over to watch?" The two have made their way to the far wall. They find a space and lean against it.

"Yeah," answers Ottilla. "And then remember that time her dad came out and almost caught them? So you pulled interference—went right up to him and started asking him about who was going to kick off for the Hawkeyes."

"Oh yeah, I forgot."

"You were quite the neighborhood heroine for that one."

"Yeah, for a whole week."

They laugh.

"Oh my God, Bumpy Nelson!" exclaims Desiree. "I hadn't thought about Bumpy Nelson in years. Remember how he figured out how to get up on the roof of Kum-and-Go and then squeeze in through that vent? He was always selling cigarettes and Snickers to us kids."

"Yeah, for a quarter. Mom'd be gone, and you used to buy them for me."

"Your mom—how's she doing? She still the party girl?"

"No. She sobered up, started going to meetings. Got herself a husband—rich old farmer type."

"Really? Good for her."

"Yeah, they're up north of Independence. They're sitting on 320 acres up there."

"Wow, money bags. You like him? You two get along?"

Ottilla snorts. "Not hardly. I was willing, but he wasn't having any part. By the time they were getting together I was . . . I wasn't identifying as a female anymore."

Desiree pulls back and looks wary again.

"Uh, okay . . ."

"Yeah, he had a lot of trouble with that one. He wasn't too impressed with me being black either, but me coming out as a male? That was the real deal-breaker for him. He wouldn't ever call me by my name. He kept away, pointing his thumb, referring to me as He-She."

Desiree stops and faces Ottilla. "Wait a minute, let me get this straight. You went through identifying *what?*"

Ottilla sighs. "It's complicated."

"None of my business," exclaims Desiree, looking down.

"No, if you want to hear, I'll tell you the whole story sometime." Ottilla gives a quick look at the inmates around them. "It's just kind of long and complicated."

Desiree touches Ottilla's arm. "No, that's okay. No problem. Whenever you feel comfortable."

The two of them start to walk again. Desiree's face clears. "I'm remembering now how you used to like to think you were a boy. I just thought it was some little-kid thing."

"No, it hung in there."

There's a pause.

Before the silence can turn awkward Desiree changes the subject. "So give me the skinny on your mom and the farmer."

"I don't really know very much. I'm not on particularly knowledgeable terms. Back when they had first gotten married, I drove out to the farm for the first time. I didn't know their phone number, and I wanted to tell mom how I was moving to Chicago. I come up and he met me at the door, telling me I didn't have to waste my time casing the joint because he had already gotten his power tools under lock and key."

"God, what a creep-o! Didn't your mom stick up for you? You and her used to be tight."

"Whenever she'd be home."

"Yeah, I remember how she wasn't around that much."

The two have found a place to sit underneath the out-of-bounds tape on the stairs leading to the second-floor balcony.

"We were tight back when you were still living there. But by the time I'm talking about, she was pretty much through with me," says Ottilla, expressionlessly. "I turned fifteen, and I wasn't willing to identify, like I said, so I was going through all that just at about the time she's starting up with the farmer. So I was getting in a little bit of trouble."

"Like . . . ?"

"I was lucky. Never got caught actually *doing* anything. Just truancy or whatever. But the school was calling her up, so she was saying I got my father's blood and I was being a threat to her sobriety. Then she was saying how me wanting to turn male was just me acting out."

"God, poor Tillie."

Ottilla face remains remote. "I was like, fine. Okay. I was tight inside Cedar Rapids by then, got my introduction and got myself hooked up with the Disciples in Chicago. They were Bronzeville, over on the South Side? And they didn't care boy

TANGLEWIRE: a women's prison novel | 149

or girl. Whichever way—as long as I had some tight Cedar Rapids connections to move their product for them."

"So you had gone full time?"

"Oo-ooh, yeah. By then I was generating income, big time. Or big time for me." Ottilla shakes off the lack of effect and smiles. "But you got to understand this is all history." A light comes into her eyes. "Here's my real story—my central story: I was lying in my cell in MCC Chicago, I'd been finally charged, and the judge wouldn't give me bail, and I was totally dope sick—kicking for my first time. I hadn't been through it before, so I wasn't sure if it was even ever going to end, you know?"

"Heroin?"

"Yeah, tar. I'd been banging."

"So what was kicking like?"

Ottilla studies the ceiling for a moment. "You know what it feels like when you chew on a ball of crumple-up tin foil?"

Desiree shudders.

"It was like that except that it's all the way up through your body. And it goes oo-o-on and oo-o-on. Feels like it takes you hours just to get yourself through one little minute."

Desiree is both sympathetic and fascinated.

"I was at the point," continues Ottilla, "where I couldn't handle any more. So I'm in the middle of my total-torture phase and I'm not even believing in God, but I called out to Him anyway. I was just starting to beg Him . . ."

"Oka-ay."

"He came."

Ottilla's eyes film over with otherworldliness.

"It was God. He came down. Like . . . over me! I don't even know how to describe it. When I was a kid, in the winter I had a big eiderdown from my grandma. It was a little bit like that. But it wasn't like just regular-old warm or anything. I mean, it was like that but it was some kind of warm that was like part-warm, part-joy. And He came over me, and then at the same time He came all through me. And He lifted my dope-sick up like—" she snaps her fingers—"like I had never even *been* dope-sick, and He just filled me up with Him."

"O-ka-aay," says Desiree, removed and cautious again.

Ottilla is studying the floor at her feet.

"It's an out-of-this-world kind of feeling, but it doesn't actually feel strange like drugs or anything because it's like something you've always *known* really well. You kind of like. . . *recognize* it. It's like something you used to know way back when, and you've been looking for it ever since you can remember. But it's like you've been looking for it on the *earth*, and they don't make it down here. They try to fake it with their crack and their heroin and their liquor and whatever. But it always comes out wrong. It comes out like this cheap, crappy imitation."

Desiree's elbows are on her knees, her chin in her hands. She is looking out onto the milling inmates. Her expression is noncommittal.

Ottilla is wrapped up in testimony.

"I've got Him in my heart now. I belong to Him. So when I'm telling you about my past and everything? I just want you to understand that that's all history. It doesn't have anything to with how I am anymore."

Desiree leans away and sees something of interest, off in a far corner of the room.

"Hey, Dessie. Hey, I'm sorry I'm going on like this. Come on. You want to walk around a little bit?"

The outside edge of the room has been cleared into a track, and dozens of pairs of women are walking it. Desiree and Ottilla join, all the time under surreptitious scrutiny. It is noted again that except for Ottilla's smooth face and a softness around the lips and chin, she could pass for a man. There is the male forehead and the shoulders, the hands and feet. She carries herself like a man, but she isn't *quite*. She's something in between.

Word has gotten out that she's a Christian, and she's doing her time straight. Except now she and Dessie are . . . hmm.

Rogo looking on, is still huddled in a group with Asia B and her friends.

"She's been telling me," Rogo reports, "how Dessie is this one babysitter she was having back over in Ohio or Illinois or wherever. They used to hang with each other."

The women nod knowingly. They pass it around: "That new boy—Ottilla? She and Dessie come from the same hometown. They know each other from back in the day. They're catching up on their news."

On the gym track Desiree gives Ottilla a playful hip-bump. "So, Cedar Rapids boy, how'd you make it in the big city? Did you miss good-old C.R.?"

"Not really. I kept traveling back on business, but I was happier in Chicago. I fit in better."

The two, deep in conversation, are still totally unaware of the attention.

"So then, when did you actually start dealing?"

Ottilla relaxes and gives a chuckle. "All the way back, middle school. Seventh grade. Mom was slinging her weed—"

"No! Your mom was dealing? Not even! When?"

"Always."

"Way back even when I knew her?"

"Yep. Ever since I can remember. She never did business out of the house. She had her little waitress job and she kept the business part away. But she had a grower-connect who didn't want to keep the product where he grew, so she was stashing it for him—getting in pounds."

"I went into your house a couple times; I never smelled."

"That was because the guy that we bought the house from? Back in the fifties he had thought that World War III was coming or something, and he had put in a bomb shelter off to the side of the basement."

"Ah."

"She usually kept the door locked, when I was a kid and I always used to try to sneak in there because it smelled like Christmas trees."

"So it wasn't that funky stuff everyone was pushing back then?"

"No, it was quality—pretty-color green."

"Hairy?"

"There was some hair," says Ottilla carefully.

"Some?"

"Yeah, *some*."

They look at each other and smile.

"Anyway, back in those days mom was drinking—getting messed up—so I could pinch the key and she never would know."

"When was all this going on?"

"When I first started at McKinley. I was feeling like this freak, kind of? I wasn't really a girl, but I wasn't a boy either."

"Poor Tillie," says Desiree, tongue-in-cheek but with real sympathy.

"Yeah I know, huh. And the white kids thought I should hang with the black kids, and the black kids thought I should hang with the white kids."

"Poor *Tillie!*"

"Yeah, I know, but I solved my problem. I started slinging."

"That'll *do* it!" exclaims Desiree.

"Selling cheap."

"*That'll* do it! So like, how much were you charging?"

"Ten dollars a finger—seven if you treated me right. I got re-eeal popular."

They both laugh.

"Then, after a while, I started getting inventive and I'd make up names, like I'd say, 'This stuff is genuine Lamb's Breath,' then next week I'd be like, 'I got this new stuff coming in—it's Maui Madness.'"

"*Maui Madness?*"

"Hey, give me a break. I was in eighth *grade*."

"And it was all the same stuff," Desiree laughs.

"Yeah, they probably kind of knew but they'd be so happy, getting to brag on a name to their friends. It wasn't like I was trying to up my income level or anything; I just wanted to be, whatever. You know?"

"Yeah, I know."

"It worked. I turned into the most popular kid in McKinley."

"I'll bet."

"I had, like, seniors from Metro coming over, meeting me after school."

"That must have been after I graduated or I would have heard."

"Yeah, you were gone by then. I remember you got prom queen; that was the last I heard. I didn't see you around."

"I got this apartment in Czech Village—me and my girlfriend Dottie Babinski? You probably didn't know—she was from Marion. Anyway . . . and then . . ."

Desiree pauses and looks away.

"Do you remember who Danté Dixon was?"

"You mean, ballplayer Danté Dixon?"

"The one and only."

"Yeah."

"We were together."

"No! You and Dixon? You're kidding!"

"Yeah, we had this big thing going. We were, like, in *lo-oove*."

"You two? Wow, I never heard. I did business with him for a little minute but he stuck me bad."

"Stuck you like how?"

"Like, I'd done a little business-- sold him a couple grams of powder by then but this time he was wanting an eight ball, and we're at Denny's, and he said his money guy was out in the car, had to look at it. Then he never came back."

"Oh God, I'm sorry."

"Wasn't your fault."

"He never told me that he pulled shit like that. You do anything about it?"

"I didn't have any muscle behind me back then so no, I didn't try to collect or anything; I just left it there. Actually I decided it was a good thing that I'd gotten off so light. If he'd had a little more patience, he could have probably ripped me off for an ounce."

They laugh.

"That was the spring of '88, and I was about to split for Chicago anyway."

"Spring of '88? He and I were just about getting together. I lived with him from June up until, like, October of '90. Which was when we got popped. We were actually going to get married, if you can believe it."

"Man! You and Dixon!"

"Yeah," says Desiree ruefully. "Me and Dixon. Ha!"

"So you got popped behind him, right?"

"Yeah, I'm passed out on Xanax in the back seat of the Eldorado, and apparently he just happens to be driving past this Wells Fargo, and so then he just happens to get it into his head that he has to go in and rob it."

"And . . ."

"And so they caught up with him like, seven miles down the road."

"Did he try to outrun?"

"Couldn't! He was out of gas!"

Ottilla lets out a bark of laughter. "What? He went up into a bank on an empty tank?"

"Yeah, didn't have any money—it had got stolen. That was the reason he had to go up in there in the first place. Then I guess he was intent on getting on down the road, then—oops—up come the cops on him."

"So you're asleep through the whole crime, so what were they charging *you* with?"

"I'm embarrassed to even tell you, like, how big of a total chump I even was. I got charged with planning and organizing. He told them it was me."

"*No-oo.*"

"Yep."

"Wait a minute. He told them *what?*"

"Yeah, he told them that I had planned out the whole robbery, and that he didn't want to but I had talked him into doing it."

"How *could* he?"

"He told me later that he just did that, because of how much he loved me. So then I couldn't be with anyone while he was down, but that was just total bullshit. He didn't care about me or how he was ruining my life or anything. He just gave me up to get the years off of *his* time."

Ottilla fists clench. "I got God in my heart and I'm not hating any more, but if I was going to hate, I would hate that kind of snitch. Bad enough you give up your people behind the *truth*. But *lying* on them?"

"Yeah, I know, huh."

"Then the cops, and the lawyers, and everything? They *know* it's a lie, but they encourage. They act like they approve of you now because you're changing your life around—coming over to the good side."

Ottilla shakes her head.

"It just really depresses me about the system, the way they tell you how you're a good person now because your lying on your friends and betraying them. Even just clean-snitching's bad enough."

Desiree falls silent now, walking and looking moodily off at the high, iron slat-webbed window across the room. She changes the subject. "So you were operating out of Chicago, and they got you on a drug conspiracy charge, right?

Ottilla walks a few paces with her head down. "No," she says. "I'm actually in here on a one-eighty-seven."

Desiree frowns. "One-eighty-seven? What's a one-eighty-seven?"

"Homicide."

They continue to walk, looking at their feet. Desiree doesn't say anything.

"It was just a job for the Disciples," Ottilla finally says. "I didn't go all depraved or violent or anything. I'm not dangerous."

"Oh, no! I wasn't thinking you were dangerous," says Desiree. She gives Ottilla's arm a quick, reassuring squeeze. "It's just. . . like, you seem kind of mannerly or whatever. I'm not able to envision you, you know. Whatever."

"You're seeing me now after God came into my heart. I was a totally different person back then. He changed me."

Silence.

"If it's okay with you, Tillie . . . I know it's super-important to you, but that kind of God-talk? It has always pretty much creeped me out. I'm sorry. It's nothing against you personally. It's like this personal issue-thing that I have."

"Sorry. Okay."

Inside Unit Two the dogs and their handlers have left, but up on the third tier, a trio of CERTS in camouflage are still in their rubber search-gloves, going through lockers. A shaved head is removing a bottle of Elmer's glue. He documents it, tosses it into the plastic bin at his feet, then moves on to search a picnic thermos. He unscrews, reaches in, digs among the ice cubes, and finds a saran wrap of salami slices. He throws it into a garbage bag.

"How you doing?" calls a voice from outside of the room.

"Just about done," answers the shaved head, and he picks up the garbage bag and scoots the bin with his foot out into the walkway.

"Finding any hand grenades?" asks his partner. "Any firearms?"

"No," says the shaved head, peeling off his gloves. "Just the one AK-47 under the bed." He throws the search gloves in the garbage.

The third camouflage emerges from a room. "You think this might be some kind of an explosive device?" he asks. He's holding up a six-inch white tube, saran-wrapped, tape-encased, and stuffed with sanitary padding. He puts it under his nose and sniffs, causing general merriment.

The lead member puts his plastic bin under his arm and looks down the tier toward the TV room.

"Just about done?" he calls.

"Be a minute," comes another voice.

Inside a walk-in closet off the TV room, the overalled worker on a ladder is reaching up into a corner near the ceiling and replacing a foot-square, cut-out section of wall. It's centered with a raw, bottle-cap-sized hole. The worker directs a small flashlight into the hole and nods to himself. He reaches into his back pocket for the caulking tube, beads the four lines, and performs a quick scrape-over with a putty knife. Finally he touches up with paint from an open can.

"I just about got it," he calls again.

He tops the paint can, steps down, folds the ladder, picks up from the floor a discarded carton, and stuffs it into his tool kit. He notices a dusting of white on the floor and scuffs at it with his boot. Finally he shoulders the ladder and backs out of the closet.

The CERT team waiting on the walkway is amusing itself. One is stretching out a dingy pair of lace underpants, causing them to dance. Another pokes at the crotch area with the stuffed tube.

The workman with the ladder approaches and they all head for the stairs.

YARD IS OPEN. YARD IS NOW OPEN.

ALL INMATES. RETURN TO YOUR UNITS.

REPEAT: ALL INMATES. UNITS.

GET READY FOR STAND-UP COUNT

The compound, cleared of dogs and camouflage uniforms, is once again alive with inmates. They dread to discover the damage that has been done to their property.

They stream anxiously back to their units.

CHAPTER 5

It's a few day after the search, and the evening meal is over. Ottilla and Desiree have joined the parade of inmates walking the main-yard square. They pass Iris and Emilia sitting on their bench. Desiree waves.

"That's Iris Engels," says Desiree. 'She's our legal beaver, or eagle, or whoever."

"Yeah, I met her. Hey, wait a minute. What was her last name?"

"Engels. Iris Engels."

"Where's she from?"

"New York, I'm pretty sure. Yeah, New York City. She was a defense lawyer on the streets, and she does really good work in here for us. I heard how last year, she got this Native American inmate immediate release?"

They keep walking but Ottilla is looking off.

"The crime occurred, Desiree continues, "on a reservation, and Iris challenged the Feds on their jurisdiction or whatever. So the judge said that she was supposed to be under tribal law, and Iris was the only one to catch it. The ruling came down and bang, the lady was out of here in three days."

Ottilla walks on thoughtfully.

"What's on your mind?" asks Desiree.

"When I was on the street, I heard about this New York lawyer, and I'm pretty sure that was the same name."

"What did you hear?"

Ottilla sighs and looks around. He lowers her voice. "The Disciples—those were my Chicago people. They were affiliated with some Bloods who were operating out of the Bronx, but I guess leadership was in Manhattan or whatever. Anyway, they were getting their money laundered in Belize."

"What's Belize?"

"It's one of those countries down there underneath Mexico? Except they speak English instead of Spanish. Anyway, the Bloods got the whole deal set up through this lady lawyer, and I'm pretty sure the name was Iris Engels."

"I wonder if it was her."

"She got it arranged with this moneyman that she knew who had started up a bank down there. You could walk in carrying your stash of cash—suitcase full—didn't matter how big. And they'd enter it on their books and give you a number and keep your name secret, and you didn't have to report to the IRS or anything."

"Cool!"

"Yeah, plus, she had connections with some charter-flight people, and she set up private trips where it was okay to bring weapons so the Bloods could take their security along with the money."

"Wow! Iris was big time."

"Yeah," says Ottilla sardonically "Big time. When the shi—when the arrests—came down, she rolled right over. Told where all the money was and then set it up with the banker guy so the Feds could come in and confiscate."

Desiree looks skeptical.

"So you heard about this from all the way over in Chicago?"

"The only reason was, when word got out that Engels was rolling, New York felt like they needed out-of-town help, so they put out a call to this Disciple I knew—Shorty-D. They wanted him to move in and take care of it."

"Except it never did happen because there she is right there, sitting on the bench."

"Shh," cautions Ottilla. She and Dessie have rounded the corner past Unit Two and are approaching Iris and Emilia again.

"She can't hear us." Desiree protests. She gives them a stylized little wave.

When they're out of earshot, Ottilla looks back guiltily. "I probably shouldn't even be talking."

"It's just me." Desiree's looks up. "So?"

Ottilla looks down at her expectant face.

"So Shorty said okay, he'd come in, but he kept putting it off, putting it off. He wasn't comfortable with the logistics—moving into new territory like that, coming up on a white lady."

"And?"

"Actually," Ottilla continues in wryly amused tone, "I was speculating at the time that maybe New York had gotten a little bit of a wrong impression over Shorty's expertise."

"Like how?"

"Like there had been this other time a while back when Shorty had gone to meet with the Bloods—cement some connections?"

Ottilla breaks off. "Hey Dessie, are you sure you're interested? This isn't exactly your scene."

"Absolutely. I love to hear. I love your stories."

Ottilla looks around and lowers his voice.

"Okay. Anyway, back when Shorty did his first trip to New York? I was speculating that he might have misrepresented himself a little bit—you know? Kind of made them think he had all the experience?"

"But he didn't?"

"Not really. When he first joined up, he had done a couple little—" Ottilla breaks off. "Anyway, after the call he was stalling and stalling, finding excuses not to go up in there, and then he got popped on his own charge and then that was all I heard."

"You're sure Iris Engels was the name?"

"It stuck in my mind because of how Shorty was obsessing."

"And you think it's the same Iris?"

"How many Iris-Engel, New York lawyer-ladies you think there are?"

Desiree has no idea.

"That's not even all I heard."

They have moved to the far side of the yard and Ottilla speaks in normal tones.

"I heard that New York was really out for her because this one guy—a guy they called Phatface Rick? He had all his cash sitting down there. In Belize. I guess it was like, a few hundred thou."

Desiree whistles.

"Yeah, I know, but a couple months before the arrests had came down, he . . ."

"Phatface?"

"Yeah, Phatface. He had taken a hit so he was in a coma on life support, and nobody knew where his money-number was at so nobody could go down to Belize for him to withdraw or whatever. But then after all the shi—after all the arrests came down? When the paperwork finally came back on how much the feds had confiscated? It came up short the exact same amount that this guy in the coma was supposed to have stashed."

"Whoo-ee." Desiree's voice takes on a Hollywood crime-boss tone. "So maybe our friend ended up with some bucks out of the deal."

"If nobody gets at her. I never heard what happen to Phatface—last I heard they weren't expecting him to come round, and everyone involved is put away now, and they're probably all pretty enraged but they can't get to her with her in a woman's prison."

"So she's safe in a woman's institution," Desiree says as though reciting a movie plot, "where they can't get close to her, huh?"

"I'm not sure how it works. That group—they're all down but they like to think they've still got the control. And maybe they're able to be keeping it tight on the street. But a job like Engles—it would be heavy, getting someone to move on her. If it was state, maybe, but in federal? I don't think they would be able to tap any of the bit—of their women. Almost have to go out and find themselves a guard."

"We could give them Uranus's name."

"Who?"

"Williamson. That one guard that stomped me. She'd be really good at—oh my God,"

Desiree covers her face with her hands. She looks guiltily to the far side of the yard.

"What am I talking about? Erase! Just kidding. Erase! Hey, Iris," she calls softly, "I was just *ki-iidding*." And then, "I really like Iris. She's been really, really good to me."

They walk on in silence.

"Probably not the same Iris after all," submits Desiree.

"Whatever. I shouldn't be talking about all that sh—stuff, anyway."

"Tillie, you can actually utter the word 'shit' in front of me."

Ottilla sighs. "I'm trying to clean up my act, now that I'm representing Christ."

"Tii-illie! Don't go there. I'm not *into* it."

"And here's me, focusing on old crime stories instead of Christ."

"*Tii-ilie!* Don't start!"

"Okay, okay. But listen, Dessie, don't go telling anyone about any of this, promise? I don't want it getting back to Ms. Iris that I was spreading her dirt. Probably shouldn't have said anything."

"Oh, Tillie," Desiree hugs her arm. "Remember when we were kids? You were always trusting me with all your secrets. And I would never have ever in my life repeated one word. Remember?"

"Yeah, I know Dessie. I just—I don't have a feeling for what it's okay to talk about in this place, you know? What to be telling anybody? I should probably be doing some praying about it."

"Tii-illie!"

"Okay, okay."

CHAPTER 6

A few evenings later Iris and Emilia are again on their bench in front of Unit Twelve when Desiree joins them.

"So is the Big O doing chapel again?" asks Iris. "I thought Bible study was Tuesdays."

"It is. She says somebody over in Unit Seven needs prayer. Whatever." Desiree adds a little snort.

Iris groans.

"Is good to pray," insists Emilia.

Iris pats Emilia on the arm. "Yes, Emmy, praying's good, praying's good."

Emilia shrugs off Iris's hand and pulls away with a frown.

"Sorry, Emmy," says Iris genuinely, giving Emilia's thigh a squeeze. "I'm not talking about your faith. I just have trouble with the born-again types."

They sit in silence, watching the evening parade.

Asia B and Rogo are among the walkers. Rogo, in her headset, is dancing, snapping her fingers. She throws a taunt at Asia B. who reaches over to smack her. Rogo dances away.

"So how long are you expecting the Jesus phase to last?" Iris asks.

"Who knows? All's I know is, it's getting really boring."

"Give it time," advises Iris. "She'll get over it. She'll get in the mix. Probably happen behind a relationship."

"I don't know."

"Actually," says Iris, glancing at Desiree sideway, "it looks like from where I'm sitting that she's getting a little something going with you."

"Oo-ooh, no. I don't swing that way. Besides, that's not anything like what we're about. We're just friends."

"I know, but I thought, you know. It might help to get her over her Jesus addiction. That's what friends are for."

"Ha! Not!"

Over past the Drug Building in front of the Trauma Unit, the Fatback Sisters—who have been holding hands and bouncing—stop on silent command. They turn to face each other and start to perform one of their clapping games. The space on the sidewalk is theirs to control.

That's the way,

Uh huh, uh huh,

We li-iike it,

Uh huh, uh huh.

A small, amused crowd has gathered.

"By the by," says Desiree casually, "she told me not to mention it, but I think you need to know if stuff like this is out there on the streets. Ottilla thinks she heard about you. Were you ever laundering any money for anybody or anything?"

Iris almost imperceptibly stiffens, and Emilia throws her a sideways glance. Desiree doesn't notice.

The Fatbacks are hopping backward and forward now, and Iris is captivated. She watches, her head tipped, her expression whimsical.

Peace, Punch,

Captain Crunch. Brick Wall, waterfall

Girl, you think you know it all

You don't. [beat-beat]

I do. [beat-beat]

"Launder?" Iris repeats vaguely, her eyes on the Sisters. "I'm sorry, I didn't quite . . ."

So POOF with the attitude

POOF with the attitude.

"Launder money. Ottilla said she heard about how some New York lawyer with your name was doing it for the Bloods or whatever."

Iris pulls her reluctant attention off the Sisters. She laughs and says with kindly affection, "Dessie, do you know how many lawyers in the New York phone book have the name *Engels?*" She separates her palms to illustrate. "Last time I counted there were over thirty."

She smiles gently at Desiree and then refocuses on the Sisters.

Talk to the hand cause the girl not speaking
Talk to the hand cause the girl not thinking.

"Yeah, probably." Desiree looks embarrassed.

Just then, from the corner of her eye, something catches her attention. Officer Ferguson—a unit over, carrying two weighty textbooks—is greeting a group of inmates. Bits of his conversation carry as he moves from one to the next.

"Well, hello there, Ms. Thomas. You're the Georgia girl, right? And how are you this fine evening? Are you adjusting to our Connecticut weather? See, it's not so bad as you thought. You'll get through your time."

Elbow elbow
Wrist wrist
Fly like a birdy
Kiss kiss

"Uh, Ms. Garcia, you're looking especially fine tonight. Did you ever get that correspondence approved between you and your husband? Where was he serving? Oh yeah, he's up there in Allenwood. You've got to just keep on your case manager. She'll get at the paperwork so long as you keep pushing."

See my pinkie
See my thumb
See my fist you better run

"Ms., uh, Ms., Johnson, isn't it? Oh John*ston*. I was close. Got your acceptance into the drug program?"

Desiree isn't ignoring Ferguson this time. She is watching closely and through half-closed, cynical eyes.   "Just look at Mr. Operator, doing his jive act."

"You two are through? When did that happen? You'll have to tell me!"

"I found out how he was actually this total horn dog."

"Sounds about right."

"So, hey Iris," asks Desiree, overdoing the gaiety, "which one you think he's after now?"

"Can't be Johnston," speculates Iris. "Johnston's too butch. Hey, I'll bet he's working his way toward the fish."

"That newbie white girl?"

"Yeah, I'm not sure when she got here."

"Tuesday they bringing her in," offers Emilia. "Me, I seeing her come."

"Yeah," says Iris, "must have been with that last airlift."

A twenty-something with long legs and full breasts is standing apart from the group. Her stiff beige uniform and black oxfords are alone in an ocean of sweat suits and tennis shoes. Her face, speckled with jailhouse, junk-food blemish, is unenhanced by makeup. Her blond ends are crisp, and each quarter-inch of her stretch of dark root represents a month in County Correctional.

She is currently passing through new-inmate purgatory. The inmate in purgatory is a ghost. She walks up to the living but is not visible to them. She tries to strike up a conversation but they don't hear; they move past. She's often even mute to the officers.

This one, ever since she arrived, has been struggling to recapture her street-sassy, biker-chick self, but all she can come up with is the nine-year-old Dora, sitting alone in the lunchroom... Standing alone on the playground....

"Yeah, watch how he's edging on over."

Ferguson flicks a quick look at Desiree, but makes his steady way toward the new inmate. They watch from the bench as he gives her a formal little bow. "Welcome to our fair institution." He maneuvers a complicated textbook shift, affirming their weightiness.

The new girl is trying not to reveal how heart-stoppingly gratifying is his attention.

"And you are Ms . . . ?

"Uh, I'm Pandora. Pandora Pearson."

"Ms. Pearson. I can see that you haven't quite settled in yet, but you are certainly looking fine."

Pandora, the former Dora, is time-shifted again, now from fourth to seventh grade. She's no longer on the playground; she's in the hall outside of social studies. Her bare arm tingles under the electrifying scrape of a calloused, ninth-grade hand.

Dyane Hoskins. He is sanctifying her with a new name. "Dora? I'll bet your real friends call you Panda. Can I call you Panda?"

Panda!

She's reliving the christening. It's firing a crimson rush through her body. The feeling as she had experienced it back then was not entirely strange. She had recognized its shadow from Technicolor passion scenes at the Triplex. But this was full strength; it coursed through her body and for years after that initial rush she had searched, but the boys and the drugs never could do the same thing for her.

Until now!

"Panda," She croaks and clears her throat. "I'm Panda."

"Welcome. Welcome, Ms. Pearson. Uh, Panda." Ferguson reaches out to touch her arm.

The same touch as Dyane had touched back then. Her legs tremble.

"We officers, we're not supposed to use first names but, just now? Just for this one day, can I call you Panda?"

Pandora nods.

Ferguson looks deeply into her eyes and smiles. "Unless I'm mistaken, you just arrived, right?"

Panda clenches her thighs and nods again.

Back on the bench, Emilia is the one to notice the far side of the compound. Something unusual again. She points. "Oh oh, *mira!*"

At the head of the yard, half a football field away, a pair officers is on the march. They stride forward with military purpose. They wear black uniforms and they carry side arms. None of the regular guards are ever armed. The sight is electrifying. It freezes all in its path."

"What-the-hell is *that?*" asks Desiree.

"Shh," says Iris. "It's SIS."

"What the hell is SIS?"

"Special Investigations. Shh!"

The inmates see the black suits and the guns, and one by one they freeze.

Shimmy-shimmy coco-pops,

shimmy-shimmy wow

Shimmy-shimmy coco-pops,

shimmy . . .

The Sisters fall silent. Arms out from their sides, they step off the sidewalk. Unnecessarily, for SIS is stalking across the brown lawn.

On the far side of the compound square, Captain Carter sticks his head out of his office door, does a double take, and starts off in pursuit.

"Hey, what are you doing?"

The black suits ignore him.

Ferguson, his back turned, is by now one of the few on the compound who is unaware of the alien presence. Pandora, facing out, sees the marchers, but she's new. If they'd been dressed in spacesuits it would have seemed no more bizarro-world to her than the symmetrically scarified Africans and the Spanish-caterwauling blonds and the Fatback Sisters.

And *he's* talking to her. She clears her throat. "I just got air-lifted," she stammers, aware that she is blushing, "day before yesterday."

"Poor Panda. That Con Air trip is brutal. That is no joke for you ladies. You managing to recover? No?"

He tilts his head and looks deeply into her eyes once more.

"Not yet? Poor Panda."

As side-armed black suits close in, the inmates nearby widen their eyes, spread their arms palms out, and back away carefully. A few tentatively raise their hands to their shoulders.

"Hold it," The captain has caught up and is at their heels. "You running wild up in here, you putting you feet on my compound. Where you getting your authority?"

"Warden's office," snaps SIS without turning.

Ferguson, although his attention is focused on Panda, becomes aware of the voices and the surrounding tension. He stiffens as he hears the crunching boots and the creaking of leather holsters. He swings around just as the black-suits halt.

"Officer Ferguson? You are LeBron Ferguson?" They grab him underarm.

"Ferguson's *my* officer," calls out the captain. "You bring him in, you come through *me*."

The black suits ignore him. One of them scowls around at the hyper-alert but blank-faced inmates.

"Hey you, clear off here."

The inmates, careful about quick movements, back away.

Except Pandora who, unable to separate what appears to be cause and effect— Ferguson's act of friendship and his arrest—is shocked into catatonia.

"Get away! Back away," shouts a suit, angrily pointing at her.

She's frozen.

"Get!"

She stumbles backward and stands swaying.

The captain steps out in front, puffing from the run..

"This man right here is my officer." He makes an ineffectual feint in Ferguson's direction.

"He's our man now."

"You got paperwork on this? Let me see the paperwork."

"Don't need it."

"What do you mean don't. . . ."

The armed men disregard him. One of them secures the captive. Ferguson holds tight to his textbooks as they swing him around to march back across the compound.

"This one is out of the warden's office," a black suit tosses over his shoulder at the captain.

The captain goes face-savingly blank. Then he along with the inmates watch Ferguson's ignominious march across the lawn of the compound.

He struggles to keep his books under his arm, but before the halfway mark, *Developmental Psychology: Part II* slips and falls to the sidewalk.

Just after it, *Social Organizations in a Changing Society* flaps open. Ferguson tries to latch on to it by its front cover but fails.

It falls. Sprawled open, onto the lawn.

Back on the bench, Desiree is the first to move. She rises and starts to stumble blindly toward her unit. Iris leaps up and goes after her. She grabs Desiree by the arm, all the time smiling as though the two are sharing a bit of play.

"No, Dessie," she exhorts through her teeth. "Pull it together. Smile!"

Desiree with a blanched, pinched face makes a halfhearted attempt to shake Iris off.

"Smile! Everyone's watching,"

Desiree twists to free herself, then suddenly surrenders. She turns and crumbles against Iris.

"No, Dessie!" Iris hisses through her grin. She laughs a carefree laugh over Desiree's shoulder and playfully pushes her away.

"I'm going to die."

"No, you're not. Smile!

She playfully punches Desiree's arm.

"You're thinking that was because of you?" she asks through her laugh.

Desiree doesn't react.

"Come on. We've got to talk." Iris playfully tugs the collar of Desiree's coat.

"For God sake, smile."

Desiree slowly becomes aware of her presentation. The laugh she returns is more a tortured yelp, but she play-pushes Iris back and the two throw their arms around each other.

"Oh God, I'm sorry. Did anyone see me?" Desiree asks, her face a distorted grin.

"No, they were all watching Ferguson."

"Ferguson! Oh God. I'm going to die."

"Smile! No, you're not."

"How'd you know that was behind me?"

"I guessed and good girl, you never said a word. Did you tell anyone else?"

"*No!*"

"Good girl."

"Oh God, I'm going to die. I didn't understand they'd actually—oh God, Bronie!"

Iris stops Desiree and turns her. "Who's Bronie?"

"LaBron! Ferguson!"

"*Bronie?*"

Desiree pauses. Her eyes skitter in thought, then her face relaxes and she issues a bark of genuine laughter.

Iris grabs her arm. "Come on. You've got to unload. Hurry, it's getting late. They're going be closing the track."

They head past the recreation building to the penitentiary's only private-conversation area.

Iris makes a show of shoulder-nudging Desiree, who sidesteps and nudges back.

They laugh.

Such is their lightness of spirit as they make their way to the track.

CHAPTER 7

The weeks before Christmas, visits are usually down but the loudspeaker has been booming names all Sunday morning. To Iris it's just background noise. She's lying on her bunk with a magazine.

Emilia bursts in holding a pair of crocheted stuffed animals.

Iris lays *The New Republic* open on her chest.

"Hey, what's going on?"

One of Emilia's animals is vaguely rabbit-like with long pink ears. The other is all face with a huge blue nose.

"*Mira*! Is finish!" She holds them out.

"What in the hell *are* they?"

"Is Ren and is Stimpy. Is a cartoon from on the TV. Emanuel, he say—" Emilia holds an air phone to her ear—"'Oh, Auntie Em, my favorite is Stimpy.' Eiana, she saying to me she love Ren." Emilia dumps both of them onto Iris's lap.

"Which is which?"

"Is Stimpy; is Ren."

"What did they use to get the ears to stick up?"

"CMS electrical wire"

"And they're stuffed with—let me guess—sanitary pads."

"Bingo!"

"Careful they don't catch you stuffing. Staff is really bitching about how we're going through the pads. They say old Ms. Gains keeps claiming her issue every month and McKinley, he sits there, trying to get up the nerve to tell her she doesn't need them and she just stares him down."

Emilia laughs merrily. "Ms. Gains, she is selling one pad—one ramen."

TAMERA JENKINS, MARIA GOMEZ, MARGARET ABBOT.
REPORT TO VISITING ROOM. JENKINS, GOMEZ, ABBOT.
REPORT TO THE VISITING ROOM.

Iris hugs the two stuffed cartoon figures. "These are my babies. They're mine. I'm kidnapping."

"No, can't have!" Emilia moves in to rescue. The two tumble on the bed and wrestle.

"You're tearing up my magazine!"

"Then give my babies!" Emilia howls. "My babies, they cry and cry—I gonna save them."

She rises, goes to her laundry bag, and snatches a loose sock. She unhooks her combination lock and stuffs it into the toe. With a hand on a cocked hip and a bad-guy squint, she starts swinging the lock-in-the-sock with menace.

ENGELS. IRIS ENGELS REPORT TO THE VISITING ROOM.

Emilia freezes in midswing.

"Yikes!" Iris throws the toys to the floor and leaps up. "Oh my God. Who in the hell? Rats! I'm not even dressed!"

They both spring into action. Iris toes off her still-laced tennis shoes and shuffles under the bed for her oxfords. Emilia snatches the uniform hanging off the side of Iris's locker and, holding the hanger in her mouth, starts to unbutton.

"You are saying, 'Too early, go back to bed,'" she reminds Iris righteously through the hanger hook. "Is good luck I already finish ironing up."

"Yes, you were right," admits Iris pulling the sweat suit top over her head. "You're a doll. Thank you."

"You welcome."

"Let me think. Weinstein? Ha! On Sunday? Grace and Howard? No, they're in . . . It's got to be Irene again."

Emilia takes the shirt off the hanger and holds it out to Iris, jiggling it impatiently. "*Apresura!*"

IRIS ENGELS, REPORT TO THE VISITING ROOM.

Dressed now, Iris using the toilet bowl for a parlor seat, lifts her face. There's a clear plastic makeup bag on her lap.

Emilia daps lipstick on her cheeks, wets and blends. She snaps her fingers. "Eye-brow pencil!"

"No, no time." Iris claws at her hair.

"No!" Emilia pulls Iris's arms away and closes in with a brush.

Finally, almost out the door: "Your watch!"

Holding the door open with her foot, Iris swings around, tears at the Velcro watchband and throws it at the bed.

"Your ID!"

There's ensues a scene of total panic, groping locker shelves and under the bed. Finally, with a yip of triumph, Emilia pulls it out of a shirt pocket in the laundry. Clutching it Iris rushes out of the room and down the hall toward the door.

ENGELS! REPORT TO THE VISITING ROOM. NOW!

Emilia standing in the room with her hands on her hips and her face up, calls out to the ceiling.

"Engels is coming, Mr. Officer!"

CHAPTER 8

The visiting room is again crowded—the same mild chaos, with children at the play area scampering and parents shouting after them.

Iris and Irene embrace and find a vacant table-and-chair set in a far corner.

"I got my holiday shopping done down there, can you believe?" exclaims Irene. "Mom wasn't doing well Tuesday and Wednesday. They had to sedate."

"What was wrong?"

"Just agitation. They say it's a common occurrence; we just have to wait it out. But they have all the good shops in Miami now, same as New York except down there it's seventy-eight degrees. So I got back into New York this morning, and I had all my Hanukkah done already. I decided to just hop a train—come on out."

"I'm so glad," says Iris. "What are you getting the kids?"

"Noah has been begging for this new electricy thing you carry around in your pocket called Newton's Message something-something. Message Pad? Nine hundred dolla, if you can believe."

"What does it do?"

"Now that I'm a little confused about. Noah goes on about handwriting recognition? So I guess it turns handwriting into typewriting or something? Although why you'd want to do that . . . I say, 'Noah, why don't you just skip writing it out and type it in the first place?'"

"Does it have any connection with the World Wide Web?"

"Apparently not. I told you how we got him a home computer last year? So that's what that's for. You can use it to type messages to people on the web or over the web or into the web or something. I say, 'Noah, wouldn't it be better to just call them up?'

Irene sighs and throws up her hands. "He rolls his eyes. He says they've gotten it to where you can order books and buy them over the web now. I say, 'Why? Why would you want to? We've got Borders just down the road.'"

"How about Chelsea?"

"She's been begging for a TV in her room because she's in love with *Sabrina the Teenage Witch*, but Noah never wants to let her watch and he calls it *Sabrina the Teenage Bitch*, and Chelsea goes, 'Mo-om, Noah's using inappropriate lang-uage,' and then they start fighting."

"So you relented."

"Note to self: I've got to call the cable company. Get her room wired."

"What else is Chelsea getting?"

Mostly clothes. *The Limited Too* in Miami has gone all preteen, so I could do a one-stop. She wanted a pair of overalls. I say, 'Like the ones the farmers wear?' So then *she* rolls *her* eyes. I'm telling you Iris," says Irene shrugging of her coat, "the older they get, the more their eyes roll around their heads."

Irene hangs her coat over the back of her chair.

"And big sweaters with sleeves that go down over the hands. I guess if you're eleven, you can't have your hands showing. And I got her a watch ring, which no-body will be able to see because of her sleeves."

"But she'll know it's there."

"Presumably. And she wanted glow-in-the-dark stars to put on her ceiling, which I thought was rather sweet but I don't know who's going to put them up there."

"How are sales at Fromagerie?"

"I called Diane from the airport. She says way up. So far twenty-seven percent over last year. And Josh told me back *when* that nobody's going to pay $9.50 for a hunk of cheese. Ha! Mr. Financial Advisor."

Irene looks pleased with herself. "Fromagerie will be well into the black this year," she states with satisfaction.

"Good. I'm proud of you, making it with your own business. When are you going to start selling franchises?"

"Ha! Like in two-thousand ten."

But, change-the-subject, you said Mom's not doing so well?"

Irene sighs. "That first day I got in, she didn't have any idea who I was. She was just anxious about someone or something called Lana. Did we ever have a dog named Lana?"

"I don't remember a Lana."

"Because she kept asking if I was sure I hadn't let Lana out. I kept saying, 'Who's Lana?' and she just kept asking again. I couldn't tell whether she was worried because I *had* let Lana out or because I hadn't."

Irene leans across the small table. "But then on Thursday she was better—she knew who I was, at least, but she kept saying"—Irene puts on a creaky voice—"'Now tell me again, where am I? Where am I living?'"

"Poor mom. Did she mention me?"

Irene takes a breath and starts to shake her head.

Iris jumps in, "Oh, of course she didn't. Why did I even . . ." Iris tries to turn it into a joke. "Maybe she thought I was Lana."

Her laugh is strained.

"No, she didn't mention you, but then she didn't mention Dad either. I'm not sure if that's an improvement or a regression."

"I wouldn't guess she's getting any better."

"No. She's regressing. I'm thinking it's a waste of energy for me to even take the trip down any more. It certainly doesn't do *her* any good. Might even make her worse. Probably I'm just trying to prove that I'm the good daughter . . ."

"*Still* the good daughter."

"Yes, as a matter fact. Still the good daughter."

"Always were."

"Iris, are you still fixated? I mean, I know you *used* to jeer but haven't you sort of *outgrown*?"

"I didn't jeer. I just pointed out."

"You jeered. Trust me, you jeered."

"Well if I did, that was because you were always acting so smug. You always used to playact at you being the good little girl. Used to drive me nuts, how you'd work it."

"Yeah, well I don't have to 'playact' *these* days, do I? She turns her head significantly left and right. "Now everyone, look: one is the good girl; one is the bad girl. Can you guess?"

Iris's face crumbles.

"Oh, I'm sorry! Here we go again. Do we always have to do this? Here, where's my purse? I've got a tissue."

Iris puts her face in her hands. "No, my fault. It's just talking about Mom. I guess it kind of churns up old feelings."

"Hey, let me go get you a soda. SunChips? I remembered to stop for change."

"You know what I've been craving?" asks Iris, wiping her nose. "Cheese

Whizzes."

"You mean in the ones in the neon orange?"

"Yeah, those. They don't sell them on commissary, and when I came in just now I saw them in the machine, and I got this big wave of longing."

"Well, come on. Let's go."

The rise.

" Now remember, Iris," says Irene in a tone of official warning, "Do not touch the money."

They start to make their way to the front of the visiting room"

"I won't touch," says Iris, "but can I just look at it?"

"You can look at it out of the corner of your eye. These are called 'quarters.'"

"Okay now. . .*quarters.* Who's that sideways guy on there?"

Iris and Irene are back at their table. Iris rips open her Cheese Whizzes and pops a Dr. Pepper.

Irene looks around. "I don't see that banker lady from Baltimore. How's she getting along? Are they still giving her a hard time?"

"Rebecca Kaplan? Not so much any more. They've mostly settled into the silent treatment."

"Okay, I'll bite. What's the silent treatment?"

"When she speaks and they act like she didn't. Like she isn't there. Maybe she'll ask someone, for instance, where can you get an extra commissary slip? When's the library's open? Everyone just keeps a blank face and walks on past."

"That's terrible. I just feel so bad for her!"

"Yeah, well it's better than them bumping her out of line or sniffing the air—'Somebody's around here's got a terrible odor.'"

"That's cruel! They aren't doing it anymore?"

"Not that I've witnessed; just the silent treatment. Actually, it's probably good for her. She's not being so reactive anymore. Besides, I think she'll be okay because I heard she's getting out of food service early-- they need her in education. She'll be teaching GED math, and some of her hazers might even be in her class. She can patronize the hell out of them; there won't be anything they can do."

Irene looks around again, singling out the beige uniforms within the family groups. "I must say, none of you bad women look very dangerous."

"Ha! We're deceptive. See that frumpy little middle-class-looking woman? No, over in the lawyer room—that glassed-off section."

"Really? Talking to that guy in the suit?"

"Her lawyer, yeah. She's in here for murdering her husband."

"*Really?*"

"She's fighting her conviction."

"Wow. So do you think she did it?"

"I have no idea. She's an interesting case."

"Oh, good. I love a good crime story."

"She's Russian, actually. Tatyana. She and her husband and a partner—all Russian—they owned a chemical plant in New Jersey. The husband turned up murdered, and she and the partner got convicted."

Irene stretches around again to get a better view.

"So you thinks she might not have done it?"

"I'm not sure, Irene. When inmates first come in, they really want to talk about their case and I'm interested. I listen and I can usually kind of guess at the backstory. But with her, I can't figure it out."

"How come?"

"If you're in jail for killing your husband and you didn't do it, wouldn't that kind of be the focus of your narrative? That you're innocent? You didn't kill him?"

"Mine would."

"You know," says Iris, crumpling her Cheese Whizzes bag and using it to wipe the orange off her fingers, "female inmates are usually pretty frank about what they did and didn't do. I mean, I'm not saying they don't complain about outcomes. There's always enough arbitrary weirdness in the system for them to feel victimized. But if they actually committed a crime, they're pretty apt to say so. Except for the two or three percent of federal inmates . . ."

Irene has turned her head and is rolling her eyes.

"What? What's wrong?"

"No, go on. You know how I love your legal lectures."

"I don't give legal—"

"Iris, you *always* give legal lectures. And I always learn something. Go on. Really. I want to hear about the tubby little Russian."

"You're sure? Anyway, if they're guilty, they usually admit they did it. Or that they did *some* of it. *Something.*"

Irene, elbows on the table, weaves her fingers together and rests her chin on them. She opens her eyes wide.

Iris goes into mock lecture mode. "*Except . . .*" She holds up a finger. "Except for the two or three percent who took it to trial. With them I can't tell."

"Why not?"

"Because of the process. If they did it, they've been denying so long, their reality changes. They . . . forget. But then, if they *didn't* do it, they can still be so wrapped up in process, they've lost track of their main issue. So it can make them sound guilty whether they are or not."

"Iris, are you sure only two or three percent of the women are going to trial?"

"Yep, look it up. You've been watching too much TV. On TV you get falsely accused, next scene you're in trial, next scene the jury comes back not guilty. In real life your lawyer's telling you that he's gotten the prosecution down to five years and unless you plead guilty, you'll do twenty."

Iris pauses.

"I can tell you don't believe me."

"So you're saying that that all over the country, perfectly innocent people are pleading guilty."

"Yep. In a federal court, anyway. Let me set you the scene: You can't raise bail, so you're sitting in a concrete pod twenty-three hours a day. Your court-appointed lawyer tells you the courts are overcrowded, and if you insist on a trial it's going to be two to three years. And then he tells you they've lined up witnesses ready to lie and testify against you—"

"Why do you people do that to each other?"

"As they say in here, '*duh*.' For a sentence reduction.'"

"They just lie?"

The prosecutor feeds them the lie—'We think this is the way it happened. This is how the crime went down—' and the detainee feeds it back to them."

"Don't any of them feel horrible?"

"Some. But the prosecution messes with their minds. They tell them all about how the assistance indicates that they're finally ready to turn their lives around. They insist it's an act of courage. They congratulate them on how they've been stepping up to the plate."

"They *believe* it?"

"Kind of. It's coming from the representation of justice—all educated and wearing a good suit. First time in their life that someone like that has treated them nice."

Irene looks distressed.

"Then he assures them that the other person's going to plead out anyway, so they won't have to actually stand up in court and testify. Just say that they're *ready* to testify, so here—sign here."

"Whew!"

"Then of course he's going back to his office crowing, about how they're all scumbags."

"Iris, I can't really believe. . . ."

"Believe. So in the meantime, that other innocent person in her pod—*her* lawyer is telling her how she's going to lose anyway because her friend's going to testify, so she caves in and she pleads guilty and she takes her five years."

"Okay, but those ones who do decide to have a trial. They're usually innocent, right?"

Iris sighed. "You'd think, wouldn't you? Since I've been down, I've talked to maybe five or six women who took it to trial. And I'm not sure about any of them."

"Why?"

"I think some of them craved the idea of starring in a courtroom drama—borderline-personality thing. But sometimes it's hard to tell whether you're looking at a guilty woman with a personality disorder or an innocent woman who's been traumatized by the process."

"Okay, okay, so the little Russian lady?"

"Tatyana? Well, like I say, she's Russian, which adds a whole nother layer of ambiguity. But reading between the lines, I think what happened is that the husband turned up murdered--she's never told me how—but that made it a *state* crime."

"Ahh, not federal."

"Right. But I'm assuming that the state of New Jersey, found enough evidence to convict the partner. At which point the partner realized—or was told—that he could get his sentence reduced if he said that she was in back of it. True or not, who knows?"

They look over at the Russian, who is talking loudly to her lawyer and waving her hands.

"Except in New Jersey, if he was the one who did the actual *killing* part, they couldn't get her. So they had to call in Feds or she was going to walk."

"Why?"

"New Jersey doesn't have a conspiracy law. The Feds do. They knew that if they could move it into the federal court system, they could charge her with *conspiracy* to commit murder. The murder itself is a state crime, but as luck would have it, the Feds could take jurisdiction."

Iris pauses in the lecture.

"Why?" prods Irene.

"Because they could charge her under the new domestic violence act, which Congress had just passed. So that was the pathway for the feds take over. And it worked because—there's Tatyana."

"I don't catch."

"Congress federalized the crime of domestic violence. So if a spouse kills a spouse, the Feds can take over if they choose to. In her case, they did. They used the new law and charged her with conspiracy to commit murder."

"And she's denying she conspired?"

"No, that's the problem." Iris sighs. "When she talked to me about her case, she never got around to mentioning anything about *that* one way or the other. What she's all hung up about—I'll bet it's what she's yelling about right now—is that Congress called the law the 'Violence Against Women Act.' But they charged her with violence against a *man*. So she's convinced that it can't apply to her. She can't get it into her head that it's just the name."

Irene stretches around to get a view of the woman again. "So she's not denying that she killed her husband; she's just denying that her husband was a woman."

"Yep, you got it."

They share a moment of sisterly amusement.

"My guess would be that she and the partners were lovers, and she probably at least knew the murder was going to happen. But through all the years of legal process, she kind of has forgotten that that's what she's supposed to be denying."

Irene laughs.

" But like I say, Iris continues, "there's a chance that the partner was lying and she's perfectly innocent, and all through those same years she just lost track. She forgot that her not doing it is actually vital part of her story. So now she's enraged, but it's over how the victim was a man and they charged her with violence against a women."

"So does she want you to help?"

"No, I can't work with any of the women who went to trial. You need the trial transcript, and it's too much paperwork. There isn't any space to keep it."

"Yeah, you already told me."

"Besides, she's got a high-powered, post-conviction team and it's new, unsettled law. They'll challenge the jurisdiction. Probably won't get anywhere, but she's convinced that it's the name of the legislation that is the perfect ground for appeal. The lawyers are all idiots because they won't listen to her. I suspect she's driving that poor guy over there nuts."

"How many years did she get?"

"Thirty-plus. And she's sixty so, it's pretty much life."

"And you think she did it."

"I *think*. But I really can't tell. Jury's out."

"Well, whether or not, that was a good crime story." Irene stretches and looks at her watch.

"Time to go?"

"Not yet. There's a four-forty that will get me to the airport in time. Should we get some candy? Come on. When we were kids, you liked Butterfingers and I was the Mars gal. When I come in here it's the only time I let myself eat candy bars. I suffer for my sister."

"For your poor sister in the slammer."

"Right. That's the one."

Iris reaches up to her chin and checks a crumble of Butterfinger.

Irene nibbles the end of a Mars bar. She looks around the room. "So who's that older lady over there with all the family? No, over there, with the long straight hair." She nods toward a table filled with three generations.

"The Latin one? I don't know her. She's just a regular Spanish momie. Why?"

"She looks kind of hippie or artsy or something."

"No, it's just her flower-child earrings. They're inmate originals. You can order the fixings—the seed beads and the ear hooks from crafts."

"Huh. Inmates make those? Does crafts just only let you order jewelry stuff?"

"No, you can get crayons and construction paper and those plastic needle-point sheets with the big holes? Lots of uncool stuff."

"So everyone in here is doing kiddy crafts."

"Everyone crochets, but they sell yarn and hooks out of the commissary. You have to have the money upfront to order from the craft catalog, and then it takes months to come in. Then you need a craft locker in the rec or it will get confiscated, and they only have enough craft lockers for half of us."

Iris crumbles the two candy wrappers.

"It's a pain," she goes on, "but anyway, the seed beads are the biggest deal because you can sell your projects to other inmates. It's the only jewelry we're allowed. Except wedding rings."

Iris glances at the long dangles on the Spanish woman. "I guess now that I'm looking, those earrings do make her look a little countercultural. She isn't."

"So what in the world would a woman like that have ever done to get herself arrested?"

"I've never talked to her but believe me, she's here on drug conspiracy. One of the men in her family. Maybe she accepted cash when her husband was out? Or told someone when he'd be back? Answered the phone?"

"That's silly, Iris. You don't go to jail for answering a telephone."

"You surely do. Especially if you're Spanish. The Feds round up whole families because they live together and they can get them on conspiracy."

"And they put them here in maximum security?"

"We're actually medium. It's medium and camp. There isn't a maximum for women. We're not bad enough. We don't rate."

"*Whichever* security. Anyway I still can't believe . . ."

"No, really, Irene. I know it sounds like some inmate, poor-us, tall-tale, but answering a phone is truly all it takes if you're Spanish. It wouldn't happen to a middle-class Anglo family. Even if, maybe the son was dealing out of the basement or somewhere? They'd probably just take the property and let the parents slide."

"So why don't the women just tell the men to go some other place to deal their drugs?"

"Irene, this generation of Spanish women—they don't have any say. A lot of them tell me that they're freer in here then they were out there. In here when a guard gets mad is no problemo. He isn't allowed to lay hands."

"Isn't it hard on them to get their kids taken away?"

"Yeah, but look over there. There's always relatives. They miss their kids, especially at first, but they don't have to worry about them."

"So it's not a bad thing for them to go to jail?"

"No, actually it is. It's terrible. They're not citizens, and they're going to get deported. They'll get dumped off at the Bogota airport. Some of the younger ones—they've been here since they were little kids—they lost touch with their relatives, they don't know where they're going to go or how they're going to support themselves. Or, that's what they say. It might be partly Spanish victim-drama; I don't have a clue. But I know for sure deportation means losing your kids."

"Can't they take their kids?"

"Certainly not on the deportation flight. They could send for them, but if the kids were born citizens that would be depriving them of their future—the American dream. And the parents aren't allowed back in to visit. They may never see them again."

"Yeah, but hey, speaking of deportation, I just remembered. What's the word on your little roommate from Colombia? Any luck?"

A shadow passes over Iris's face. "Emilia? Not a word. We're still waiting to hear from the congressman."

"So what was her crime? Did *she* just answer the phone?"

"No, she was more involved. She got arrested with her younger sister. They'd rented an apartment in Virginia and working as clerics at the Colombian embassy.

They were from Medellin, and they had some kind of family ties with the cartel. She says everyone in Medellin does."

"Were they dealing drugs?"

"Ironically, she says the reason the two of them got into trouble was because they *weren't*. They were straight—didn't sell; didn't party. So when the cartel needed a spot to store product, their place came up. Mind you, I'm sure they were paid off, but she implies that they didn't have a choice."

"So if they were good girls, why didn't they go to the police?"

"Against the Medellin cartel? Are you kidding? They'd been here for less than a year. Back there the police work for the cartels."

Irene sighs. "That's so sad. I hope they let her stay. Where's the sister? Is she . . ."

"Irene, I'm sorry, but technically I'm her council, and she's made me promise over and over not to talk about it. I've probably broken confidence by just even saying this much."

"Well, okay. I just I hope you can work it out for her."

"So do I."

CHAPTER 9

GOOD MORNING, LADIES. TIME TO GET UP.

ALL RISE FOR STAND-UP COUNT. OUT OF BED. STAND UP.

There is the turn-off beep, then a back-on.

OH, MERRY CHRISTMAS, LADIES.

REPEAT. MERRY CHRISTMAS. ENJOY YOUR CHRISTMAS, LADIES

THAT IS A DIRECT ORDER.

Iris has been awake this morning for an hour. She's sitting up in her bed, drinking instant coffee and reading The New Yorker. Emilia—on the upper bunk, sleepy-eyed, a tousle of hair hanging down—peeks over the side.

"Merry Christmas."

"Iris smiles. "Merry Christmas, babe."

Emilia scrambles down to quickly use the bathroom before the officers arrive for count. Then with her thermal top on, she wrestles into her bra. She pulls her sweatshirt over it and pulls on her pants.

They hear the guards enter their building to count, and they both stand.

As the counting guards finish and exit the unit, Iris starts to lie back down.

"No," insists Emilia, grabbing her and lifting her back into a standing position. "Count is not clear."

Iris makes a face. "Rule freak."

"Is Christmas morning. We are being good girls on Christmas."

"Okay, but they better hurry."

The two women stand waiting. Iris taps her foot, looks at the ceiling, and sighs. Then just before she gives up:

CLEAR. COUNT'S CLEAR.

LADIES, PREPARE TO EXIT YOUR UNITS FOR CHRISTMAS DINNER.

Emilia sings, "Christmas, Christmas, *Feliz Navidad!*" while doing a monkey dance, hopping on one foot and flapping her hands. Then she switches over to a chicken dance, pumping elbow-wings. "Puck-puck-puck," she squawks. "Me, I am the Cornish hen. Christmas dinner! Puck-puck-puck."

"Christmas in the penitentiary," Iris laughs at her and muses and repeats, "Christmas in the Penitentiary. Who would have thought?" She counts on her fingers. "My fifth Cornish game hen."

As the common area fills, the two go to their lockers to bring out gifts. Emilia has wrapped Iris's crocheted hat and scarf in taped-together, hand-decorated yellow legal pad. Emilia's earrings and bracelet set are tucked into empty dental-floss boxes.

"You go get in line, Babe. Save me a place. I have to use the bathroom."

Emilia, in her new earrings, is lined up at the front door of Unit Twelve. She beckons to Iris wearing her new hat and scarf.

The door is unlocked, and as the officer opens it the inmates pause in wonder. They gasp and blink at the shimmering whiteness and call to each other. "Look at the snow! Snow for Christmas!"

"Nieve. Ha nevado!"

"I'm der-ee-eaming of a whi-iite . . ."

"Fel-iiiz Navid-aaad."

"Better not pout; better not cry-yy . . ."

They stream out onto a white compound, making fresh tracks on the sidewalk. The a.m. work crew had not been roused on a holiday morning and it sleeted last night, then froze, then snowed. The woman, especially those from tropical climates, have hilarious trouble staying upright.

Emilia slips and screams. Iris grabs her arm. "No, keep your feet flat. Walk like a duck."

Emilia flaps a free elbow and quacks as she goose steps. A Colombian matron in front of them skids and nearly falls, and the three of them—Iris, Emilia, and the matron—almost incapacitated with laughter, cling to one another, fighting for footing.

The stream of inmates, eager for a place in line, laughs and swerves around them.

"Careful!"

"*Cuidado*!"

"Don't fall!"

As the three merrily wrestle, they hear approaching keys. The buzz-cut officer is closing in.

"Inappropriate contact, ladies," he calls out sternly on his way past.

It douses their laughter. They stand and stare at each other openmouthed, then at his back, Emilia calls.

"Merry Christmas, officer,"

"*Feliz Navidad*," calls the matron.

"And Merry Christmas to you too, sir," calls Iris.

He doesn't hear. He keeps marching.

CHAPTER 10

It's Christmas afternoon, and inmates in brown coats, pulling bright new crochet over ear and around necks, are straggling out of the dining room. Word has spread that there's no pat-down officer.

"How you get them to give up a second one of those little chickens?" asks a freshman on the way out of the dining hall.

"You got to be slick," instructs a junior. "Go back around end-of-the line, come up like you ain't eat yet. Mr. Uniform, he ain't going to notice you because all the sisters look alike."

A Spanish woman at the center of a group of friends tips herself backward to accentuate the small lump poking out from the front of her waistline.

"Mira! Estoy embarazada."

"El bebé de la Navidad!"

"Los pollos bebé de la Navidad!" and the group falls into gales.

Desiree and Ottilla exit together in deep conversation. "You can't keep to all the rules. It's impossible," Desiree protests.

"I'm going to try," replies Ottilla. "I lived lawless up to now. It's about time I tried doing it the other way."

"You mean you're going to do all your time without ever having, like, one little crumb of kitchen food in your property?"

"I'm going to try."

"So how are you ever going to do forty-something years without ever having anyone borrow anything from you? Your roommate runs out of creamer, you're going to tell her, 'Nope. Can't help you out. 'Gainst the *ru*-lles.'"

Ottilla sighs and doesn't respond.

"If you follow all the rules, you'll be turning yourself into a total asshole; that's what you'll be doing."

"I know Rogo says that too. I'm going to have to pray for guidance," Ottilla admits.

The sidewalks have been tracked clear, the ice has melted in places, leaving safe areas to step on. The majority of the population is out making the compound rounds and enjoying the holiday white.

Desiree and Ottilla join the others, walking side-by-side. Inmates cast sidelong glances at the couple and comment quietly to each other:

"That Big Boy right there, she be getting herself out of the chapel these days. She be socializing."

"Ain't nothing going on."

"Ha! I'll *bet* ain't nothing going on. Look at them."

"Ottilla, she loves Jesus. And Dessie, she don't go that way."

"Yeah, Dessie been saying how they just good homies."

"Wait and see. Wait and see."

Desiree, since she got out of seg, is no longer the compound's stuck-up blonde. She was victimized by the administration and beaten down by a guard; therefore the population—even the blacks—give her grace. Among the young whites and Spanish, she's close to being the compound's sweetheart.

Ottilla, on the other hand, as Danbury's most male inmate, has enjoyed star role from the beginning. It's fitting now that the two have paired off, and the narrative of Dessie and Tillie playing together as children inspires layers of tender inmate sentiment.

The compound takes note of them but Desiree and Ottilla themselves are unaware.

"At least I know one thing," says Ottilla. "If it's in the BOP rule book that I'm not supposed to take food out of the dining room, I'm not going to do that at least."

Desiree defiantly pats the bump at the side of her waist, and Ottilla looks at it.

"It's my Cornish game hen," Desiree defends. "I couldn't finish it. What am I supposed to do? Throw it away? Let it go to waste? I was raised to believe," she continues primly, "that it is a sin to waste food."

"I don't care if *you* do it," Ottilla hastens to insist. "I don't care if *anyone* does. It just isn't the right thing for *me*."

"It's against the rules to have a girlfriend too," teases Desiree. "You going to keep that rule?"

Ottilla colors slightly. "You're not supposed to have relations. BOP can't make rules about your feelings."

"So you're going to do your forty-five years—"

Forty-one."

"So you're going to do your forty-one years without ever having any sex? Ever again?"

Ottilla is quiet, trying to form her words.

"You know, some people are born different—like, maybe they're born deaf? So until they get to heaven, they never get to hear music or birds or anything?"

"Yeah, no birds. So?"

"Well, I think some people are born where sex isn't the right thing for them. They're born so that when they grow up, sex is twisted wrong. It doesn't turn out to be the correct thing for them to do. They can love but . . . You know what I mean?"

"I don't even have a *clue*."

"Those last couple years on the streets? I was going through my gender reassignment and it turned me into something . . . evil. I mean in regards to sex."

"Wow! You, *evil*? Come on, *Tillie*."

"No, really. Before I started in on the hormones, I was okay. I was attracted to women and had girlfriends and everything, but I was pretty much . . . I wasn't twisted about it or anything. I mean, I'd have, sexual feelings but I'd also feel kindness and, you know, friendship. I'd see someone and I'd feel like I'd want to really talk to that person—get to know her."

Desiree nods.

"But then, after I started—oh, never mind. I don't like to go there."

"Come on, Tillie, talk to me."

Ottilla walks in silence, studying her feet. Then she looks up at Desiree's earnest expression.

"After the hormones really kicked in, I'd want to . . . it made me into a bad person, you know? Like, I got *mean*. And the worst thing was, I really *liked* it. I liked being mean. It was exciting. I don't hardly ever feel that way anymore. Or I'll only get a little wave—a flashback. Then I pray real quick, and it turns into a memory instead of a feeling. You know?"

"No, I actually don't. Actually, I have no idea."

"Because I'm not saying it very well. There's a lot of background you need before you can understand. Anyway, long story short, sex isn't something for me."

"Forever?"

"Yep, and I'm in exactly the right place for that. God put me in a place where people aren't allowed to have physical relations, and I'm really fine with that."

"You're going to feel different. I'll bet."

"No I won't For me it's a good thing. I was just born wrong. Or, not *wrong*. Different. Like I was born a girl on the outside, but ever since I can remember, inside myself I'm a boy. I used to tell you about it, remember?"

"Yeah, I remember. I thought it was just a stage or whatever."

"No, it never went away. After I grew up it got even stronger. It really messed up my attitude toward life. I thought if I could get the money to afford the hormones and the surgery and everything, then I would be like other guys—like I was *supposed* to be. And I thought *then* I'd finally be happy. So then I managed to jump through all their hoops and they started letting me have the testosterone—"

"Testosterone? Was it like a pill?"

"No, injection. But then after I'd been doing it for almost a year, I was really getting full-blown into it, and it started giving me this evil attitude."

"So then you went wild and committed your crime?"

"No. No! Not at all. That was on assignment."

"So that wasn't any part of any evilness?"

"Well, maybe. Maybe if I hadn't been on the hormones I'd have turned the job down. I don't know. I just know at the time I was happy to be asked."

They continue their walk.

"What happened with the hormones?"

Ottilla sighs.

"Actually when I got arrested it was more like I got *rescued*. Because the testosterone was turning me wicked. And if I had gone ahead and finished the whole reassignment thing? It would have been really bad. I would not have been in a good situation."

"Like how?"

"I had only gotten my top part done, thank God. I had finally gotten up enough money for the other, but believe me, if I'd gotten a chance to go ahead and get the bottom surgery? Whew!"

Ottilla whisks her forehead.

" I actually had my appointment at the time the feds came, so it was perfect timing."

Desiree involuntarily glances down at Ottilla's crotch.   "Why?   What was perfect?"

"Because if they'd come for me a couple of months later, I wouldn't be here in a woman's prison. They would have put me in with the men. Probably Leavenworth or Terre Haute or somewhere."

"Wow!"

"Exactly. A female prison is just so much of a better place to do your time. I can relax, not worry about anyone coming up on me. And I can just concentrate on getting my mind and my heart closer to God."

Desiree makes a face that Ottilla doesn't see.

"So I'm thanking Him," Ottilla continues sincerely, "for pulling me up off the streets and putting me in here where it's possible to live a life where He can stay in my heart—where I won't lose my joy. So yeah, I'll be following the rules."

"Okay, I get it. No relationship because rules. But guess what? It's in the rules," and Desiree points it out with attitude, laying down a trump card, "that if you see someone else breaking the rules, it is required that you go and report that person. So how about *that* rule?"

"You know, Dessie," says Ottilla, giving her a playful push off the sidewalk, "I read that whole regulation handbook, and I never did see that one in there."

"Well, read it again," says Desiree without conviction.

Ottilla grins. They walk in silence for a while.

Finally Desiree asks, "But what if it was in there?"

"I wouldn't be keeping that one," says Ottilla. "Snitching? Betraying? That's heinous. That would be the quickest way to lose my joy. For sure."

"But what if God wanted you to? Like for stopping harm to others or whatever."

"If I saw someone hurting somebody and I couldn't do anything myself, I'd call in the authorities but that's not what I mean. I'm talking about turning in friends and colleagues for your own personal gain."

"But like I said. Pretend it was a rule. And God was wanting you to keep the rules."

"It isn't, so I don't have to worry."

COUNT TIME. GO TO YOUR ROOMS, LADIES.

EVERYONE IN YOUR ROOMS FOR AFTERNOON COUNT.

The two make an about-face on the wintry sidewalk and head back toward Unit Two.

"Hey Dessie, you sure you don't want to go to our Christmas concert tonight? You would be getting the privilege to hear me sing in the choir."

She nudges Desiree again.

"Now see, that would be a real special treat for you."

Desiree is shaking her head.

"Warden Coleman is saying," Ottilla continues, "that us choir ladies have invented a new worship style. She says we're doing gospel improv. So, there! Are you tempted?"

"Let me check." Desiree wets her finger and holds it to the wind.

"Nope. Not tempted."

"She'll be on the piano. You'd like to hear her play. She does that up-and-down-the-keyboard gospel-roll thing."

"No, really Tillie, I mean it. Going to church gives me the creeps. But," Desiree hastens to add, "that's just me. I'm sure it's right for others. It's just—maybe I've got my personal issues?"

COUNT TIME. EVERYONE IN YOUR UNITS.

"Lets talk about it sometime, okay?"

"Okay, you tell me about your hormone-gender-reassignment problem, and I'll tell you about my church problem."

They high five. Ottilla holds open the door to their unit with one hand, the other at the waist, and bows. Desiree turns up her nose and sniffs and sweeps in.

The inmates exchange knowing glances. They nod at each other.

CHAPTER 11

A half-hour later Ottilla and Rogo are on their bunks ready to stand for the opening door and the counting guards.

"Last Christmas?" answers Ottilla. "Last Christmas I woke up and grabbed my works and shoved off. Christmas high."

"Didn't go see your mom?"

"No, I was going to drive over, say hi, but on Christmas Eve she wasn't picking up, then I couldn't get an answer next morning, so I figured I'd just do my Christmas on the nod."

"Where she been? Ever find out?"

"She called the next day. I was surprised. First time since she got married that she ever called *me*. I guess Franklin—that's her husband-- he had had another stroke. She had been over to Iowa City at the hospital."

"He pull through?"

"Yeah, but he's totally paralyzed up. So how about *your* last Christmas?"

"Last Christmas? Last Christmas I was sitting in Roanoke County, waiting all day for Moms to come Then all evening I was standing in the phone line. Her car battery had went dead."

Ottilla is silent, looking up at the mattress springs. "So it sure could be worse than this," she says.

"Could be worse. Sure could. I guess we adjusting to our fate."

"Actually," admits Ottilla, "This Christmas I'm feeling pretty blessed."

"That's good. Probably helping, how you're getting yourself your new friends and all."

Ottilla is silent.

"I see," suggests Rogo casually, "where you and Johansson are getting deep. You two, maybe . . . fixing to be that way?"

"Not *that* way. She's my oldest friend. She was my idol all the time when I was growing up."

"Your idol?"

"Yeah, kind of. My star? My rock star? I couldn't figure why all the other kids were going on about Madonna or Newton-John or anybody when we had Dessie, and she was prettier and she was right down the block. For all my primary school years, she was the center of my life. Then she moved on and I moved on but I never forgot, you know? She always stayed with me."

Rogo is silent.

Ottilla sits up now and idly twirls her combination lock.

"So then I walk into prison, and I don't know how it's going to be in here. I'm thinking it's going to be nothing nice. And I'm praying for God to stay with me and get me through. So then—there she is."

"Yeah, down in the mud getting the shit kicked out."

"I know, but the prayer had just left my lips, so it felt like it was a sign, or a gift, or something. I thought maybe it might not even be *real*. Like I was having mirages or whatever. That's why I kept asking who she was."

They hear the guards opening the doors and they break off the conversation. Ottilla rises, and Rogo scrambles down to the toilet seat and onto the floor to stand beside her. The guards are down the walkway.

"But don't get it wrong," insists Ottilla just above a whisper. "It's nothing like you're trying to say. We haven't even brought up that discussion. We'll be keeping it straight. We neither of us want it the other way."

The guards are getting closer.

"I don't know," says Rogo, teasing. "You two looking *go-ood*."

"Seven, eight . . . quiet, ladies. No talking."

They both go silent and pull into military attention.

CHAPTER 12

"—give thanks for our dear sister, Warden Coleman, here accompanying this congregation of voices, raised to You in praise. And finally dear Lord, on this Christmas evening we thank you that even in times of darkness, you are here with each and every one of us. You say in your book that you come to set the prisoner free. When we are free in Jesus our shackles fall away, and we are free indeed."

Scattered amens from the inmate congregation.

The chapel is overflowing. The nave is full; a line stands at the rear against the wall. The visiting minister's sapphire-blue suit almost perfectly matches the choir robes of the twenty-odd inmates seated behind him. The robe of Warden Coleman at the piano is a deep purple topped with a crisp white collar.

All heads are bowed.

"Praise be to the Lord. In Jesus's name, Amen."

There's a call of responding *amens*, and the room rustles into life.

"Sister Coleman? I hear you have a few words for the ladies here."

The warden rises and moves around the piano bench and to the podium. "Why I thank you, Brother Lewis. Thank you for offering up your Christmas evening to come in to give us your words of loving inspiration. Big hand? Let's give a big hand for Reverend Lewis."

They applaud.

"First I want to praise the Lord for sending me here to this institution so I could meet all you beautiful ladies. And I want to praise you all for warmly welcoming me."

The inmates' faces shine.

The warden leans toward them on the podium.

"I've got a little confession to make to you all tonight. My little confession is that at one season of my life, I wanted to be a preacher. Yes, I did!" insists the warden as though quelling protest. "I wasn't going to be any old Warden Coleman. I was going to be"—she straightens tall and her voice deepens—"the Reverend Coleman." She laughs at her folly.

The audience, unsure, responds with a titter.

"But the Lord had a differing plan in His mind for me, and so today I am here with you not as your reverend but as your warden—as your Warden Coleman."

She puts a hand to her heart and gives and small half-bow.

"Even so," she continues her hand still over her heart, "as Warden Coleman I want to assure all you ladies that the center of my heart [*patting*] is not over at that administration building." She points her other arm to her left. "The center of my heart [*patting*] is right here in this chapel."

She points to the floor.

"Yes it is. The center of my heart is here, and so last October, when I first came to Danbury, I was thrilled and amazed to find a choir of angels. Yes, ladies, you heard me right. That's what I said: a choir of angels waiting to welcome me."

She turns to the choir and gestures. "And so now for our Christmas closing, this beautiful choir of Danbury angles will raise up their voices in musical praise."

Applause.

The warden, beaming, returns to her piano and begins to trickle out background chords. The choir rises and moves down. The director, a heavyset inmate, hair straightened into a crisp shelf, moves to the front and turns to address the congregation.

"We ladies of the Danbury chapel choir have been hard at work composing our special Christmas offering. So tonight we are ready and eager to share, through this music, the individual testimonies of the truths of what we hold in our hearts."

She turns and raises her arms.

Whee-een . . . Jesus came into my heart,

(On Christmas day.)

When Jesus came in-to my heart

(On Christmas day.)

The front and back rows of singers alternate lines. Now they all hold the last chord as one of the members moves to the front. The piano tinkles and the rest of the choir hums as she talk-sings:

I am grateful to be here to day with Je-e-sus.

He pick me up off the stre-e-et.

He walk me and su-po-ort me.

Jesus, He my sa-a-vior.

She moves back as another inmate takes her place.

I am lucky-to-be-alive-at-all-today with Je-e-sus.

He save me from my da-ark-ness.

He is walking all my steps with me.

He take me down the path of ri-geous-ness.

Then another:

I do one day-at-a-time with Je-e-s-us.

He be my su-ppo-ort group.

He pick me to my feet when I am do-o-own.

I do one-day-at-a-time with Je-e-sus.

A women beside Ottilla in the back row moves forward:

Jesus, He my do-oc-tor.

He heal me in my hos-pi-tal.

He give me my med-ica-a-tion.

Jesus, He my do-oc-tor.

Ottilla moves to the front now and sings in a high vibrant tenor:

Jesus is my res-cu-er.

He released me from with-dra-a-wal.

He visit me in my pri-son cel-ll.

He fill my body with His-healing lo-o-ove.

At this the choir comes together—rolling piano and rousing chorus.

Whe-e—en . . .

JESUS! Came into, my heart.

When JESUS! Came into, my heart.

Floods of Joy, o'er my soul, like the sea billows ro-ooo-oll,

When Je-s-us. Came in-to. My heart.

The chapel rocks with applause.

CHAPTER 13

"She's got Bible study class," Desiree answers, sitting down on the bench a few weeks later.

It's early evening and although it's bright under the arc lights, the edges of the snow-covered compound are slipping into shadow. The three—Iris, Emilia and Desiree—watch a pair of female officers performing haphazard pat-downs. Some inmates are beckoned with crooking fingers; some are waved past.

The pile of bags at their feet is skimpy tonight. Word flowed through the dining hall that the searching guards were out, and now the floor under the tables is scattered with bags. The p.m. kitchen cleaners will bring them out as the garbage, and with any luck they'll be retrieved later from behind the dumpsters.

Just now a female guard is extracting a roll of saran-wrapped carrot sticks from inside an inmate's waistband. She shakes a "naughty naughty" finger.

"Talk about infantilizing," comments Iris. "Uranus was more fun to watch. I actually kind of miss her style. I guess you don't, huh, Dessie?"

"No, I can get along without," agrees Desiree.

"Are you missing the Ferguson style?" teases Emilia.

Desiree doesn't reply.

"Sorry!" cries Emilia.

"I don't mind," says Desiree stoically. "He was just another creep."

"By the by," says Iris. "I overheard a couple of case managers talking about him. I guess they're throwing the book—charging him with statutory. Probably get three or four years after he pleads out. Which he has to, since his crime is documented in a video."

Desiree stiffens and looks alarmed. "What about me in it?"

"Don't worry," says Iris quickly. "They'd fuzz out your face, but it's not going to be presented anyway. He'll plead."

"Oh God, I'd die if that video gets shown to some actual *jury*," moans Desiree.

"It won't. There's not going to be any trial. He'd lose and then he'd get fifteen to twenty."

"God, what a creep. I can't believe I actually—oh well."

"The officers were saying that the judge wouldn't let him out on his own recog, and the wife wouldn't put up the house, so he was sitting in Fairfield County for a while. But they finally let him go home for Christmas."

"Merry Christmas, Fergusons," says Desiree bitterly.

"Yeah, I'll bet that was a warm celebration under the Ferguson Christmas tree."

Desiree's sits in silence, her face twisted in amused spite. Emilia glances over in concern.

"Is Ms. Dessie and Mr. Ottilla being like that?" she asks, holding up crossed fingers and trying to twinkle.

Desiree shakes off her thoughts. She reaches across Iris and play-slaps Emilia's leg.

"No, not like *that*."

"Now, I don't know," says Iris in mock warning. "You two are looking like you're getting pre-ee-tty tight."

"I'm straight and she's a Christian, and so there you go—*poof*! Nothing happening."

"She's looking pretty enamored. Jesus would be some heavy competition, Dessie, but I bet you could beat him out."

"I don't want to beat him out. I don't go that way."

But it wouldn't be like you'd be totally *going* that way. She's actually kind of . . . male, don't you think? For all practical purposes?"

"Not for *all* practical purposes. Down there she's still, whatever. She was going to get reassignment surgery," Desiree reminds them, "before she got arrested."

They sit in thought.

The two officers finish up and gather their meager winnings to walk them over to the dumpster.

"I wonder how that kind of medical operation would even work," muses Iris.

Desiree's face is increasingly troubled.

"I don't want to even think about it. Yuck."

"They can expand the clitoris . . ."

"What's 'clitoris,'" asks Emilia, and Iris whispers in her ear. Emilia looks troubled.

"Then," Iris continues, "I think—can carve a new penis. From the vagina? No, that can't be right. Maybe they make a tube?"

They sit silently looking out onto the compound, their faces clouded with aversion.

"Well, she got arrested, so it never did happen," says Desiree.

"Maybe they take some intestines or something," Iris goes on thoughtfully, acting it out with her hands, "and then they . . . sculpt it into a penis? Somehow?"

"Eww," exclaims Desiree.

"Like is a sausage?" asks Emilia.

"Yeah, I don't know. Can that be right? I'll have to get a book sent in."

They sit in contemplation. It's Emilia who breaks the silence.

"When they making it, how they going to stuff it up with?"

There is a long, thoughtful pause. Iris keeps her deadpan expression and speaks tonelessly.

"Sanitary pads."

"Look at those ladies over there on that bench," says Rogo as she and Asia B wander out of the dining room.

"They be busting themselves up over something or the other, " comments Asia.

"Those inmates, there, they having way too much fun for prison." Rogo observes.

"Wa-ay too much fun," agrees Asia B.

CHAPTER 14

It's after dinner the next day and Desiree and Ottilla have managed to secure a table-and-chair set in Unit Two's common area. They're playing Canasta.

At the surrounding tables are inmates visiting, crocheting, and writing letters home—some illustrating them with crayon cartoon characters. Up on the top tier, a pair of Asian women are separating strands of yarn for baby blankets. The hanging ball, a weighting and stabilizing pencil poked through the middle, spins as the two above form the new single-strand balls. Back toward the rear, a trio of lithe black women is bumping hips and singing in lilting island.

In every life we have some trouble

When you worry you make it double

Don't worry, be happy.

In the front entrance an inmate holds open the door, bringing in the cold. She turns and drags in a net laundry bag filled with cans of mackerel and ramen noodles and coffee creamer. On top rests a large clear plastic bag of fiberfill batting.

"Ladies! Look! They got in the polyfill!"

"*Mira! Relleno. Que les dieron en polyfilla!*"

"No more sanitary pads!"

"Way to go, commissary! Good timing! Christmas is over so *now* you get the fiberfill!"

It's a commotion, and inmates up and down the tiers poke their head out of their curtain doors. A second inmate comes through the door with fiberfill, and there's general celebration.

"Bet you never pictured prison," Desiree says to Ottilla, "with all the inmates cheering for stuffing material."

"No, that I never did," agrees Ottilla as she deals out a hand. "Guess I'm going to have to learn how to make stuffed animals."

"Yeah, now that you don't have to stuff them with sanitary pads—break any, ahem, *rules*."

Ottilla smiles at her cards.

"Better learn to crochet first, Tillie. They don't let you out till you learn how."

"I got some time. I probably don't have to start right yet."

"Oops, sorry, Tillie! I wasn't trying to rub it in about your sentence or anything. I didn't mean . . . you know."

"I got a hefty one all right," Ottilla smiles in good cheer.

"God, Tillie, I don't see how you can take it so well," says Desiree, sorting her cards. "If I was looking at your kind of time, I'd be having a totally depressive incident."

"Makes the difference when you got God in here." Ottilla fist bumps her heart. "As long as He's giving me my joy, whatever else is fine. It makes me happy to be right here where I am."

Desiree shakes her head and lays down a three of diamonds. "So do you mind if I ask: how'd they ever catch you?"

"Got rolled over on like everybody else in here. One of the Disciples got popped, and he knew about how I got the assignment. He was facing a lot of years, so he was looking to lighten the load."

Ottilla picks up the three and lays down three jacks.

Desiree pulls a card from the deck. "Another thing I don't understand," she says. "You said you were affiliated, so how'd you ever get hooked on heroin? Were the Disciples letting you *use*? I thought it was their big no-no. Like 'never get high on your own supply.'"

Ottilla laughs. "Hey girl, you gots the gang-slang. You down."

Dessie gives a three-finger sign.

"No, I never did use until I stopped slinging," Ottilla answers. She lays her last card and picks up the deck to shuffle. "The feds had got a warrant behind that original crime, and they busted into my crib. But then they left me hanging out on the streets for almost a year before they brought me in."

"So you didn't start using until then?"

"Yeah, I was on the testosterone so I didn't have to hustle down any rigs. Feds wanted them on the search, but they had to leave them be when I showed them my 'script. So then—I was muscle-packing the hormones—so then all's I had to do was learn how to find a vein. And then, lucky me, I had a tight connect right up on the fifth floor of my apartment building. Didn't even have to walk out onto the street."

"So how long were you on it?" asks Desiree, picking up the jack and adding it to her hand. "The heroin."

"The feds came in on me, September of 1994. They left me on the streets through that winter—watching, trying to catch me doing business. I stayed cool, but I switched over from hormones to smack because my life was over, so why not?"

"Did they ever work on you to get you to cooperate?"

"At first. While they were searching my crib, couple of them sat me down, told me how they had me dead to rights, etcetera."

Ottilla shuffles the cards and deals them out with care.

Desiree waits through the pause.

"Anyway," Ottilla finally continues, "they were telling me they had me on that other thing, and they were going on and on at me about how much time I was looking at and how they could help me but I had to want to help myself."

"That was how they came at me too," agrees Desiree. "But at that point in time I was still too zonked out on zees to understand what they were even talking about. They were like, going on and on—how much trouble I was in, blah blah. So here's how zonked I was: I thought they were on my case because I was *high*. So I was concentrating on acting normal. I wasn't even trying to talk."

"You had no idea?"

"None! At that point I was totally unaware that Danté had done any robbery, so I was just like, 'duh.'"

"When did you find out?" asks Ottilla.

"That night on the jailhouse TV. The news was on and I was like, 'Oh my God, that's Danté! That's me!'"

"I'll bet it was kind of surprising."

"*Kind of!* I almost fainted." Desiree laughs and lays down on her hand. "Canasta. Here, your deal."

Desiree writes down the score. Ottilla shuffles the cards and deals.

"But anyways," says Desiree, sorting her hand, "you were telling your story. So last I heard, they were searching your place and they didn't find anything, right? No money, even?"

"No, I kept everything in a different spot. They told me how I was looking at inside for the rest of my natural life, but I could make it easier on myself, etcetera. I just looked at them. Then they left, said goodbye, walked out. I'm like, 'What the hell was *that?'*

Ottilla studies her hand.

"But then I went to this lawyer," she continues, who had done work for the Disciples. He told me that their strategy was that they probably didn't have any slam-dunk on me, but if they left me alone and just watched and followed, they could catch me pushing. So then that would allow them to work me on the other charge--get me to plead out easier. He warned me they were going to be watching me tight so I closed down operations. I just pretty much holed up."

Desiree is totally attentive. She has stopped sorting her hand and is leaning forward. "So they were watching you but you were just staying inside all that time just doing heroin?"

"Oh, I got up and about every now and then, but I just wasn't doing any business. They did pull me over right after on 80, thinking I was making a run. I opened up the trunk—told them to go ahead."

"Were you going to Cedar Rapids?"

"No, I was on the way to the farm to see my mom, tell her I might be going away for a while. Ask her if I could FedEx her my cash."

"So was her husband still being like that?"

"Nah, he had had his first stroke by then, and he wasn't having the ability to be much of any way. My mom was taking care of him."

"So he had the nurse and she had the purse."

Ottilla laughs. "Pretty much. He had, like zero leverage anymore. He was right there in the dining room—mom had turned it into a bedroom. I didn't even step in to say hi or anything, but I talked loud so he'd know it was me in his house. I was still carrying around my hard heart back in those days. If I had a chance to do it now I'd—"

Desiree interrupts. "Okay, Tillie, not to mind me changing the subject, but can you tell me about that thing that they got you for?" She adds hastily, "You don't have to if you'd rather not. I won't tell anybody if you need to keep it private."

"I don't care if you tell anyone. I'm not hiding. I just hope you aren't going to come down on me. You know it's a homicide, right?"

"Yeah, you told me, but I was wondering some more about it," says Desiree in a casual voice as she involves herself in her hand.

"Hey, like I said, Dessie, I'm not dangerous. It wasn't like I went into some murder-rage or anything. It was just, back then the Disciples were my people, so it was just a thing I did for them. I was on assignment."

"And you had to, right? Because they ordered you?"

"No, truthfully Dessie? It wasn't like that."

"Oh, yeah, I remember how you told me that one time how you could have turned it down."

"Actually, they weren't *able* to order me because I was never a full-fledged member. I couldn't be as long as I was a girl, so that gave me another big motivation for my transition. Sounds kind of sick now—like how my big aim in my life was to become a member of an outlaw gang. But at the time they were my family—they respected me. They were good to me, you know?"

"Oh, I understand. Especially after how your mom had rejected you and all."

"They told me that they had gotten together and decided that I had leadership abilities, and after I was finished up with all my reassignment procedures, I could be a member of the Black Disciple Nation, and I could start working up in the organization. They always really encouraged me—they knew the procedure was expensive, so they were always cutting me special prices and all."

"So they didn't order you, but . . ."

"That thing they were asking me to do? That would ordinarily have been up to C-Note—he was in charge of discipline. He would have ordinarily taken care of it. But in this particular case—it was this kind of special circumstance."

Ottilla lays down a card.

"And at that point in time," she continues, "when they came to me, I was really getting into the testosterone and it was changing up my attitude. Making me aggressive. Erasing my inhibitions or whatever. So I'm like, 'Sure, why not?' I was actually kind of proud of how they were needing me."

Ottilla looks off for a moment to where a group of Jamaicans are dancing.

The landlord say your rent is late
He may have to litigate
Don't worry, be happy.

Desiree waits.

"But no, Dessie, it was on me. I could have turned them down. They'd have probably found another way around, so it's not like the actual victim would still be—you know? Whatever."

"Whatever," Desiree says, looking up over her cards at Ottilla and locking eyes with her. "You did what you had to do at the time."

"And it all worked out like it was supposed to. I mean, I understand now that in the end, if I had said no, that other person probably wouldn't be around anyway. And I would never have come to know the Lord."

Desiree turns, shielding her face with her cards, and rolls her eyes at the wall.

Ain't got no cash, ain't got no style
Ain't got no girl to make you smile

But don't worry be happy

"And then I wouldn't be in here with you, would I?" says Ottilla, reaching over to tap her wrist. "So it's all good. I don't worry; I be happy."

Desiree pulls a funny face.

"Hey, Dessie, what are you got up in there? Play your card."

CHAPTER 15

The sun is coming up, a.m. count has cleared, and a sprinkling of hardy inmates, bundled for winter, stream from their units and head for the tracks. Ottilla and Desiree emerge from Unit Two. Their matching, multicolor, crocheted hats and scarfs are incongruously bright against the washed-out brown of their prison-issue jackets. Their breath steams in the air.

"See," says Ottilla, gesturing broadly, "We almost have the track to ourselves."

"No doubt. I can see why." Desiree hunches into her coat and shivers. "What I'd like to know is, what am I doing at this ungodly hour?"

"It's not ungodly; it's godly! Look at that sunrise. Now that's a godly sunrise."

There's a growing river of orange and pink on the horizon. It twinkles on the razor wire and colors the track.

"Yeah, yeah. What's godly this time of day is me in my bed, concentrating on the inside of my eyelids."

She shivers again.

"Come on. You'll warm up. You'd be fine if you hadn't been out partying all night. So how was it?"

Dessie smiles. "It was great. It was so nice of them to do that for me. Iris got permission to close down the law library, and Emmy had stashed a shower curtain, and she printed NONVIOLENT real big in magic marker, and she hung it up. And then she blew up a whole bunch of search gloves and hung them around for balloons."

"Blown-up gloves? Sounds weird."

"No, they were actually cute. She decorated them. She glittered all up the palms and painted the fingers and everything."

"Hmm."

"You know, Tillie, after you've been down for a while, you learn to appreciate the simple things in life."

"That's simple? Balloons are simple. Blown-up rubber gloves with glitter are something, maybe. But they aren't *simple*."

"Emmy's were. Or, they were way cool, anyway. Then Iris brought chilaquiles and chips and dip and she got a couple commissary gals to drop us off ice cream. You should have come."

"How could I miss Bible study?" asks Ottilla, playfully. "We're on first *Corinthians*."

"*Woo-woo!*"

"Hey, Dessie," and Ottilla gives her a playful little shove, "don't knock it. You would have enjoyed the part where Paul was saying how women have to keep quiet in church."

"You know something, Tillie? Me keeping quiet in church? That's just never going to be an issue."

"Now don't say never, Dessie. I can see you in church just praising and singing . . ."

"And then you woke *up*."

Ottilla chuckles. They walk in companionable silence,

"But that is nice," admits Ottilla, "that they gave you the party."

"I know, huh? Iris did all my paperwork for practically free, and then she throws me a party. She's been really good to me. I wish you liked her better. She talks good about you. She's always encouraging us in our friendship."

"She makes me maybe just a little uncomfortable. But that's just me. I like that she helped you get redesignated."

"I know. Now that I'm not violent anymore, I get me my whole year off."

"But you have to make it through the drug program."

"Yeah, but I will. I don't care what their rules are over there, I'm following. I'm motivated."

"So, when will they be moving you over to the Drug Building?"

"Probably not for two or three months, unless someone gets kicked out. The beds are all filled; they just started up their new cohort."

"But you're in for sure."

"Yep. I got interviewed; they told me yesterday. I'm lucky. This one girl I knew who worked in the laundry? She was trying to get accepted but she didn't have any proof of substance abuse in her PSI, so she said how she totally had to jump through hoops, trying to get her mom to hustle some shrink to confirm she was an addict."

"Did she ever make it?"

Desiree rewraps her scarf. "Yeah, but then she fucked up and got kicked out and then they transferred her out to California."

"How'd she fu—mess up?"

"Relationship or something. But I got in, no hassle because: DWI! Which is totally weird. You get drunk in a bar and you try to drive home, but they catch you, so that makes it how you get out of prison a year early."

Ottilla chuckles. "That's the system. Got to love it."

"I'm loving this time, anyway. Iris did the math last night and with good time, etcetera, my new date is now—wait for it, folks: January 10, 1998. I am sooo short. One little year and I am so gone."

"Cedar Rapids?"

"Des Moines first for halfway house. When you do the program, they have to give you your full six months halfway. That's plus the year. So, if Iris hadn't gotten me the redesignation, my date was going to be, like, June of 1999."

"Eighteen months off. That's pretty good."

"I'm lucky. Iris told me last night that them giving me my nonviolence wasn't any sure thing. She said regional goes over your record and decides it on an individual basis."

They walk for a while in silence, their breaths steaming in the chill morning air.

"So, I'm still not quite getting it," says Ottilla. "You proved that you were an addict, but if you hadn't gotten that violence thing off your paperwork, they wouldn't have let you have any treatment for your addiction?"

"Oh, they'd have let me in to the *program*, but I wouldn't have gotten any year off. So, I would have never have even applied."

The two walk briskly, Ottilla setting the pace. Desiree gives a small skip to keep up.

"The program is supposed to be a bitch," Desiree continues, a little out of breath. "It's all these classes and meetings. They let you out of your regular job and everything, but you get a strike if you're late for a meeting or for any other tiny, little infraction—three strikes, you're out. They say it's jail inside of jail. Plus, everybody's snitching on everybody."

"Why snitching?"

"Because according to them, that's the only way you can get well."

"You're kidding!"

"No, they call snitching 'assuming a leadership position.' They say when you go to the counselors and tell on someone, you're taking the responsibility to help that other person out while in recovery."

"So," said Ottilla, "then that other person gets kicked out of treatment. How's *that* supposed to help?"

"Helps the others learn consequences? I don't know. Anyway, they say it's a selfless act of community service, or whatever."

"They got *that* dead wrong. Every snitch I ever heard was snitching to help out *themselves*. How are they trying to call that service? It's the opposite of service. It's hurting someone else for your own advantage. It's *sinful*."

"Hey, they're the experts. They're saying that's how you get cured."

"If that's the way, I'll stay sick."

They walk in silence.

"It's God that cures addictions anyway," offers Ottilla. "He cured me. And He most definitely didn't do it by having me snitch out my friends."

"*Beep beep!*"

A jogger in thermal shirtsleeves, mittens, and scarf over her headset is coming up from behind. They step away to let her pass.

"Yeah, right, whatever," says Desiree dismissively. She looks off toward the razor wire. "What time is it, anyway? They're giving out bananas. Dining hall closes at eight."

"We got time."

Desiree is silent. Her face is turned away.

Ottilla finally nudges her. "So who all was at the party?"

"It was mostly just Iris and me and Emmy," says Desiree eager for the subject change, "but then a bunch of people dropped in. We got caught up on the news. I guess Cortez? She's that little short girl with the tits that's a Unit Two orderly?"

"I have no idea."

"Anyway, she was going with this one white girl—Buzby? You probably might not know her; they call her 'Buzz-Buzz.' Anyway, Cortez found out about how Buzz-Buzz was messing with this other Spanish chick over in Unit Five, so she knew Buzz-Buzz would be pissing dirty, so she drops a revenge kite. And so the officer, just to be evil, showed Buzz-Buzz the snitch kite with Cortez's handwriting all over it. So, Buzz-Buzz, she's sitting there waiting for the test to come back, and Cortez doesn't know Buzz-Buzz knows and—Tillie? Ah, *Ti*-iillie! Earth to Tillie."

"Sorry. I was looking at the sunrise. See over there? Where it's all lavender? And then see how there's that little streak of orange?"

"I'd probably appreciate it a lot more if I didn't have to look at it through all that wire."

"The wire makes it even prettier."

"Yeah, woo-woo."

"*Beep beep.*"

The move.

"By the way, Tillie," Desiree says back on the trail, "I was mentioning to Iris about your case?" She adds quickly, "You said you didn't mind if I talked to her about it, remember?"

"I don't mind."

"It was just Iris and Emilia there, before anyone else came. Iris was saying that she didn't understand why a homicide charge went federal. She said that it would be federal only if it was, like, a hate crime. Otherwise she said it's always state unless the incident occurs on a military base or a federal park or a post office or whatever."

Ottilla is silent.

"So anyway," Desiree asks lightly, "did you commit your crime in the post office?"

Ottilla's voice turns formal. "Actually, it became a federal case because at the time of the occurrence, the victim was scheduled to act as a prosecution witness in a federal trial. So that turned it federal. "

"Oh, okay. I'll tell her that. If you don't mind."

A dozen more inmates have joined them on the track. Ottilla, silent, walks a pace removed. She's lost in the sunrise again. It's turning a spectacular golden-edged salmon.

"The actual crime," says Desiree, "it was behind snitching, right? On the Disciples?"

"Yeah."

Desiree lays a hand on Ottilla's arm. "The guy that you—you know—whatever. The victim? He wasn't any friend of yours or anything, I mean, like, did you know him?"

They walk in silence.

"It wasn't a him."

They walk in silence.

Finally, Desiree takes a deep breath and moves closer. She gives Ottilla's arm a small hug. "If you ever feel the need to talk about it, Tillie, I'm always right here. You understand that, don't you?"

"Okay, thanks." And then, breaking free and turning to her, "Hey Dessie, it's getting that time. We'd better get on over there if you want your banana."

CHAPTER 16

It's evening, and out past the compound square the tangle of wire captures glints from the setting sun. It's a little too chilly on the yard for most of the inmates to gather, but Iris and Emilia—their chins tucked inside matching crocheted scarfs—sit in quiet companionship on their bench.

They survey the scene. The dining room is closing and the two shakedown officers gather up bags of salad vegetables and move toward dumpsters.

"The prison's lovely, dark, and deep," intones Iris in mock grandiosity.

"Is getting dark," agrees Emilia amiably.

"And miles to go before I sleep."

"So, you gonna climbing over the wire?"

"And miles to go . . . Probably not tonight."

Desiree comes striding up.

"Ta da," and she ceremoniously opens one side of her coat. "Guess what I have, ladies and gentlemen, hidden here under my sweatshirt."

"Single malt scotch?" asks Iris.

"A baby!" cries Emilia.

"Ta da." Desiree reaches under her sweat pants waist band and pulls out an industrial cone of thread. It's nearly empty—an eighth-inch wrapping of beige—but Emilia squeals and snatches it.

"*Muchas-muchas!*" She cradles and rocks it and sends it air kisses.

"That's wonderful. No more us separating dental floss, huh, Emmy?"

"Careful," warns Desiree looking around and moving in.

Across the compound an officer is heading in their direction. Emilia tucks the cone under her coat and caresses the bump. "How you gonna getting it?" she asks.

"Jimenez over at laundry traded it out in exchange for if you peg up her new roomie a couple pairs of pants."

"*No problemo.*"

"She's sitting there on the sewing machine," comments Iris. "Why doesn't she peg them herself?"

"Because O'Donnell says if he catches her one more time, he'll send her back to the folding tables. I'll bring the pants over for you tomorrow."

"Good."

"Oh, and by the by, Emmy, what are you charging for thongs? Out on the streets I was trying to wear them for a little minute before I got popped and they felt really . . . weird. But now everyone's saying how panty lines are so out, and if you wear the thongs for a while you to get used to them. So now that I'm getting out early, I'm thinking I better practice up."

"Free!" exclaims Emilia. "You bringing me the panties."

"Thanks, Emmy, you're a doll. Barlow wants some too.

"You just made Barlow up a couple of them, didn't you Emmy?" asks Iris. "Did they get confiscated already?"

"Yeah, it was snoopy Wilson again shaking lockers. A male wouldn't ever have even noticed."

"It's still two ramens, one mackerel."

"Okay, I'll let her know."

Iris makes room on the bench. "Come on, sit, we need to talk."

Dessie sits.

"You're not going to want the hear this," says Iris behind her hand, "but I've got to warn you that it's starting to get out about you setting up Ferguson."

"What! Who? Who's saying it?"

"I'm not going to mention names. It's just around."

"Oh my God! No! Is it really?"

"Yeah, probably one of the guards told an inmate."

"Oh, God, no!" Dessie puts her face in her hands. "I'm going to die."

"Don't worry! I think I squelched it. I told everyone they got the wrong gal. I said yes, he got snitched but it wasn't you—it was Lydia McCormick. I said that they were having a thing, but then she ratted him to get a transfer because of her sick kid."

"Good. Whew! Did they believe?"

"Yeah, actually, they did. Because of the way she got shipped out like that. I reminded them that always, when they catch a guard with an inmate, that inmate is gone. They always ship them. I'm amazed," says Iris, lowering her voice, "how you're still here."

Desiree looks around and then leans in. "I told them I wouldn't cooperate unless I could stay," she whispers.

"Good on you. Except they don't always keep their promises."

"The warden told me I'm supposed to spread it around that she does. Except I don't know how I'm supposed to because, why am I supposed to *know* that she does? She didn't explain that part."

Iris chuckles. "The lady is not a lineal thinker. Anyway, McCormick disappeared overnight, so it made sense to everyone."

"Whew. Thanks."

"But frankly, Dessie," says Iris speaking in a normal tone, "no one wanted to think it was you anyway. You're popular, and they like to see you and Tillie together and everything. It's all around about how you two were neighborhood pals. They love it. You're kind of the compound princess these days."

Desiree blushes.

"So, what's going on with you and the big O?"

"Oh news!" says Desiree looking around. She lowers her voice. "Remember how you were wondering about how Tillie got her murder charge to go federal?"

"Yes."

"Well, she says the—whatever, the victim? Was just happening to be a witness for some big-deal federal trial that was coming up."

"Ah ha. That'll do it. Supposed to be testifying against a Disciple?"

"Exactly."

"But I wonder how she got to the guy. They usually put their witnesses in protective custody."

"I have no idea. It wasn't like she was being all anxious to talk about it or anything. But one thing she did say."

Desiree pauses.

"Yes?"

"It wasn't a guy. It was a girl."

"Oh, better and better," says Iris, clapping her hands. "You know how I love a good crime story."

"She wasn't exactly, like, bubbling all over about it."

"You'll get it out of her, Dessie."

"Yeah, she probably will tell me eventually. I remember when she was a little kid and there'd be some big thing going on with the other kids. Like someone was lifting from K-Mart or smoking pot or whatever. She'd always start out saying she shouldn't and making me promise and everything, and then she'd always tell me."

"Well, good. When she does spill it, you've got to be sure and share. By the way, has she mentioned any more about her sex change?"

"Not really. She's mostly too busy talking about Jesus. But I'll get her around."

"You know," says Iris turning to include Emilia, "I had my sister send in a book, and I was wrong about how they do that bottom operation. That procedure I was talking about with the vaginal lining?"

Desiree and Emilia nod and lean in.

"I got it mixed up. That was what they do to penises to change men into women."

"What? How?"

"They turn the penis inside out and line the new vagina with it."

"You're kidding!"

Emilia shudders violently and hides her face in Iris's shoulder while Desiree puts her hand over her mouth. "Oh. My. God," She exclaims through her fingers. "What some people will do with their bodies! What do they . . . ? Do they, like, carve a hole out up in there or something?"

"They do. It does sound a little intense."

"So why do they even *let* them? They won't let them stick powder up their nose, but it's okay if they want to turn their dicks inside out and shove them up—Jesus!"

"It's certainly extreme. I hadn't really focused on it before I started reading, and it made me start thinking how important a thing it must *be* for them."

Desiree snorts.

"No, really. I was realizing if they're willing to go through all that to have a body that matches their identity . . . I tried to imagine how they must be *yearning*."

"Yeah, well, how about them yearning to match up with the identity they are when they're high on cocaine?"

Emilia laughs.

"Dessie! I'm shocked at you. You're asking our legal system to make even a *modicum* of sense!"

"Yeah, shame on me."

"Anyway," comments Iris, "to me, Ottilla's current attitude doesn't make any *more* sense. She's believing in some God out there who put her in somebody else's body? Except now she's all happy to stay living inside it. Isn't it a little perverse to believe in a God who gets involved in your sexuality? And then who gets into punishing you for trying to change it?"

"I don't think she was actually saying that God was punishing her for *trying*," says Desiree a touch defensively. "Except it's all confusing because in her case if she had changed, she'd be punished by getting sent to Leavenworth. But I don't know if she thinks that would have been God or that would have been the system or whatever."

"I give up." Iris throws up her hands. "I just hope the poor girl—uh, *guy* gets over it."

A chilly breeze has come up and Desiree gathers her coat around her and zips it up. "Yeah, huh, whatever," she says, her chin inside the top of her zipper. "But you were talking about a man switching over to a woman. What kind of operation are they going to do on a woman?"

"The book mostly focused on the man-to-woman thing, but I guess there's a couple of ways for the other. Sometimes they construct a penis out of some forearm skin or thigh or something. But not always, because they say that just the testosterone is supposed to bulk up the clitoris. It enlarges it? So they just have to cut it loose . . . from something up in there. Which allows it to be more prominent."

"So, like, does it stick out when you're walking around?"

"I have no idea. Does Tillie's stick out?"

"Ewww, gross! I'm not even thinking about . . ."

"Is sticking out too far," reminds Emilia in a practical voice, "they not gonna let her into Danbury."

"Huh. I wonder how far is too far. You could ask her," suggests Iris.

"What? Yeah, like I'm supposed to go up and say: 'Hey Tillie, how far's your clit sticking out?' I don't think so."

"Yes, but I have faith in you, Dessie. You'll get her to talk about it."

"I'm thinking no. Tillie's kind of, delicate or whatever. Not delicate—*proper*. When she was a kid even. I would tease her, and I would try to get her to tell me the little-kid dirty jokes, but she wouldn't, and when she had to go pee she was always all, 'I have to go use the restroom.' I'm pretty sure she's never going to chit-chat me up about the size of her clitoris."

"I'm so sorry, Dessie," sighs Iris. "I guess you'll just have do your own private research."

"No! Not me!" exclaims Desiree. "No way. This bitch here? " She raises her arm up, points at the top of her head, and speaks urban. "This bitch ain't into no clit. It ain't going that way."

"How 'bout is sticking out?" suggests Emilia innocently.

"*Especially* is sticking out." Desiree cocks her head side-to-side. "This bitch? This bitch is strictly-dickly. Besides"—she continues in her own voice—"after Ferg . . . after all the other, whatever. Danté, whatever. I promised myself, no more burning coal. The loving's great, but it is so not worth it."

"But really, Dessie," objects Iris, "think about it. The Big O's more white than anything else. So you wouldn't be going that way, and she's—excuse me. *He's*— actually more *male* than anything else. So you wouldn't be going *that* way either. I was just thinking that maybe if you two could engage in a few therapy sessions it would help her—I mean *him*—to transition out of the Jesus-freak phase."

"Tillie's female, and she's black, and she just *lo-oves* her Jesus. So that's that."

"And she's totally hooked on you."

Desiree rises, shrugs, and raises her palms up helplessly. "Then the poor baby is shit out of luck."

She starts to turn away. "Hey Emmy, I'll bring Jimenez's pants over tomorrow. And next Tuesday's when I'm due for my new underwear issue for my thongs."

"Gracias for my new thread."

"Think about you and Big O," says Iris to Desiree's back.

Desiree doesn't turn around.

"Yeah-yeah-yeah."

CHAPTER 17

There's been a January thaw. It's clear tonight and unseasonably warm. Most of the inmates are outdoors taking advantage of the weather, and the recreation building isn't as crowded as usual. On the court are a half-dozen inmates playing pick-up basketball. In the far corner a group of Spanish matrons in headsets, arms folded and out, faces raised dreamily, eyes closed, sway and slide.

Off to the left, a tall inmate surrounded by a group of fans sits on a front-row bleacher tuning a guitar. She has a shadow mustache, and her bleached thatch of hair is short at the sides. The pant legs of her sweat suit are tucked into prison-issue high tops.

Boots in the gym are against regulation—tennis shoes only—but the two recreation specialists on duty tonight overlook the guitar-player's infraction. They favor the compound boys. They join the rest of the staff's constant complaints about the new population. They hark back to the golden days when Danbury was full of *real* inmates.

Just now, one is commenting out of the corner of his mouth about the bounce of an overweight ball player. They have positioned themselves where they can also keep an eye on the weight room next door—the place where conflict is most likely to arise. Sadly, for the past year what conflict arises, arises high-pitched and nonphysical.

Added to the sad dearth of male-on-male competition, the gym has been reduced to a social area. Tonight in the middle of the bleachers is a tightly gathered group of Asian women pulling strands of yarn from crocheted bags, fingers flashing, laughing, talking in their own language.

A group of blue-black village Africans are easily distinguished from their American cousins by their darker complexions and by their formal, intonated English. Just now they're discussing the Nigerian penal system.

"Is very much more superior than this prison, Danbury. Ten thousand naira—fifty dollar, you pay, you will be a free person."

"My uncle in Bama Town—he is the one they say kill his cousin? He is being a free person for eight thousand naira."

"O-ooo!"

"O-ooo! Bama Town prison is one A-plus prison."

Ottilla and Desiree, alone in conversation, are perched up in one of the lofty corners.

"Did they just give you the works and let you figure it out?"

"No, that first month I had to go down to the doctor's office to get the injections. Then they decided my reactions were okay, and they taught me how to fix myself."

"So how long did it take to start working?"

"I started seeing the changes right away."

"Changes like what?"

"Like I started getting muscled up—my bones started to get thicker. I got taller. My feet grew a couple of sizes."

Desiree sits close to Ottilla, wrapped in attention. "Wow! Just a couple little shots can do that for you?"

"Yeah. Testosterone is wicked."

"So you weren't always the bohunk, huh?"

Ottilla reddens slightly and laughs. "Naw, I used to be a flimsy little thing."

"Then you must have shrunken up from when I remembered. You were a big girl back then."

"Yeah, I actually always was, but the meds grew me a couple of inches."

"Really? Like, how soon after you started?"

"I was noticing changes just after that first month. My skin started getting, you know, thicker? I was starting to get bigger pores. I'd look at my hands and my knuckles would have gotten bigger just, like, overnight it seemed like. Creases in them and everything."

"Okay," says Desiree giggling, "so first you got the new knuckle-creases."

"No, actually, funnier than that. First thing I saw happening was my toes. I was starting to grow hair on them."

"No! Hairy toes? So you got a sex change on your knuckles and your toes."

"Hey, don't laugh, " Ottilla says, in mock indignation, "It was a big deal."

"Okay, knuckles and toes. So, then what?"

"Seemed like after a couple a months—you got to remember, Dessie," Ottilla becomes serious, "all this was happening before I found God. I wouldn't have ever tried to do it if I'd known Him."

Desiree stretches out her legs and pigeons her toes and examines her tennis shoes.

"But anyway, I was building up new muscle mass every day, it seemed like. Veins were popping out on my arms. Hair on my legs. Beard. My shoulders got wider. My voice got deeper."

She has Desiree's attention again. "So how much of all that went away after you stopped?"

"Most of it. My height and my bones didn't go back. I've still got the hands and feet."

Ottilla stretches fingers and makes a fist.

Desiree pokes her. "What about the hairy toes?"

"Hairy toes had to go."

"Oh, that's just so sad. What about all your female, you know, your parts?"

"By then I had the money together from, you know—my business? Except the docs wanted me to wait on my bottom operation until I had grown into my changes some more. But after a couple of months they decided I would be ready for my top."

Ottilla pauses and looks away.

"So you got the top done…" prompts Desiree."

"Actually, I had to postpone, and then it took a while to get back qualified for my top surgery because the doctors were assuming that I was postponing because I was having second thoughts. Like I was wanting to back out or whatever? And I couldn't very well explain it was for a job I had to do."

"So you told them . . ."

"That I had a family situation. I had quit my therapist as soon as she okayed me for surgery, but then she got called back into the picture and she knew I wasn't telling the whole story, except she couldn't really go out on a limb and tell them that I was emotionally prepared either. So they all decided I'd better wait until I was totally committed, blah, blah, blah."

Ottilla stares off onto the basketball court.

"So why was it really that you had to postpone?"

Ottilla replies without taking her eyes off the ball game. "The Disciples needed me to do this thing for them. Which it probably isn't right for me to talk about right at this minute."

"Yeah?" prods Desiree.

"Well, actually, it was the thing that got me in here." Ottilla looks down between her feet, inspecting the gym floor through the bleacher slats.

Desiree moves closer and nestles Ottilla's arm.

"You don't have to talk unless you want, but it might make you feel better. We've all done shit in our lives, Tillie."

Ottilla sighs. "Yeah, I know and I wasn't acting out of rage or hatred or anything. It was an assignment. And I probably would have tried to back out, but after I'd gotten started transitioning—after the hormones kicked in and all? That was about the time they came to me, and by that time it felt, like, 'I'm on it. I got this one,' you know?"

"No. Tell me."

"I had never met the top brass before. I'd just seen them around. But they called me in. They had this apartment up on the top floor of Robert Taylor."

"Robert Taylor?"

"That was the projects where they operated out of. I heard they got it all torn down now. Anyway, they had gotten me up there and they told me the wolves was at their door, and they had to make a move and they were thinking I might could contribute. They had come up with a plan but they were needing me to make it happen. And I listened to them, and the testosterone came up on me with an attitude, you know? So when they presented it to me, I was more into like, 'Yea-ah. Got to be done. Let's do it.'"

Desiree snuggles closer.

"I hate to tell you this, but at that point in my life I took it like a compliment—I was real proud that they came to me, because it was the first time I had gotten recognition by leadership, and I got caught up in the adventure. It sounded like, you know, *fun*."

She looks down at Desiree, who is looking up with admiration.

"I knew it was wrong, kind of. But, it wasn't *really*, because I had thrown my loyalty in with the Disciples and they were telling me it had to happen. Plus, I was already living outlaw. I mean, I was slinging and at that time in my life, slinging was, like, normal. Know what I mean? I mean *I* was; everyone I knew was. I'd come up with my mom doing it. So like, in the eyes of the law, drug dealing was wrong, but it didn't *feel* wrong. Or not as long as I was honest and didn't deal dirty—come up wrong on anybody or anything. At that time it felt like who was being a good citizen was the guy who was being an honest dealer."

Ottilla is no longer speaking distantly and Desiree is all attention.

"Back then I'd think about it—this was when I was in therapy before I started my reassignment. And I remember realizing how citizens would say, 'When you're dealing drugs, you're ruining lives.' And I'd think about that, and then I'd go down to the Stop 'n' Shop and I'd see all those ruined old guys, lined up in there, buying their pack of Kools and their bottle of Night Train and I'd think, that clerk in there is slinging junk the same as me. We aren't doing any different. We're both clerks."

"Except you were making more money," comments Desiree lightly.

"Yeah, but it was me taking the risks. Besides, I didn't flash. I lived quiet. I rented a little efficiency in a building down a few blocks from the projects. I was driving an old '82 Buick, all rusted out."

"O-ooh *slick*. A *Bu-ick*!"

Ottilla laughs. "Hey, girl, be easy. At first the Disciples, they were like you. They were always on to me about my ride, chiding me how I'm rolling in a granny-go-to-church. I'd tell them, 'yeah,' I'd tell them, 'so you in your shiny new Explorers and your Lincolns? How many times you getting your asses pulled over? Now, me? Not ever. I'm rolling 80--Chicago to Iowa--couple times a week, and I *never* been stopped.'"

"Yeah, huh."

"Actually, I always had on my good-hair wig and a lace top and all, but I considered it was the Buick that kept me moving on my way."

"Yeah," Desiree contributes, "after Danté went out and bought his '90 Eldorado? He was always getting pulled over."

"See? Anyway, the Disciples, they come round to respect how I'm willing to go humble for my business. But the truth was, I was trying to save up my money for my surgery."

"How much?"

"Forty to fifty. Over and above the therapy sessions and the hormones and everything which in and of itself was up in the thousands."

"Whew!"

"And remember, I wasn't moving kilos or anything—I was just o-zing—maybe make seven, eight hundred a run."

"So, when did you decide to get your change done? How old were you?"

"I was eleven, actually."

"Eleven!"

"Yeah, it was the year before you moved away. I saw this program on channel two about transsexuals and it made me have this feeling come over me. Like everything shifted inside."

"Channel two? Like public-broadcasting channel two?"

"Yep, don't laugh."

"So PBS changed your life."

"Yeah, I know. Funny, huh. Before I saw the special, I had always known that I was a boy inside ever since I could remember. But up until then, me thinking that felt kind of normal? Or whatever? My mom, she never made any big deal over me not being girlie—hating on frilly dresses and dolls and stuff. She let me be, you know? And in my feelings I was different anyway because I was black but I never did meet my dad, and mom was white, and everyone I knew was white, and I talked white. So I always sort of felt like I was white. Even though I wasn't. It was like the same thing. I felt like I was a boy, even though I wasn't."

Desiree nods. "I can totally see that."

"So I had always got those two things about myself mixed up, you know? I never was *anyway* who I actually *was*. So feeling like a boy was just another part of the deal. Or something."

"Yeah, I remember now!" Desiree laughed. "For a while there you kept insisting your name was Max. You were making everyone call you Max."

Ottilla laughed too. "Yeah, my Max phase. You were the first one go along. You would see me coming, and you would call like, 'Hey, Ma-aax. Let's go get some Frosty Nerds.'"

"Oh, God, Frosty Nerds. I forgot Frosty Nerds."

"And don't forget Cry Baby Extra Sours."

Desiree laughs lovingly and puckers her mouth. "I'm still tasting."

"Anyway, you started calling me Max, so then everyone did. Mom even went along. That was the summer before I went into fifth grade. Except then, school and my teacher? She wasn't having any part of *that*."

"Yeah, I remember you dropped the whole thing and we went back to 'Tillie.' But then you saw PBS?"

"Yeah, and it gave me this big shift in my feelings. The program—it talked about how some people knew that they were born inside of the wrong body. That they were, like, actually a different sex than their body was. They were saying how some Asian cultures explained it through a faulty reincarceration incident or whatever. Like a male soul had messed up and gotten stuck inside a female body by mistake."

"Wow."

"I know. That part really blew my mind. And they talked about the surgery and they showed before-and-after. They mostly just had men-to-women, but there was this one woman-to-man. That was the first time I separated it in my mind—my skin-color identity thing and my sex-identity thing. And I got this big realization: I realized I couldn't change the color of my skin, but I could change my gender."

Desiree nods.

"So from then on I vowed to myself that when I grew up, I was going to get a sex change. Because I thought at that time, that was the only way I was ever going to feel right. But course then I found God, so--."

"Wow," interrupts Desiree," I had no idea back then that you were going through all that. You seemed like such a happy little kid."

"Yeah, I always was happy whenever you were around." Ottilla shoves her playfully.

Desiree smiles.

"No. I was usually happy enough. But then after I turned teen and I got the idea in my head that I was born into the wrong body, it started making me discontented. Like every little problem I blamed on my mixed-up, identity. It felt like life was going to be wonderful after I got myself switched over. So all through high school I had a mission: I was going to turn eighteen, and I was going to get my hormone therapy, and then I'd get my reassignment surgery—uh, my *confirmation* therapy. My shrink, she always told me to say 'confirmation.'"

"When did you start seeing a shrink?"

"Just right after I turned eighteen, when I moved to Chicago. I researched and found out that I had to get the changeover okayed by a qualified therapist before any endocrinologists—that's the hormone doctor—would give me any hormones. So I found this shrink that specialized in transgender."

"Just transgender? Were there enough of you guys?"

"Clients. Yeah, I guess. I *think* she just did us. I'd see other clients in the waiting room. Every one of them were men trying to go female. I could look at them and tell."

"So what did she council you about?"

Ottilla laughs. "Boy, she sure wanted me to stick with my gender issues. Nothing else about my life. She charged two-hundred a session, so when I'd pull her out my cash instead of my checkbook or my plastic or anything she always looked uncomfortable. She was always real careful to stay away from my current occupation—like how I was making my living and whatnot."

"She didn't want to know if it was dirty money."

"Yup. First we did my childhood—like my gender issues. How did my mom deal with it? How were the other kids? Then my adolescence and then I graduate high school—bang. Abrupt halt."

Desiree laughs.

"But it was all good because I wasn't going to her for any emotional counseling or anything. I just had to get the right shrink to do the right paperwork so I could get my gender right—start my transition. Uh, *confirmation*."

"What was the conformation consisting of?"

"The hormones were the next step."

"You told me about physical changes but you were kind of saying you were mentally changed as well?"

There's a pause. Ottilla looks down at her feet and goes silent.

Desiree waits.

Finally, "Maybe I'll want to talk about it later."

From the court comes the sound of female exhortation and the dribble of a ball. The Asian women laugh and chatter. Down on the bottom row the guitar player's fans are sitting around her on the floor, swaying, listening to a plaintive county correctional lament.

The hookers are cursing,

The drunk drivers snore.

The shoplifter's crying on this

cold jail house floor,

I need you now, Momma like never before.

Rock me to sleep, Momma,

Rock me to sleep.

Desiree breaks the silence. "So you were, uh, eleven when you decided?" asks Desiree. "Before you were a teenager, even?"

"Yeah, from that time, after the TV program, that was all I ever wanted—to get myself turned into a male. I had started hooking up with the Disciples before I graduated even, and I was always saving up for my surgery. Except sh—stuff kept happening.

"Like?"

Mom started programming like I told you—doing AA. And she was on my case because she had decided that she had changed up her lifestyle so I was supposed to change up my lifestyle, and I didn't trust her not to go through my stuff anymore, so I kept my savings in the trunk of my Camaro."

"You were driving a Camaro? Cool."

"It was just an old beat up '69 ZL1 that I got for a couple hundred. Except then, bang, it gets stolen. Right off of Metro High parking lot."

"Oh wow! Did the police ever get it back?"

"I never even called it in. I had weed in the trunk along with all my savings so I was too paranoid. I just went down to MV and took my name off it."

"So there went all your money?"

"Yeah, whoever finally jimmied open the trunk—made his day. So that was my first setback. Then this one time after I had moved to Chicago, my apartment got busted in and they took the safe. So I found this other spot to keep my new safe in, and I had to start again. Then another time I invested big on a shipment that went south, and I had to start again."

Down below, the singer belts the chorus.

Rock me to sleep, I remember the joy,

Curling up

On your lap

In that old Lazy Boy.

The group sings along.

I was safe

In a love

They can never destroy.

Rock me to sleep, Momma,

Rock me to sleep.

"My Cedar Rapids people—it took me a couple of years to find anyone with any discipline. The ones I had at first, they were perpetually broke so I had to front them if I wanted them to move anything for me, and they were always coming up wrong with the money, doing the excuse thing like they just got robbed or they're still trying to collect or whatever."

"Yep, that's Cedar Rapids."

"I was always having to lecture, 'First rule, you don't front a front,' and they were always like, 'Yeah, we know.' Except it would be ninety-seven degrees out there and them with their long sleeves on."

"Long sleeves?"

"Covering up their tracks."

"Duh. Trying to hide that's why the money wasn't right?"

"Yeah, I had to eat a lot of their fu—excuse me, their mess ups—until then I found a tight connect."

"So who was that? Would it be anyone I would know?"

COUNT TIME. CLEAR THE COMPOUND. CLEAR THE
COMPOUND, LADIES. TIME FOR EVENING COUNT.

Ottilla and Desiree rise and begin to step down the bleachers.

"Probably not. She lived over in Hiawatha. She had a couple little kids, didn't party—just a little weed was all—and she had tight connections inside Rockwell Collins. Then she got up next to Quaker Oats. She moved a lot of product. They weren't drug testing yet."

"Yeah, I remember how all those union factory guys, didn't they just *love* their cocaine? It was their big-time high-life or whatever. Pulling out their little vials, pouring lines on the back of their hands like they were Hollywood."

"Yeah," agrees Ottilla with a laugh, "those were the customers all right. They had already gotten their campers and their speed boats, so now it's like, they were moving on up to cocaine."

"Yeah, they all just thought they were so cool. Especially when they managed to get next to Danté. He was always dissing them—treating them like dirt. Plus, then they'd see me with, they'd want to flip out. But all's they could do was like, nadda—zip—because of how bad they needed to keep their cool connect. Me and Danté, we would always just *laugh*."

The two of them leave the rec and walk out into the compound night, back to Unit Two.

"Good times in C.R.," says Ottilla.

"Good times in C.R."

Desiree hugs Ottilla's arm.

CHAPTER 18

"All's I'm doing is telling you what got passed on to me, know what I mean?"

The afternoon stand-up count had just cleared, and Ottilla and Rogo sit down—Ottilla on her bed, Rogo on the toilet bowl.

"It's just not true," Ottilla is insisting. "Who did you ever hear it from?"

"Ms. Asia B," answers Rogo with a show of reluctance, "but she say, don't put out my name on it. She whoop me up-side, I go catching her up into any kind of messy."

"Dessie's not a snitch," says Ottilla loudly. "I know her. I've known her for years, and I know she's a hundred percent stand-up."

"Shh! Okay, Asia B just said to warn you, so that's all's I'm doing. She say, warn your roomie to take it cautious, if you two be starting up a thing."

"We aren't starting up a thing. We're friends, and that's the way it is, and Dessie is not a snitch."

"Hey don't get mad at me. I was just repeating—"

"So who's she supposed to be snitching on? She's not up in any mix; she doesn't know any dirt to snitch. Let's see, only thing she knows is she know somebody with nail polish. She's been getting her toenails done. But why would she drop any cop-out on her polish lady? She'd be dropped it on herself. She wouldn't do it anyway."

"Yeah, you probably right on that."

"She was just saying how lucky it was she didn't have any polish on when they stripped her out for seg. They'd have been all over her case trying to get her to give them up the name."

"Ms. Asia wasn't referring to no little contraband."

"Well then, what?"

Out in the common area an officer has come in and thrown a crate of mail on the desk. "Mail call." He starts to call names. "Jackson—Estella—Gust—Gustafson . . ."

There's a general exit for the common area.

"No really," insists Ottilla. "Who was she supposed to be snitching on?"

"I better ain't say, know what I mean? You be going to go right back to Dessie and then my ass is in it."

"I won't repeat it to her. Tell me the rest."

"You gots to promise. Word?"

"Word."

"Word?"

"Word."

Okay, Asia B, she say it's all over the compound that Dessie was messing with that one guard? That one got his ass marched off? Word is, she was doing him, and then staff got to her while she was in seg, and she rolled and set him up."

Ottilla laughs in relief. "Whew! You had me going there for a little minute." She laughs again. "If you're saying *that's* the story? I know *that's* bunk. Not even. Not even one little tiny—" Ottilla squeezes her thumb and index finger. "Whew!" She wipes her forehead.

"You promised not to tell her," warns Rogo.

"I won't. I won't. I won't say a thing. I wouldn't ever want to repeat something like that back at her *anyway*. She'd be, oh, man she'd be wigging out, charging around, trying to find out who started it."

"That's why you can't be criminating Ms. Asia B. Know what I mean?"

"Munoz —Schaefer —O'Neill."

"Hey Rogo, no problem."

"Word?"

"Cortez¬¬—Garcia."

"Word."

Ottilla shakes her head in wonder.

"I am telling you, the rumors that get started up in this place."

CHAPTER 19

Next evening, on the compound square beside Unit Six, a pair of older Spanish women are dancing, their eyes heavenward in ecstasy. Down past rec, a trio of African Americans with pelvises thrust forward and thighs spread, dance-play at shimming one another off the sidewalk. Outside of the Drug Building a group of inmates are gathered to gossip. They laugh at a ponytail speedwalking past, belting out:

Been a lo-oong, lonely, lonely, lonely, lonely, lonely—her voice quavering out into the night, the singer oblivious inside her headset.

Ottilla and Desiree join the parade of inmates walking the square. "Just a couple of rounds," says Ottilla. "I promised Tamika and Alicia and this other gal—I forgot her name—that I'd work over their fractions with them. They're taking their GED test tomorrow."

"Okay, that's cool. It's Thursday, I'm going up to watch *Friends* pretty soon, anyway."

"Every time I look in the TV room it's all Spanish momies watching soaps. I didn't think that TV up there even knows how to *speak* English "

"It does on Thursday white-girl night. Last week Phoebe was giving hair cuts and messing everybody up, and us inmates were all saying she ought to go over here and work in the beauty shop."

"We wouldn't want you missing *that*."

"No, we certainly would not."

Ottilla picks up the pace and Desiree does a half-skip. "Hey, Tillie, you were telling me yesterday about how you started in on your hormones and they changed up your attitude for behind when the Disciples wanted you."

"Yeah, but I was thinking last night, later after count? I hadn't really brought God into it when I was telling you, and that was the whole point of the story."

Desiree rolls her eyes.

"I mean, later," Ottilla explains, "after He came to me and I started knowing Him and everything? At that point I understood that He had made me exactly the way I was supposed to be. And it hadn't been His part of His plan for me to try to change myself."

"Just a sec." The two are coming up on Iris and Emilia's bench. "I got to talk to Iris." Desiree steps away and Ottilla waits for her.

"I'm not just *saying* that," apologizes Desiree to Iris. "They really were out."

"Oh, of course," says Iris. "I believe you. No hurry. Any time they get it back in stock."

Desiree returns to Ottilla. "I owe Iris a foundation," she explains. "I think it must have been for Emilia. She was wanting 'medium suntan,' and I don't thinks Iris even wears makeup. Except commissary had run out."

The two continue their walk.

"Those Colombian women," comments Ottilla, "they sure can spend the time getting their faces ready in the morning."

"I know, huh. When I lived over in five where they had public restrooms and all? You could almost never get a mirror in the mornings. The Spanish totally bogarted. And to tell you the truth. I couldn't see how it helped them out that much anyway. Sometimes they'd end up putting it on so thick, they'd almost be looking like clowns. I'd wanted to say, 'La—dies, who are you trying to impress? You're in the pen-i-*ten*-tiary.'"

"I suppose it's a culture thing."

"Yeah, but it bugs me how they get so superior about it. I had this one Colombian tell me once, I swear she was acting all sympathetic and all"—Desiree assumes an unconvincing accent—"You Norte ladies, you could be pretty too if you would just *try*."

Desiree snorts and does another skip. Ottilla slows her pace.

"Not all of them," offers Ottilla. "Emilia doesn't seem like that."

"No, Emilia is a total sweetheart."

"Plus, I love the Spanish who convert to Protestant. They really get into worshiping. When we're all together like that with the Holy Spirit coming down, we're all sisters."

"Whatever."

They walk in silence.

Desiree indicates up ahead. "Speaking of sisters."

The Fatback Sisters have taken over the sidewalk and are bouncing to their headsets, shouting out fragments of song together:

Hard like an erection,
Hard like an erection.

They stop singing to concentrate on their headset, a finger in the air as they wait, wait, belt out:

I'm fuckin' the sluts and hoes,
The bigger the butts the tighter the clothes.

Ottilla and Desiree maneuver their way around.

"You know something, Dessie?" says Ottilla. "Like I was trying to say just now, I was thinking last night after we talked, and I realized I had maybe represented my past situation wrong. I might have given you the impression that transgendering was a good thing. I was representing the way that I'd seen it at the time, when in actuality I came to understand it was like, my original sin. It was what led to everything else."

"Original? So like what you're saying is, you would never have gotten into any big-time dealing if it hadn't been for you wanting a sex change?"

Ottilla sighs. "You know, I really wonder about that. Looking back, it seems that way. It seems like that was what drove me and all, but I can't say for sure. I don't know what I would have done otherwise. When I first turned senior, Mom told me I should go in and ask the guidance counselor about college scholarships. I was really good at math, you know? And I was trying to tell the counselor that, but it was like he didn't hear it. He just gave me a bunch of college brochures on women's athletic programs."

"Oh God, so was Koslosky still there?"

"Yep. That would be him."

"He was totally worthless. He couldn't even have guidance-counseled Einstein. He'd have probably put him into appliance repair."

Ottilla laughs.

"Plus," Desiree adds, "he was always trying to get next to you so he could brush against you and shit."

"He never tried to brush up against me," says Ottilla, and they both laugh.

Halfway down the compound circle a couple of inmates have started jogging, trying to clear the sidewalk for themselves. The night fills with indignant protests.

"Hey, no running!"

"No running on the compound!"

LADIES, SLOW IT DOWN.

NO RUNNING ON THE COMPOUND.

"I'd like to *think*," Ottilla goes on, "that I'd have done something else if I hadn't wanted to buy my sex change, but I can't really say that for sure. I remember back then I was getting into my black gangsta act. It gave me stature in high school."

"You was the man."

"Yeah, I was the man. So I already had the role model. Then mom—with her recovery and all—she made me kind of think: 'You think I'm bad? Okay, I'll *be* bad.' So I can't truthfully say it was all behind the sex change."

Desiree and Ottilla have rounded the compound and come up behind the Fatback Sisters again, who are facing each other. They've switched over to a playground chant.

Shimmy shimmy cocoa pop

Shimmy-shimmy, rock-rock

I like coffee, I like tea

I like the boy and

The boys like me!

"What I do know now," Ottilla continues, "is that it was wrong to rebelling against the body that God put me in. When I finally got my shrink to give the okay and I started injecting the hormones? The effect on me was—it was really bad. Like it was turning me wicked. And the worst thing was, I liked it. It felt really good."

"Like how?"

"Like I started getting all these cocky, arrogant-energy feelings. I'd start wanting to strut around, get in peoples faces. Like people on the streets, disrespecting and getting in my way? I wouldn't have even noticed before. Now I'm getting into these, like, anger flashes. Fantasize about hurting people, imagine punching them out."

"Wow."

"And before, if I'd get really upset I'd want to cry. Now I'd get angry; I'd want to punch out a wall. And the thing was, all those changes were feeling like they were a step up."

"A step up?"

"Yeah. From the place I'd been at before. I felt like I was really improving myself."

"Huh. Did it affect your sexuality or whatever? Your sex drive?"

"Big time. I mean, it wasn't just how it made me hornier, which it did. It brought my attitude over to a whole nother place. I started thinking of women—I mean, it's not just that I thought about them more often—but I thought about them *different*. I mean, the way they even looked started changing."

"Wow, really? Like how?"

"Yeah, they got soft—softer or sexier or something? But at the same time, they were more like *things*. Before, I'd see a pretty girl, and I'd be wanting to talk to her. Thought she'd be interesting to get to know. Now all's I'd want to do was just jump on her, grab her, turn her into my sex slave."

"Wow! That's intense."

"And it felt really good. It felt like this was how I was supposed to feel—all ruthless and powerful and whatever. I understood things I never could figure out before. Like how come men would want so much to be rulers and kings and sh— stuff."

"*Kings?*"

"Yeah, kings. Like in history class. Teachers would actually act like it was okay or amusing or something, how those ruler guys used to go out and kill because they were securing their power. You know, like it was perfectly okay to kill—even your own *family* members—if the *reason* you were killing them was that it could make you the king."

"Yeah, I guess so."

"The teachers would kind of smile about it, and I wouldn't ever be able to understand. Like, why would you want to go out and kill your own people for *that*? Now if it was money? *That* maybe I could understand a little bit—wanting to have more stuff. I mean, don't get me wrong. I personally wasn't behind possessions badly enough to go out and kill anybody, but I could see it."

"Yeah, I guess I can too."

"But to go out and kill your own *folks*? Like your *brother* or something? Just so you could get to be the ruler over a country? I mean, what was *that* about? Ruling a country didn't sound like something you'd even want to do. It just sounded like *work*."

Desiree laughs. "But then after you started shooting the hormones, you wanted to be a king?"

"I could *understand* wanting. I mean the power rush and whatever—being the number one? Having everyone in the whole nation under your control? I got it."

Desiree and Ottilla come up on the Sisters again. They've gathered a small audience. Desiree and Ottilla make their way around it.

Up, down, side to side
Up, down, shake a little ride
P.O.P. spells POP!

"So up until that point," says Ottilla, "I'd been totally laid back as far as my position with the Disciples. But after the testosterone kicked in, I started getting ambitious, you know?"

"No. Like how?"

"Like I was wanting to pick up the pace. Stake out my own territory. I started thinking about handing Iowa off, getting assigned a high rise. Iowa was slow—my market there was still mostly powder, you know? And by then the high rises had gone rock. Which shoved the action up a couple-notches."

"Yeah, I know. Danté was one of the first in C.R. to get into moving crack. I mean, some of his people were still basing and cooking it up themselves. But those rockers, they could be a trip— out of control, begging for fronts, bringing over their shop-lifts all the time and shit. Danté had to come down hard."

"I know. Before my hormones, I thought crack wasn't my area. I mean, we're talking mommas taking food out of their babies' mouths, selling their car seats and playpens and everything. I didn't want any part. But the chemicals started getting me ambitious—more territorial—wanting more action."

"How long after you started?"

"Close to a year."

"So what did you do about it?"

"The Disciple leadership, they heard how I was getting restless and they called this conference. I wasn't there; they just told me. And they decided I could be a full-fledged member after I'd finished my transition. They said that while I was still a female—well, they said 'bitch'—they couldn't give me my own buildings or anything because all the other bitches would be saying, 'if she can do, why can't we?' So they came and told me they decided that after I'd gotten my transition completed they'd make me full-fledged and they'd start upping me my responsibility, see how I played."

"But you said you were looking more male by then. Couldn't you just pass?"

"No, I had big boobs. I'd try to strap them down, but they were too big to hide. I'd been putting it off a little bit—getting my top operation. Maybe I was apprehensive or whatever? But by that point I'd been long enough on my hormones, and I told the endocrinologist I was ready."

Desiree stops and turns to Ottilla.

"But Tillie, you just said the other day that you had to postpone the operation because of the Disciples."

Ottilla sighs. "Yeah, that's another whole part of the story."

Desiree waits.

"Hey, what time is it?" Ottilla grabs Desiree's wrist and looks at her watch. "Ten after! I promised the GED girls I'd be over in education. I'm late already."

"Now, Tillie, You've got to promise you'll finish telling."

"Can't promise— "

"Til-llie!"

"Okay. Promise."

CHAPTER 20

Warden Coleman is in her office, talking on the telephone. Her voice rings with only barely suppressed joy. "Yes, indeed, and my immediate priority is the well-being and safety of my population. First I get to know them, let them know I'm on their side so as to immediately establish a climate of cooperation....

"Why thank you, sir. I understand that my methods may be considered just a little bit unorthodox in certain quarters. But I do not believe in keeping my inmate relationships at arm's length. When I'm given a new assignment, I hit the ground running in that I immediately begin to build mutual trust.

"Right you are, sir, and because of my efforts at building trust, my inmates are uniquely willing, I believe, to work with me in *achieving* that safe and secure environment....

"Why thank you, sir. Coming from you, that means a lot to me."

As the warden hangs up the phone, there is a light rap on the door and the captain's black face appears at the office door window. He opens the door and steps aside to allow Desiree to enter. She comes in hesitantly.

"Ah, Captain Carter? This won't take long. Don't go too far away. Why, hello Ms. Johansson, sit down. You happened to arrive at just the right moment."

The warden looks at her phone fondly. "That was Deputy Direc—no names." She holds up a forestalling hand. "I'm not going to mention any names. I'll just say, that was a *big* name. I'll leave it at that. But I can tell you that individual was extremely impressed with the changes we are making here and the job we are doing."

The warden gently adjusts the position of her desk phone. Her cheeks have flushed. The color picks up the mauve in her designer scarf.

"This is coming right out of DC," she confides, leaning over and inviting Desiree to share in the excitement. "The BOP is instituting a reemphasis in policy. The director—and let me add that he has the encouragement of his congressional committee—the director is actively seeking to ascertain and to bring to the forefront any and all issues of inmate safety."

The warden's long earrings vibrate along with the purple and gold beads of her extensions. Desiree pulls her attention away from them and focuses on her lap.

"This institution no longer intends to turn a blind eye to abusive behavior on the part of bad-apple correctional officers. Few as they might be. And just now—as you walked in—it was the deputy director on the phone thanking me for the work that I'm doing."

Desiree scratches at a speck on the leg of her uniform.

"Ms. Johansson, I'm glad you let me know you wanted a one-on-one but let me take the opportunity to thank you again for your willingness to put yourself out on the front line, so to speak. To help assure that other women in this institution will never be made to suffer the kind of abuse that you suffered. What you did took courage and we appreciate it."

Desiree's looks up. Her eyes shift uncomfortably.

"Ah,' continues the warden, "I understand that your BOP security redesignation came right on through?"

Desiree nods.

"See, we keep our promises. And I have to emphasize, Ms. Johansson, that this was a redesignation that *probably* could not have occurred without a little head wind from this office. Regional was very impressed when I told them about the way you had so courageously stepped forward. They agreed that the kind of leadership you displayed deserves recognition. And because of that, they made a decision to manipulate policy. Let's just say that you went that extra mile for us and we are going that extra mile for you."

The warden smiles and tilts her head inquiringly. "Now what's the little something on your mind?"

"I've been kind of flipping out," answers Desiree, "over what's going to be happening to that video. It totally freaks me to think of me on there while a whole bunch of people are watching me."

"That tape is in the hands of the prosecution, Ms. Johansson, but as I emphasized from the beginning, your face is blanked out and there are no other distinguishing features. I personally had that tape redacted before it was handed over and I can assure you, your identity is secure."

The Warden takes off her pink-framed glasses and smiles at Desiree with maternal fondness. Desiree remains silent but she doesn't look entirely convinced.

"Now if you would indeed be required to testify." admits the warden, picking up her glasses and twirling them. "If the case ever went to trial—but I've been assured that because of *your* effort in coming forward and cooperating, a trial is not going to happen. As we speak," The Warden taps her watch with a long purple fingernail, "Correctional Officer Ferguson—uh, correction: *former* Correctional Officer Ferguson—and the district attorney are plea-bargaining. So as I promised from the beginning, your identity in this will be kept entirely confidential."

"Thank you, Warden Coleman," says Desiree looking down. She spreads her fingers and talks to her nails. "I just have to tell you, it gives me the creeps every time I think about me on that tape with everybody sitting there, watching."

"I understand your concern, Ms. Johansson, and I can assure you that you have nothing to fret over." The Warden leans forward. "Now Ms. Johansson, again, I want to thank you, but I also want to find out if there is anything else we can do to make this reentry of yours more comfortable."

Desiree looks confused.

"Here, back into the general population," explains the warden. "You'll be moving over to the Drug Building, but until then, if a bed opens up somewhere else, would you like us to find more comfortable housing for you? I understand that Unit Two can get just a little bit nasty up in there."

"No, I'm fine in Two as long as I'm in there where I don't have to have any roommate."

"Fine. I'm sure we'll be able to keep you in that situation, Ms. Johansson. We can't give you an absolute guarantee, but we can certainly try. And in the meantime, I'd like to remind you that if you see or hear of other situations on this compound that are threatening to the quality of life and safety for you ladies, my door is always open. Just drop me a cop-out again—here take a couple of forms with you." She slides a few sheets across the desk. "I assume that we're probably both a just a little bit interested in keeping communications on the down-low."

Desiree nods and folds her paperwork.

"Ain't nobody's business but our own, right, Ms. Johansson?"

Desiree nods carefully and the warden rises.

"Again, I want to thank you—not just in the name of administration, but in the name of the entire inmate population—for stepping forward to help us keep all you ladies in a safe and secure environment. Ms. Johansson, let's be certain that this line of acquaintanceship is ongoing, shall we? If you see any other behavior that you find disturbing."

"Uh, okay."

Warden walks around to the office door. "Captain Carter? Oh, there you are. I believe this young lady needs an escort."

CHAPTER 21

"Ra-aags. Rags for sale. Anybody want to buy any rags?"

Desiree, in uniform and work boots, carrying a stuffed khaki duffel bag, enters the law library calling out like a street vendor. "I've got worn-out sheets. I've got stained underwear."

Iris, at her desk, looks over her reading glasses and Emilia at the typewriter laughs.

"I don't know about the underwear. Do we need any rags?" Iris asks Emilia.

"Possible, yes." Emilia leaves her typewriter and opens a metal storage cabinet stocked with cleaning supplies. On the bottom shelf is a pile of rags. "Nasty," she confirms. She gathers them and holds them at arm's length and walks them to the trash can.

"Help yourself," offers Desiree, and gestures expansively at the duffel bag at her feet.

Emilia unzips and begins to pick through the crumpled-up pile of torn sheets and toweling. She becomes involved with the task. Pushing the bag over to a library table, she starts to sort and fold."

"Got a second?" Iris asks Desiree.

"Yeah. I can stay a little minute. O'Donnell never expects me back when I'm on my rag-run. He always just looks at his watch and goes, 'Get back for stand-up count.'"

"Sit down. What's new? We haven't had a chance to talk for a while."

"Yeah, I know, huh. I didn't want to tell you last night in front of everybody but

Coleman—as in: ta-dum! The warden!—called me in yesterday. She sent Captain Carter over to pull me out of laundry. I mean, like he walks in there and everybody just totally tenses up. And Carter's standing there at the door and he goes, 'Johansson?' and I'm like, *Oh my God!* and all the other whole crew—they're, like, pretending they aren't even noticing. Then when I get back, I have to make up this whole story how, no big deal, Captain Carter just was needing me to sign paperwork on the Uranus thing. I'm thinking they believed."

"What's she like—the warden?" asked Iris. "I've never actually had a face-to-face."

Emilia is intent at pulling rags out of the duffel bag, folding and sorting.

Desiree looks her way. "Hey babe, thanks for doing that for me."

"No problem,"

"So what's Coleman like?" prompts Iris.

"I guess she's okay." Desiree pulls up a chair close to Iris's desk. "Although I have no understanding of what's going on with all the makeup and the nails and shit. Whew!"

"Yeah, I've never had the privilege but I imagine Coleman up close might be a little much."

"Scary."

"So what did she want?"

"She said she just called me in to thank me for the Ferguson thing, but it seemed like it was mostly her wanting to make sure I knew that I got my redesignation due to her, pulling on her strings or whatever. Of course she didn't mention it was you that did all the paperwork. She took all the credit."

"And you should give it to her. I'm sure she expedited. That kind of thing happens slowly, if it happens. Yours went through like that." Otilla snapped her fingers. "She told you that she had helped it along?"

"That's what she said. Then she asked if I wanted her to move me out of Two. I'm like, 'I'm fine in Two until I get over to the Drug Building.' But then I asked her can she fix it so I don't have any roommates. I wasn't really thinking I was going to be able to stay in there alone but she's like, 'No problem.'"

"Wow. You got juice, baby. She promise anything else? Push-up bra? Cognac?"

"Perfume!" chimes in Emilia. "Tell her, Obsession!"

Desiree laughs. "Yeah, maybe if I go out and set her up another officer, she'll bring me in half a gram of coke."

They laugh.

"She really emphasized," continued Desiree, "how she wants my help and assistance if I see any other blah blah blah."

"Huh, You know, Dessie, if I were you, I would pretty much leave the assistance-thing be."

"Oh, don't worry, I have no intention of turning into any warden's little pet snitch. That's not my M.O. That is not the way ah ro-oll."

"Uh-oh! Now she's talking sister again."

"You down," comments Emilia

"Keep it tight, sister," advises Iris, "Those administration types know how to sweet talk an inmate."

"Yeah, I know, huh? She tried it on me, I just kept going, 'Sor-rry. I got nothing for you. 'Sor-rry.'"

Iris moves her reading glasses up to the top of her head and, with her elbows on the desk, leans toward Desiree.

"Other than that, what's the news? I swear, whenever I need to get my gossip fix, I go to you. You are so tuned in. So anybody over there in two get caught naked?"

"I wish."

"But so how are things going between you and the big boy? Has she started professing her undying love?"

"Yep, sure has. For Jesus. I'm out of the competition."

"Can't compete with a Jewish hippy?"

"Who's the—oh, ha-ha. No I can't. But," Desiree pauses and looks around the room. Then in a whisper: "I finally got it out of Tillie about the details of how her homicide went down."

"Oh good!" says Iris. "I need my crime-story fix."

"So, you know," says Desiree, leaning in, her voice still lowered, "how Tillie was always saying how she didn't want to talk about her crime? But I knew she kind of did? You know? So anyway, yesterday evening she came upstairs to pay me back my can of tuna, and I finally got the whole story out of her. And it is really weird."

"Cool!" says Iris. "This one's going to be even better than the sex change."

"And I think it's even got a little kink in it."

"Perfect!"

"Anyway, this was all taking place a year and a half before she got popped. She was scheduled for her reassignment surgery for her top part that next week. You know—for getting rid of her boobs."

"And—?"

"But before it came up, some of the higher-ups in the Disciples call her to their high-rise apartment. I guess they had this whole top floor of the projects—Robert Taylor or something? Anyway it was for meetings, and it's this bare room with just folding chairs, and it's kind of dark in there or whatever. And there's four or five top Disciple officers and six more whatevers standing against the walls with weapons, and leadership's sitting in the room and they're all, really totally serious."

Iris's eye slips over the wall clock.

"Yeah, come on."

"And the leadership, they're telling her how they've heard good things about her sense of discipline, and they know how she's transitioning and they think that's cool, and they say they're ready to welcome her into the Disciples as a brother, etcetera. But they tell her that in the meantime, they need her help with a job. And here's the big thing. They still need her to be a woman until it's done."

Iris leans in.

Emilia stops folding.

"She said she was pretty much feeling mentally male by then. She had been on her hormones for, like, a year or whatever? And she was getting taller and starting to get muscled up, and her whiskers were coming in and her body hair and whatever. But she had kept her wig and women's clothes for when she went on her drug runs because then she wouldn't get pulled over on the highway."

"Yeah, go on. You told me about that."

Desiree takes a deep breath. "Anyway. *Apparently* there was this chick—she had been with one of the Disciples at one point in time and she had like, been involved. She knew shit, and the guy she had been with was getting held at MCC waiting on his trial and everything, but they had someone inside the attorney general's office, and they found out that the girlfriend was turning state's evidence. She was like this main witness or whatever, and without her testimony they probably weren't going to have enough for a conviction."

Iris is all attention. "The feds were just leaving this woman out on the streets?"

"I guess, no. They had her holed up over on the east side in this hotel. Except the Disciples tracked her down—*some*how. Tillie didn't go into that part."

"Wasn't she guarded?"

"Yeah, but the fed guard—he would just hang out downstairs in the hotel's, whatever—waiting room or whatever."

"Lobby."

"Yeah, lobby. So anyway, this chick—they would let her go out clubbing every night, and the feds would just follow and watch and everything, and every so often, she would pick up a women. Take her back to the hotel. I'm not quite getting the woman part, if she used to be with a Disciple. Probably she went both ways."

"I'm guessing they told her no men. Wouldn't let her take any men up to her room. But she needed help whiling away her lonely nights."

"Yeah, whatever. Oh, I forgot this part. It was a lessie bar she always went to.

Just down the block from the hotel."

"Probably she refused to stay alone in her hotel room at night," Iris speculates, "and it was a place where they thought she could party and be safe."

"Right. So anyway, you can see how Tillie's going to be fitting in if she's still a woman."

"Yeah, I'm getting it."

"So Tillie says she dressed up real sexy. I guess that was how the chick swung. She wasn't into butch or anything. So Tillie's in her wig and her mini skirt and her glam halter-top, and shit. She said her boobs were like double D. Can you imagine Tillie with big tits?

"No, not really."

Dessie wrinkles her nose in distaste. "Like, yuck! Freaky!"

"It sounds as if you really got her into the story."

"Yeah, I did, except she'd keep having her second thoughts about having fun telling it, and so then she'd have to go into her self-criticism/Jesus mode, which was totally boring. But whatever."

"What you'll put up with for a good crime story."

"Yeah, huh. Anyway, I could tell she was getting into telling me. So anyway, I guess Tillie picked the chick up—she said no problem whatsoever. Just talked her up the first night; walked out with her on the next. And so of course they had this federal escort behind them all the way back to the hotel, and she says when they got back to the hotel there was this drama because the FBI stopped them and did this a metal detection wand thingie over Tillie's purse. Tillie had to act all indignant, like 'what the shit,' and the chick started cussing out the FBI, and I guess it ended up being quite the little scene."

Desiree pauses and looks around the law library again. Emilia is reaching back down into the duffel bag. It's nearly empty.

"So here's where the story gets kind of . . . I don't know. Tillie? She kind of passed over the specifics. You know how she is. Doesn't like to talk about raunch. I didn't want to interrupt for details because by this time she had went off into some remembrance thing— I didn't want to snap her out, so this part here I'm just guessing."

The three women bend in closer and Desiree lowers her voice.

"I guess they started to go at it and Tillie had a couple of these plastic handcuffs in her purse, which naturally the FBI didn't detect and I'm assuming she told the chick it was for sexual games or whatever. I guess the chick let Tillie cuff her. She was going to cuff her to the bedpost but there weren't any posts, just this head-board. So Tillie—like it was a joke or whatever—she got her to go down onto the floor and got cuffed up to the bed rail."

"At which point, yeah."

"Yeah, and here's where it gets freaky. Tillie kind of liked telling about it—about how the chick looked and shit—but at the same time she's like, talking to *herself*. She's like, reliving or whatever. And she had already told me how the hormones were working her attitude. I mean, like, she started looking at women different, like the drug was turning women into her toys or her sex slaves."

"Yeah, you told me."

"And she was saying the hormones had made her hands real strong—plus she'd been working out on her grip and then, this is the point where she goes all vague. Like she didn't quite spell out the total picture. But I think at that point in time—like while she was doing her strangling thing or whatever? She got this big hormone surge? So I think what she was—she was like confessing that she actually got off. Like—she came while she was in the middle of doing it."

The room is silent.

"Hum, interesting," says Iris.

More silence.

"Poor Ottilla," Emilia finally sighs. She bows her head, whispers to herself in Spanish and makes the sign of the cross. Then she slowly goes back to the rags—sheets in one pile, toweling in the other.

"It's hard for me to really picture the whole thing in my mind," says Desiree, "her doing that, the way she is now, because she's so straight or gentlemanly of whatever. I mean, she's like, the opposite of the kind of person who would get into it, you know? Like, strangling another person? I guess those hormones shots really must have done a number on her personality."

"Poor Tillie," repeats Emilia softly.

Desiree looks around the room. "God," she exclaims, "if Tillie knew I was telling, she would absolutely kill me."

"I wouldn't put it that way if I were you."

"Oh yeah, ha-ha. Tillie would be hugely *pissed* if she knew I was telling you. You guys can not tell a soul!"

She looks toward Emilia.

"Emmy! Promise."

"Promise," says Emilia in a small voice.

Desiree takes a breath to continue the story.

"I'm going into my shrink act, and I'm like: 'So how do you feel about that?' And so Tillie snaps out of her memory-trippy thing, and she starts going off into like, some sort of philosophy trip. And it's like she got totally past the part about how she got off, and she started to say she doesn't think that the homicide in and of itself was a sin in the eyes of God. She says she was like a soldier on the battlefield who follows orders and she was following orders. She says she killed an enemy who was guilty of traitorship or whatever."

Desiree leans back in her chair.

"But she says her original sin was trying to change— she goes like, 'who God made me.' Taking her hormone therapy and getting the operations and shit. She says the hormones had the affect of giving her over to evil thoughts or turning her over to evil impulses or whatever."

"That's a new one. Hormones made me do it—the testosterone defense. Somebody's going to try that someday." Iris looks into the distance. "Hmm, you could argue that men are responsible for ninety percent of society's murders, the difference between the male and female temperament lies in this one hormone. Hmmm."

"Except," Desiree says, "I'm not quite understanding all her thought processes. She isn't beating herself up behind the murder. She's saying her mistake was trying to change into a man. Which led to the murder. And the murder was under orders, so it wasn't a sin, so I give up."

"Sex change as the original sin?"

"Yeah, I know. She was saying the Old Testament's full of homicides with God giving the orders to His authority figures who give the orders to whoever."

"She's right about that," agrees Iris. "They're killing each other for God all over Old Testament. However, what they are not doing is injecting testosterone."

"Yeah. Tillie says that when someone's in a position over you it's because God has put them there, and you go into battle to kill or whatever if they tell you to. Because God's— *whatever* —is making it right, or whatever. She says God's authority trumps man's laws."

"Ha," snorts Iris. "Tell that to my uncle the rabbi."

"Yeah, I know, huh. But she says on the other hand, God had made her perfect and she was going against God's design by trying to change herself into something that He did not intend for her to be." Desiree straightens up. "So that's what she says, anyway. So I guess God's telling her she doesn't get to have a dick."

The tension in the law library dissipates.

"Oh, Lord," Desiree intones in a sing-song whine, "*won't you buy me some balls and a dick?*"

Iris laughs. Emilia looks at Desiree in puzzlement."

"What 'balls and a dick' is? American toy?'

"In a way," says Iris and throws Desiree a silent *shh.*

"That's a really interesting story," says Iris, pressuring Desiree out of a giggle. "I always know you're going to have interesting info. Anything else?"

"Nothing. Zada." says Desiree seriously. "That was when they called count, so that was that. But I'll get more out of her, not to worry."

"I'm all a-quiver," says Iris. "Can't wait."

Desiree rises. "Got to go. O'Donnell's going to be sending out a search party."

"Hey Dessie," teases Iris, "now that Tillie is presenting as a manly-man, any second thoughts on starting things up?"

"Not really," says Desiree. "I mean, I admit it—I've started to get, like, these kind of waves or whatever. Every now and again. Except then it flashes into my mind what she's like——you know—down there? And that pretty much puts the ki-bosh. I just can't go that way, you know?"

"Maybe you wouldn't have to look down there," suggest Iris.

"Yeah, maybe, but then, how would—you know. Oh, never mind."

"Dessie, all over this compound—all over this *world*—women are managing to have sex with each other. I'll bet if you two get started, Tillie would know how to go about things."

Desiree points up. "Not while Jesus is up there looking down through the ceiling."

"Maybe Jesus likes to watch."

"Yeah, sure, I'll explain to Tillie how Jesus wants to watch us having sex. That'll go over big."

Iris spreads her palms upward. "Who knows?"

The rags have been carefully folded and are back into the duffel bag. Desiree picks it up and heaves it over her shoulder.

"Hey, thanks big-time, Emmy."

"Be too bad to be wasting that private room of yours," reminds Iris, "since it happens to be the only one on the whole compound."

"How 'bout Tom Cruise gets sentenced in here, and I'll think on it," offers Desiree.

Iris offers "How 'bout Joey Ramone, *I'll* think on it."

"How 'bout Eugenio Derbez?" chimes in Emilia.

Desiree and Iris look at her, then at each other.

"Who?"

"Who?"

Emilia sighs dramatically and puts her hand over her heart. "Is my lover. Eugenio, he is so-ooo wanting me."

Iris and Desiree are mystified. "Who the hell is he?"

"Eugenio Derbez," Emilia insists and does a valley girl *duh*. "Is everyone knowing my Eugenio. He is my bomb—my big Spanish movie star."

"Oh, *movie* star. *O-kay!*"

"Good one, Emilia,"

"You had us," says Iris and Desiree catches on her face an unguarded gaze of tenderness.

She smiles to herself and heads for the door. Then, as she's on her way out, she turns and sticks her head back into the room.

"About Tillie and you know—the thing. Don't. Tell. Anybody."

"We won't."

"Promise, you guys?"

"Promise."

"Promise."

CHAPTER 22

The dining room at lunch is crowded with inmates dressed in workday beige. Ottilla and Desiree, carrying full trays, move down the aisle between the tables, looking for a place to sit. Desiree pauses in silent question. The table's empty space is down a couple inmates toward the middle, but the two next to the aisle are happy to oblige a favored couple. They scoot their trays and shift over.

Desiree lifts the top of her hamburger bun and pokes her fork at the small patty. "See! I knew I could find it somewhere. *There's* the beef."

"Seek and ye shall find," recites Ottilla.

Desiree covers her ears and cowers. "Oh no, Tillie, please. Not at lunch. It's so early!"

"Okay, how about, *In the beginning was the word and the word was . . .*"

"No! Mercy!" Desiree pleads covering her ears and doing a horror-movie writhe.

Ottilla laughingly relents. "Okay, I'll save it for dinner."

"And I'm in my room eating mackerel."

Neither of them notices how their back-and-forth is attracting glances around the dining hall. Everyone enjoys seeing them together.

Desiree takes a bite of her burger. "So then we don't get a chance to talk for only this one day, and so then all of a sudden you're working over at UNICOR. I didn't even know you had *applied*. I thought you said your mom was sending you in your money."

She is. I'm not doing it for the money."

"So why?"

"Because there's actual *work* over there. Food service was driving me crazy."

"You never said any complaints or anything. I thought you were okay with it. "

"Yeah, well I wasn't trying to fixate. I was working on my acceptance skills."

"So was anyone in the kitchen giving you a bad time or anything?"

"No, no. Not really. But I really did not like it. I would report at four a.m. which I wouldn't have minded except I get over there so that I can do . . . *nothing*. I was assigned to wipe down the service line. That's it! Five minutes before and after breakfast. If I go real slow, I can stretch it out to ten minutes."

Desiree gestures with her hamburger.

"Some inmates are perfectly contented with no work, Tillie."

"Well, it was driving me nuts. First day I'm thinking I can help somebody else out, keep myself busy? So I go over to the toaster, offer to pitch in? They act like I'm trespassing on their personal property or whatever. I'm like, 'Okay, okay! I was just trying to help.'"

Desiree laughs. "I know. People are weird about their jobs. At the laundry you do not shelve somebody else's shirts or make up somebody's bedrolls or anything. Total no-no."

"I know, over in food service they were like"—Ottilla goes into a scratchy, la-dy-voice vernacular—"'I know you new here and you ain't know no better, but child, you got to know 'bout how to keep you place. You can't be hustling up in here, trying to run up privileges where you ain't got no business.'"

"Hey you did that good. Yay, Tillie!" She waves a floppy French fry. "You can talk the talk after all. Now let's hear you do some brother."

Ottilla deepens her voice. "Hey, baby, I ain't going to li-iie. You is looking fi-iine."

"Don't!" Desiree laughs, putting her hands over her ears again. "You're sounding like—you're sounding like Danté."

"Oops, sorry." Ottilla pauses and takes a bite.

"No problem. He is not even in my thought patterns any more. So go on with your food service ordeal."

"So over in the kitchen, it was like, the higher up you climbed the more work they rewarded you with. The lady who had been there for, like, *ever*—she was doing five jobs—cracking eggs, flipping pancakes, measuring the oatmeal—whatever. If you tried to go near, she'd scream like you're trying to snatch up her baby."

"That would be Ms. Ida, right?"

"Yeah, that's Ms. Ida."

"I heard that Henley is just sitting there, letting her go off on everybody all over the kitchen."

"They say she's getting worse and worse. They told me that in my case, she was actually treating me good. Man, I sure couldn't tell. Anyway, some of the new inmates, they'd find a little spot in the storage area or wherever, curl up, and go to sleep. Mr. Henley, he'd walk right past, practically step on them, act like he wasn't even seeing them. But then someone would go up to him and snitch them out? He'd go back and start *yelling*."

Desiree laughs. "Sounds about right."

"Yeah, to you. You been down for a while. To me it seemed total lunacy—first him trying not to notice? Then him trying to notice and going off? I felt like it was an alien civilization."

"Desiree laughed and sucks milk from her carton. "I know, first month or so, this place is La La Land."

"Then finally after I had figured out what the logic was, it made it easier on me. What I came up with was that staff was always supposed to honor their snitches. So Henley, he isn't caring about his workers sleeping on the job, but if anyone comes up to him and snitches them out, he has the obligation to go over and yell."

"Yeah, sounds right."

"Then I figured that the rules say they got to keep us all assigned to a job, but there's too many of us in here now because of the war on drugs and there isn't enough work. So work's a premium, and the more sonority you get on a job, the more work they let you do. So for me, I was low-dog. I had to just stand around. For like, hours. I said to Mr. Henley that I would rather be on a chain gang, busting up rocks."

"So how does he go?"

"He goes, 'welcome to the penitentiary.' So I'm standing there, trying to wrap my mind. I was telling him I was wanting it to be *like* a penitentiary; he's saying, 'Welcome . . . ' It didn't make a lick-a sense."

"So," says Desiree pertly, wagging another fry, "Welcome to the penitentiary."

"Don't you start."

"I know. They all say that except for O'Donnell in laundry. He keeps yelling,"— Desiree does a deep voice—"'This is jail, not Yale.'"

"Jail, not Yale? I like that. Makes sense, anyway."

"Yeah, especially after I found out how Yale is right there," Desiree gestures with her French fry, "up the road." Desiree puts the fry in her mouth and starts to peel off her cupcake wrapper.

"Yale's around here? I didn't know that. I'm not hardly even aware what state I'm in. They just dropped me down."

"I know. If they told us we were in Minnesota, we'd believe them, huh?"

"Probably. Except for the addresses on our mail."

"But anyway, I remember now how you did mention a couple of weeks ago how you were going to try to get out of food service, and I'm like, good luck on that. They're not letting you out until you've put in your six months."

"I know. That's what Henley told me. But I was praying on it in the chapel last Sunday after service. I'd been trying to remind myself that I was in prison and things were not supposed to go the way I wanted them to. So I was concentrating on accepting, but I was getting a little confused because I was praying for *more* work, and that didn't feel like me wanting it easy—or me not accepting the consequences of my criminal act."

Desiree, with a removed expression, inspects her cupcake, turning it from side to side.

"So then," Ottilla continues ignoring Desiree's flagging interest, "I was trying to figure out, did I have any right to pray over how they hadn't given me hard enough labor? I couldn't get my head around it. So I just started praying for a better attitude."

Desiree, her eyes elsewhere, takes a bite.

"Then I was there praying, trying to understand, and I overheard a couple of the ladies—they were off in that little side room?"

Desiree shrugs. "I've never been up there."

"Oh, yeah, that's right. But so anyway, they were right there close and they were talking about how in UNICOR, staff is always pushing you to work harder. They were saying, 'Mighty-Whitey, up in there? He be like the devil. That man, he going to work you like you a He-brew slave.'"

Desiree has to laugh at the imitation.

Ottilla has finished the salad and is working on her hamburger. "So I took it as a sign, and Monday after work I go over to UNICOR and I get right in to see Mighty Whitey—that's Mr. Whitely. He looked me over, asked me if I could lift fifty-pound cartons. I told him all day long, and two days later I'm on the call-out."

"That is so totally amazing. Nothing in here happens that fast. They must have needed you ba-aad."

"They did. The forklift's out—waiting on parts? And I guess a couple warehouse women, their backs kept going bad on them. They had their medical excuses and all, but Mighty Whitey—this was last week—he ordered them to move the cartons anyway. So they went on sit-down, and he called the captain and they took them to seg. So all the orders were backing up."

"Couldn't he just get his other workers?"

"I guess everyone was siding with the sit-downs who had had their medicals, and everyone else was threatening to do it too. So I came at the exact right moment. I get to work by myself, and I'm loving it. There's piles to do."

"Sounds thrilling."

Ottilla takes a fork of Jell-O. "It's a blessing. I'm accepting it as a gift."

"Tillie, not to change the subject but why do you always go for the Jell-O instead of the cupcakes?"

"Because it—"

ROCHELLE GOODEN, REPORT TO THE CAPTAIN'S OFFICE.

REPEAT: ROCHELLE GOODEN.

REPORT TO THE CAPTAIN'S OFFICE.

Ottilla freezes. "Did they say Rochelle Gooden? Oh sh—oh shoot! That's my bunkie! That's Rogo. Why are they—God, I hope that doesn't means she's in any trouble."

"If they're calling her to the captain's office," says Desiree darkly, "that probably *is* what it's going to mean."

CHAPTER 23

It's the end of the workday, and Ottilla with the rest of the UNICORE crew is stalled in the line waiting to pass through the metal detector. An older woman has set it off and is being patted down and then sent around and back in her stocking feet.

She talks overhead to the machine. "Mr. Buzzer, ain't you never going to remember how I got metal in my *orthopedic* shoes?" She looks down and addresses the line. "That devil up in there? He could piss off the Good Humor man."

They laugh.

The inmate in line behind Ottilla is young—a short, busty blonde. She slides a quick a look around and then does a fake stumble, bumping her front into Ottilla's back. "Hey, I'm sorry," she apologizes.

Ottilla turns and smiles. "No problem."

"I'm Darleen Davis. I'm over in assemblies."

"I'm Ottilla Cassidy. I just started in warehouse."

"I know. So Ottilla, can I call you O?"

"Well, I wouldn't prefer. They used to call me that on the streets, but I turned my life over to Christ, so it doesn't fit my M.O. anymore. I'm Ottilla now, if that's okay."

"Sure," answers Darleen brightly. She pauses but before Ottilla can turn away, "I'm going over to the rec before count. Mr. Castagno is having b-ball tapes on. Want to go over and watch some nets?"

"No thanks. Another time. My roomie got called to the captain's office. I need to go to back to the crib and make sure she's okay."

Ottilla clears the metal detector.

"See you around," he calls to her.

Inside Unit Two Rogo lies on her top bunk beside her discarded headset. She stares up at the network of pipes crawling the ceiling. A tear quivers on her cheekbone.

"Want to talk about it?" asks Ottilla, hanging up her coat.

Rogo stays silent for a moment. Ottilla unbuttons her uniform, eyes on Rogo.

There's a pause. Rogo swipes at the tear. "I don't know," she says. "Ain't nothing nice."

"You in trouble with the captain?" asks Ottilla quietly.

Her thermal is stained at the armpits. She takes it off and stuffs it, along with the shirt, into one of a pair of laundry bags hanging from the foot of the bunk. Her torso is lean and male. The two crescent-shaped scars under her nipples have almost disappeared.

Rogo doesn't answer. Then: "Ain't the captain."

"Captain's not involved?" asks Ottilla, pulling on a tee shirt.

"Oh, he involved. Captain, he up in there, he be all, 'Ms. Gooden, come in and have a seat, Ms. Gooden. Can I get you a sodie-pop, Ms. Godden?' I'm saying to myself—I'm like, 'Uh-oh, he talking to me this way, ain't nothing good happening right here.' Be fucking with my morale, know what I mean?"

Rogo relaxes a little. Ottilla reaches over to the toilet paper holder, pulls off a length, and hands it up. Rogo blows her nose, then turns onto her side and props up her head.

"So then the Captain, he be escorting me into his back room while he's doing his want-a-sodie thing. I see he just be fronting, because back up in there is this other nigga—light-skinned? Be all honky-correct, wearing one of those starched-up white-boy suits. Captain Carter, he be all like, 'Ms. Gooden, this gentleman is hoping you might be in a position to give him some assistance.' And I'm all—I'm thinking to myself—position? What position? I ain't *in* no position. I hit the compound; I am squeaky, know what I mean? Ms. Asia B, she ain't let me be in no position."

Ottilla nods.

The act of narration is lightening Rogo's mood. "Then Captain Carter, he be all, 'Anything you say in this office, is strictly blah blah, Ms. Godden. It will go no further than blah blah.' Captain Carter, he be all like, 'This gentleman here is interviewing with permission from the BOP. He has come up from Washington to have a word with you. I'll let him introduce himself.'"

As Rogo gets into the rhythm of the story and as her mood eases, she starts speaking with animation. "So then the light-skinned nigga, he standing up, shaking my hand and shit, he be pulling out his badge and shit. He goes like," Rogo deepens her voice, 'I am here on behalf of the FBI.'"

"FBI!" Ottilla, who has been leaning against her locker, straightens up.

"I know, I'm like, 'Whoo-ee, girl, your ass in trouble. Going to be some Biblical shit coming down right here.'"   Rogo looks around quickly and lowers her voice back into an undertone. "He start it off all gentleman, trying to be slick. He goes, 'how you doing, how they treating you up in here, got everything you need?' Like that. I know I'm in it now, he be shooting me that kind of shit."

Ottilla waits.

"So then he going on about how this other inmate up in North Carolina, Butner, he got sentenced to seventeen years. And he going on and all this time, I am having no comprehension. I'm like, why he telling me about a nigga I ain't even know?"

Rogo's voice has risen.

"He just go on about how finally this brother, he decide he is going to step up to the plate, share his knowledge, so forth and so on. So the FBI nigga, he's saying he personally got to working on behalf with the courts, this-that-and-the-other. Long story short, he gets Butner down to sixty-two months. So now the Butner brother, what with his time served, this-that-and-the-other, he got less than a year to go before he out the door and me, I'm thinking, '*What the fuck?*'"

Rogo is still leaning over her bunk. Her voice is rising. "He is going on about how the FBI help a brother out—now the FBI can help a sister out. Cause he ain't think I need to be doing the kind of years that I got sentenced."

"What did you say to him?"

"I ain't say *nothing*, know what I mean? Just sit there, let a nigga talk."

COUNT TIME. ALL INMATES IN YOUR UNITS.

ALL INMATES: FOUR O'CLOCK, STAND-UP COUNT.

Rogo sits up and slides down off her bunk, landing lightly on the floor.

"Long story short," she goes on in a husky whisper, "the dude's wanting information, about a thing went down with Mojo. My cousin."

Rogo goes silent, staring up at the ceiling.

"You don't have to talk."

"That's okay. You the best friend I got. Anyway, went down, like, over a year before I got popped. FBI, he saying he understand it wasn't my mix, but he figuring I might be in my cousin's confidentials."

Rogo looks away and lowers her voice even more. "Then he trying to tell me how I got popped? How it was Mojo laid me down on that one. He was saying Mojo had set me up. Knew the shit was coming down—knew the Feds was coming up on my crib next morning."

"Do you think it's true?"

"Man, *I* don't know. I told you how my cousin gets a last-minute call—his Grandma Booker need a ride to the funeral. Mojo, at the time he took the call—he got himself one of those new cell phones--be riding and talking at the same time, know what I mean? So he gets the call, he riding with the shit. So on his way, he drop it off at my place."

"What was it? Just product?"

"No, the little bit of stash they got was mine. He just laid down the Glock 9 that had got outfitted with a silencer."

"Why was he riding around heavy?"

"He say he just did business with a dude up over past Vinton. He coming up my way, he gets the grandma call."

"So your cousin didn't come back for his sh—for his stuff that night?"

"I told him not if he going to be late. I had to work seven a.m., man."

"And the Feds came early the next morning?"

"Yeah. Yeah they did. Come in busting, waking up the whole building. Then the lawyer Mojo bought me turned out worthless, know what I mean? She just sat there, didn't do nothing, let them enhance me for the silencer. At that time I didn't know shit, but then when I come up in here, Ms. Iris, she telling me how the silencer was a legitimate class III device in the Commonwealth of Virginia—she's going to file the paperwork, try to knock me down the extra sixty."

"But now the FBI's got you wondering about your cousin."

"First I thought, 'Na-aw—man's prevaricating.' Grandma and Grandpa Gooden raised us up together, we brother and sister, man. How Mojo going to set up his own sister?"

Rogo leans onto a locker. She now has her sweatshirt on over her tee.

"But then, I don't know. If the shit was going to have to come down, in reality the shit actually should have come down behind Mojo. I mean, he be the man; I wasn't deep. I just be doing a little transport, mostly up to Richmond. Earn me a couple bucks, know what I mean? I wasn't into no big-time slinging."

Rogo pauses for a moment. "Well, okay, truth: I would move a couple eights to my supervisor up in Popeye's every little now and again—weren't no thang. Always showed up on time for my work. Supervisor saying I'm class A."

"But your cousin didn't get busted."

"Still out there as of—I talked to moms last Sunday. Mojo, he telling me he had it from the inside, the reason I'm popped, that was behind this one little thing I did couple months back with a nigga over East Roanoke. Mojo say Roanoke was the responsible individual—say he going to take care of him for me, soon as he find him."

"So today? What else did the FBI say?"

First he goes, 'Huh, Ms. Gooden, huh we're all friends here. You call me Nathan, I'll call you Rogo.'"

Rogo barks a joyless laugh.

"So I'm thinking, uh-oh. Shit's coming down. Then like I say, the dude starts telling me how I got set up. He's saying, 'At the time of your arrest, Ms. Gooden, why do you think we did not make inquires about a certain Mr. Mordell Johnson. AKA Mojo?' He's like, 'Why is it that we did not ask you to give us information concerning your cousin? I'll tell you why.'"

Rogo starts to sit on Ottilla's bunk but stops herself and looks for permission.

Ottilla nods and sits on the toilet.

"Me," Rogo continues, "I'm not saying anything. I just sit there be ignorant and FBI is going, 'The answer to that, Ms. Gooden, is because we already knew. At that time, we had had your cousin under supervision for well over a year. We knew about his activities. We had all the information we needed to put your Mr. Mojo away for a goodly number of years. And the reason we didn't do it, Ms. Gooden, is because your cousin was working with us. Your cousin was securing time on the streets for himself by giving us information. Your Mojo knew if he kept bringing us the bodies, we'd let him stay out there. In other words, Rochelle, Mojo rolled right over on you.'"

Ottilla sighs. "Rogo, you do understand that they lie, don't you? They know they're authority figures—like a pastor or a teacher or whatever, speaking truth. They play on that. I don't know about the guy you just talked to—I can't call him out for certain—but just because he's saying all that? That doesn't mean it's true."

"Yeah, I know. And I do remember this: that first time they questioning, they was asking me shit on Mojo. Asking on a lot of folk, know what I mean? Mojo included. But at the time, I'm not giving up word-one. I'm just ask for a lawyer. After a couple hours they give up, take me back to the holding cell. I'm only just up in there until next morning I see the judge. Grandma Gooden, she be down with my cash bail, coming up from Mojo."

"So if the FBI is supposed to know all about Mojo's activities, what they want out of *you*?"

"Long story short," Rogo looks around the room and lowers her voice again. "About maybe a year before all the shit come down, a dude come to town, got an introduction from some Bloods up in Richmond, got the triple O ink on the shoulder, got the body language—all the authentic shit. He telling Mojo he be tied in with Black Miami, can get him hooked up right—right product, right price. At the time, Mojo's just slinging the Mexican coming up out of Texas—it's okay quality, better than most of the shit in town, but he ain't get it direct. Before he lays hands, it stepped on couple times."

Ottilla listens attentively.

Rogo is in the rhythm of the narrative. "Everybody know Miami got the quality, got the price, but Miami buttoned up. Mojo, he can't even get close down there. The shit this new dude brung is quality. So Mojo, he check out the dude, check out the connections, seem okay; he order up half a K—move it like"—she snaps her fingers—"order up another whole one, he getting so now he retailing o-zee's over to the competition. A Trey or two is coming to Mojo now, wanting what he got. So he order himself up a couple more Ks, happen again, know what I mean? Except, long story short: Mojo, he's getting word on the dude and, long story short, the dude . . ."

Rogo is silent. She finally finishes in a low voice. "He ain't around no more."

The sound of the front door opening and keys rattling bring Ottilla and Rogo to their feet. They both stand wordlessly at attention until the counting guards have gone past and are up the metal stairway.

But in the hiatus, Rogo has become weighed down again. "Hey, Tillie," she says with a catch in her voice, "I can't be laying all this shit down top-a you. Ain't any-none of your problem."

"Hey no, that's fine, Rogo. I'm not a lawyer or anything, but if I can help . . . Unless you think you need to keep things to yourself. Maybe you're not comfort-able . . ."

"No, man, it's not that way. I'm trusting you up in this place, and I'm trusting Ms. Asia B and that's it. Except I ain't laying this kind-a shit over onto Ms. Asia's. She be taking it too heavy."

They hear a counting officer's laugh. The other one joins in, and the two slam out the back door.

Rogo sits on the toilet and puts her head in her hands, "Dude's going to be coming back round up here tomorrow. He say he giving me overnight to think on my situation, know what I mean? I can't figure what's right."

"You need some prayer, Rogo. You shouldn't try to do this alone. You need to ask for help."

Rogo scratches her head violently. "Maybe. But I ain't been practicing up on my praying."

"You don't need practice. He's waiting for you to come to Him for help. He's ready any time. You just got to ask. Maybe if you tried over at the chapel? You'd get more into the feeling of it?"

"I ain't never been. Kind of a public area up in there, ain't it?

"No, nobody hardly comes after dinner. If you want, I'll go with."

Rogo pauses.

"Appreciate it," she finally says in a small voice.

COUNT'S CLEAR.

CHAPTER 24

It's after dinner. Iris and Emilia are on the bench. Desiree joins them.

Asia B approaches. She has pulled a white do-rag issue scarf off her head and worries it now, twisting it around her fingers.

"She just say it's the FBI—can't say no more right now. Then she's heading off with the Big O. I'm scared for that child."

"The FBI doesn't come in here to punish anyone," reassures Iris. "They're probably looking for information from her."

"I talked to Tillie after dinner," Desiree offers. "She said she was taking Rogo to the chapel for 'prayer.'"

"She ain't never been a praying kind of child. If Big O be getting Rogo up over into the chapel, that child is going through some evil."

"She is tell you the story later," assures Emilia.

"She sure ain't tell me now. She in the dinner line, I ask, 'What trouble you got yourself into? What's that capt'n wanting with you?' She's saying, 'Ain't no captain, be the FBI up in here from off the street.' She say, 'they just be doing they 'li'l thing.' She say, 'you ain't be fretting your head on me, Ms. Asia B.' I say, 'How I ain't fretting my head? You got me fretting all over my *body*.'"

Desiree gets up. "Gotta go. If you see Tillie, tell her if she wants to talk, I'll be in my room."

A group of black women approach. "Hey Asia B, what's up with Rogo?"

"Yeah, what Captain Carter want?"

Asia B waves her hand dismissively. "I having no idea. He probably just got himself a little paperwork issue. Can't be nothing bad. Rogo—that girl just do her time. She ain't be up in no shit."

"No doubt."

"Truth."

The group hovers, unsatisfied, but when nothing else is forthcoming, they wander off.

As soon as they are out of earshot, Asia B asks, "What you thinking about all this, Ms. Iris?"

Iris shakes her head. "I'm pretty sure they're not trying to find out anything going on here in Danbury. They're almost certainly looking for information from the streets. Do you know how affiliated she was out there?"

"She ain't affiliated none whatsoever. Except she got a cousin she grow up with. That cousin—he all up in some dirt. So I'm thinking, if the suits wanting information out of Rogo's mouth, be concerning that cousin."

"I didn't see anything in her paperwork," says Iris. "It wouldn't appear that when they were working out her plea agreement her lawyer had much leverage. She got points for taking responsibility, but if she had given them information, they probably wouldn't have enhanced her on the silencer."

Asia B snorted. "What that kind of child be wanting with no silencer on no weapon? That child—she ain't be no *silencer* kind of child. She just be a dancing-her music, popping-her-fingers kind of child. When they haul her in, the way it happen to *her* mind, she just be caught up in some harmful luck. Be all happenstance—how they finding all that cousin-shit up in her place. I ain't about to saying nothing at her, but I suspecting she got her little ass set up. I'm saying to myself: how it going to be, the one time that cousin stashing weapons be the one time they busting in? That don't sound right to my ear."

"No doubt," agrees Iris.

"Truth," agrees Emilia.

"I'm relieved Ottilla taking the child under her wing. Rogo, she got nothing but respect for that one. Be like her big brother."

CHAPTER 25

It's evening, and Desiree lies on her bottom bunk wearing a set of thermals. Beside her flip-flops on the floor, an issue of *People* is half separated from its cover. She is intent on a crochet project. With her tongue's tip showing from the side of her mouth, she's working out the mechanics of the stitches.

"Knock, knock."

"Enter."

Desiree's shower-curtain door is pulled open, and Ottilla pokes her head into the room. "Hey Dessie, have you seen Valdez anywhere around?"

"Delores or Maria?"

"Maria," says Ottilla, holding up a paperback copy of *This Present Darkness*. "She asked to read this next."

"Come on in, Tillie. Last I saw her she was over at rec. No, that was yesterday. I haven't seen her today."

Ottilla starts to withdraw.

"No, Tillie, don't go away. I need a break."

Ottilla enters a bit tentatively.

"Come on, sit down."

"So you're starting to crochet," Ottilla observes. "What are you making?"

"A scarf. Blanca showed me how to do 'the first row and now I'm rocking it. Cause like they say," she chants, "'You got to stay 'till you learn to crochet.'"

"Yeah, I heard that one." Ottilla sits on the brushed steel toilet seat, resting the book on her lap.

"And I am looking *short*. I am at the door. I'm down to two hundred and eighty-seven and a wake-up."

"But who's counting," agrees Ottilla.

"Hey, Boo, you are learning the lingo, girl. You getting it down."

"Yeah," replies Ottilla in mock Ebonics, "I be a for-real penitentiary mama. Excepting I ain't learnt no cro-chet."

"You got time, Boo-Boo."

"Yeah, I got time."

Desiree frowns at her work. Then she says lightly, "Hey Tillie, what's going on with Rogo?"

Ottilla sighs. "Poor Rogo. She's torn up. You know how the FBI came in on Wednesday and said he'd be back next day? All day on Thursday, Rogo was a basket case waiting to get called. Now she figures she's got to sweat it out over the weekend."

Desiree does the last stitch on the row and rests the project on her lap.

"Poor Rogo," she says.

"Yeah. I'm teaching her this method—when I was at MCC, a volunteer from the streets gave me this book. It shows how, instead of ignoring your fear and pushing it away, how you own it. First you isolate it—locate where it's at in your body. Then you let yourself have the experience of it and let the original fear-lie come up for recognition. Then you offer the whole package up—ask God to take it away."

Desiree snorts. "If your fear package is that you're waiting for FBI to come for you, I'm not seeing how that's a fear *lie*. Sounds like a fear truth."

"Yeah but it's fear based on an original—oh, never mind."

"So is that—is it helping?"

"It's helping, but she's still shaky."

"Maybe the FBI's trying to get her shaky. They do that, you know. Maybe he isn't even coming back."

"He knows Rogo isn't going any place so he's going let her stew would be my guess. But he's coming back."

"How do you even know?"

"'Cause they have street-word that Rogo's got info behind a cold case, and they're wanting it bad."

"Yeah but how would Rogo even *know* anything? I mean, *Rogo*?"

"She knows."

"But Asia B says Rogo wasn't up in any mix. What information could Rogo possibly . . ."

"It's not her; it's her cousin who was the player."

Ottilla shifts uncomfortably and picks at the cover of her book.

"Rogo just helped."

"Helped do what? Come on, Tillie, are you sure she isn't just making shit up?"

"I wish."

"No, really, Tillie. Maybe you're taking this too seriously? I mean, like w*hat*?"

Ottilla sighs again and says reluctantly, "I guess back in '93, the Feds sent an undercover into Mojo's—that's the cousin—into his operation. So the undercover—he was good at it. Was getting in deep. But then someone from Richmond knew a guy in DC and found out the guy was DEA or FBI or whatever—anyway, he was a fed. So I guess Mojo drove up all the way to DC to make sure. See the paperwork for himself and everything-—so he could absolutely confirm that the information was right. So then, you know."

"What?"

"Well, I guess Mojo took care of it."

There's a silence.

"So how does Rogo come in?" asks Desiree casually, not looking up. She picks up the crochet and moves her thumb to count the last row.

Ottilla doesn't respond.

"I'm sure Rogo didn't actually help . . . with the whatever. With all the taking-care-whatever."

"Yeah, kind of."

Desiree with her head down continues to finger her stitches.

There's a silence.

Finally Ottilla says in a low voice, "Rogo helped to get rid of the evidence."

There's another pause. "Heavy duty," says Desiree. "What did they do with . . . the evidence?"

Ottilla sighs. She ignores the question. "Poor Rogo. I'm really getting to know her. She acts all goofy-hip-hop and everything, but underneath she's really emotional and sensitive. And now she's pretty torn up."

Ottilla fingers the book on her lap.

There is a silence.

"...there, four, five." Desiree is murmuring the count. Then, casually, "tore up, how?"

Ottilla sighs.

" Over in the chapel yesterday after we got through praying about it—after she ran the whole scene down, it kind of came to her—to both of us—that without the evidence, the Feds can't prove there even was any crime. The guy could have just run off down to Mexico with a woman or something."

Desiree asks, "So it's just Rogo and Mojo who know about the whatever?"

She takes Ottilla's silence as an affirmative.

"So even if the cousin is rolling," she adds, as though filling in a story plot, "he's not going to roll that way. So the Fed is probably lying, trying to get her to talk."

"Exactly. Mojo's not going to be telling on himself. He knows how they catch you up in a possession, you can give them names for the narcotics charge and you lighten the load. But they got no mercy if you put a gun on a Fed. Mojo, he is well aware."

"Yeah, huh."

Ottilla leans forward. "You got to understand, Rogo had no idea until after the fact that anything was even going down. That part was all Mojo. It was afterward when Mojo needed her help. Couldn't trust anyone else."

"So . . ."

"So, I shouldn't be telling you any of this. It wasn't even like Rogo was telling *me*. It was almost like she was confessing to God or something. I didn't even *want* to know."

Ottilla concentrates on finger-shuffling pages.

"I understand, Tillie. This is some heavy-duty shit for you to deal with. "

"Heavy duty for *Rogo*. Look," says Ottilla earnestly leaning forward and putting *This Present Darkness* down on the floor at her feet. "This is absolutely just between the two of us. This isn't just regular jailhouse gossip. This is serious. Rogo's in deep."

"Oh, Tillie, I understand. I wouldn't ever tell anyone in here about this kind of shit. These inmates are worthless. Look what they did to me, making up shit about showers and shit. You can't trust them with anything."

"That's what Rogo says."

"I mean, I might repeat it around, like, which bitch is hooking up with which bitch or whatever. But when it's serious shit, I'm tight."

Ottilla studies her feet."

"You know, Tillie, I haven't mentioned this but when I was in seg they were really working me for information—promising me shit and everything? I told them, 'Sorry.' I said, 'If you want to find out shit, go find out yourself.' I'm telling you this because I keep my mouth shut. I'd never, ever repeat anything like this. To anybody."

"I know, Dessie. I remember, when I was young, you were the only person in the neighborhood that I really felt like I could talk to. I remember I'd tell you about like, who was cutting school, who was shoplifting, who was getting into the liquor cabinet."

Ottilla smiles over at her.

"It always felt so good to come and talk to you. Mom wasn't usually around, back in those days, and I used to get all anxious when I'd come on things like that. But it made me feel like everything was okay again after I'd unload on you. Plus, I knew I could trust you."

Ottilla sits back.

"Of course, if I'd known God back in those days . . . But back then, you were like, a stability figure. My stability."

"That's sweet, Tillie. I had no idea. I just liked it when you were around. You were my little buddy. Remember I'd call you that? 'L'il Buddy?'"

"Yeah. Remember that one summer how you were teaching me all the names of the birds?"

"Oh, that's right. My aunt had sent me this book. We got our juncos and our waxwings down that summer."

"I loved it. Remember how you used to take me up to the cemetery and read me the tombstones?"

"Yeah."

"Remember that time I had to go to the bathroom so you took me into the bushes and there was this couple, you know?"

"Oh, I'd forgotten all about that."

"I was like six or something, and I was all confused about what they were doing and you tried to explain but it wasn't seeming to me like they were *loving* or any-thing—it just being ugly with each other. I was like, 'No way!' You were like 'Way!'"

They both laugh.

"And then—I think that was when I told you my big secret: I told you how I felt like I was somebody totally different on the inside than I was outside."

"I don't remember that part."

"I do. You said, no problem. You said if it was my insides, I could be anyone I wanted to be in there. You said it was my own private place where nobody could come in who wasn't welcome. You said that you were like that too because inside you, you were a big rodeo star. You told me that you were the only rodeo rider in the circuit who could stay on Mr. T."

"Mr. T!" cries Desiree. She drops her crochet and sits up and hugs her knees. "Oh my God! I'd forgotten all about Mr. T. That was during my rodeo phase. I must have been, what? Like, eleven or something?"

"Yeah, anyway, after you told me about you and Mr. T. you said I was perfectly okay. You told me that if in your heart, you knew you were the only rider in the rodeo who could stay on Mr. T., then in *my* heart, I could be a white boy. I remember how it really made me feel, 'Whew!' But you said to never tell any grown-up. You said they would ruin the whole thing. So I never did."

"Oh God, Tillie, look where it all got us! Sitting here together in a penitentiary."

"Yeah, but because of all that I found God, so it's all good. Dessie, I don't mean to change the subject, but it's been heavy on my mind lately and I feel like I'm called upon to say something. So have you ever thought about trying out going to church and . . ."

"Tillie! Don't. You. Even. Start!"

"K-okay. Sorry. I couldn't help it. He's done so much for me, and He's wanting to do the same thing . . ."

"Tillie!" Desiree looks very dark.

"Okay. Feels like if I could help you . . . You were, like, almost my guardian angel to me when I was a kid."

There's an uncomfortable pause.

Desiree has colored a little. She starts patting around on the bedclothes for a missing crochet hook.

"I'm just wanting to repay you," says Ottilla.

"You can repay by quitting with the God talk," she answers in schoolmarm firmness.

Ottilla sighs and picks up the book up from the floor and starts to rise.

"It's going to be count pretty soon. I guess I'd better get back down; see how Rogo's doing."

Desiree finds the hook. She holds it up in victory and her scowl disappears. She leans over toward Ottilla now with a smile and an eager expression.

"Tillie, sit! You never finished about Rogo. Last I heard, Rogo and Mojo? They were in the middle of doing, like this dirty deed or whatever."

"Yeah, and I probably should be leaving the whole thing right there," Ottilla says, but she slowly sits down again on the toilet.

"Now really, Tillie," Desiree asks, "are you sure Rogo isn't making this whole thing up? I mean like, just to make herself big-time or something?"

"No she's not making it up."

"So how can you tell?"

"She's been putting in too much, like, real-life detail," says Ottilla as though to herself. She sits back and leans against the sink, crossing her legs at the ankles, stretches them down the aisle between the footlockers and the bunk. She studies her flip-flopped toes, wiggling one and then another."

Desiree frees herself from her blanket, crawls out of bed, rises and slides the white shower curtain shut.

"No, leave it open. We've not supposed to be in anyone's room with it closed."

Desiree sighs and rolls her eyes and slides it back open. She sits back. Ottilla's toe is level with her thigh, and Desiree reaches over and squeezes it.

"Detail like how?" she asks in idle curiosity.

"Like, how Rogo and Mojo were raised up together. They lived with their grandparents, I guess, about fourteen miles out of town, out on this tobacco farm. She says the soil's played now out and it's all fallow and grown over, but back then it was still good. They sharecropped."

Ottilla stops and stares past the open shower curtain doorway, over across the high-ceiling common area. Desiree's third floor room is almost level with the grilled, ten-foot bank of windows.

"Okay . . ."

"But, see, Rogo's grandparents—they're both dead now and the property's—I guess It's wrapped up in some legal dispute or something and it's just, like, sitting there. But back in the day, besides the tobacco they had a little half-acre garden out back—greens and tomatoes and whatever. Rogo said her grandma had these special corn seeds passed down in the family. She says the ears were runty but sweet, almost like candy. She says no way can you get corn like that anymore."

Desiree is patient.

"But I guess anyway," Ottilla lowers her voice, "I guess there was this cistern out back there for watering the garden during dry spells?" She stops and focuses on her toes again.

Desiree sits very still, her arms around her knees.

"So anyway, I guess when Rogo was young, some neighbor kid had fallen in? The way I understand, the kid didn't get drowned or anything—the water was low at the time—but so anyway, the Grandpa—he had to cover it. So he starts making a form for the concrete—bending plywood into a circle? Rogo really went into details. It made a big impression. Measuring. They had to do math to get it the right size. So then the grandpa pours the concrete cover to fit over top of the cistern."

Desiree waits in silence.

"Rogo, she said till the end of his days that Grandpa was cursing himself for pouring the concrete so deep. Because when he needed to water the garden? It was always too heavy—took all three of them—Rogo and Mojo and the grandpa every time they had to move it off and then back on again."

Ottilla breaks off the narrative.

There is silence in the room. From around them echo the voices of scores of inmates talking and playing and calling out to one another.

The two sit in silence.

"And . . . ?" prompts Desiree. Ottilla doesn't respond, so Desiree finishes for her, as though coming to the end of a bedtime story.

"But then they grew up and Rogo and Mojo grew up to be big and strong, and they were big and strong enough to move the cistern lid... al-ll by themselves."

Both of them are silent again.

COUNT TIME, LADIES.

ALL INMATES, BACK TO YOUR ROOMS.

NINE P.M. COUNT.

Ottilla startles and springs up off the toilet bowl. Desiree slings the blanket off her legs and rises, scattering needlework and the crochet hook onto the floor. Ottilla is nearly out the door but Desiree stops her and guides her into a turn. The two face each other in the narrow floor space between the bunks and the footlockers. Desiree moves a half step forward, raises her arms and presses herself gingerly against Ottilla. Ottilla, facing the toilet, stiffens. She stares over the sink at her own distorted face in the stainless steel mirror.

Desiree moves her body away but rests her head on Ottilla's chest and Ottilla relaxes slightly, looking down onto Desiree's off-center pony tail. She allows Desiree to sway her back and forth for a moment.

Desiree says into Ottilla's shoulder, "I'm glad you finally got to unload. That's a lot for you to have to be carrying around by yourself, Tillie."

"This is probably inappropriate contact," says Ottilla, her body stiff.

"Probably is."

They hear echoing through the cavernous steel and concrete hall, the rattle of the TV and the inmate voices.

Ottilla frees herself. "So if it's hard for me, think about what it's like for Rogo."

"It's just good that she has you."

COUNT TIME, LADIES. IN YOUR ROOMS.

"I don't even have to tell you—this stays here, right?"

Desiree rolls her eyes. "Come *on*, Tillie."

"Just making sure . . "

"Du-uuh."

CHAPTER 26

It's meatloaf for lunch, and the dining hall is not crowded. Back in the '80s an inmate had found a mouse foot in her meatloaf, and ever since Danbury's meatloaf has been mouse loaf. The inmates curl their noses over it, and today the majority are in their units making do from commissary.

Iris is eating however, and Emilia, performing an innocent room scan, is busy under the table, stuffing a plastic bread bag with carrot sticks and slices of green onion.

Desiree, carrying a picked-over tray, passes and Iris flags her down.

"Hey Dess, do you have a minute? I need to go over some details behind your release date. I think the BOP might be messing it up. Can you get permission to come over to the library this afternoon?"

"Is it something we can do after dinner?"

"Probably not. That place is turning into a mad house in the evenings. The minute I walk in, everyone needs my help."

"Yeah, I know, huh. Okay. I think maybe O'Donnell might let me out of laundry for a little while if I tell him it's behind my date. He's in a good mood today. We're all teasing him how it's because his wife was nice to him and he got some last night."

Iris looks up quickly. "He doesn't shut conversation like that down? He let's you ladies talk to him that way?"

"Not usually." Desiree squeezes a sitting space at the end of the bench. She put's her tray on the table. "He's usually all, 'Okay, ladies, don't push it. That's enough.' But today he's all . . ." Desiree pulls the corners of her mouth into an exaggerated grin.

Iris goes back to her plate, and spoons up some banana pudding. "I've been hearing rumors and I'm wondering," she says, inspecting the contents of her spoon, "if any of the laundry cuties over there are getting lucky."

"Nope, maybe with each other, but not with O'Donnell. He's a totally straight arrow. Like a new Spanish girl comes in and tries to come on to him all sexy? He'll just tell her to get a bucket and go back and swab down behind the washers. He don't play."

"That's so sad for you all. That big hunk of man going to waste."

"Yeah, I know, huh." Desiree rises with her tray. "He's not going to come on to me but he'll probably let me come —ha- ha—to the law library."

"Ha ha."

"Ha ha," agrees Emilia.

Iris is in the law library with Pandora Pearson, the new inmate.

"So Ms. Pearson—uh, Pandora . . ."

"Panda," the inmate corrects.

"Panda, let's see . . ." Iris flips through the stapled pages of Panda's Presentence Investigation Report. "So what was the date that they sentenced you?"

"It was somewhere in the fall."

"Okay, I got it here. November 1996. So you're well within your year."

"My year?"

"They only give you a year now to file a 2255. I'll read through to look for possible ineffective. Let's see, you're here on a FUFI, but they enhanced you for weapons? I'm not understanding."

"A FUFI? What's a FUFI?"

"Fraudulent Use of a Financial Instrument."

"No, they got me for credit cards."

"Yes, that's the financial instrument. So," Iris skims the pages, "I'm not understanding where the weapon comes in."

"That was because of Wizard. He had . . .

"Wizard?"

"The guy I was with. He had this weapon and it was on him when he broke in."

"Broke into a property?"

"Yeah, there was this house over on South Bradford, and he'd scoped it out and he really didn't think there was anyone in there but as it turned out, there was this one old guy."

Iris listens with a professionally neutral expression.

"Wizard said how the guy was just sitting in bed in the dark so that was how they charged Wizard with brandishing. I mean he had no intention whatsoever of hurting anybody. The guy was old, and Wizard isn't the kind of person who's into violence against senior citizens. He said the individual was just fine when he left."

"Okay, let's back up. What's all this got to do with credit card fraud?"

"That was where we got them. The old guy didn't have any money but he told Wizard where."

"Where . . . ?"

"Where the credit cards were. Wizard was just in there looking for jewelry or coins or whatever. But the old guy told him. He told him right where they were in the drawer and he told him, just take them."

"I'll bet he did."

"Yeah, he actually did. Wizard says . . ."

"Okay, wait. I'm still not understanding what that's got to do . . ."

"Well after we got home, I told Wizard how the credit cards were going to be bunk because the old guy was going to call them in and all. But then the next day they were saying on the news how somebody-somebody, was in a coma from corneal arrest as a result of a break-in, and they said South Bradford so we knew probably they were referring to Wizard's activity. Except they got that part wrong because when Wizard left, the old guy was just fine. So the coma was not the result of Wizard."

Iris sighs. "Go on."

"So anyway, we realized that with the coma happening and everything, the old guy maybe hadn't gotten a chance to report the credit cards. So Wizard calls, and all three of them were good so we went out. First we picked up some gear at the Harley shop, and then we went to Circuit City for car speakers, but then we decided we should move out of the Delaware area, so we went over to Jersey City to go to Zale's."

"So you crossed state lines."

"Yeah. But then we were at Zale's and I had my watch picked out and everything, but I'm starting to get nervous when they said the computer was slow. But I just stood there like an idiot, because I thought if we left and walked out they'd know something was weird."

"But the weapon?"

"It was in my purse. Wizard had this hole in his jacket and the 22 kept falling through into the lining, so he put it in my purse. So then they popped us at Zale's, but that clerk—I swear—he did not even know I *had* any gun in there. But they got him on paper saying how I opened my purse and disclosed it in the threatening manner and he was traumatized or whatever, which was just total bullshit because I didn't even want him to see it."

"I agree that it doesn't make a lot of sense. Why would you threaten the clerk with a gun while you're buying jewelry with a stolen credit card?

"Exactly!"

"Your lawyer must have objected."

"See, that was where I didn't understand. I was getting charged by the Feds but Wizard, he was getting charged by Delaware. My lawyer said Delaware was trying to drag it out to give the victim a chance to die so they could charge Wizard with felony murder, and she said that if that happened, they were thinking about charging me as accomplice. But she got them to make a verbal commitment if we didn't fight the Feds over the weapons charge."

"So what proof was Delaware offering that you were an accomplice?"

"Just Wizard saying how I was waiting out in the car and shit, but she said it was unsettled law, and if the victim did die, them prevailing with me on the felony murder could go either way. So she was like, let's not slow down the process—let's get me off their radar and let the Feds get me sentenced."

Iris pauses over a section. "Hmm, it's pretty unusual, bargaining between the Feds and the State. She might have done you a big favor."

Iris pauses over a section of the paperwork and looks up. "Did the victim ever die?"

"Not the last I heard. My phone numbers just went through day before yesterday, and I still can't get ahold of my cousin because he's temporarily disconnected or whatever."

Iris sighs again and massages her temples. "Okay. Keep trying to find out. The agreement with the state was off the record, so I might have grounds for ineffective here. She let the weapon enhancement go unchallenged, and I could argue that it's antithetical that you would threaten with a weapon while trying to use a stolen credit card. But I'm hesitant to do it because if it's going to motivate the state to swoop in . . ."

The door to the law library opens and Desiree sticks her head in. "See, I told you O'Donnell was going to let me out."

Iris looks up from the paperwork. "Hey, Dess, could you wait for just a second? Uh, Panda, why don't you just leave all this here with me. I'm going to have to just assume that Delaware has a felony murder statute because I can't access state law from in here. But I also have no way to research how exposed you might be to the charge of accomplice."

Iris sighs again, flipping through the pages and looking concerned. "The weapon enhancement is weak, and it's moving you way up to level twenty-six. Trouble is, if the victim dies and in the meantime the state appoints some new hot-shot prosecutor . . ."

Iris taps her pencil eraser on the desktop and looks out the window. Finally she closes the stapled stack of paperwork.

"I'm thinking we should probably just postpone as long as we can—let Delaware do its thing. We've got, what? Nine months before we need to file. But in the meantime, do keep trying to find out what's happening with the victim."

Pandora rises. "I will. I'll keep calling. Mom doesn't have a clue about any of this so I can't ask her, but I did ask if she would go through my stuff and find my address book and send me some numbers so I can get my people on my phone list."

"I'll really need to know before I can proceed. But like I say, we've got time."

"Thank you very much. I'll come back in tomorrow or day after . . . Oh, by the way, my money finally got on my books last week. I'm supposed to turn in my commissary list tonight, so what can I . . . how much do you think . . . ?"

"Panda, I don't charge. This is my service to the population. But," Iris sits back and casually stretches out her legs. "if you want to remember my secretary here."

Emilia turns around in her secretary chair and performs a deprecating little wave.

"It's absolutely your choice," Iris goes on, "but if you feel like contributing a typewriter ribbon . . . And poor Emmy has an addiction to hair care products. Emmy, how's your conditioner holding out?"

Emilia with an apologetic smile holds up a squeezed thumb and finger.

"The girl can go through the conditioner," says Iris looking at Emilia's blue-black sheet of hair with a mixture of exasperation and parental satisfaction.

"A woman has hair for glory and pride," pipes up Emilia saucily. She turns back to her typing.

Iris smiles. "You mean a woman's hair is her pride and glory?"

"Same thing," sasses Emilia over her shoulder.

"I personally don't see the difference between Suave and Pantene," says Iris, turning back to Pandora, "but Emilia insists. So Panda, if you think about it, you might mark an extra Pantene? Except if you haven't gotten your shampoo yet, I think they only let you buy one at a time. But they'll let you get a Suave and a Pantene so maybe—"

"I already got all my hygienes," says Pandora, "so no problem." She hesitates. "I was looking at the commissary list, but I don't remember any typewriter ribbons. So is that a commissary item or . . . ?"

"They list them way over on the back of the page. They're between the denture adhesive and the Preparation-X."

"Preparation-X?"

Iris spreads her hands in helplessness. "Hey, don't ask. They sell it by the carton. The Spanish women use it on their faces. They say it reduces pores and tightens wrinkles."

Pandora is unsure how to respond. She glances at Emilia's back and gives a hesitant chuckle. Emilia, speaking over the rattle of her typewriter, "Is working. Is the reason how we are keeping beautiful."

Pandora has left the law library and Desiree has taken her place. Desiree is paging through her paperwork while Iris scribbles a column of figures.

"Yeah, you're right," says Desiree, flipping the pages. "Initially they did lock me up in Poke County before they transported me to Linn. I almost forgot because it was such of a nightmare type of experience."

Desiree pushes the stapled report back to Iris.

"They reference it here," says Iris, tapping with her pencil, "but if I'm calculating right, they didn't include your Polk County time when they were computing your release date."

"Huh. So that changes my date to earlier?"

"I think. Let's get this straight. Before they transferred you to Linn County, you were in Polk County for how long? Can you remember how long you were there?"

"Yeah, it's coming back. It was exactly one week and one day. It was all day Tuesday, then through that next week and until Wednesday. I remember because the Altoona cops, after they got me all interrogated, etcetera, I heard them saying that they needed to wait until after midnight to check us in —that would be into Polk County—so they just left me in the interrogation room and I was still pretty zonked, so I curled up on the floor and went to sleep."

"Your paperwork doesn't specify how long you were there; it just mentions it. But you know for sure it was eight days?"

"Yeah because that next Monday, while I was sitting there in Polk County, I heard them saying how it had gone Federal so they couldn't keep me there at Polk and they needed to get me transferred over to Linn. But they only had space in the van for one other inmate, and so they had got Dixon transported—that was Danté—but now they wouldn't have any driver available until Wednesday."

"Okay, I just wanted to make sure, because if you were in Polk County for more than 24 hours it counts as time served. It's a good thing we caught this now. It can take months to get them to fix it. You're going to have to walk this paperwork over to Ahern. He's upstairs in that area to your left of food service."

"Thanks, Iris." Desiree gathers up the papers.

Desiree moves toward the door, but Iris stops her. "By the way, do you have another minute?"

Desiree pauses. Her eyes flick between the door and the chair. "Probably," she admits cautiously.

"You are so tuned in," says Iris in pseudo chagrin, "Here I'm always having to go to you to find out what's happening on the compound."

Desiree shrugs and looks modestly down at her shoes.

"So do you have any word at all on what's going on with Rogo? Rogo won't say anything, and Asia B is about out of her mind."

Desiree pauses. "Kind of." She looks around the room. "It's pretty heavy-duty confidential," she says doubtfully. "I probably better not say anything?"

"If you aren't comfortable . . ."

"No, it's not that! It's how I absolutely promised—dead mother's grave, etcetera—but you know what?"

Desiree sits back down again. "Actually, in my opinion, Rogo should be coming to you and unloading all this anyway. She's kind of in trouble, a little bit, and she needs some advice, and you're the only person on this compound who can give her anything that's actually worth anything. I'm going to strongly advise Ottilla on how Rogo needs to come and talk to you."

"I'm not certain I could help but I could try."

"Yeah, huh. So maybe if I start to filling you in a little bit."

Iris nods.

"Just so you could be thinking over Rogo's options or whatever."

"That might be helpful."

"But Iris, really, when Rogo comes, you really really can't let her know you know anything."

"I'm good at playing it dumb."

Desiree looks at her watch. "I probably got another half hour before O'Donnell starts freaking." She settles back into her chair and leans across Iris's desk. She lowers her voice. "See, actually, the deal is . . ." She scans the room again. "The deal is," she repeats, "about a year before Rogo got popped . . ."

CHAPTER 27

It's a couple of weekends later, nine-thirty on a Saturday morning, and the visiting room is beginning to fill. On the right side of the room an elderly couple sits in conversation with a young, beige-uniformed inmate.

"Your Uncle Norman and Aunt Thelma? It was last week they stopped over from Vermont. They were on their way down to visit Kenny and—Henry, what's that gal's name that Kenny got married to? Sheila? Yeah, Kenny and Sheila. Anyway, Thelma isn't doing so well. She's having trouble getting around. She's supposed to be due for her hip replacement, but the doctor wants her to take off the weight."

At the entrance, an elderly, gray-haired Spanish woman enters with a baby in her arms. A young inmate rushes over, hastily greets the older woman and eagerly reaches for the baby. The inmate croons and rocks the mewing bundle, her nose buried deep in the baby's neck.

At another table a pair of forty-something white women in peasant blouses and long, graying hippy hair sit with a young African American.

"Food ain't that bad if you eat off the commissary," the inmate offers politely, then seems to intuit she's given a less-than-satisfactory response. "Sometimes it's going to be nasty," she hastens to reassure them. "I've seen bugs in it and shit."

Both visitors lean in and cluck sympathetically.

Iris and her sister Irene are sitting silently side by side toward the back of the room. They aren't looking at each other. Irene looks away at the far ceiling, and Iris carefully coaxes a curl from her Cheetos bag. She takes a sip from her Dr. Pepper and sighs. "Look Irene, I laid it out so carefully. I just need your *address*, so I don't see the problem. I will *not* be living with you."

"I know you said that but Josh—he still . . ."

"They won't let me relocate unless I submit a new address, and it has to be a relative. But that doesn't mean I'm actually going to be moving in. I just need . . ."

"Yeah, I know you kept emphasizing that, but Josh and I don't quite understand why. We get it that you don't want live in New York anymore, but why involve us?"

"Because you're the only other address I've *got*. I can't very well give them mom's nursing home."

"So why go through the bother? Why don't you just let them put you down in New York and then turn around and go wherever you want to go?"

"Because they won't *let* me. The judge gave me three years of post-release supervision. So I wouldn't be *able* to leave. My supervision would be keeping me in New York."

Irene sighs.

"Look," Iris says, "I wouldn't ask if I didn't really need your help. I can't go back to New York, okay?"

"How do you mean 'can't'?"

Iris looks at her orange fingers and wipes them with a tissue.

"I burned a few bridges."

"What bridges? Are you saying that you would—what? Have criminals going after you? Oh boy, that's just great, Iris. I'll go home and explain how you need to move in with us because you need to hide out from gang members. Josh will just be so thrilled."

"No, no Irene! Stop! God, you get dramatic. I was referring to bridges within the legal community. They took away my license, but I've been hoping to be able to clerk. I wouldn't be able to in New York."

"Why not? They would remember? After eight years?"

"Oooh, yeah, they'd remember. It was a big deal. It's not as if I did anything that half of the defense lawyers wouldn't have done—actually *do*. But I got caught, you see. So that makes me a pariah. So if I hope to be meaningfully employed, I have to relocate. And they'll only relocate me if I can give them a relative's address."

Irene looks uneasy.

"But if they just plop you down in Philadelphia, you'll *have* to come live with us."

"No. Not at all! I'll be in the halfway house until I find a job, and from there I'll get my own place. I will not be moving in with you, I promise. So please, just explain to Josh that all I'm needing is your address."

"Iris, he's still going to be apprehensive. Thinking of you there in Philadelphia and our home being a possible fallback, and he—"

Iris bristles. "Apprehensive! Why? I told you I will never—"

"He's concerned about you. He's worried about your lack of resources. He says by next year's release date there probably won't be anything left from your funds, and he's afraid you'll have to rely on us. I mean we'll help with what we can, but as far as actually . . . We're trying to build up college funds for Noah and Chelsea. They're the ones who will be needing our resources and next year they'll still be at highly impressionable ages."

"What do you mean, impressionable? What? I'm a bad influence? You think I'd be fucking turning them into little *criminals!*"

"See! The language! That's exactly—"

"Oops, sorry. I'll be sweetly turning them into little criminals. Does that sound better?"

"Yes, as a matter of fact, it does. Josh is troubled over you bringing the penitentiary into our home and when you use language like that, it just goes to prove."

Iris sighs wearily. "Would you please go home and assure your poor, dear, put-upon husband that his nefarious sister-in-law would rather go to a homeless shelter than—"

"Iris, don't! You don't have any right to be that way. You're doing it again. You're acting like we're the bad people and you're totally the blameless one. News alert, Iris: Look around." She spread her hands. "This is a prison. You're the prisoner; I'm the visitor."

"Oh, thank you so much for the information, Irene. I never would have realized, if you hadn't—"

"And all the time you were being a criminal, you just thought you were just so cool, consorting with all your creepy gang members and your creepy black Basquait-somebodies and your creepy Warhol warehouse or whatever. And always letting me know how beneath you I was, with my little middle-class family in my little middle-class suburbs."

"I never . . ."

"Yes you did! You most assuredly did! And whenever you used to mention Josh, you'd always say, 'So how's the little insurance agent,' like he was some kind of a joke or something.

"I never said 'little.'"

"You didn't have to. It was right there in your tone of voice, and so now that you ruined your life and disgraced your family and landed yourself right smack in the middle of a penitentiary, you still expect us to treat you like, aren't you just *so* special. You expect that none of us should even ever acknowledge—"

Irene trails off weakly because Iris is hunched over in tears. "Why do we *do* this to each other? I've got another Kleenex somewhere in here."

Iris's shoulders shake, and Irene finds a tissue. "I'm sorry, Iris."

There is a pause as Iris finally pulls herself together. She blows her nose and looks up. "Factory," she says through her tissue.

"*What?*"

"Not the Warhol warehouse," she enunciates in exaggerated schoolteacher. "It was the *factory.*"

Irene replies in the same tone. "O-ooh, okay. It was a *factory.*"

"This is important," insists Iris.

Irene catches the spirit. "And he's not an insurance agent; he's a financial *advisor.*"

They look at each other with affection.

"But you're right," admits Irene, finally. "He is kind of short."

"And," admits Iris, "it wasn't really a factory anymore. By the time I got there they weren't actually making anything. Everyone was always stoned, just sitting there. Like on a shelf? So it actually was more like a warehouse."

They both chuckle ruefully.

"Irene," says Iris, blowing her nose. "I'm really sorry for the way I was back in those days. I was pretty high on myself—living on the edge. It wasn't really me."

"Yes, I know, Iris. I realize that."

"I'm sure there were times when I was a superior bitch, but I'm not like that any more. This place has gotten things back in proportion for me. And I just really thank you, Irene, for sticking by me even after I was bitchy to you and messed up my life and everything."

Irene reaches and clasps her hand. "What else could I do?"

Iris smiles painfully. "You could have disowned me."

"We're family. That's not what we do."

They sit in silence.

"But honestly Iris," says Irene finally, "what *are* your plans? Can you support yourself just being a law clerk? You used to have expensive tastes."

"Not anymore. Prison has taught me to live simply. And Irene, I probably shouldn't even tell you this, but I do have some fallback."

"Fallback! You mean money? I thought the government took it all."

"There were actually some funds that were . . . that were actually not available to the government at that time."

"You have money stashed?"

"I do, but it isn't anything I'm going to be able to get my hands on right away."

"Why?"

"Well, I have to be off paper."

"Off paper?"

"That's prison language for finishing your supervised release. They don't ordinarily let you out of the country when you're on paper, and I'll have to travel to access. It's in an offshore trust."

Irene still looks confused. "Where?"

"Belize. In Central America."

"*Central A*—what's it doing down there?"

"At this moment?" says Iris feigning a look at a watch-less wrist. "It's compounding interest at seven and a half, waiting for me to come get it."

"How did you manage?"

"There's this New York investor who set up a private bank down there, and I got to know him."

"How well do you know him?"

"Really well."

"Really, *really*?"

Iris holds up two entwined fingers.

Irene nods slowly and gives her sister a knowing look. "And here Josh and I thought you didn't get involved. You know, with men."

"Oh, you do what you do," says Iris waving her hands in airy dismissal. "Anyway, there's enough there," she continues, "to—let's put it this way: for me to be very, very comfortable. But not until after I get off paper."

"So, like, how much?"

Iris mouths a figure. "That's the original investment."

Irene breathes, "At seven and a half?"

"Guaranteed."

Irene leans over warmly and puts her hand over Iris's. "I'm just so glad you're not going to be a total. You know."

"What? Bag lady?"

"Yeah. Pushing around a grocery cart with all your stuff."

"Talking Yiddish to myself?"

"*Singing* Yiddish."

They laugh, sharing a sister-joke from their childhood.

"I'll talk to Josh about the address—not in Yiddish. I'll talk to him in English."

"And remind him all I want is an address. I'm not going to freeload."

The penitentiary visiting room is filling up. Over in the children's area, a pair of preschoolers starts to fight over a toy wheelbarrow. Their inmate mothers rush over, eager for a chance to parent.

Suddenly the visiting room officer at his desk points and bellows, "That's *it*. That's enough over there."

Everyone startles and look around. The room falls silent.

"Inappropriate contact. Read your rule book or leave."

There's a moment of confusion as the room tries to make sense out of the two options.

"That means you," the officer continues, singling out a young couple wearing matching wedding rings.

"What in the world were they doing?" asks Irene.

"Probably just getting too close to each other. We're only allowed contact on the way in and the way out."

"I'll make a note of that," says Irene wryly.

The visiting room relaxes and returns to conversation.   "Should we get our picture taken?" Irene nods toward the photo area.

"I didn't buy picture tickets. I didn't expect that you'd be coming again so soon."

Iris and Irene watch as a young, pale inmate along with a middle-aged rendition of herself stand insecure and hesitating at the head of the photo line.

The Spanish inmate photographer beckons the couple in arrogant, impatient gestures. She points and orders the two into position with a show of aggravation.

The two blush and attempt to comply. They pose by clasping each other's waists.

"Not! No, no! It is no touching allowed," shouts the photographer as though dealing with unruly insubordinates.

The two redden and spring apart. The photographer flicks an approval-seeking glance at the officer.

"My Lord, that was rude!" exclaims Irene.

"Cruz should not be doing that to Wilson in front of her mother," says Iris.

"What was she being so bitchy about?"

Iris sighs. "She was emulating the officer. Some of the inmates, they come in here, they were riding rich and high on the streets and now all of a sudden they're stripped of all the trappings—back to being underlings. So they try to reestablish stature by acting like the officers. You notice the tone of voice she used? Total imitation."

"You'd think they'd want to *fight* the power, not imitate it."

"Women in prison don't fight the power. They sneak around it. They aren't rebels like men. Or like the inmate men in the novels and movies, anyway. I really haven't figured out how gender-specific it is—prisoners taking on the characteristics of keepers."

Iris looks off into the distance.

"Bettelheim," she continues speculatively, "reported in the concentration camp men acting that way—trying to mirror the guards. So maybe it's universal." She looks back to Irene. "But it isn't in the movie version because what gives good story is *fighting* the system. So prisoners trying to please the guards by acting like them haven't entered the prison narrative."

"Who's Beatleheim?"

"Bettelheim. Never mind. Just someone I read somewhere. Anyway, that was one of the things that surprised me most when I was first down—the way inmates were trying to model their keepers."

"Are they, like, doing it to try to be good people? Rehabilitate themselves?"

Iris shakes her head decisively. "No, just in the eyes of the staff. They aren't striving for any actual virtue; just the trappings. They've all got their little get-over hustles, believe me. But at the same time, they're hungry for staff approval. And when the staff gives them a little taste, they use it—well, *some* of them use it—as permission to tyrannize. They don't want virtue. They want to head up the pecking order."

"Everyone's like that?"

"Oh no, of course not. Actually, I think it's a little more of a Colombian thing, but there's so many Colombians in here that they set the tone."

"Iris, aren't you sounding, maybe, just a little bit racist?"

Iris sighs. "No, Irene. Not in here. Nobody's superior or inferior on the basis of race. But we sort ourselves out that way. We belong to tribes. We're tribal. And God help the white lady, coming in deciding she's a citizen of the world—that the quality of her friendship . . ." Iris sits up and puts a hand on her midsection to orate, "is not 'strained but falleth like the gentle rains from heaven onto the just and the unjust.'"

"*Woo-wee*, aren't we the literate one."

"Yeah, but then after it falleth, shit be coming down on the bitch."

They both laugh.

"In a few months she's as tribal as everyone else."

"Speaking of, how's that Jewish Security-and-Loan gal doing?"

"Rebecca? She's better. She's learning how to be an inmate. She's not quite there, but in another month I think she'll be ready to have a conversation with."

"Shouldn't you be tribal and be helping her?"

"For one thing, there's no Jewish tribe in here. There aren't enough of us. We're white. And for another, Jew or no Jew, she hasn't been ready to take advice from me. It would just be a huge energy drain."

"If you say so," says Irene skeptically. Then idly, "So what about you and that Colombian girl you've been so worried about? Doesn't that count as you bestowing friendship outside the tribe?"

"No, after you've been down awhile, it's okay to form trans-tribal relationships. You can cross over."

"But if she's Colombian, isn't she one of those inmates that's into ordering people around and everything?"

"No, not Emmy."

Irene notes her sister's softened expression. "She's a good gal, huh?"

"Yup, a good gal."

"You been trying to keep her from getting deported. Is that going anywhere?"

"I'm feeling very positive. I'm working on it. I'm pretty sure I may have gotten it arranged."

"What are you doing? Are you getting someone to intervene or . . ."

"Kind of." says Iris vaguely, cleaning off the table. She whisks away the crumbs and crushes her empty Cheetos bag. She puts her Dr. Pepper to her ear, shakes, and looks for a garbage can.

"Oh, did I mention?" she says, returning, dusting off her hands, "They're having their inmate talent show next week. It's our big annual event."

"Talent show? That's sweet that they actually let you do that."

"They encourage it. It engages the population in positive, community-building, activities."

"What do you girls do? Sing and dance?"

"The ladies? Mostly. That and lip sync. You put your order into recreation and they'll order the sound track."

"Sounds like fun."

Iris pitty-pats her chest. "Thrilling! We're just all so-oo excited."

"Do *you* perform? Any talent thing?"

"Yeah, sure. I stand up and read section three, line seven of the Sentencing Commission Guidelines."

Irene laughs and puts on her coat. "I remember how when we were kids you used to sing."

"Not anymore," says Iris firmly, handing Irene her purse. "I'm a fan girl. My contribution is, I clap and cheer."

CHAPTER 28

Iris and Emilia, in the dining room with their lunch trays, are just starting to eat. Desiree, walking by with a full tray, pauses.

"Come on, join," says Iris making room.

"Okay. I was waiting out there for Tillie, but I guess they're letting UNICORE out late again. Except she was saying she was finally having her first Team after work, and maybe they moved it up and that's where she is."

"I didn't hear them call her. Who's she got for Team?"

"Angelino's her case manager. I'm not sure who's her counselor, but of course she's got Cervantes."

"That's another big Unit-Two downside," says Iris. "You get crazy Cervantes for your unit manager."

"He sure doesn't bother me," says Desiree. "He won't even look at me."

"Yeah, you're attractive. Attractive inmates are Jezebels. Actually, come to think, Cervantes and Ottilla might hit it off. Who knows?"

"Tillie hasn't actually met up with any of them."

"She hasn't had *Team*?"

"They were all on vacation or conference or wherever when she first got here, and then she got overlooked. I told her it was like this big rule that she was supposed to have Team in her first two weeks, and that them skipping her over was a total infraction against BOP policy. She said she wouldn't snitch them out."

"Ha-ha." Iris inspects a spoonful of baked beans and changes the subject. "Tonight's the night. Are you and the big boy planning to step out? Hot date?"

"Yeah, sure. Hot date!" Desiree fans her face.

"Hey, it's Danbury's happening of the year."

"Yeah, watching the Fatback Sisters jiggle their asses."

"Now Dessie, the evening promises so very much more. I understand that Yanina's going to sing, and Romero is working up her sign-dance routine."

Emilia pipes up, "Miss LaShonda singing tonight. *His Eye Is On the Sparrow.* Me, I believe is gonna be very beautiful."

"You're right Emmy," says Iris, turning to her. "LaShonda is wonderful."

"Is the warden going to be with her on the piano?" asks Desiree.

"No, I hear she has an engagement. She's sending her love."

"Aww," says Desiree.

"Now, Dessie, don't be like that. She wishes us nothing but the best. We're her family."

"Yeah, ri-*iight.*" Desiree takes a bite of hot dog.

"Anyway, *His Eye* sounds like right up your big boy's alley."

"Yeah, Tillie'll get into it. I actually had to talk her into going. She was thinking about staying in the unit, saying how peaceful it is when it's all quiet and everything."

Iris gets a speculative look on her face. "Actually, I hadn't thought about it but tonight would be an excellent opportunity for you and the Big O to spend some quality time. The unit's all cleared out, you two up there alone? Might be the one time you could get her relaxed enough."

Desiree rolls her eyes and draws a big X in the air with her finger.

"Come on. Be healthy for her. Get her mind off the Jesus-jive. Start getting her past."

"Yeah whatever, but who says *I'm* ready? To be with a *woman?*"

"You said you were having fantasies."

"Not fantasies, *dreams!* Last night I had this other one. It was like me and Tillie, we were in the laundry, back on the folding tables? And we were making out and we were almost getting there, and O'Donnell, he comes in and he starts yelling, 'Johansson, I told you to unload those dryers!'"

They all laugh.

"I really wish I wouldn't do that. It gets me so I'm uncomfortable for the whole rest of the morning. It's like, a total pain."

"You're in your room alone. Why don't you take care of yourself?"

Dessie blushes. "I've tried to go there a couple of times, but I always get this image of my mom sitting there watching me. It never works."

Iris sighs. "Poor Dessie, you need therapy too. Anyway, tonight would be perfect timing."

"Naw, I'll take a pass. I had trouble enough getting her to say she'd go. So now I'm supposed to turn around and . . . Nah. Won't work."

"And we wouldn't want to miss the Fatback Sisters."

"Shh," says Desiree pretending to look around. "Tillie might hear. We don't get to make fun of the Fatbacks in front of Tillie. She says they're God's special children."

"Tillie is right," chimes in Emilia staunchly.

"Really?" teases Desiree flicking a conspiratorial look at Iris. "God likes them big?" Desiree and Iris share amused glances.

"So, Emmy," Iris adds slyly, "Are you trying to tells us that God is a fat-back man?"

Emilia, her face blank, busies herself cleaning up napkins and crumbs.

"Sorry!" Iris exclaims. "Sorry, Emmy, take it back. I apologize."

WORK CALL, LADIES,

ALL INMATES REPORT TO YOUR WORK AREAS.

They start toward the exit with their trays. Iris, close to Emilia, leans in. "I'm sorry, Babe. I was out of line."

"Is okay," says Emilia.

CHAPTER 19

The common area of Unit Two is alive with activity. The mood is festive. The cavernous space rattles with Spanish exhortations and African American vernacular, and white trash-talk. The chatter melds together and bounces off the concrete.

An inmate hurries down the stairs, wielding a hanger with a kitchen white shirt, starched stiff with ironed-in sugar water. She halts on the landing and turns. "Hey, Calhoun, do these pants make my ass look fat?"

"No, you're looking fine, girl. Break a leg! You're going to knock 'em dead."

"Another ascends with a handful of a wrinkled do-rags. "How long's the ironing-line?"

"Ha! Don't even try."

Down below, the common area is crowded with inmates clutching their clear plastic makeup bags, grooming themselves, and grooming each other. They hold out their small, filmy acrylic mirrors from commissary, tilting and shifting, striving for a clear image. They adjust the roll of their bangs and they rub Wet 'n Wild lipstick under their cheekbones and they use broom straws to separate clumps of commissary mascara. One of the younger inmates with a red marking pencil (contraband), licks it and outlines her lips. Another uses sandpaper (contraband) to scruff the lead of her yellow pencil (legal) before she lines her eyes.

"Hey Coco Pop, your bunkie still works over at commissary? She say when they're going to getting in the white-girl eyebrow pencils?"

"Like, the same time as when they get in the white-girl face powder," says Coco Pop, dabbing talcum powder on a zit. "Like, maybe in the year 2000?"

The black women section off one another's hair and replenish with pomade and Hair Food. Frizzy roots are being oiled and coaxed into the bases of dreadlocks, and cornrows are being braided against varying shades of scalp. Over beside one wall, a Spanish eyebrow-shaping expert with a length of thread closes in on a brow, twists, and pulls.

"*Es terminado*," she announces with a flourish, and another woman slides into the plucking chair.

In her room in the middle of the first floor, Ottilla—in her sweat suit—is lying on her bottom bunk reading. She looks up as Rogo enters, spreading *Prince Caspian* on her chest.

Rogo has edges of panic in her eyes.

"Hey you, what's wrong?"

"I've been trying to call my Mojo cousin for ever since the feds come up in here. He just ring-ring-ring. So then I'm finally getting Aunt Tamika's number approved, so she trying to tell me how Mojo disappeared."

"Disappeared? Like, for how long?"

"Maybe four-five days? She say only way she found out is Lil' Mookie, he was passing by Mojo's crib and he was hearing Massacre up in there hollering."

"Massacre?"

"Mojo's German shepherd. Anyway, door wasn't locked so Mookie, he go in, poke around up in there, the phone ring, he pick up on Aunt Tamika. He reporting to her how Mojo seems like he took off. Safe's open, Explorer's gone, dog going crazy, poop all over the place. Aunt Tamika, she come all the way downtown to get Massacre. She can't bring him over to her place—Uncle Lester got the allergies, know what I mean? So she had to commit him into the animal shelter. They locking him up till Mojo come bail him out."

"Do you think Mojo got arrested?"

"No way. They come for Mojo, it's going to be the SWAT-team--body armor, rousing up the whole neighborhood. And like Aunt Tamika's saying, Massacre still be alive. They come for Mojo, they taking down the dog."

"So what does your aunt think?"

"She don't know. She say last time she talking to Mojo, she passing it on how it look like the authorities be out route 122, poking round Grandpa's old farm. They be out in their white zippy-suits—whole mess of them. She passing the news on to Mojo, next she hear Mojo gone. She saying how she ain't supposing the farm got nothing to do, then, bang—the phone time me out. Going to make me wait my thirty minutes, by then Aunt Tamika be gone. She about to take off overnight down to Greensboro."

"You worried?"

"Yeah, I'm worried. I can't understand what would steer the police out to Grandpa's except . . . you know."

OTTILLA CASSIDY,

REPORT TO YOUR UNIT MANAGER.

"Oh-oh. What's that? Now you in trouble?"

"No, I think they're calling me for Team." Ottilla leans over and puts her book under her bed.

INMATE CASSIDY: CERVANTE'S OFFICE.

"Damn . . . darn, I shouldn't have changed. I forgot. Ms. Stephenson told me they were going to try to work me in before count. Where'd I put my uniform?"

She pulls the beige pants and shirt from her laundry bag and shakes them out.

Rogo, to get out of her way, hops onto the toilet rim, the sink, then over to her bunk. Ottilla finishes buttoning her shirt and sits on her bunk to pry off her tennis shoes. She jams her feet past the tied laces of her prison-issue oxfords and stands. She slaps her breast pocket.

"Where's my ID?"

"Over there, up top your locker. No, under the Bible."

Ottilla, on her way out, pauses, reaching over and laying a hand on Rogo's calf. She squeezes and gives it a shake.

"You'll be okay?"

Rogo nods unconvincingly.

"You try to pray on it," advises Ottilla. "I'll be praying on my way over."

Ottilla is sitting with her trio of Team members around the office manager's conference table.

"We're running a little late, and we're going to try to get you back for count, Ms. Cassidy. From what we see here, you seem to be making a very satisfactory adjustment."

Ms. Stephenson, Ottilla's counselor, is a young African American with a warm smile.

"We could only wish that all our newly arrived inmates, especially the ladies such as yourself, who come in with, ah, your level of history, could adapt into institutional life. Let's see, it says here that your activities center around the chapel—choir, Bible study—that's very good, very positive."

She glances up at the Unit Manager, Mr. Cervantes, sitting impassive at the head of the table. He's a burly, dark-complexioned man, midforties with slightly misaligned features. His full head of black hair rises from a low widow's peak. His hands are folded in front of him.

"We suggest," Stephenson continues, "that you consider taking one of our extended learning classes. Ms. Rogers from Unit One has put together an African American history class. I believe this quarter she's focusing on reconstruction? We're also lucky enough to have a professor from Barnard college coming in, volunteering her time twice a month for a poetry workshop. You might be interested in that."

Ottilla nods. "Thank you, Ms. Stephenson. I'll look into it."

Stephenson sits back and nods across the table. "I'll let you take over, Margaret."

"Let's see here."

Ms. Angelino flips through the pages in front of her. She's a large, middle-aged white women in a no-nonsense navy blue suit, a little tight across the chest. "Let's see, you've got your phone set up, we've activated your numbers. No one on your visiting list yet?" She peers over her glasses. "You're looking at a good bit of time here, and we always encourage the ladies not to lose contact. You want to do everything possible to maintain a relationship with your family members, even— *especially*—you long-termers. Hmm, no siblings. I see your mother and father . . ."

"Stepfather."

"Oh, yes, stepfather. They live in Iowa? That must feel like a very long ways away, doesn't it?"

Ottilla nods neutrally.

"But we strongly advise you not to let yourself become isolated. Remember to get that information to me so I can get your family members approved. You never know; they might suddenly have the opportunity to come east. It would be too bad if we couldn't get them approved in time. You want to get those names submitted to my office."

Ottilla gives another noncommittal nod.

"You have your high school degree. Huh, now how did you get into UNICOR already?" She's puzzled. "Oh, I remember! You're the one that Whitely went all gangbusters over."

She turns to the other two counselors.

"Whitely came into my office couple weeks ago, and I honestly thought he was losing his marbles. I was sitting there with paperwork backed up to here, but he wasn't going to leave until I dug out Cassidy's file. I tried to tell him I'd get to it when I get to it, but I swear, the man was about to pound my desk." She chuckles. "I thought I was going to have to call the captain on him."

The other counselor laughs sympathetically. The Unit Manager at the head of the table looks off into the distance.

"That Whitely, he's quite the character," agrees Stephenson.

Angelino turns to back Ottilla. "We don't have a work report on you from UNI-COR yet. I hope you've managed to stay on Whitely's good side. I hear he's been experiencing a little inmate insubordination over there."

"We get along good."

"Let's hope it stays that way. He's not supposed to be the easiest. Am I hearing correctly that they call him 'Mighty-Whitey?'"

Ottilla's eyes shift between the two counselors.

Angelino chuckles, bouncing slightly under her suit jacket. "Mighty-Whitey," she savors and addresses Stephenson again. "He said he wanted someone over there who wasn't a pussy willow. Don't quote me on that. Those were *his* words, not mine."

She turns back and sizes up Ottilla's shoulders.

"He must have wanted this one pretty bad, all the fuss he made. So you're satisfied with the job assignment? Everything okay?"

"Yes, Ma'am, I like it. Plenty to do."

"Good. I just wish some of our other inmates had your kind of work attitude, Ms. Cassidy. Our job would be a lot easier if all of our ladies managed to adjust to Danbury as smoothly has you seem . . . Hmm, let's see . . . moving along here. You've some long years ahead of you. We're sorry to see that, but it does make you eligible down the line for preferred housing. Hmm, I'll tell you what I'll do."

She looks up and leans toward Ottilla.

"We try to recognize inmates such as yourself who present with a positive attitude. I think as soon as a bed opens up, we're going to try to get you out of the projects." She looks over at Cervantes. "Does that make sense to you, Javier? I would be bumping her up over a few other heads."

Cervantes appears not to have heard her.

"So I think that's what we'll do. Now, you won't be on the call-out tomorrow or the next day. You can't expect to move for a month or two, but you never know when a bed is going to open up."

She looks up from the paperwork and chuckles again. "In here, anything can happen."

Stephenson laughs in merry acknowledgement.

"And usually does," finishes Angelino with satisfaction. "Now," she goes on, "if you feel you need help in adjusting, we strongly advise that you put in a cop-out to Ms. Alphorn, our psychiatrist. She'll be more then willing to help with any issues including," her eyes flick down to her paperwork, "any possible sexual-orientation type of confusion that you might find yourself going through."

"Thank you, ma'am but honestly? I've got to tell you that I won't be needing help with any of that. I've found a relationship with Christ. He came to me when I was in Chicago MCC, and He's making me . . . He's adjusting me. He works with me on my orientation stuff. He's not finished with me yet—I'm still a work in progress—but anyway, He's my psychiatrist. I don't need any other, but thank you."

"Uh, well, yes. Uh, that's good." The two staffers exchange quick glances, then look with foreboding up to the head of the table.

Cervantes is coming alive. He sits up and leans forward. His face has a Latino cast, but his eyes are startlingly blue. He hones in on Ottilla.

"Now that's exactly the testimony we want to hear, Ms. Cassidy," he says, studying Ottilla for the first time. "Thank you for those inspirational and stirring words." Cervantes's voice does not match his face. He speaks in a musical tenor and with only the barest hint of Spanish inflections.

"It's a glorious thing," he goes on, "that you have given your heart to our Lord, and I know this personally because at one time in my life I was also headed down the wrong path. If I had not found Christ, I might be sitting across that table where you are now. It's never too late, Cassidy, but if you had only found Him before you committed the terrible deed that brought you here . . ." Cervantes points with an index finger to the paperwork in front of him. "If you had only found Him first, you wouldn't need to be here today."

Ottilla nods in happy accord.

"I know in my heart," Cervantes continues, leaning forward, his face alive, "that if every young person who wanders astray could find the Lord—could find Him before they set off down a path that brings them to terrible places such as this, we wouldn't need to *build* penitentiaries."

The other two staffers, their faces carefully blank, sit with their eyes down. Stephenson, her legs stretched to the side of the table, studies the toe of a high heel. Angelino concentrates on her hands, twisting the pair of embedded rings on a finger.

"We wouldn't need any jail cells or courts or paddy wagons or any such instruments of incarceration," he intones. His speech is beginning to find a cadence. "We could set our policemen to repairing our streets and tending our parks. We could move our lawyers and judges out of the courtroom and into the schools to instruct our children. We could send our jailors out to tend the sick. And I believe *that* time is coming. The lion will lie down with the lamb. I'm looking for it to happen in my lifetime. Do you feel the same way, Cassidy? Are we on the same page?"

Ottilla's face is alight. "Oh, I absolutely do, sir. I appreciate you taking the time to minister this way."

"I feel the Holy Spirit in this room right now." Cervantes shivers lightly. "I beg pardon. I have to apologize to my staff here. I'm not supposed to proselytize on government time. The BOP frowns on that, don't they?"

Cervantes tries to meet the women's eyes, but they are stuffing paperwork into their briefcases. Ottilla, however, gazes at Cervantes, flushed with pleasure.

"When I see an inmate like you, Cassidy, who has found the Lord and turned her life around? The Spirit just takes over."

"It means a lot to me, sir, to find someone who has the same kind of relationship with Christ that I do. The chaplain and the nun here, they're fine people, but they're not really . . . To meet someone like you in here, someone who's on fire—I just never expected. Thank you."

"We've got to let these two women go home to their families, but Cassidy, I'd like to have a further word with you. Perhaps if you'll step back into my office for a minute?"

Stephenson and Angelino, still carefully neutral, look at each other. They stand to leave.

COUNT TIME. ALL INMATES RETURN TO YOUR
UNITS. COUNT. STAND-UP COUNT.

Ottilla starts and turns to the door.

Cervantes stops her. "No that's all right, Cassidy. Don't worry. I'll call over and let them know you're here with me."

Back in the office, Cervantes sits at his desk. "Here, take a chair. I'm happy to hear your confession of faith, but I see from your records that you have a history of gang-affiliated violence."

"Yes, sir. That's past."

"I'm sure it is, but we have another situation here. Frankly, Cassidy, from my point of view it's even more disturbing. I'm referring to your history of gender maladjustment."

"I had a *history*. God cured me, and now it feels right for me to be the way He made me."

"I'm relieved to hear that, Cassidy. I'm relieved to hear that. And I'm sure you are convinced it is true, but I keep an eye on my compound. Whether you know it or not, I've been observing you."

Cervantes stares at Ottilla steadily and pauses, waiting for a response.

Ottilla is confused. "Ah, yes sir?" she responds hesitantly.

"I confess that I've been a little bit concerned."

Ottilla reddens. "In what way, sir?"

"You may not have been aware, but as I say, you've been under my observation. I've seen you with Johansson."

Ottilla looks even more confused.

"And I can't help but suspect that your relationship is headed down into dangerous territory—into enemy territory."

"No! Not at all, sir! It's not anything like . . ."

Cervantes holds up his hand.

"I know, I know. Perhaps right now you feel nothing but pure friendship for the individual in question. And frankly, Ms. Cassidy, if you hadn't confessed your faith, we wouldn't be having this conversation. This is between the two of us. I'm probably stepping a little out of line here, Cassidy, so bear with me."

Ottilla nods uncertainly.

"Just how well do you know Johansson?"

"Very well, sir. We grew up together. We lived on the same block. I've known her for years."

"And you assume she has told you everything about herself."

"Absolutely, sir. She told me all about how she got in here and . . ."

"So she told you how she masterminded a bank robbery?"

"No sir, that was not the way it happened. She was . . ."

"Yes, yes. I'm sure she has her own version. Everyone's innocent, of course."

"I'm not sure I've found that to be true, but in the case of Dessie—"

Cervantes hushes Ottilla with a finger to his lips. He leans across his desk and fixes Ottilla with a bright blue gaze.

"And of course, your ah, *Dessie* has confided to you all about herself and Officer Ferguson?"

"Officer who?"

"Ah, I thought not." Cervantes slaps his desk. He leans in. "This is something that is going to come as a shock, "but it's something you need to be aware of. Again, I'm stepping over the line. This is not the kind of information . . . What I'm telling you stays in this office."

Cervantes pauses, fixing Ottilla with an intense gaze.

Finally Ottilla nods slowly.

"I'm sorry to have to tell you this, but your—your *friend*, your Dessie—she set herself about seducing one of our officers, Officer Ferguson. Stop, stop. Sit down. You need to hear about this."

Ottilla sits again slowly.

"I believe you arrived here at just about the time that our Officer Ferguson was escorted off the compound? You may or may not have heard, but the reason he was arrested was that he had stumbled and allowed himself to become entrapped into a sexual relationship. With an inmate. Ah, I see you are unaware. The inmate in question, I'm sorry to have to report to you, is your very own Dessie—Ms. Johansson.

Ottilla's posture is rigidly .

"Yes, I see you're shocked. You should be. I'm just glad the Lord has given me an opportunity here to warn you about her."

"Beg your pardon, sir, but are you sure?"

"Oh, I'm sure, Ms. Cassidy. I'd be in a position to know now, wouldn't I? She tempted a good officer, and she led him into sin and then she deliberately—*deliberately*—posed in the *act*. In the very act. She posed right there in front of Warden Coleman's video camera, and from what I hear—and I hear it from people in the know--she seemed to be enjoying the experience. Quite a bit."

Ottilla doesn't move. Her face is totally blank.

"Now I'm not saying that Officer Ferguson is blameless. He was a trained officer of this institution. He was warned about inmates like Johansson, and he should have been strong enough to put the temptation aside. But the fact remains that your Ms. Johansson led a dedicated officer into sin and ruination. At this very moment, he's sitting in prison and his children are growing up without their father. All because of your, ah, *Dessie*."

Cervantes inspects Ottilla's face.

"Did Johansson tell you about her redesignation? Did she tell you how the BOP no longer recognizes her as violent?"

Ottilla nods slowly, involuntarily.

"And how now after she has completed the drug program, she's eligible for the mandated year sentence reduction? I see she has told you about that. Well, that was her reward, Ms. Cassidy, and in my opinion, it's a pure travesty. An inmate entraps an officer—against all prison regulations. She seduces him, but then rather than being punished by the BOP, that individual is *rewarded* by the BOP. Does that make any sense to you, Cassidy?"

Ottilla doesn't respond.

"Well, it certainly doesn't make sense to me because it's *wrong*. I don't make policy here. I have to accept it. but don't have to like it."

Cervantes leans over his desk again and lowers his voice.

"Now it's been my experience that in institutions like Danbury, inmates—especially long-time inmates such as yourself—can be tempted into unnatural relationships. No, no, I'm just warning you. I've seen it happen. It's unfortunate, but it's true. And while I believe—while I am *sure*—there is nothing like that going on between you and Johansson *yet*, I want to warn you." Cervantes pauses again.

Ottilla's face is stiff and pale.

"You're dealing here, Ms. Cassidy, with a defective, destructive personality. A very destructive personality and I've seen enough to know. You're stepping out into some dangerous waters. Mark my words, she may very well try—and if I know my inmate, she *will* try—to lead you into sin."

Cervantes rises and holds up a finger. "Be forewarned."

Ottilla slowly stands.

"This conversation is against policy—it didn't happen," says Cervantes moving from around his desk. "I'm speaking to you as fellow Christian, not as a Unit Manager. I'm giving you this information because it's my duty as a Christian to forewarn and to advise. I'm sure, Ms. Cassidy, that you're thinking now that you're strong enough to resist the kind of temptation that I'm warning you about. Perhaps you haven't even been tempted. Yet. But she will try to tempt you—to make a move on you. I assure you, she will try."

Cervantes opens the office door and lowers his voice. "And if Johansson ever did manage to entice you into committing....into luring you into one of her her little honey traps? Why, I wouldn't be at all surprised if she trotted right over and..." Cervantes gives a cynical bark of a laugh, she *confessed* to her friend, the warden, all about it."

Ottilla stands in the doorway, her expression still blank, staring past Cervantes at the hall wall.

" Then next thing you know," the unit manager says with satisfaction, "there you will be with a leading role in one of her little home movies. In *another* of her little home movie."

He ushers Ottilla out.

"Be forewarned," Cervantes repeats.

Ottilla is curled on her bunk with her army blanket over her head.

CHAPTER 30

Rogo, carrying her commissary baseball cap and wearing a new multicolored, crocheted, stiff-sided fez, pushes aside the shower-curtain door of the room and enters.

"Whew! There you are! You absent at count, you absent at chow? I ain't going to lie, I scared. I was afraid they locking you down or something."

Ottilla doesn't move.

"Hey, Tillie, up. Time for the show. Wake on up and get yourself correct. You stepping out along over there with Ms. Dessie, know what I mean? She going to be along *for* you."

Ottilla doesn't move.

Rogo poses in front of the stainless steel mirror, tipping her head and examining, first from the left, then the right. "Ms. Asia B, she finally got Ms. Jackson to crochet me up my kufi hat like she promising. What you think?"

Ottilla doesn't move.

"Hey Tillie, how you laying there like that? Get your ass up out-a the bed."

Desiree appears, standing in the doorway. "Hey Tillie, what's going on?" She looks at Rogo. "How long has she been asleep?"

Rogo, turns away from the mirror and squats in front of her locker to twirl the lock. "Been sleeping like that since I come in."

Desiree would like to step into the room, but Rogo is taking up the floor space. She waits until Rogo has stashed her baseball cap, slammed the locker, and reset the lock. Then, to allow Desiree to enter, she climbs onto the toilet seat, up to the sink, and over to her bunk.

"Come on, Tillie," Desiree carols in a mom voice. "Time to get up."

When Ottilla doesn't stir, Desiree sits on the edge of the bed, puts her hand on Ottilla's shoulder and shakes gently.

Ottilla jerks away from Desiree's touch and emits a negative bark.

Desiree removes her hand in insulted injury. "Okay, okay! God, talk about rude!"

Ottilla pulls the blanket more securely over her head and curls herself up tighter.

Desiree rises in indignation. "What is with her?" she asks Rogo.

Rogo shrugs. "She ain't speaking to me, neither."

Desiree is still indignant. "Whatever her problem is, tell her to get over it. If we don't get to rec, we won't even get a seat. I'm out of here."

On her way, Desiree turns and studies Ottilla's inert form. She relents.

"If she pulls it together," she says to Rogo, "tell her," and she leans toward Ottilla and enunciates, "to get over there because I'm saving her a place."

The rec room is brightly lit and crowded with excited inmates. The basketball court is filled with rows of folding chairs and inmates in gray sweat suits. Up front is a knockdown stage on which Mr. Castagnola, head of recreation, and a couple of inmate assistants are setting up sound system. The black fabric covering the five-feet-tall early '70s speakers is loose and peeling.

Desiree scans the folding chairs. The front row still has seating, but it's roped off for performers. Inmates in kitchen whites are claiming them fast. The rest of the folding chairs are filled.

Making her way through the crowded court, Desiree finally spots Iris and Emilia sitting off to the back on a ground-level row of bleacher. She waves and they signal and squeeze over to make room.

"Where's the Big O?" asks Iris.

"She's on her bunk. She won't get up. She's going through something or other."

"Is she sick?" asks Iris.

"Who knows? I've never seen her like that. She's all up under her blanket. Won't show her face."

"Is feeling some kind of way," suggests Emilia.

"Yeah, you got it, Emmy," says Desiree. "She's feeling some kind of way, but whichever kind of way, it is a pain. She looked like she was asleep so I tried to wake her up. I thought she was going to growl my head off."

Testing, one-two-three. Testing.

"I suspect she's going through some sort of a religious crisis," diagnoses Iris. "I've seen it when people in here come down off their God-high. Some of them can sink pretty low. It's been my observation that bonding with another inmate is the best way for them to pull themselves up out of it."

"Yeah, well, she's got Rogo. They're totally buddy-buddy. Actually, more sister-sister. Brother-brother? Whichever. They're tight."

Testing, one-two-three. Testing . . .

"Now that," says Iris archly "is not the kind of bonding to which I was referring."

Back in Unit Two Rogo, still wearing her multicolored kufi, sits on Ottilla's bunk and rests her hand on the curled-up figure. "Come on, bunkie, how you be doing this way?"

Ottilla sighs deeply and uncurls. She pulls the blanket off and rubs her hands over her face. She sits up. "Yeah, I'll get past it. I got some kind of... news, I guess you'd call it. Over at Team."

"What? You in trouble up in there?"

"No, no. Cervantes? Unit manager?" Ottilla sighs deeply. "He was warning me away from Dessie."

"Cervantes talking smack on Dessie in *Team*?"

"No, he talked to me after in private. He was saying like she's going to try to entrap me to get me in trouble or something. So now I'm all confused. She has never ever acted like that around me."

"Well, you know her better than he does."

"Yeah, but then he also passed some information on to me about her. He wasn't just dishing dirt. He knows the Lord, and he was just trying to warn me, you know? As a Christian. I don't want to believe it, but I got no choice. He's in the position, you know?"

Rogo nods. "I probably know what he be telling you. I ain't never trying to mention it. You didn't know nothing, and I ain't being the one to fuck you over with it, know what I mean? He's talking how she be messy with that officer, right?"

Ottilla nods.

"That was past, man. All over by time you get in here."

"I had a different vision of her, I guess. I never saw her in that way."

"Asia B, she say that after an inmate be down for a while, that inmate going to take comfort where she find it. Dessie lonely, officer come on to her, promising her contraband off the streets, whatnot? You don't want to be judging on her too harsh."

"It's not that so much. It's that Mr. Cervantes told me she went over to the warden and snitched him out."

"Yeah, I was hearing some kind of grapevine shit, but I ain't necessarily believe. According to Ms. Asia, Ferguson was up on coochie all over the compound, could have been any number of bitches snitching out his ass. Don't needing to be Dessie."

"Mr. Cervantes had inside information. He's in the position."

There's a disturbance out in the common area—the slamming of doors, stomping, the rattle of chains.

"Okay, heads up," calls a male voice. "We're looking for a Rochelle Gooden."

Ottilla and Rogo freeze and lock eyes.

"If Rochelle Gooden doesn't come out, we're going to go in after her." Then, conversationally, "She's supposed to be on the ground floor."

"Hey Daniels," comments a second male voice. "So where the hell is everyone? Goddamn place deserted. What makes you think Godden . . ."

"Rochelle Gooden," calls Daniels in a loud and taunting voice, "this is your favorite FBI Officer. Come out, come out, wherever you are."

Rogo and Ottilla hear heavy footfalls and the sliding open of shower curtains.

"Hey you! Git!" yelps a creaky voice.

"Pardon us, ma'am."

Another curtain slides open, then back.

"My thinking is, she ain't even. . . ."

The curtain to their room opens. Rogo and Ottilla are clutching each other.

"Aha. Gooden!" Then over his shoulder. "See I told you. This is her, Duffy."

He crooks his finger at Rogo and says, as though to a reluctant child, "Gooden, now you be a good girl. Here you go. Turn around, that's right. Let's see those wrists. Atta girl."

"Ow!"

"Oops, sorry, too tight? Well, tsk-tsk."

Ottilla crouches on the toilet seat. Agent Daniels, moving the handcuffed Rogo backward, pulls her past the shower curtain and out the door.

Ottilla rises to follow.

The two are in the common area and Daniels, from behind, roughly prods Rogo forward. Then after a few steps, he stops and plucks the kufi off Rogo's head. She jerks around.

The agent smiles and moves the hat disdainfully under his nostrils. Holding it away at arm's length like a soiled tissue, he drops it.

Rogo's face shows nothing.

Daniels crooks the handcuff chain with his finger, jerks it high, bending Rogo over and then pulling her up.

"Ow!"

"This is how it works, Gooden. You put a gun on one of our guys, you get your li'l arm sockets hurt a li'l bit."

"I didn't—what I do?"

"Uh, like, we found a certain *body*? Think! Does that ring a bell for you? Body? DEA agent?" He leans close to Rogo's ear.

"Here's a little advice, Gooden: Homicide 101."

He enunciates as if to a child.

"When you decide to do an agent? And there is a bullet? Remaining in the body? You, uh, you, g*et rid of your weapon*. You do not *keep* your weapon; you get rid of your weapon. You want to throw your weapon *away*."

"Wasn't me. I didn't do no—"

"Sure-sure, my cousin made me do it, right? Don't worry, Gooden, we've got an all-points out for Modell Johnson. We'll get our Mr. Mojo. But in the meantime here, you've got yourself in a little position now, don't you? Did you ever hear about this thing called a lab report? Concerning a certain hand-held weapon you claimed? In your property?"

"Ow!"

"This way, Gooden. Hey Duffy, go open that door."

Agent Daniels pushes a reluctant Rogo. They begin to move up the aisle of the inmate-deserted common area.

But not quite deserted, for beside the door—making themselves small—huddles a pair of inmates. The whites of their eyes are showing; they cringe against the entrance wall.

Now or never.

They dash for the door and scoot through.

Mrs. Caruthers, a heavy-set, elderly African American, stands in her doorway, holding a tissue to her nose. Her head swings ponderously between the players as she comments to herself.

"Now, this here ain't right. Why that devil-man be trifling with our child?"

No one notices her.

Ottilla has followed Rogo into the common area. She picks up Rogo's kufi and shakes and dusts it.

The agent shoves Rogo between the shoulder blades and then yo-yos her back. Ottilla slips around to Rogo's far side, puts a hand on her shoulder and squeezes it.

Daniels pushes Rogo down the aisle and Ottilla keeps pace.

"You! Inmate! Step *away* from the inmate."

Ottilla takes her hand off of Rogo's shoulder and moves aside but only half a step.

"Now if you want to tell us at this late date," Daniels is saying, administering a rough poke between the shoulder blades, "about how you got all confused—how that gun was your *cousin's* gun after all? Why we'd be willing . . ."

The outer door crashes open, and the large body of Captain Carter fills the doorway.

He's huffing.

"What in the fuck are you doing on my compound?" he yells trying to catch his breath.

"Apprehending my suspect."

"Why wasn't I notified?"

Carter stomps into the common area.

"I am responsible for the security of this institution. When you come up in here, you go through my office. You think you can bypass around me? This is my compound; you seizing *my* inmate."

The Captain steps forward as though to grab Rogo, but Duffy steps between.

"You're out of the loop, Carter," says Daniels. "You can just go back and relax. We're in control on this one. We have the authority."

"From who?" squawks Carter, his voice rising a register. "Where you getting any some kind of *authority?*"

"Straight from the warden's office."

"Warden?"

"Don't believe it? Call her."

Daniels reaches for the book-sized phone buckled to his belt and feints as though to unsnap it.

"What the fuck you going through *Coleman? I'm* in control."

Ottilla step in and puts her hand back on Rogo's shoulder.

"Not on this one. We tried, Carter," Daniels is jeering at him. "We went to you, remember? You couldn't give us shit. Warden Coleman gave us our information. She gave us the body and sure enough, right where she reported. Now she's given us permission."

"Wait a minute, Coleman gave you the *what?*"

The two men continue to argue as Rogo slowly turns toward Ottilla. Her neutral expression as she looks at Ottilla is changing slowly. It's becoming one of shocked recognition.

Ottilla meets her eyes squarely for a beat then slowly, as though coming into realization, her eyes widen, her gaze flickers, her face goes slack, and lowers her head.

"Christian, ha!" hisses Rogo. "You a ratting, rotten *hypocrite*,"

Ottilla's face is to the ground.

"You ain't no Christian. You nothing but a motherfucking *snitch*!"

Rogo looks down at the hand resting on her shoulder and sneers. Her eyes narrow at it in contempt. She hacks and spits. Ottilla turns away blindly.

Agent Daniels, still warding off the captain, moves his captive on toward the door. Rogo strides through the common area, her chin raised high, her face twisted into a cynical sneer. She marches out the door.

With the kufi in one hand, spittle on the other, Ottilla stumbles back into her room. Still clutching the kufi, she falls to her knees in front of the toilet bowl. Her shoulders begin to convulse.

On the recreation stage a white-suited performer, one barefoot raised, is twirling to the static-degraded sound system's closing chords of *Unbreak My Heart*. She is performing an art-dance/sign-language combo and so her arms, rather than being flung wide, form a circle in front of her.

She twirls again, then lowers into a squat, tipping slightly sideways, her fingers busy while she teeters and resists the urge to prop herself. She catches her balance as two fingers come to rest over her heart. The sound system achieves a crescendo and the performer spreads her arms, bends over, and stretches out onto the floor.

The applause, enriched with art-of-signing virtue, rises and continues to applaud. The uplift is in no way diminished by the fact that no one on the compound has a hearing impairment.

As the signer trips away, signing her thanks, the inmate moderator, a tall young woman of indeterminate ethnicity, strides to the center stage.

"Thank you, Sonia. That was beautiful. Let's give up another hand." She makes clapping motions using her mic.

"So now, ladies and gentlemen—er, excuse me—my mistake—*ladies*. We aren't counting you, Mr. Castagnola."

Heads turn to the entrance. There are a few titters.

Mr. Castagnola, the rec specialist in a plaid shirt, khakis riding low, stands impassively with his arms crossed. He tries but can't quite hide a glimmer of pleasure.

Over toward the back of the room, on the first row of bleachers, Iris, Emilia, and Desiree have their heads together.

"I think it's Herrera next," says Iris.

"Hey," comments Desiree. "As long as she isn't going to go into one of her sex-climaxes."

"She singing very beautiful," protests Emilia.

"Shh," interrupts Iris, her eyes on the far side of the room. "Something's going on."

The Unit Two witnesses have entered, rushing past Castagnola. Their faces radiate important news. They scurry, each to her own empty folding chair, one to the left, one to the middle, and begin to passionately whisper. The news is met with a gasp.

"Something happened out there," says Iris. "I can't imagine . . ."

"And now let me introduce to you," says the on-stage moderator, "our own queen of the tango, or the rumba, or whatever." The mic emits a shriek and she covers it. "One of those numbers down there. Let me introduce Danbury's own, Yanina *Herrera*. Take it away, Yani!"

The middle-aged Argentinian widow, composed now that no pat-down officer is arousing her, steps onto the stage. Off in back, her assistant works the sound system. Chords of Spanish guitars rise. Yanina tips her head up, closes her eyes, spreads her arms, and breaks into passionate song.

Yo vide una garza mora

Dandole combate a un rio

Iris, still keeping track of the spread of news, leans toward to Emilia.

"What's going on over there? Can you get a bead on it?"

"*Silencioso!*" exclaims Emilia, her eyes closed. On her face is an expression of ecstasy.

"Oops, sorry." Iris nudges Desiree and signals toward Emilia with her eyes.

Asi es como se enamora

Asi es como se enamora

Emilia is transported, but not alone. All around the auditorium Colombian women are hushed. Some of the younger African Americans try to vocalize low-grade disregard but are hissed down. For once they fall silence.

Luna, luna, luna, llena menguante

Luna, luna, luna, llena menguante

The ecstatic Yanina belts the vibrato-laden notes filling the room.

Her pitch is only slightly sharp.

In Unit Two Ottilla is in her room on her bunk again, but she's no longer hiding under her blanket. She's propped up; her head rests against the iron pipe of a headboard. Her eyes are open wide; her face is rigid.

Mrs. Caruthers, the neighbor home with a cold, pokes her large black face through the shower curtain.

"Now ain't that something shameful? Why those no-good po-lice be trying to criminate our girl?"

Ottilla doesn't respond.

"That li'l girl, she ain't done no-any such of a thing."

Ottilla doesn't respond.

"Those . . ." Ms. Caruthers's voice trails off.

Ottilla stares. Her face is chiseled, locked in. Her eyes, off past the curtain-en-shrouded, paint-encrusted iron slats, are focused on something far away.

Mrs. Caruthers withdraws, shaking her head and muttering to herself. She slides the curtain closed.

Yanini has retired, and a beautiful young African American is singing a cappella in a high, delicate soprano.

I sing because I'm happy,
I sing because I'm free.
For His eye is on the sparrow,
And I know He's . . . wa--tching . . . me.

She finishes and bows her head.

The audience, which been respectful but perhaps a bit restless, applauds and cheers.

"And now," says the moderator, striding back to center stage, "We have our own Charity Moreland! She's singing a number that went right to the top of the charts here at Danbury FCI. She composed it under the inspiration of you Danbury ladies, right here—right in this very recreation center. Am I right, Moreland? Didn't you get your AC/DC on right here? From the Danbury ladies? So let's give it up for... *Charity!*"

The clapping and whistling dies; the room goes quiets. The sound system is silent, and the singer—holding a prison-issue guitar—strums the opening chords.

She has worked on her appearance. The compound is accustomed to seeing the five-foot, ten-inch inmate in unisex mufti, but she's been femmed-up now for the show. There is thick black around her eyes, bright-blue glitter shadow, fuchsia cheeks and lips. Her hair, normally a bleached fade, has been waxed into pink melted-crayon spikes.

The look is perilously close to camp-infused drag queen, but the performance is dignified by the voice. It's transformed through her prison sentence from a sensitive, folksong vibrato to a rough-edged vernacular. But it's still strong and true. It fills the auditorium.

> *Got the concrete on my yard*
> *Got the green-baloney sandwich on my plate.*
> *Got the carceration khaki,*
> *Got the house that measure six-by-eight.*
> *I rebuke my situation, ain't adjusted to my fate.*

A few veterans know the lyrics. They clap and sing.

> *Got the thirty months behind me,*
> *Got the other thirty-seven left to do.*
> *Looking out on past the concrete got the Tanglewire view.*
> *And when I contemplate my view I get so*
> *Tan-gle--wire blue.*

Desiree leans across Iris to Emilia. "How's she going to get that stuff out of her hair?"

"Maybe she use black ladies . . . uh, ironing, uh . . ." Emilia air-carves a hot comb.

"Yeah that might work."

> *Mother-loving tanglewire,*
> *He twisting lazy in the sun.*
> *He got them thousand razors calling,*
> *Ya'll come, and take that ru-uun, hon. But I re-*
> *Mark on what the old cons say,*
> *Before I instigate that climb,*
> *The feet don't never touch the free world while*
> *the body's doing Fed-er-al time.*
> *The feet ain't never touch'n street side,*
> *Till you finish up your fed-er-al time.*

Iris still has an eye on the spreading news. She watches Asia B squatting behind the back row of folding chairs in intense conversation with Ms. Jasmine. Ms. Jasmine recoils in horror and claps her hand over her mouth.

Asia, still squatting, turns and scans the room. She catches sight of Iris, rises and scurries over.

Iris leans forward. "What? What's happened?" she mouths over the music.

Asia crouches and whispers into Iris's ear, and Iris jerks away in alarm. She cups her hand around Asia's ear and whispers an urgent question. Asia shakes her head and expresses helpless ignorance.

Morning's here is nasty,

Got to line up for my shower and my shave.

The singer lets her guitar hang, raises her mic, and air-shaves her underarm.

Pay me eighteen cents an hour,

Gonna work me like a He-brew slave.

Taken sick the Doc he grin, he diagnoses

Me my ear-ly grave.

Desiree, to Iris's left and insensitive to the unfolding drama, is leaning around past Asia's ample squatting figure to watch the stage. Iris hip-bumps Emilia aside to squeeze in room for Asia on the bleacher.

Asia puts her face in her hands and her shoulders start to heave as, from the stage comes an amplified, desolation-yodel.

Mother-loving tanglewire—

He twisting lazy in the sun.

He got them thousand razors calling,

Ya'll come and take that ru-uun, hon.

But let me ponder what the old cons say,

Before I execute that climb:

The feet don't never touch the free world while the

Body's doing Fed-er-al time.

Yo' feet ain't never feel no freedom fore you

Finish up your Fede-ral time.

The singer strums the closing chords and softens her voice.

I rebuke my situation

Ain't adjusted to my fate.

Her fans in the audience rise, cheering and whistling, and now Desiree is free to focus on the situation beside her. Asia B has gotten herself under control, but she is still in obvious distress.

"Dear Lordy, what I going to tell her people? I promised them I'd take care of that child."

Iris takes Asia's face in her hands, turns it, and shakes it gently. "Asia, there was nothing you could do. It was out of your control."

A group from the folding chairs is calling Asia B urgently, beckoning her. Asia B breaks away and scurries over to them.

"What?" screams Desiree when she hears the news. And then, "Oh my God! Poor Tillie!"

"I know. If she wasn't feeling that great in the first place . . ."

"Oh. Poor Tillie!"

Up on the stage the moderator is blowing into a nonresponsive mic and slapping it against her hand.

"She must be just dying," moans Desiree. "Rogo was like her little brother. What in the world . . ." she trails off. Then, "Oh God, maybe it's because of . . ." She clutches Iris's arm.

Meanwhile there's trouble on stage.

"What in the hell is wrong with this thing?" come the moderator's curse over exasperated *Oh no's* and *Not again's* from the audience. She sends an entreating look Castagnola's way.

He shrugs.

A trio of Spanish inmates leave their front row seat to hop onto the stage. They consult around the controls.

Desiree is still clinging to Iris's arm. "Iris, I wasn't supposed to tell anyone about, you know, the Rogo thing. If Tillie finds out—oh, God, Iris, you—you and Emmy? You guys have to pretend like you don't—like you don't know anything."

"Don't know what?" asks Iris extracting her arm. She mimes a lip-zip. Desiree looks across to Emilia who zips likewise.

On the stage the Spanish inmates doctoring the sound system jump as it emits a shriek.

"I can't imagine what Tillie is going through."

"She probably shouldn't be going through it alone."

"I don't know. Last I saw her she was acting like she *wanted* to be alone."

"That was before Rogo," says Iris with conviction.

The sound system seems to be healed, and a fourth Spanish inmate has joined the trio. She and the sound system mechanics move center stage and pose, heads down, fingers over their heads ready to keep snap the beat, feet ready to twirl.

"And now," calls out the moderator, "for some salsa! Take it away, ladies."

The system thumps and goes dead again. The kick-starting four slump. But then the beat rolls, and they spring into a spirited salsa.

"Dessie, trust me. The boy needs comfort."

"Yeah, she probably does need a friend." Desiree glances uncertainly toward the rec's guarded door. "I'd maybe try to go back over there, but I don't know if I can get past Castagnola. I'm not sure he's letting anyone out."

"He'll have to let you if you do the chick number on him."

Desiree stands up and snaps her fingers. "Which is, uh . . . "

"Tell him that you just started your period."

Desiree grins and tosses an a-okay.

She heads for the door.

In Unit Two Ottilla is propped on her bunk, staring out past the vinyl-shrouded, paint-encrusted iron slats forming the inner wall of her room. Her face is sculpted and locked in.

Desiree pushes past the shower-curtain door and closes it behind her. She seats herself gingerly on the edge of the bed, placing a tentative hand on Ottilla's thigh. Ottilla flinches slightly. Otherwise she doesn't react.

"Tillie, talk to me." And then, shaking Ottilla's thigh, "Come on, Tillie. Earth to Tillie. It's me, Dessie."

Ottilla, as though with great effort, shifts focus over onto Desiree's face. She frowns and squints as though against a glare and shifts her eyes away.

Desiree leans over to intercept Ottilla's gaze. "Tillie, I heard about Rogo."

She gently massages Ottilla's thigh. Ottilla moves her eyes down to Desiree's hand and stares at it.

Desiree stops massaging. "We need to talk about it."

Ottilla's eyes shift away again, over past Desiree's shoulder.

"Tillie, remember when we were kids back in Oak Hill? How you always used to come to me and . . ."

The shower curtain behind Desiree slides open. Mrs. Caruthers with a tissue and a raw nose, wearing her sheet like a toga, is standing in the doorway.

"Ottilla, she ain't ready to talk just yet," Caruthers advises Desiree. "She be grieving. That li'l Rogo roommate of hers went and got herself busted."

"I know," says Desiree with impatience.

"Got herself busted by the street po-lice," overrides the neighbor." They come in, cuffed her right up, took her straight out the compound."

"I know, I know," says Desiree with barely concealed irritation, not turning.

"Ottilla, she can't be talking to no one right just yet," repeats Ms. Caruthers. "She be set in her grief. She need herself a little time to heal herself up."

Desiree rolls her eyes, totally exasperated, and stands up.

"I'll be up in my room. Tillie, you shouldn't be alone. You need to come up and talk to me, okay?"

Ottilla doesn't move.

Desiree shoves past Mrs. Caruthers but turns back to Ottilla. "I'm taking that as a 'yes.' You need to talk. You be up to see me. That's a direct order."

Up on the third level of Unit Two, at the far end of the tier, Desiree stands on the walkway. She leans over the railing and looks down on the empty common area. Nothing moves. From somewhere echoes the slam of a foot locker, then silence. Desiree sighs and turns to her room. She goes in and slides the shower curtain closed.

She sits on her bunk and twirls her combination lock. Opening her locker, she takes out a tee shirt. She lays the shirt on her knee, stretches to pull her sweatshirt over her head, and then pulls the tee down over her prison-issue sports bra. The neckband of the tee has been ripped off, and it exposes one shoulder. She looks down and sees the graying bra strap. With the tee still enclosing her arms, Desiree wiggles her way out of the bra and slides it out through a sleeve.

She turns back to her locker, digs deep into the top shelf's far corner, and pulls out a crumpled Nacho bag. She opens it and shakes out a white cotton thong done up with beige hand stitching. She pulls her sweatpants and underpants off as one and step into the thong. She adjusts the strip in back, frowns, wiggles, and readjusts. She looks down at her exposed flesh, tucks in some stray pubic hairs, and turns to the toilet bowl. Supporting herself on the sink, she climbs onto the rim. She stands, balancing precariously, trying to eke out an image of herself from the small steel mirror.

She frowns, shakes her head, climbs down, and goes back to her locker. She finds a pair of thermal long johns and pulls them on over the thong.

She positions herself on her bunk but then gets back up immediately to slide her curtain half open.

She finds a copy of *US* magazine under her bed and arranges herself back on her bunk, turning the pages idly.

Her eyes keep being pulled to the doorway.

Now from the stairs comes the echoing sound of footfalls. Desiree comes to attention. She tugs her neckline back over to expose a shoulder. She looks down to inspect her thermals, makes a face, and arranges her crocheted blanket over them.

The footsteps are nearing the final tier. Desiree spreads her magazine over her chest and puts on a welcoming face.

The steps rush past.

Damn! Just that new girl. Piper? No, Pandora.

Desiree listens as Pandora rustles around in a room a few door down and slams a locker.

"Hey Panda," Desiree calls before Pandora can make it past again. Pandora halts immediately.

Wow! Desiree Johansson knows my name?

"What you up to?" asks Desiree.

Pandora holds up a tampon. "Coco Pop's starting to leak. I said I'd run back over."

"Hey Panda Bear, could you do me a solid?"

Panda Bear!

"On the way out—you know who Tillie is, don't you? Ottilla Cassidy?"

"Sure. She lives down the bottom tier, right?"

"Right. On the way out, would you stop by her room and tell her I'm waiting for her?"

Pandora takes in Dessie's bare shoulder and her gracefully arranged legs.

Wow! She's wanting her to come up so they can . . . .

She tries for a blasé attitude but can't hide the naughty glee. "I'm on it," she assures Desiree.

The moderator is back on stage.

"And now ladies, the act we've all been waiting for. You all know them, but I'm going to introduce them anyway. Drumroll—ta-tum. The *FATBACK SISTERS!*" The room erupts with stomping and whistling.

The two sisters in the front row rise and turn. They giggle and wiggle fingers in little-girl salutes. They turn to the stage and set out, jouncing together to an interior beat. All the way, and up the stairs to the stage, they slap thighs-hands-thighs.

Their four backups in shorts and tees are there ahead of them, clustered rear stage around the tape deck. To fill the hiatus as the backups nurse and coax the sound system, the Sisters take control, striking poses for the audience.

First they do steamy babes—pelvises thrust, one leg resting on tiptoe to profile a thigh, thumbs tucked to bracket breasts.

Then, as the laughter and whistles peak, they become alpha males, stance wide, testicles a-jiggle, signing against their crotches.

Then back to cheesecake—arms behind their heads and backs curved in languor.

The audience loves it.

"You go, girls!

"Yay-yay, Fatbacks!"

"Da Sisters is da bomb," someone yells, and others clap and take up the chant.

"Da Sisters is da bomb."

The sound system lets off a shriek. They turn expectantly. Nothing. The Sisters shrug and look at each other.

Miss Mary Mack, Mack, Mack.

All dressed in—

A sound system squeals *Eee—eeek!* The synthesized beat comes booming out from the oversized speakers, and the Sisters put down their hands and scurry stage rear, exchanging places with the four backups.

"It's Biggie!" call out the backups into their air mics. Then they begin their weave in and out across the stage performing referee and cheerleading gestures and pausing for free shots.

The Sisters have found their props—toilet paper tubes—one is a mic, the other a cigar stuffed with painted-tissue. They bend their heads to accept a backup who drapes them with glittered, construction-paper chains.

In proper attire they stride upstage, transforming themselves into the personification of suppressed danger. And now as Biggie's voice starts to rasp, the whole stage—the Sisters and the backups—halt and solemnly bend forward.

"Yeah . . . Mother [bleep]" and the back-ups lip-sync an exaggerated enunciation of the opening-line bleep-out.

"better know . . . huh, huh."

The audience cheers.

Lock your windows, close your doors.

Biggie Smalls, huh . . . yeah.

The audience cheers again.

The Fatback Sisters are embodying the two ages of B.I.G.—old Notorious and young Biggie. They hold their cardboard rolls with one hand, performing splayed-finger gestures with the other as they nod portentously to the beat. Their eyes are half-closed; their heads are tilted as they stride back and forth.

Old Notorious opens the narrative:

My man Inf left a Tec and a nine at my crib

Turned himself in, he had to do a bid

A one-to-three, he be home the end of '93

I'm ready to get this paper, G, you with me?

Young Biggie steps forward:

Mother[bleep]ing right, my pocket's looking kind of tight

And I'm stressed, yo Biggie let me get the vest

Old Notorious, flicking air ash off his cigar, admonishes his younger self:

No need for that, just grab the [bleep]ing gat

The first pocket that's fat, the Tec is to his back

Word is bond, I'mma smoke him, you don't fake no moves (what?)

Treat it like a boxing: stick and move, stick and move.

On the downstairs level of Unit Two, Pandora with her tampon has slowed her trot. Most of the rooms have been left with curtains open, deserted.

Now, which room . . . ?

Three doors down from the entrance is a closed curtain and she hovers outside it. She raises an automatic fist, but she can't knock on a curtain. She's too new to be confident of protocol, but still she is emboldened by her assignment—an insider mission.

She slides the curtain open.

Ah.

Ottilla is propped on the bed. Her expression remains fixed as Panda opens the curtain, but her eyes move and Pandora takes this as permission to enter.

"Hey, Tillie, Dessie's up there in her room? And she told me how you're down here, like, *waiting* for her? To get ready to—you know. So she's actually ready for you now, so you can actually just go up there now, and, whatever." Panda purses a kiss-kiss.

Ottilla fails to respond.

"She's totally up there in bed waiting for you."

No response.

Perhaps her delivery lacks in pizzazz? Pandora shimmies and swings out a pelvis. She licks an index finger and tests the temperature of her hip.

"*Sᴋᴋ-ᴋᴋ.*"

At the sound of the sizzle, Ottilla's expression changes from vacancy to fury. She swings her legs onto the floor and rises, crouching slightly, head forward, arms down, hands forming fists.

Pandora beholds Ottilla change. She sees the face redden, then deform into twisted rage. She backs out of the room. She flees.

The Ottilla who ascends the stairs is no longer a female. His anger is mixed with grim, mission-oriented commitment, and he tackles stairs like the leg of an obstacle race—two, then three steps at a time. He flings himself around the last landing.

In the rec, the audience is loving the act. The black girls know the words, and they clap and follow the beat and mouth along. The Spanish women are amused by the flash and prance. The older white women distance themselves with quizzical amusement, but the younger ones are right there. They clap and bob with the rhythm, finding a lyric every now and again and mouthing it.

Over beside the door Mr. Castagnola, his arms folded, leaning against the wall, has forgotten he is supposed to condescend. He's all attention. The corner of his mouth twitches, and his eyes are dancing.

Young Biggie takes center stage:

Nigga, you ain't got to explain shit
I've been robbing motha [bleep]a since the slave ships

Old Notorious steps forward. His cigar has become a mic.

Yes love, love your [bleep]ing attitude
Because the nigga play pussy,
that's the nigga that's getting screwed
And bruised up the pistol whipping
Welts on the neck from the necklace stripping
I'm dipping up the block and I'm a robbing bitches too
Up the herringbones and bamboos
I wouldn't give a [bleep] if you're pregnant
Give me the baby rings and the #1 Mom pendant.

The backup singers amble around the stage, loping in and out, stopping occasionally to throw up their arms in random gestures.

Young Biggie's do-rag over her corn rows has slipped to one side. She ignores it.

I'm slamming niggas like Shaquille, shit is real
When it's time to eat a meal I rob and steal
'cos Mom Duke ain't giving me shit
so for the bread and butter I leave niggas in the gutter.
Huh, word to mother, I'm dangerous
Crazier than a bag of [bleep]ing Angel Dust
When I bust my gat, mother[bleep]ers take dirt naps.
I'm all that and a dime sack, where the paper at?

As young Biggie finishes the verse, one of the backups stops and bends over the sound system. The music halts, the two Biggies step away in favor of the backups holding up a signboard. The board is filled with a large half-circle encrusted with gold-glitter.

The audience puzzles, ready to accept, but . . .

A back up elucidates out into the hesitation, "*Biggie went gold!*"

Of co-oourse!

The audience claps and cheers, and the music starts again. Old Notorious takes up the narrative.

Big up, big up, it's a stick up, stick up
and I'm shooting niggas quick if you hiccup

In Unit Two Desiree never has a chance to grasp what it was that had burst through the door and hurdled itself onto her. There is, in the back of her mind, only a faint understanding that it is Tillie.

But it isn't *Tillie*. It's a transmogrified, nightmarish version. She has made instinctive moves to ward it off, but so quickly has come the clamp of iron around her neck, the pop of a breaking bone, and the creep of muddy red over her eyes . . .

Her writhings are child's play, her clawings, little love scratches. She is distantly aware of shuddering from the thing on top of her—some horrible travesty of erotic completion, but it's happening to someone else. Somewhere else. It seems no longer pertinent.

It doesn't matter.

Hold up, he got a [bleep]ing bitch in the car
Fur coats and diamonds, she thinks she a superstar.

INMATE DOWN. INMATE DOWN.

Mr. Castagno straightens and turns and rushes out the door.

Oh, Biggie, let me jack her, I kick her in the back,

Hit her with the gat.

On stage Notorious steps in front of young biggie, who steps away.

Yo chill, Shorty, let me do that . . .
Just get the [bleep]ing car keys and cruise up the block.
The bitch act shocked, getting shot on the spot.
(Oh shit! The cops!) Be cool, fool.

INMATE DOWN. ALL OFFICERS REPORT AT
ONCE TO UNIT TWO. INMATE DOWN.

PART 3: CHAPTER 1

"Come in, Engels," says Warden Coleman. "Have a seat."

The warden is dressed in a fuchsia suit that matches her nails and her lipstick. A patterned scarf at her neck picks up the lime green of her earrings and her upswept glasses.

Iris finds herself once again suppressing the urge to squint.

"Now first I need your input concerning the emotional state of the compound. I hope all you ladies are managing to settle back down and adjust to the shock."

"I'm not a psychiatrist, but I haven't noticed evidence of trauma," replies Iris. "It's a population that has, perhaps, become somewhat inured to violent incident of the . . ."

"Is there anyone out there," overrides the warden, "who is in need special help? I received a positive response from regional when I submitted my request for a grief-counseling specialist. It's been a couple of weeks, but nothing ever expedites that quickly in the BOP, does it?"

"If I hear about anyone having trouble, I'll drop a cop-out."

"Please do."

The warden rearranges papers on her desk, letting the silence build. She clears her throat.

"Now first, she announces as though reading a bulletin "I'm feel led to repeat my town hall message: Nobody on this compound is at fault. I don't want any of the ladies of this population to say to themselves, 'if I had only done this, or if I had only done *that*, I might have prevented a tragic incident. I don't want any of you to feel you are in any way responsible. And that includes you, Ms. Engels."

The warden takes off her glasses and leans across the desk.

"There is no way you could have prevented the tragedy. The incident transpired, due to the fact that BOP authorities who were in a position to know better, sent us a walking time bomb. Plain and simple. A walking time bomb. Cassidy was waiting to explode. If it hadn't been Ms. Johansson, it would have been someone else."

Iris nods wisely.

"She was pretty tightly wound. I have to confess, she made me uneasy. Again, I'm no psychiatrist, but I agree that she was unstable. Except actually Warden Coleman, why I requested a meeting was to find out—"

"Somebody up in Designation made a error in judgment. A *lethal* error in judgment. A *deadly* error in judgment," continues the warden. "Trust and believe, I've filed my complaint over the matter. A strongly *worded* complaint, I might add."

The warden waves and indicates with her glasses.

"A volatile personality, with her criminal history and her identity issues? She should never, *ever* have been placed in open population. She needed to go straight to lockdown at Carswell."

The warden seems to be working herself up. "I said it before and I'll say it again: that individual was a walking time bomb. That is a fact. And it's a fact that went unrecognized—*criminally* unrecognized—by those whose responsibility it was to recognize. And now everybody—me personally, you, and the rest of the ladies have to live with the consequences."

"Everyone except for Desiree Johansson," says Iris dryly.

The warden stiffens. "I was not aware, Ms. Engels, that this would be the preferred occasion for tasteless humor."

She puts her glasses back on but peers at Iris sternly over the rims. "I'm a little disap—"

"I'm sorry. That was totally inappropriate," Iris looks down and begins to pluck at lint on her pant leg. "It was probably just . . . my defense mechanism? Johansson was a friend. I guess I'm still in shock."

The warden relaxes and puts her glasses on. "Why, yes. I suppose we all have our own style of grieving."

"But what I really want to know . . ."

"Ms. Engels, I have some very positive news for you."

Iris looks up eagerly.

"You're going to be very pleased. Due the cooperation you have offered and the viability of information you provided to the proper authorities, the Attorney General has approached your judge in New York. I believe it was suggested that you may have exposed yourself to retaliation? From the population? Over my objection, I might add. I know my population and I sense no personal threat to you whatsoever, but I believe something there was some such suggestion in the FBI report. I suspect they were pushing the envelope in your favor, so to speak."

Iris looks back down.

"Anyway, the judge has agreed to give you time served—immediate release. So as soon as the BOP can process your paperwork—and that should be in just a few weeks now . . ."

"That's wonderful, but you remember what I actually requested was—"

"Further," overrides the warden, "the judge has agreed that you have obviously rehabilitated yourself to the extent that he feels comfortable in relieving you of all your supervisionary obligations. You will be free and clear; your probationary duration is lifted."

"But what about Rivera? Immigration is coming Thursday! We haven't heard."

"Ms. Engels, I'm afraid you might have your priorities just a little out of line? I am informing you that the courts have secured your immediate release and you—"

"But that wasn't the agreement!" Iris protests. "You were here, Warden Coleman. You were here. You heard!"

The warden is shaking her head.

"You remember," Iris continues in distress, " how I insisted before I told them anything... I asked them—I asked them *specifically*—if they had authority to lift Emilia's deportation order, and they *assured* me. You heard them, *remember*? They said they could get it done. They *promised*!"

"Well, as it transpires, that seems not to have been the case. Apparently they did approach immigration, and as it transpires, there wasn't an actual pathway . . ."

Iris crumbles. "But that was the whole point. Of everything. Oh God, I promised. She's counting—"

"Ms. Engels, I'm a little disappointed in you. I appreciate that you and—what's the little inmate's name? Rivera? I appreciate that you two may have formed an attachment, but . . ."

Iris shakes her head violently. She has been sitting next to Warden Coleman's desk, and now she throws herself, head down, across it.

The warden jerks back in alarm, then relaxes.

"Take it from me," she addresses Iris's head in a condescending tone, "these penitentiary relationships—I understand that they can be quite intense but—*guess what*? They don't *last*."

Warden Coleman smiles down at the top of Iris's head. She makes a move, but pulls her hand back.

"Now I'm sure, Ms. Engels, that you feel the, uh, 'friendship' that you've established with this inmate is 'unique.'"

Iris, face down on the desk, shakes her head violently.

"When Rivera is released, even if they would let her stay in this country, she'd be out there; you'd be in here, she'd be forming alternative relationships. Why, as it is, I'd be willing to gamble that within a week or two she'll be finding herself a nice Colombian boy. . . ."

"No that doesn't have anything to do with it. You don't understand."

"Ms. Engels, I confess I'm a little surprised at your reaction. I had placed you in my mind as one of our more mature—"

"What am I going to tell her?" Iris asks desperately into the desk. Her shoulders start to shake.

"Now Ms. Engels, I understand that you are still under the emotional influence of a violent death, but I would not have expected quite this level of hysteria. Of course Rivera would prefer to stay in this country. They all would prefer to stay in this country. But perhaps they all should have thought of that before . . ."

The warden breaks off the sentence. She sighs and looks down at Iris's head again. She pulls some tissue from the box on her desk and changes her tone.

"Rivera will manage just fine in Colombia. Why, the child might even be better off there among her own people."

Iris rears up. Her eyes are narrow slits.

"No, she won't," she hisses.

The warden, tissue extended, shrinks away.

"Let me tell you the story," Iris says, striving for control. Her face is still wet, but she takes the tissue and sits up straight.

"Emilia and her sister were from Cali but they lived in Bogotá," Iris begins as through reciting an official legal narrative. "The brothers of the family had gotten involved with the cartel; the cartel tried to enlist the sisters as mules. In response, the two of them fled the country."

The warden takes a breath to interrupt, but Iris holds up her hand.

"They relocated to Virginia and found jobs at the embassy. The cartel learned where they were and it started taking over their apartment—using it as a storage house. Eventually it evolved into meeting place."

The warden sighs, but she's silent.

"Everyone was arrested," recites Iris. "The sisters feared for their lives and were too terrified to cooperate, but eventually they were persuaded on the assurance— on the absolute *assurance*—that when they completed their sentences, they would be sheltered here under the witness protection program instead of being deported."

322 | PATRICIA COYNE

"Well all that's very interesting but . . ."

Iris holds up her hand.

"But then the next year Congress passed an amendment to the Immigration Act that closed off judicial exemptions. Their lawyers wrote to inform them that the FBI was no longer able. So . . ."

Iris leans in and looks deeply into the warden's eyes.

"Emilia's sister was released last year. They put her on a plane to Bogota. She got off the plane and she was gunned down. At the *airport*. In front of her *mother*."

The warden takes in the implications.

"Yes, well, I can see it's an unfortunate situation that Ms. Rivera is finding herself in, but Ms. Engels, you are not responsible for her, and you must not lose track of the fact that you've been fully recompensed. Immediate release without supervision! It seems to me that Washington is being more than fair."

"But that wasn't the *deal*. The deal was if the information proved out, they'd take care of Emilia."

"And Ms. Engels," says the warden as though looking for advantage, "why weren't you a little more forthcoming about all of this?"

Iris voice is beginning to shake again. She looks away and talks to the file cabinet.

"I was respecting Emmy. She believes this Spanish thing that the more you speak it out, the more it's going to happen."

Iris lets out a moan.

"Oh, I don't know." She puts her head in her hands. "All I know is, I've got to go back to the room and. . .she thinks it all arranged. I've got to tell her. . . Oh, God!"

"Well, I still think you might have shared a little of the background."

Iris looks up.

Her face is wet again but she says flatly, as though making a statement, "And Warden Coleman, you *do* believe that if I'd explained the everything—if I'd given them the whole story—that would have made a difference.

The warden is silent.

"*Right?*"

The warden's eyes falter. She looks away.

CHAPTER 2

It's a wintery Connecticut day, but there's a spring breeze moving across the compound. The inmates milling around the noontime square waiting for the work call are still zipped into their brown, prison-issue coats, but the snow is starting to melt and the piles of snow that edge the sidewalk are thawing.

The pat-down operation in front of the dining room is in full swing, with inmates lined up in front of the two officers—one the young military buzz-cut, the other an older, a heavy-set female. A few wilted bags of salad-bar vegetables are lying disconsolately in the mud at their feet.

An inmate steps out of line and attempts to slither away toward her unit.

"Hey, you!" yells the female officer, "Get back over here." She snaps her fingers and points at the ground. "Get over here."

The guard is rewarded with a cookie. She fingers it as though to avoid contamination and drops it on her pile.

Yanina, the Argentinian cabaret singer with a wicked grin on her face, has joined the male officer's line. When it's her turn, she steps up, shimmies her shoulders, and spreads her arms. She does a whole-body sigh and looks heavenward, preparing to be transported.

"Get out of here, Herrera," growls the officer, not quite achieving a tone of disgust.

She droops, disconsolate.

"Go! Git!" he yells.

Yanina, in desolation, slumps off to her friends. Out of his line of vision, she grins at the group of women and flashes her coat open for a glimpse of a plastic bag. There is silent celebration as the group heads for their unit.

Iris watches the scene from her bench in front of her Unit Twelve. She sits alone, arms folded. She hears the door open and starts to turns toward it. It's an Asian from the second floor.

Iris turns back.

A patted-down Pandora approaches Iris hesitantly.

"Sit," Iris tells her. "Heard anything from home?"

"No, that old guy's still in a coma. Wizard's still sitting in county."

"Okay. Keep trying. But in the meantime, do you have any good gossip for me? That's your job, remember?"

"Yeah, actually, have you heard about the Fatback Sisters?"

"I heard they got caught . . . what? After midnight count? I haven't heard any details."

"Coco Pop heard some of the officers talking. They were laughing their heads off. They were saying that the officer who caught them? She had just transferred from the Air Force, and her name tag was missing and she thought is was back where she had just counted so she went back in and she saw the one Fatback lying there on her back with her bare legs up and a big old head of hair in the middle."

Iris makes a face.

"So at first," Pandora giggles, "she thought there was just the *one*. She didn't realize she was looking at two of them and she they say she almost passed out and I guess now she's supposed to be going through trauma or PTSD something. She's in counseling."

Iris smiles. "Poor lady."

"Maybe they'll have to commit her into treatment, huh?"

"We can only hope. Perhaps she'll never recover."

"Yeah, huh."

"I suppose when the Sisters get out of the hole, they're finally going to have to break them up—put them in separate units. There's going to be total hysteria."

"You think?"

"I know. I was here when they first came in and they tried to separate them. The shrink finally overroad admissions."

Iris pats Panda's shoulder. "That was a good one, Panda. Keep up the good work."

Iris sees Asia B approaching with a friend.

"Hey, sorry Panda. I've got some business to talk over with Asia. Stop by the law library when you get a chance."

"So what's the word on Rogo?" Iris asks after the two newcomers have settled themselves into Panda's seat.

"Still sitting in the hole at MCC New York," replied Asia. "I guess they finally decided they were going to process her there instead of back in Roanoke. She's only getting the one phone a week, but last her momma heard, nothing new."

"Do you suppose she's finally able to come to terms with the fact that it was— what's his name? That cousin . . ."

"Mojo."

"Yeah, that Mojo gave her up?"

"I ain't got no notion. All's I know is that child is ruined. She going to be locked-and-gone all her natural life. Cause you just know that Mojo—he going to stick that homicide *onto* her. His people say he be out on escape? Ha! Mark my words, they got him tucked away somewhere and he be a-running that lying mouth of his."

"Poor Rogo. She got a bad deal."

"That child did not deserve it."

"No she didn't." Iris leans across Asia. "Hey, Tanya, what's the word on Cassidy? She's still on suicide watch, right?"

"Yeah, but I hear she's getting moved over to seg today."

"How can they? Isn't she still on the tube?"

"No, she eating. Jazzy, she went on her suicide-watch shift last night. She say Ottilla eating, but she still ain't talking, just looking at the ceiling. She get up every little while to pee is all."

"But they're moving her over to seg?"

"Yeah, until her transfer goes through. Jazzy, she say how the shrink come round, tell the officer they have to move her on out until the marshals come. They got another suicide needing the bed."

"Who that?" asks Asia B.

"Some new inmate from admissions. Shrink say Ottilla still got a little bit of the akinesia. Going to get her into treatment up at Carswell, FMC, but she ain't be a danger to herself no more.

INMATE EMILIA RIVERA, REPORT TO R&D.

RIVERA, RECEIVING AND DISCHARGE.

Iris starts.

"My Lord," exclaims Asia B, "That's your roommate they calling? What they wanting with her?"

"Immigration's coming today." Iris turns to the unit door. "She's in there packing out. She'd better hurry."

"Why ain't you and that child say nothing about how she be out the gate today?"

"She didn't want any drama. Some of the Colombian women were going to throw her a party last night, but she told them no, she wouldn't come if they did."

"My Lord, you ought to be in there, helping your child pack out."

Iris looks at her lap and her eyes start to well. "She said she wanted to be alone."

There's an uncomfortable silence. Asia B and Tanya study the compound.

"Shame how you be losing your people," Asia B finally ventures. "First Dessie, now Emmy."

There's another silence.

Iris finds the tissue in her pocket and blows her nose.

"So," says Asia B in an upbeat tone, "you ain't got that much time left your own self, do you? How soon you be out the gate?"

Iris doesn't answer right away. "Oh, I don't know," she says finally, "I guess I've still got, something like, I don't know. A couple of years?"

"Now Ms. Iris, you ain't holding onto the correct attitude. You got to be working your countdown. You got to *own* your date."

The door to Unit Twelve opens and they turn and rise as Emilia steps out in her gray sweat suit, carrying a bulging, multicolor crochet tote bag.

INMATE EMILIA RIVERA, REPORT IMMEDIATELY.

DISPATCH. IMMEDIATELY.

"Ay-yi-yi! Is gonna mad at me."

"Who cares?" says Iris. "They're not going to have Rivera to kick around any more. Hey, why don't you just let them leave without you."

"They will find me."

"Yeah, probably. Come on, give me the bag. Let's get over there."

Across the compound, outside the door marked R&D, Iris puts the tote bag on the ground. She puts her arms around Emilia and rests her chin on top of Emilia's head. She sways her back and forth.

"Bye, Babe. Sorry I couldn't make it work out for you."

"You try," assures Emilia.

Iris breaks away. "You've got my sister's number, right? Where is it? Okay, call. The minute you get to your mom's. Okay? Promise?"

"I call," recited Emilia, "first thing, *de la casa de mi madre.*"

RIVERA! DISPATCH! NOW!

Iris is trying hard to control herself.

"Sorry, this is not like me"—she angrily wipes at a tear—"I'll be hearing from you. Trust me. We will absolutely be talking again."

Iris embraces Emilia, puts a finger under Emilia's chin, and raises it. She kisses her on the lips.

They don't notice buzz-cut, finished with his pat-down duty and marching up from the side.

"Hey, you two, "he yells, his face reddening, "cut that out!" His voice rises. "*Inappropriate contact!*"

Emilia leaps away guiltily but then gathers herself. She straightens and, giving Iris a quick side glance, she turns to face the officer. She takes a defiant, wide-legged stance, grabs ahold of a bicep and, with a raised hand, separates out the middle finger. She pumps it up once, pumps it again . . .

"Hey you, what the fuck!"

She slumps back down, grabs her tote, and scurries into R&D.

"Bye, Babe." calls Iris with a sob in her voice, "See you!"

"*Hasta ahora.*"

CHAPTER 3

Iris waits patiently outside Departure for ten-foot gate to finish their stately opening slide. She passes through, out under the Danbury Federal Correctional Institution sign. She's dressed in heels and a sleek black pant suit, white collar open at her neck. The gates roll shut again as she steps out onto the street. Her sister stands beside an SUV. They hug.

"You still haven't heard from Colombia?" Iris asks.

"Not by the time I left."

"Maybe one of the kids forgot to mention?"

"Iris," says Irene impatiently, "Can't you even say hi? No! I asked them. Yet again. And Noah says that there have been no calls from Uzbekistan or from New Guinea or from Colombia. Okay?"

"Okay, okay. Just asking." Iris throws her duffel bag in the back seat. "Whew! I made it. Snuck right out. No one knew I was leaving."

"Why didn't you tell anyone? Didn't you want to say goodbye?"

"Not really." says Iris, getting in the car. "The inmates can get struck by envy if they find out the Feds are letting you out early. I decided probably best to just disappear."

"I'll never understand that place," says Irene pulling away from the curb.

"Me neither." Iris closes her eyes and leans against the headrest. "My God," she says, inhaling, "just smell it! The inside of a car! I totally forgot."

"I'm not sure this one smells so wonderful. Chelsea spilled her milkshake last week."

The sign ahead says Interstate 84.

"Like I said," says Irene, "we would have flown you back but with you not having any ID . . ."

"I've got my prison ID," teases Iris. She stretches and digs into her pocket. "Here, want to see?"

"Throw that thing away,"

Iris gropes for the door's window crank.

"How do you get this to . . . oh, here." Iris finds the button underneath the glass and the window descends.

She leans out and breathes again. "Exhaust! Sweet! God, I love it!"

She watches her ID sail off down the road.

"I know you couldn't talk on the phone," says Irene, "but let me get it straight. You got out early because. . .? Good conduct?"

"Something like that, Irene. It's complicated. Let's just say I worked the system."

"Actually, it's Josh wanting to know. He was saying it was highly unusual but what does he know? Actually what he was really interested in is your post-release parameters. No supervision means you're free, but he was wondering how free."

"*Free*. No restrictions. But so what's my money looking like? Do I have anything?"

"Not very much. Josh was investing for a longer-term strategy, so with him liquidating now, he was saying that when we minus out what we've been sending you every month, you'll only be looking at couple thou."

"That'll work."

"Yeah, but he's worried that there's not enough to see you through any length of time. So that's why he wants to know about, you know, if you can leave the country. Get to . . ."

"Absolutely. Go as soon as I update my passport."

"So you'll be heading down there?"

"As long as you still have that envelope."

"Still in the safe."

"Good. I'll go to the Haverford post office —is that still where they process passports? First thing Monday morning. I believe you can pay extra and get it done quickly."

As they merge onto 84 West, Irene is chattering on.

". . . and Chelsea! She is so excited. She said she'd sleep up on the top bunk so you could move into her room and take the bottom. I told her, 'No way. We're putting Aunt Iris in the guest room.'"

Iris gives a happy laugh.

"After all this time in a crowded institution," Irene continues, "I reminded her that her aunt is going to need her own space."

CHAPTER 4

On the floor beside the locker of the curtained-off segregation cell, a full army duffel bag is draped with a wet towel. Beside it rests a lunch tray with an untouched bologna sandwich, an unopened potato-chip bag, and a still-stapled eight-ounce carton of milk.

The rattle of the cart comes down the hall and stops beside the door. Ottilla's segregation cell is enclosed with a sliding shower curtain but behind it, the hinged cover to the door's slot squeals opens.

"Tray."

Ottilla is lying on the bare, plastic-covered mattress of the bottom bunk. Her cheeks and neck are still scabbed from lacerations. Her hair is wet from the shower. Her eyes are fixed on the sheet-metal base of the bunk overhead.

"Cassidy, tray."

Without changing expression Ottilla swings her legs, sits up, picks up the tray, pushes aside the shower curtain, and fits the tray through the door slot. The tray disappears. The slot slams.

Ottilla pulls the curtain closed again.

"Open curtain, Cassidy."

The order is rote, and Ottilla ignores it. She lies back. Her eyes fix once more on the sheet metal.

Down the passageway an inmate, isolated inside her Walkman, warbles in a quavering vibrato.

Turn around, bright eyes.

Every now and then I fall apart

Turn around bright eyes . . .

From another cell comes a chant:

Officer, Ooofficcer! You still ain't give me my phone call. Officer, Ooo-fficcer! You still ain't give me my phone call.Officer, Ooo-fficcer! You still ain't . . ."

Ottilla's expression remains blank, but her body screams:

Shut the fuck UP! Shut the fuck UP! Shut the fuck UP!

She shudders. Her body is moving through another jolt of, as Ottilla, back when she was Omar, learned to think of as the electric jim-jams. She tries to relax against the invasion. She fails and convulses.

She wishes for the shadowland where until recently she had been resting. Her return has thrown her back into withdrawals.

She knows she deserves them.

The electricity moving through and her body subsides.

She shifts her gaze from the sheet metal and up to the ceiling. Just above the upper frame of the slats, against the front wall, stretches a line of thin, bare, base-metal piping. Interspersed with it and poking out at odd angles are a half-dozen red, daisy-wheel valve handles. Across the midcell ceiling runs a group of older pipes. The small pipes carry wiring, but many have been orphaned by electrical upgrades. The lead water pipes are replaced with alloy but still hang there. The largest pipe, a fat main water line, runs across the ceiling and escapes out into the passageway.

It catches Ottilla's interest. She feels the birth of another nerve attack, but it dies away as she focuses on the large pipe. She raises her chin to look at the stack of bedding at her feet and then at the pipe again. She sits up, feet on the floor, and with one of them pulls the duffel bag closer. She throws aside the wet towel, unzips and gropes. Her hand finds her combination lock. She retrieves it and holds it. It is open. She clicks it shut. She rests it carefully on the floor beside her feet.

She leans and reaches down to the foot of her bed where her bedding is folded. She pulls out a sheet, finds a corner, then picks up the lock and feeds the sheet corner through the u-section. She square-knots the corner off and pulls it tight.

She stands now and sets the knotted sheet on her top-bunk mattress, then moves to the toilet and steps up onto the rim. Her legs are shaky, so she steadies herself on the bedpost. She feels for the edge of the sink and steps up to it, then springs over onto the upper bunk.

In 1940 when Danbury Federal Correctional Institution was built, the ceiling height of the single cells of the Segregation Units complied with regulation. They were sixteen feet high—well within code.

But by the '90s and the raging of the drug war, the requirements of a rising inmate population shifted. It was decided by the number pushers in Washington's Bureau of Prison that Danbury was to change from a male to a female institution. With the women in residence, it was recognized that only half of the protective custody and punishment beds would be needed. Therefore the Protective Custody—the P.C. wing—of the Segregation Unit could be freed up to house the general population.

In response to its new mission, the facility doubled its toilet-paper acquisition order and added menstrual pads. The commissary ordered tampons, upped it's shampoo and reluctantly, only under direct orders, put in for rudimentary cosmetics. Contracts were posted for the hanging of privacy curtains.

When it was ordered that the single cots be replaced with army-surplus bunk beds, someone in Security & Facility Management pointed out that the square footage of the former isolation unit cells met BOP requirements for single beds only. The warning was over-ridden.

It was only going to be the females.

The order to double-cell included the whole building. It failed to specify that the decision need apply only to the general-population side of the unit. Therefore, in the changeover, both sides were hung with privacy curtains and both sides were equipped with bunk beds.

This would not have been a problem at a newer institution, but Danbury's electrical and plumbing fixtures had never been sealed off behind a finished ceiling. They remained exposed. Therefore the new top bunk of the Segregation Units offered the at-risk, or simply the adventurous inmate, access to it's pipes. It was a contravention of code, but the DC office responsible for overseeing security did not coordinate with the DC office responsible for population density. In the bureaucratic flurry created by the prison's sex-change operation, the code was ignored.

It was only going to be the females.

During final inspection, the BOP Supervisor looked at the bunks and looked at the ceiling and hesitated.

Then he shrugged.

It was only going to be the females.

The journey of the main water-line pipe begins behind the toilet bowl, goes up the cinder-block outer wall and, turning just short of the ceiling, runs across the length of the cell and out onto the walkway. There is a hand's of width of space between the main pipe and the ceiling.

Ottilla kneels on the top bunk and aims.

The lock bounces and falls into the sink. Again, and it clatters on a footlocker. The next falls cleanly to the floor.

Ottilla takes aim again, finding sustenance in the action. The voices of the hole no longer jangle through her body.

> . . . *now I'm only falling apart*
>
> *Nothing I can do*
>
> *A total eclipse of the heart*

"Officer, *Ooofficcer!* You still ain't give me my phone call. Officer, *Ooofficcer!* You ain't still give me my phone call.."

"Wilson, you're not getting shit. Now shut the fuck up!"

"*Oo-officccer!* You ain't . . ."

Ottilla's body no longer responds to it.

Regulations require that the segregation cell's curtain remain open unless an inmate is engaged on the toilet or is robing or disrobing. The guards are required to police on the half hour.

But Cassidy, at first viewed with extreme caution, has proven to be of no trouble whatsoever. Not once has she requested the time-consuming privilege of being shackled, escorted out to her hour of yard and then reshackled back to her room. She never calls them to complain. She takes her trip to the showers only when they remember to tell her to.

Indeed, the most dangerous inmate by far— *ever*— is a lamb. The guards joke about how they wish all the ladies here in the hole were in here for killing each other.

"Open curtains, Cassidy," they call out automatically as they make their rounds, cruising on past.

"Open curtains," they call again as they cruise back.

But this morning was different.

"Last day, Cassidy. Marshall's coming dark a.m. You need to get out now and get showered up."

Ottilla makes her preparations in the ominous shadow of her knowledge of God. She understands that suicide will seal her separation. She had been lavished with love and she tossed it away.

Indeed, she remembers the exact moment when she had chosen to surrender to the other power—the one that had been scratching from outside, waiting to reinvade. And as soon as she gave permission, it had come surging back, full force. It gifted her with her old friend: a gush of rage and power and sexual domination..

She is visited again by a flash of the image of purpling distorted faces, stretched-up fastened hands. Clawing fingernails. The thrill goes to her crotch.

No!

She doesn't want it there, but it's too late. She betrayed God. She had gone traitor, over to the enemy. This is where she lives now.

For a few weeks she had been enveloped in deep shade. When she emerged, she emerged dope sick. She tried to return to the shade, couldn't get back in. But she's grateful now that she has been given the strength and the courage to act.

She understands that she has placed herself back where He found her. And if it means that she will exist, even beyond death in drug-sick withdrawal, then that is right and that is fair. She only wants to get on with it.

Turn around, bright eyes. . .

"Officer, Officer!"

"Officer, Officer!"

This new mission of hers and the activity it requires is working to keep the seg voices from wiring through her. She hardly notices them. And now, after a series of tries, the lock finally slips through the space between the ceiling and the pipe.

Ottilla allows the lock's weight to pull the far corner of the sheet down. It swings out of reach. She agitates her end, trying to lure the end in.

She can't.

Ottilla fastens her sheet corner to the bedpost, crawls onto the sink, down to the toilet rim, and retrieves the toilet plunger resting there. She looks up. The lock dangles a good nine feet over her head.

Back on the top bunk, she stands on the mattress and extends the plunger handle and reaches.

It hooks. She fishes in the lock and ties it into a circle, then tightens and tests the knot. The two kitty-corner sheet ends form a large whole-sheet loop. From it she tries to tie off a smaller section, but she has not thought through the process. Before she can form a smaller loop into her strip of sheet, she needs its ends need to be free.

She tries to unpick the original knot. It refuses to relax.

She climbs down from the bunk again and selects a white athletic sock from her duffel bag. Back on top, with the sock sectioning off the large loop, the sheet forms a circle of the correct size.

Standing on the mattress she tests the new knots, then pulls the noose down past her ears and onto her neck. It rests against her collarbone. When she raises her arms to hold off the section and tug and test with the other, the knot still holds. She pulls it up to check for size and the noose fits. It stays beneath her jaw.

She looks down for a minute, takes a breath.

I'm sorry, God.

She drops.

No-oooo.

The scream is mental; it comes from inside, but not from her exactly. It comes instead from the fleshy mass of a creature. She's living in it but it doesn't feels like... her. The tip of its toe finds the toilet rim and thrashes to gain foothold, but the sheet swings away and the noose is tightened. A red fog fills her head. It is turning dark.

But somehow the darkness is not filling *her*. It is filling only the prison-body where she's been incarcerated. An invisible gate is rolling open. She moves out of her body and through it.

She's out on escape!

She escaped!

Now, from her vantage point hovering just over the body, she looks down at the poor misbegotten thing, swinging from its shabby sheet. A twitch of a foot tries to jerk her back, but the gate is rolling closed. This is her release date. She's done her time. She's out.

There's just a glancing notion that she should be in awe. But it all seems so natural.

Of course.

The *her*—the part of herself that she has always actually *been*—is rising and the sheet rock ceiling of Danbury's Segregation Unit is no longer made of a substance that can imprison her.

She is free.

She is as free from the material of the building that had enclosed her as she is from the body that had enclosed her. And this is how it's *supposed* to be. It's how she had actually been all along and she hadn't realized it. Indeed, now it seems passing strange to her that the prison and the prison-body had ever had the power to lock her in at all.

As she floats through the roof and up into the passageway of the night, she sees on the horizon . . .

It's a light.

But not really just a light, for it's a light that shines with language, and it's a light that calls to her now in a voice that is at once both high and deep. And it's a voice that sings. It sings a song she has never heard before but a song that she has always known. It sings a song in a many-chorded voice, deep and resonant, but sparkling high with anticipation.

The light sings and it's carol fills the passageway.

Is that my lovely child?
My lovely, lovely child?
Is that my lovely child?

"It's me!" Ottilla calls to it in answer.

Ah, yes. I've been waiting so long.
Ah yes. You're finally on your way.
Finally on your way.

"I'm coming."

Come here, my precious one.
Come her my precious one.
My precious, my precious.

"I'm coming."

Ah, thank you!
Ah, you at last.
Come. Please, come quickly.

"I'm coming."

Oh, so beautiful, my child.
Come, my love. Come to me.
Come back to me.

And so she does.

The End

ABOUT THE AUTHOR

"You can't write about a woman's prison unless you've been there," insists the author, "and you can't write about drug dealing unless you've done it."

Patricia Coyne has.

Convicted of drug conspiracy in the mid-nineties, she served over eleven years in three different Federal institutions.

She now lives a quite life, close to the Alaskan homestead where she was born and raised.

51722139R00192

Made in the USA
Middletown, DE
04 July 2019